Italian
BACHELORS

IRRESISTIBLE
SICILIANS

ITALIAN BACHELORS
COLLECTION

July 2017

August 2017

September 2017

October 2017

November 2017

December 2017

Italian BACHELORS

MICHELLE SMART

Published in Great Britain 2017
By Mills & Boon, an imprint of HarperCollins*Publishers*
1 London Bridge Street, London, SE1 9GF

ITALIAN BACHELORS: IRRESISTIBLE SICILIANS © 2017
Harlequin Books S.A.

What a Sicilian Husband Wants © 2014 Michelle Smart
The Sicilian's Unexpected Duty © 2014 Michelle Smart
Taming the Notorious Sicilian © 2014 Michelle Smart

ISBN: 978-0-263-93133-4

09-0917

Our policy is to use papers that are natural, renewable and recyclable products and made from wood grown in sustainable forests.
The logging and manufacturing processes conform to the legal environmental regulations of the country of origin.

Printed and bound in Spain
by CPI, Barcelona

WHAT A SICILIAN HUSBAND WANTS

MICHELLE SMART

For Luke with all my love.

Michelle Smart's love affair with books began as a baby, when she would cuddle them in her cot. This love for all things wordy has never left her. A voracious reader of all genres, her love of romance was cemented at the age of twelve when she came across her first Mills & Boon novel. That book sparked a seed and, although she didn't have the words to explain it then, she had discovered something special – that a book had the capacity to make her heart beat as if she were falling in love.

When not reading, or pretending to do the housework, Michelle loves nothing more than creating worlds of her own featuring handsome, brooding heroes and the sparkly, feisty women who can melt their frozen hearts. She hopes her books can make her readers' hearts beat a little faster too.

Michelle Smart lives in Northamptonshire with her own hero and their two young sons.

CHAPTER ONE

GRACE REACHED THE bottom of the stairs and padded bare-foot to the alarm on the wall. Working on autopilot, she punched in the code and disabled it along with the sensors running throughout the ground floor. Only once had she forgotten to deactivate it. She had still been half asleep, little more than a zombie. By the time she had walked into the kitchen, the house was making more noise than a dozen hen parties trapped in a large room consuming vast quantities of Jaeger Bombs.

She switched the kettle on and yawned loudly.

Coffee. That was what she needed—a strong dose of caffeine and a good blast of sugar.

While waiting for the kettle to boil, she pulled back the insulating curtains covering the back door and peeked through the pane of glass. Bright early-morning sunlight temporarily blinded her. Squinting, she was greeted with the sight of a thick layer of frost covering the garden. It made her skin feel cold just looking at it. She dropped the curtain sharpish.

Still shivering, she turned to the kitchen table and switched the laptop on. Leaving it to boot up, she made her coffee, adding a huge dollop of milk to cool it down quicker. She brought the mug to her lips and was about to take her first sip when the doorbell rang.

A chill that had nothing to do with the cold outside swept through her, seeping into her bones.

Every hair on her body stood to attention.

Her heart crashed against her ribs, the motion strong enough to unbalance her and slosh hot coffee over her hand and fingers.

She winced and muttered an oath, but the slight scald did her good. It snapped her to attention.

Shoving the mug on the counter, spilling more coffee in the process, she wiped her smarting hand on her dressing gown and strode to the tall cupboard in the corner. She pulled out a wicker basket, burrowed a hand under the pile of tea towels and reached for the small, cold handgun.

The doorbell rang out a second time.

The laptop now booted and ready to use, she clicked on the icon that connected to the live feed from the four surveillance cameras covering the perimeter of her house. The screen split into quarters. Only the top right-hand frame showed anything out of the ordinary.

She didn't recognise the small figure wrapped in the thick parka, woolly hat and matching scarf. The woman's knees were springing slightly and she clutched a large bag to her belly, no doubt trying to keep warm in the icy conditions.

Torn between a hard-wired wariness towards strangers and feeling sorry for the freezing woman, Grace walked cautiously down the narrow hallway and drew back the heavy curtain covering the front door. The muffled shape was opaque through the frosted glass panel. Holding the gun securely behind her back with her right hand, she fumbled open the three sliding locks, unlocked the deadbolt and loosened the safety chain. Only then did she turn the lock and pull the door one and a half inches, the exact amount of slack given by the chain.

'Sorry to bother you,' the woman said, her teeth chattering. She raised her phone. 'My car has broken down. Can I borrow your phone to call my husband, please? I can't get a signal on my mobile.'

Not surprising, Grace thought. Most of the mobile networks struggled for a signal in this small Cornish village. Luckily, her landline worked fine.

She perused the stranger for longer than was polite. The woman was a good four inches shorter than Grace and, beneath the thick clothing, only a slight thing. What she could see of her face was red from the cold.

Rationally she knew this stranger could not pose a threat. Even so...

Even so, her mind raced as she thought of a whole posse of reasons as to why it was impossible to let her in to make her call and then offer the hospitality of warmth from the ever-constant cast-iron cooker in the kitchen.

Much as she knew she should slam the door in the stranger's face and direct her to the farmhouse at the top of the drive, she could not bring herself to be so uncharitable. It would be at least another ten-minute walk for the poor thing.

'Hold on a sec,' she said, shutting the door. She stuffed the gun into the deep pocket of her dressing gown, a place she knew topped the list of most stupid places to hide a firearm. She had no choice but to place it there.

Stupid, paranoid mind. You've been hiding for too long. Can't even open a door without expecting an ambush.

She unlocked the chain and opened the door.

'Thank you so much,' the woman said, stepping straight in and stamping her feet on the welcome mat to shake off the early-morning frost clinging to them. 'I was starting to think I'd never find civilisation. The roads around here are dreadful.'

Grace forced a polite smile and shut the door behind her. The cold had already rushed into the heavily insulated house. A cold, uneasy feeling swept through her, a feeling she disregarded.

'The phone's right here,' she said, indicating the landline on the small table by the front door. 'Help yourself.'

The woman lifted the receiver and made her call, pressing a finger to her ear and speaking in a low murmur.

The conversation went on for a good few minutes. When she finished, the woman put the receiver back on the cradle and smiled at Grace. The smile didn't quite meet her eyes. 'Thanks for that. I'll get out of your hair now.'

'You're welcome to wait here for your husband,' Grace said, hating the thought of anyone being outside in such awful conditions.

'No. I need to go. He won't be long.'

'Are you sure? It's horrid out there.'

The woman backed up to the front door and reached for the handle. 'I'm sure. Thank you.' She opened the door and headed off down the driveway without so much as a goodbye.

Perplexed, Grace stared at the rapidly retreating figure for a few seconds before shutting the door and relocking it.

She shivered.

The hairs on her arms were standing to attention again.

It took a few beats before she recognised the coldness in her bones as a warning and not a pure physical reaction.

Something was off...

Standing stock-still, she strained her ears. The only noise she could detect was the thundering of her own blood careering through her at the rate of knots.

Stupid, paranoid mind.

All the same, something about the stranger's demeanour played on her mind. As she padded back to the kitchen, all she could think about was the way the woman had rushed off...

The shock of the doorbell ringing a short while earlier was nothing compared to the floor-rooting terror of finding the tall, darkly handsome man in her kitchen, a man flanked by two gorilla-resembling goons.

'Wait in the car for me,' he said to them, not taking his eyes off Grace.

The goons left immediately, departing through the back door, the same door that had been locked just ten minutes earlier...

'Good morning, *bella*.'

Bella. The way that one particular word tripped off his tongue like a caress paralysed her. The drumming in her heart was instantaneous, a memory flickering back to life at the first sound of his voice. A beautiful, velvety rich voice with a heavy Sicilian accent that made his English sing.

The drumming became a loud pump. The paralysis was replaced with a fizzing energy that cleared her head of the fog that had filled it. Without taking her eyes off him, she slid her hand into her pocket and pulled out the gun.

'I'm going to give you five seconds to get out of my house.'

Only by the tiniest flicker of a thick black eyebrow did Luca react to having a gun aimed at his chest. His firm lips twitched as he lazily placed his hands in the air. 'Or what? You'll shoot me?'

'Don't move,' she snapped, her eyes widening as, hands held aloft, he took a step towards her. 'Get back!'

It could almost be described as humorous that Luca, unarmed, was utterly unfazed while she, holding a lethal weapon in her hands, was cold with fear.

She doubted he had ever felt a solitary jolt of fear in his life.

She must not let panic control her. She had always known this day would come. Mentally and physically she had prepared for it.

'I said get back.' She tried to steady her grip on the gun but her hands were trembling so hard she had to use all her concentration to keep the aim straight.

'Is this how you greet all your guests, *bella*?' He cocked his head to one side and took another step towards her, then another, his deep-set eyes not moving from her face. At some point she had forgotten how mesmerising they were, how the thick black lashes framed eyes so dark she had once believed them to be black. Only upon the closest of inspections could a person see they were in fact a deep, dark blue, like a clear summer's night. And once you knew their colour you never forgot.

How vividly she recalled the first time she had seen those eyes close up. That had been the point when every cell of her body had come alive. That had been the point she had fallen helplessly in love.

But that had been a long time ago. Any love she felt for him had died ten months ago when the truth about him could no longer be denied.

'Only the uninvited ones.' Deliberately she made a big show of slipping the safety catch off the gun. 'I will tell you one last time, get out of my house.'

He had inched close enough for her to see the pulse in his temple throb. She had to get him out of the house *right now*.

'Put the gun away, Grace. You have no idea how to handle such a dangerous weapon.'

Having a gun pointed at him had not figured in any of the welcomes Luca had been expecting. His heart thundered beneath his chest and, while he did not believe she would shoot him, the last thing he wanted was to panic her into doing something beyond either of their control.

He could hardly credit that he had found her. Finally.

As soon as he had positively identified her photo, he had boarded the jet kept on permanent standby for this very purpose, and travelled straight to England.

Grace's face was void of expression. 'You have no idea what I'm capable of handling. How did you find me?'

Somehow he managed to quell the spike of rage her tone-less words provoked. She could be speaking to a stranger for all the emotion she conveyed. 'With great difficulty. Now put the gun down. I only want to talk to you. Nothing more.'

She made no attempt to hide her incredulity. 'You came all this way and went to all this trouble just so you could *talk* to me? If you just wanted to talk, why not knock on the door like a normal person rather than get a stooge to distract me so you can break in through the back door?'

'Because, my clever, deceitful Grace, you have led me on a merry dance around Europe. You have gone to incredible lengths to hide from me.' So successful had she been in keeping one step ahead, he'd been ready to believe she had a magic portal to vanish with whenever he got too close. Even before he'd verified the picture was truly her, he had insisted his men keep a close watch on the house with instructions to follow her if she went anywhere. Just in case. He would not let her slip through his fingers again.

'I haven't led you anywhere. If I had wanted you to find me I would have given directions.' Keeping hold of the gun with her right hand, she wiped her left down the side of her thin dressing gown, the movement pulling it open.

Her detachment was all on the surface.

A heavy thickness settled in his blood. The long py-jama bottoms and matching vest top showed off her slender, almost androgynous figure beautifully. Yet there was something softer than he remembered about her physique, a softness not matched in the coolness of her unwavering hazel eyes.

His mouth ran dry. Wetting his lips with his tongue, he continued to scrutinise her.

She had changed so much. If he had crossed her in the street he would have likely not recognised her. This, undoubtedly, had been her intention.

He had almost disregarded the photo. It had been taken mere minutes after his men arrived and strategically placed themselves out of sight of her security cameras. She had left the house for a few moments to collect her post from the box at the bottom of her driveway, bundled up in a thick, shapeless coat. They had managed to fire off a couple of shots before she had gone back inside but only one had captured part of her face.

The angle of her head had caught his attention. As he'd studied it closely a flicker in his belly had ignited. It was Grace. It was the same angle she always tilted her head when thinking, the same angle she would strike when standing in front of a large canvas with a paintbrush in her mouth. Of course, in those days, her hair had been long. And blonde. Not the short, red pixie haircut she now sported. It was a style he should find abhorrent but on Grace he found strangely compelling. Sexy.

Very sexy.

'How was I supposed to know you didn't want to be found?' he asked coolly. 'You left without a word to me or anyone. You didn't even have the courtesy to leave a note.'

'I would have thought my silence made it clear.'

Her silence had spoken volumes. But how could he not search for her? He would have searched for ever.

This was the woman who had promised to love and honour him until death did they part, not until…

That was the precise problem. He had no idea why she had simply vanished from his life.

And he could hardly credit he was now standing less than ten feet from her.

'You didn't take any of your clothes.' She hadn't taken anything. She had gone for a walk on the estate, climbed over the fence that marked the perimeter and vanished.

'Your goons would have been suspicious if I'd wandered through the vineyard with a ruddy great suitcase.'

Was that really sarcasm he detected in her voice? From Grace?

'I knew you would try to find me. That's why I have a gun—to stop you or your men from forcing me to return. Because I tell you now, I am not setting foot in Sicily again. So, unless you want to learn for yourself how good my aim is, I suggest you leave. And put your hands back up where I can see them.'

For a moment all he could do was stare in disbelief. 'What the hell happened to you?'

This was not the happy-go-lucky artist he had known and loved, the woman who had always looked at him with such happiness. He had long been accustomed to women looking at him with lust—devotion even. No one could ever accuse Grace of something as insipid as devotion yet she was the only woman who had ever made him feel her world was a better, happier place just for him being in it. She was the only woman who had ever made *his* world a happier place for being in it.

By contrast, this woman's eyes conveyed nothing but cold, hard contempt. It was like looking into the eyes of a stranger.

The wife he knew did not exist any more. Not for him.

Maybe she was the same old Grace when in the company of friends. Maybe she could still warm a cold room with a smile.

But not for him.

Her icy voice broke through the sudden haze clouding his vision. 'You know what they say: marry in haste, repent at leisure. Well, I have done nothing but repent since I left you.'

Long-ago uttered words floated back to him. *I love you more than anyone or anything. I belong to you, Luca. We belong to each other.*

His stomach heaved. He sucked in air through his nostrils, breathing deeply to quell the nausea lining his throat.

This was not his wife.

He should turn around and walk away but he deserved answers.

And he would have them. If he had to tie her to a chair for a month he would get the truth out of her.

'I'll ask you one more time—how did you find me?' She repeated her earlier question through gritted teeth.

'With the help of your friend's phone.'

For the first time her composure dropped, her jaw slackening. 'Cara?'

'Yes.'

'I don't believe you. Cara would never betray me.'

'She didn't. Her phone did. You called her on it shortly after you left me.'

Her face whitened. 'She would never have given it to you.'

'No,' he agreed, experiencing a surge of satisfaction at having broken through her cool façade. 'I regret that underhand methods were used to obtain it from her, but once we had it in our possession it was simple enough to find your number and, from that, your location.'

He made it sound so straightforward. Instead, his initial jubilation at getting her number had been doused. Her network provider had no way of getting a fix on her—her phone was not being used, had likely been thrown away or destroyed. Another dead end. Or so it had seemed until a week ago when it had unexpectedly sprung back to life. Luckily, he'd paid someone from the network to keep a watch on the number in case a miracle occurred.

It seemed miracles did happen.

'Does Cara know what you did?'

'I don't know.' He didn't care. What he did care about was the way Grace's hands were shaking. Shaking hands and guns were not a good combination. 'Give me the gun or put it down.'

'No.' She raised it higher, her eyes widening. 'I'm not putting this down until you leave. Get out of my house.'

'I'm not going anywhere, so you might as well put it down.' He kept his tone calm and took a step towards her.

'Get away from me,' she said, stepping back, her voice rising. 'Don't come any closer.'

'We both know you won't shoot me.' He lowered one of his raised hands and extended it towards her, the tips of his fingers closing in on the barrel of the gun.

'I said get away from me!' Her words came out as a screech and were immediately followed by the loud tone of his phone ringing out in his pocket.

Like a tightly coiled spring suddenly released, Grace jumped at the sound.

In the confines of the small cottage, the noise of the gun was deafening, loud enough to distract him from the bee sting on his right shoulder.

They stood in frozen silence until Grace's chest shuddered and she dropped the gun to the stone floor. It landed with a loud clang, the only noise apart from the ringing in his ears.

He had only a snapshot of time to register her white-faced shock before the wet warmth on his shoulder demanded his attention. Pulling the top of his jacket aside, he winced as a burn of pain went through him. His disbelief at the red fluid seeping through his white shirt was nothing compared to his shock when he finally comprehended that the distant ringing in his ears was not an echo from the gunshot but the wails of a baby.

She had shot him.

Dear God, she had shot him.

Through her ringing ears she could hear Lily's distant wails, a noise that seemed as far away as the moon.

She had shot him.

Her hand flew to her mouth and Grace could do nothing but stare at the blood seeping out of Luca's right shoulder.

He stared back at her with a look that could only be described as stunned.

On legs that didn't belong to her, she hurried to him. Her cold blood chilled further. Up close, the wound looked even worse. She reached out a hand, pausing before she could touch him.

'I'm so sorry,' she said dumbly, trying to clear her head of the drum banging loudly in it. 'I'll get something for the bleeding.' Her stomach churning, Grace rushed to the tall cupboard. She pulled out the same basket in which she had stored that monstrous gun and grabbed some tea towels.

Lily's cries became more distressed, the piercing sound penetrating the thick walls of the cottage and striking through Grace's heart.

Dear God, what was she going to *do*?

Could Luca even hear the cries? Or had the shock of

being shot deafened him just as it had temporarily dulled her own senses?

He had sat down at the table. His olive skin had paled considerably, the dark stubble across his jawline pronounced.

This was the closest to vulnerable she had ever seen him.

She leaned over to place a clean towel against the wound. His uninjured hand shot up and grabbed her wrist. 'What do you think you are doing?'

'Trying to stem the blood flow.'

He ground his teeth together and leaned forward so their faces were just inches apart. 'I am quite capable of tending to my own injury. Leave it with me and tend to the baby you are hiding upstairs.'

CHAPTER TWO

AT LUCA'S MENACINGLY delivered words, all the blood running through Grace's veins plunged to her feet.

White light flickered behind her eyes before she caught a waft of warm, minty breath and an enormous shudder ran through her.

'Are you in immediate danger?' She managed to drag the question out, jerking her wrist against his grip.

'No.' If anything, his hold tightened.

'Then let go of me.'

Those midnight eyes flashed before he sprang his fingers open like a remote-controlled robot.

In a murky daze, she climbed the stairs and walked into the bedroom she shared with her twelve-week-old daughter.

Lily lay flat on her back in her cot. Her thin arms were struck out like a starfish, her little legs kicking in all directions, her cute face scrunched up and bright red. Grace had no doubt that if her tear ducts had developed, Lily's cheeks would be soaked.

Scooping her out of the cot, she brought her to her chest and breathed in her daughter's sweet, innocent scent. 'Oh, Lily, I'm so sorry,' she choked out, swaying gently as she tried to soothe her. 'Your mummy has done a terrible, terrible thing.'

The implications hit her with the force of a tsunami. As

she patted Lily's bottom and murmured words of comfort, her mind raced.

She had shot Luca. She had actually shot someone; a living person. She had caused physical harm to the man she had once loved, the same man who now knew of the existence of her child.

Inhaling Lily's scent brought some control to her careering thoughts, and the fogginess clouding her brain began to abate.

Under no circumstances could she let the shock of all that had just occurred control her actions. She needed to take control, now, before it was too late.

Too late?

Who was she trying to fool? Of course it was too late.

What did she expect? That Luca would take her shooting him and hiding the existence of their child on the chin and walk away?

And she'd so nearly got away with it.

She'd managed to get hold of the gun only a couple of months ago, when she had been unable to sleep for fear of Luca's men finding them and tearing Lily away from her. She had seen the evidence of what her husband was capable of, evidence that burned her retinas and flourished in her nightmares.

The threat of prison if she were caught with an illegal firearm had not deterred her from purchasing it. She'd got it from the son of the farmer she rented the cottage from, a young man with a few unsavoury acquaintances. She hadn't cared where it came from; she was safer with it. Lily was safer with it. Knowing it was in the house allowed her to sleep. Sometimes.

Luca's men were always armed. And they were dangerous. Prison had seemed preferable to falling into their clutches.

They were also stupid. She had outwitted them before when she made her escape. She could outwit them again.

Except Luca had come for her personally, something she had not anticipated. She had imagined him like a king in his castle, waiting for his soldiers to bring his erring queen home, so she could be locked in the tower for the rest of her days.

Luca was not stupid. Luca was the sharpest person she had ever known, which made him infinitely more danger-ous than his lackeys, and much harder to outwit.

Some sixth sense had been nagging at her for weeks that it was time to move on. Why, oh, why had she not acted on it sooner?

Prison did now loom dark. Not a traditional cell of iron bars and a tiny slot for a window, but a towering pink sand-stone nightmare.

Lily finally stopped whimpering. Soothed and snug, she fixed her trusting, night-blue eyes on her mummy.

Her mummy, Grace reminded herself. This was not just about her—this was about her innocent, dependent child. The first time she had held her alone, away from the ears of midwives and obstetricians, Grace had made her daughter a promise. She had sworn she would keep her safe.

She had sworn she would never let her fall into the hands of the dangerous gangster that was Lily's father.

It was amazing how long Grace was able to drag out wash-ing and dressing into a pair of faded jeans and a long, thick purple jumper. By the time she had changed Lily's nappy and generally fussed over her, a whole hour had gone by. She would have dragged things out even longer if Lily hadn't started to grizzle, no doubt hungry for her bottle.

Mentally bracing herself, Grace straightened her spine and carried her daughter downstairs and into the kitchen.

'You took your time,' Luca said from his seat at the table. He had removed his shirt. A short, rotund man was tending his shoulder, his bald head bowed in concentration. With a snap she recognised him as Giancarlo Brescia, the Mastrangelo family doctor. His presence should not be a surprise. Luca rarely travelled anywhere without him. People who lived by the sword and all that.

'I'm surprised you didn't send one of your goons up to keep watch,' she retorted, averting her eyes.

She didn't know what she found the most disturbing: his naked torso or the bloodstains marring his smooth skin. Some had matted into the swirls of black hair covering his chest. Dimly she recalled the many happy hours lying in his arms, breathing in his musky scent, splaying her fingers through the silky hair. Once upon a time, it would have taken a crowbar to prise her away from him.

'Believe me, you are going nowhere,' he said, his voice like ice.

'That's what you think.'

He laughed. A more mirthless sound she did not think she had heard. 'Do you really think I will let you disappear again, now, when I know you have had my child?'

'Who said she was yours?'

An animalistic snarl flittered across his handsome features but he remained still, the needle penetrating his flesh making any movement on his part risky. 'Do you think I would not recognise my own blood?'

She shrugged with deliberate nonchalance and sidled past him to the fridge, keeping a tight hold of Lily. She caught sight of the bloodied bullet laid oh-so-casually on the table and winced. She winced again to see the doctor expertly sew Luca's olive skin back together.

Luca followed her gaze. His nostrils flared. 'It lodged in a bone. There shouldn't be any permanent damage.'

'That's good,' she said, blinking away her shock at the physical evidence of his wound. Thank God she hadn't eaten breakfast. It would likely have come back up. She needed to keep a level head. Needed to keep her control.

She could not let guilt eat at her, and as for compassion… what compassion did Luca ever show *his* victims?

Turning her back to him, she pulled a bottle of formula out of the fridge and popped it in the microwave. She took a deep breath and punched in the time needed. The microwave sprang to life.

'Sorry to disappoint you, but she's not yours.'

The silence that ensued felt incredibly loaded, almost as if her lie had sucked all the air from the room, making her chest tight and her lungs crave oxygen. She could feel the burn of his eyes piercing the back of her skull, sending prickles of tension racing across her skin.

The microwave pinged, startling her. Was it always so loud?

She removed the bottle and shook it.

Lily must have caught the scent of milk because she started to whimper again.

'Shh,' Grace whispered. 'You can have it in a minute. Mummy needs it to settle first.'

Finally, unable to bear the tension another second, she tossed a glance over her shoulder.

Luca's eyes were fixed on her, his face tight, his features a curious combination of fire and ice.

The doctor had finished stitching the wound together and was cleaning the blood off his shoulder.

Smothering another retch, she sucked in more air in an attempt to stabilise her queasy stomach.

'Is your conscience playing up?' Luca asked, raising a mocking brow.

'No.' She turned her face away, the heat from another lie stinging her cheeks.

'No? It should be.'

'If anyone should have a troubled conscience, it is *you*.' She snatched up the bottle. 'I'm going to the living room to feed my daughter. Shut the door behind you when you leave.'

Not bothering to look for his reaction, she strode out of the kitchen. In the small living room she turned the television on and settled on a squishy sofa.

Since Lily had been born, Grace had become addicted to daytime television. And evening television. And nighttime television. The trashier the programme, the better. Concentrating on anything with any depth had become impossible.

She switched the channel to one of those wonderful talk shows featuring a dysfunctional family spilling its dirty laundry to a braying audience and a patronising host, and the incongruity of the situation almost made her laugh.

She could imagine herself on that stage, trying to justify shooting her own husband. Trying to justify a lot of things. Like ignoring all the signs that the man she loved was nothing but a gangster.

But love had blinded her. Or should that be lust? A combination of both that should have overwhelmed her in its intensity had instead been embraced. Without a second thought, she'd opened her heart wide enough to allow Luca to step right inside and burrow deep into her soul.

She had graduated art school full of the wonder of all life had to offer. Together with her best friend Cara, they had travelled Europe, visiting many of the architectural wonders in the continent.

Sicily was magical. She had fallen in love with the island and its gregarious inhabitants. Its more nefarious history had only added to the romantic ideal she had conjured.

Cara, an outdoor lover, had dragged her along for a hike over the mountainous terrain close to Palermo. They had followed what they joked was the longest fence in the world, a fence that kept outsiders from properly appreciating the most beautiful vineyards in the whole of Europe. When they had come to a gap in the fence they had assumed— wrongly—that it gave them a right of way. As luck would have it, the gap had led into an open meadow with the most spectacular views either of them had been privileged to see. Cara had been aching to paint it, so they had opened their picnic blankets out and set up; Cara with her watercolours, Grace with her sketchbook and pencils.

She had barely made a scribble when a black Jeep tore up the hill and screeched to a stop beside them.

That was when she had met Luca.

He had got out of the Jeep and walked towards them, a gun in his hand.

She should have been terrified. He had been dressed all in black, and her mind had immediately gone into an overdrive of images of swooping vampires and flesh-eating ravens.

While Cara had sensibly turned into a gibbering wreck, Grace had been entranced. It was as if she had inadvertently stepped into a movie shoot and the head vampire had come out from his coffin to greet them.

Looking back, she could hardly credit that she had been so blasé about a man with a gun, but she hadn't felt the slightest shiver of physical danger. She'd been so naïve she had assumed *all* Sicilian men carried guns. Fool that she was, she'd thought it all somewhat romantic.

Inexplicable tears filled her eyes and she blinked them away, sniffing loudly, disturbing Lily, who was busy guzzling her milk. The poor little mite was unaware her happy little life had irrevocably changed.

Footsteps sounded down the hall, followed by the sound of the front door closing.

She held her daughter ever tighter. She would rather die than be parted from her.

Somehow she didn't think Luca had been the one to leave the house.

Her intuition was bang on the money.

He strode into the living room as if he had every right to be there. His chest was still bare; a large white bandage had been placed over the wound on his shoulder, his arm resting in a sling.

He made straight for the television and turned it off.

'I was watching that.'

His nostrils flared. Not taking his eyes off her, he reached into his back pocket and produced two passports.

Blood rushed to her head so quickly it made her dizzy. Her hold on Lily tightened as she watched him, chills crawling up her spine.

Slowly, he waved the passports at her before sliding them back into his pocket.

'Lily Elizabeth Mastrangelo.' His words were monotone yet utterly remorseless. 'Her date of birth puts her at twelve weeks old.'

He might be injured but he still exuded the latent danger she had once found so exciting.

Why did he have to loom over her so? At five feet eight Grace was taller than the average female but next to Luca she always felt tiny.

Why, oh, why had she not moved on sooner? She had got back into physical shape relatively quickly. Obviously if she was comparing her recovery with that of a super-model who managed to get back into her itsy-bitsy knickers within days, then she had been a failure.

In reality she had been fit enough to move on a month ago.

So why had she dragged it out?

Where had this abnormal lethargy come from?

Why had she not run the moment she had been fit enough?

'How dare you go through my handbag?' she said, dredging the words from a throat so arid it hurt to speak.

His eyes flashed. 'I have every right. You stole my child from me.'

Somehow she managed to grind the words out. She would not let him win. Not without a fight. 'She is not your child. I had to name you as her father because we're married.'

'Yes, she is.'

How she longed to slap the arrogant certainty from him.

'You did not have the opportunity for an affair and, besides, you loved me. Our sex life was incredible.'

A deep flush curled inside her, scattered memories of being wrapped in his arms, naked, his hard strength...

'*Loved* being the operative word,' she said, a little more breathlessly than she would have liked. '*Loved*, as in past tense. Lily is not your child.'

She refused to acknowledge his mention of the *S* word. The nightmares of the past ten months had been too great for her libido to do anything but wave a white flag. The only ache had been in her heart. And only in the dark early hours, when the world slept, did her heart acknowledge the aching absence within it.

Luca came before her and dropped to his haunches. The movement caused a fleeting wince to contort his features. The twisting sensation in her belly tightened. Being incapacitated in any form was anathema to him. She could have shot him a dozen times and he would still have the same vital, energising presence.

'*Bella*,' he said in a voice that was far too silky for comfort, 'she has the Mastrangelo hair. And you were still married to me when you conceived her. I know for a fact you did not cheat on me…'

The tension cramping inside her suddenly exploded and she met his gaze with wild eyes. How stupid was she to think for a single second he would even contemplate Lily being someone else's? Luca was so insufferably arrogant the thought of his wife cheating would be as likely as the moon being made of Stilton.

And how stupid was she to have named him as the father on the birth certificate?

'It's a bit hard to have an affair when your own husband has a tracker in your phone to monitor all your movements, and assigns two bodyguards to chaperone every single movement and report on anything the tracker fails to pick up.'

Lily had finished her bottle. She stared up at Grace, startled to hear her mother's raised voice.

Luca's lips formed a tight white line. Still on his haunches, he tilted forward. 'So you admit she is mine? You admit you wilfully kept my daughter's existence a secret?'

Forcing her voice down to a lower, calmer tone so as not to distress Lily, Grace stared at him with all the venom she could muster, willing him to feel every syllable that came from her lips like a punch to the gut. 'Yes. I hid her existence from you, and do you know what? I would do it again. Lily deserves better than to know of the monster who created half her DNA. You might be the sperm donor but *I* am her mother. She does not need you. And neither do I.'

The poison in Grace's voice cut through him, as sharp as a dagger.

Luca had taken one look at Lily and known she was his.

He could not say where this certainty had come from but there been no shadow of doubt in his mind. She was his.

He was a father.

Now his detestable wife had admitted the truth, he should feel relief. Instead, a raging burn was working its way through his system, a burn he was struggling to contain.

He would never have imagined such poison being uttered from the lips of his wife, a woman who always saw the best in people and always looked for the humanity in the face of evil.

He had never imagined she would look at him as if he were the Antichrist itself.

His guts rolled as he watched her lift their child onto her shoulder and rub her back, her movements gentle and loving.

The pain in his shoulder was immense. Once they were safely in the air he would take the painkillers Giancarlo had tried to get him to consume. Taking them would likely dull his reactions. Right now he needed every wit about him.

Unable to look at Grace a second longer, he got to his feet. 'I'm giving you half an hour.'

'For what?' she asked tightly, rubbing her nose into their daughter's thick black hair.

'To pack. Anything not packed will be left behind.'

That hateful venom came back into her voice. 'I'm not going anywhere.'

'You think not?' On legs that felt heavier than usual, he paced the small room. Somehow she had managed to cram a treadmill, an exercise bike and a rowing machine inside the tight confines. No wonder she had lost all her baby weight. No one looking at her would guess she had recently given birth. This, from the woman who had once told him with a straight face that she was allergic to exercise. 'I am not giving you a choice.'

'There is always a choice.'

Abruptly he stopped pacing and stared at her, making no attempt to hide his loathing. 'This is how we are going to play it: In exactly thirty minutes we will leave this place and return to Sicily.'

He took a breath.

Little more than an hour ago, he had been unaware Lily existed, unaware he was a father. Her thin eyelids were shut, displaying thick black Mastrangelo eyelashes.

His chest constricted, memories of his early childhood suddenly flooding him. His first memories. Waking up one morning at the age of three to find his parents missing. He remembered Bettina, his favourite maid, who was often given the task of watching over him, being red with excitement. His mother had gone to hospital to have the baby. He could still feel the eager anticipation he had experienced at that moment. Even clearer in his mind was the memory of his parents arriving home with the baby, his mother's pale, tired joy, his father's beaming pride. They had sat Pepe in Luca's arms on the sofa, and taken pictures of the small brothers together. He had been full to bursting with happiness.

Lily was the image of the baby Pepe had been.

This was his daughter.

And Grace had hidden her from him.

He looked at his wife. Her eyes were hollow, sunken, as if she hadn't slept for ten months. He was glad. Her guilt should not have allowed her any sleep.

'You call me a monster,' he continued, dropping his voice so as not to disturb the sleeping child. 'Yet I am not the one who vanished without a letter of goodbye. I'm not the one who decided her child would be better off without a father and conspired to keep me out of her life. And you have the nerve to call *me* a monster?'

Her clenched jaw loosened but her eyes remained unblinking as she said, 'I would do it again. In a heartbeat.'

Blood rushed straight to his forehead, colouring his thoughts, making his skin hot to the touch.

She had not the slightest remorse, not for anything. He could punish her, severely. He could snatch Lily from her arms and banish her from their lives and she wouldn't be able to do a single thing about it.

He could. But he wouldn't.

Luca had loved his parents equally but it had been his mother to whom he had gone with his cut knees and scrapes, his mother who had kissed his bruises better, his mother for whom a thousand hugs would never be considered enough.

Grace loved Lily. And Lily loved Grace. Already the bond between them was strong. It would take a heart of stone to break that bond.

Children needed their mothers and he refused to punish Lily for her mother's sins.

No, Grace's punishment would be of a different nature.

Blackness gripping his chest in a vice, he stalked towards her and bent over to speak in her ear. He could smell her fear through the clean scent of her skin and it gladdened him. He *wanted* her to fear him. He wanted her to curse the day she ever set foot in Sicily.

'You will never have the chance to take her away from me again. Lily belongs in Sicily with her family. You should consider yourself lucky I believe babies thrive better with their mothers or I would walk away with her right now and leave you behind to rot.' He paused before adding, deliberately, 'I would do it in a heartbeat.'

*** * ***

Grace closed her eyes tightly and clamped her lips together, trying desperately hard not to breathe. Luca's breath was hot against her ear, blowing like a whisper inside her. Tiny, tingling darts jumped across her skin, fizzing down her neck and spreading like a wave; responses that terrified her with their familiarity.

Her lungs refused to cooperate any longer and she expelled stale air, inhaling sweet clean oxygen within which she caught a faint trace of an unfamiliar cologne.

She forced her features to remain still, forced her chest to breathe in an orderly fashion. But she had no control over her heart. It jumped at the first inhalation and then pounded painfully beneath her ribs, agitating her nauseated stomach.

Luca wore one scent. He was not a man prone to vanity. Changing his cologne was not a triviality that would come on his radar.

She blinked the thought away. His mouth was still at her ear.

'You see, *bella*, you do have a choice,' he said, speaking in the same low, menacing tone. 'All I want is my daughter. Her well-being is all that matters to me. You can choose to stay in this cheap cottage, alone, or you can choose to return to Sicily with me and Lily, as a family.'

'I will *never* be part of your family again,' she said with as much vehemence as she could muster. 'I will never share your bed…'

He interrupted her with a cynical laugh. 'Let me put your mind at ease on that score. You have borne me a child. I have no need or desire to share a bed with you again. No, I will take a mistress for my physical needs. *You* will become a good Sicilian wife. You will be obedient and defer to my wishes in all things. That is the price you must pay if you wish to remain a part of Lily's life. And you will endure it with the grace that should be your namesake.'

'I hate you.'

He laughed again, a repulsive sound completely at odds with the deep, rip-roaring laughs she remembered. 'Believe me, you could not possibly hate me more than I hate you. You stole my child from me and, as you know, I am not a man who forgives people who act against me. But I am not a cruel man—if I were, I would take Lily and leave you behind without a second thought. Just as you would do to me.'

All she could do was stare at him, her heart, her pulses, her blood all pumping so hard her body trembled with the force.

He straightened to a stand, keeping his eyes locked on her. 'The *choice* is yours. Come to Sicily with me and Lily, or stay behind. But know this—if you stay, you will never see Lily again. If you come with us and then decide to leave, you will never see Lily again. If you come with us and I feel your behaviour is not befitting the role of a good Sicilian wife and mother, I will personally escort you off the estate and—'

'And I will never see Lily again,' she supplied for him dully.

He flashed his white teeth at her and inclined his head. 'So, we have an understanding. Now it is time for you to make up your mind. What is your *choice* to be?'

CHAPTER THREE

GRACE DID NOT think she had ever felt as nauseous as she did when the reinforced four-by-four came to a stop before the imposing electric gates. Two on-duty armed guards nodded at them respectfully as they drove through and into the Mastrangelo estate.

As they travelled along the smooth drive, cutting through rolling vineyards and verdant olive groves, the familiar scent of Sicilian nature at its crispest pervaded the air, flooding her with bittersweet memories.

After the freezing climate of Cornwall, a part of the UK that tended to have mild winters but was suffering from a particularly acute cold spell, the freshness of Sicily in December was a sharp contrast. The sun had yet to set, the brilliant cobalt sky unmarred by a single cloud. Her thick winter coat lay sprawled across her lap, her jumper warmth enough.

She turned her mind to her mobile phone and silently cursed.

She cursed the heavy snowstorm that had engulfed the south-west of England the previous week and made the roads so treacherous. If Lily hadn't needed to attend the local doctor's surgery for her three-month inoculation, she would never have attempted the journey. But she had. For safety's sake she had recharged the phone she had bought in Frankfurt for emergencies, and taken it with her on the hazardous bus journey, not dreaming that to do so would set in motion the wheels enabling Luca to find her. She had switched it back off the minute she returned home to her rented cottage.

She cursed that she hadn't dumped the stupid phone the moment she ended her brief calls to her mother and Cara all those months ago. She'd been in Amsterdam, waiting to catch a flight to Portugal. She'd reasoned that if Luca could trace the calls then good luck to him tracking her down at Schiphol Airport. She'd called her mum's landline but Cara only had a mobile phone. To play safe, she had advised Cara to destroy it. To play even safer, upon landing in Portugal she had hired a car and driven to Spain.

What she couldn't curse was using the phone in the first place. Her mum and Cara would have been the first people Luca contacted about her disappearance. After two weeks on the run and no contact, the guilt had been crippling her.

She looked at him now, sitting in the front passenger seat, his head turned to the side by the window. Such was his stillness she wondered if he had fallen asleep, dismissing the thought almost immediately. He had power-napped on the jet back home but his naps always evoked images of a guard dog sleeping with one ear up. He would not properly relax until he was safe inside his home.

As much as she hated him and everything he represented, Grace cursed herself too. The more she thought about the past wasted month, time she should have used moving herself and Lily to a remote Greek island as she had intended, the more she wanted to give herself a good slap.

She had watched her fill of gangster and mobster films in the ten months since fleeing Sicily, had read everything she could get her hands on about them too. *Know your enemy* had become her mantra. She had known the second

Luca found her he would not hesitate to have her dragged back to Sicily. As she had learned, it was the way of his world, where women were little more than possessions.

Which again begged the question, why? Why did she not move on when she had known the longer she stayed, the greater the trail she would be creating for him to find her? Even using Lily's inoculations as an excuse was no good—she'd had over a week since then to get her act together.

After a couple of miles they reached a larger wrought-iron gate, this one with guard shelters either side, both of which had monitors connecting to the larger security station in one of the estate cottages. From this point onwards, the ground was alarmed. Anyone who stepped onto the land triggered it, the boffins in the cottage using their technology to zoom onto the intruder. In all the time she had lived there the system had only been activated by large animals.

The head of security, Paolo, came out of the left shelter to greet Luca, tipping his cap as they exchanged a few words. When he spotted Grace in the back he nodded respectfully before returning to his station.

So he hadn't lost his job. She could not begin to describe her relief. As the person in charge of all security on the estate, losing the boss's wife was definitely on the 'do not do' list.

She leaned forward and rested a hand on the shoulder of Luca's seat. 'Thank you for letting Paolo stay in his job,' she said quietly.

He turned his head. 'If you mean the fact you were able to waltz out of the estate without an escort, then rest assured, I never blamed him for that.'

'I didn't waltz. I walked.' She had walked through acres and acres of vineyards and miles of arable land until she had found the field she was looking for. It was the same field she had inadvertently trespassed onto with Cara the day she first met Luca. The broken section of fence they had originally slipped through had long been mended. It took little effort to climb over it. It had felt prophetic, like coming full circle.

'I saw the footage. You looked as if you were going on an early-evening stroll. There was nothing in your demeanour to suggest you had no intention of returning. I give you credit, *bella*. You are a wonderful actress.'

Her coolness had been external only. As soon as she was off Mastrangelo land and no longer subject to scrutiny from the multitude of spying cameras, she had dumped the tracker-installed phone Luca had given her into a hedge and run, all the way to the nearest town. From Lebbrossi, she had taken a taxi to Palermo and caught the first flight off the island. That the first flight had been to Germany had been neither here nor there. If anything, it had done her a favour. It had made Luca's job of tracking her down difficult from the outset.

The drive veered to the right. As the four-by-four turned with it onto the straight she caught her first glimpse of the pink sandstone converted monastery. The late-afternoon sun beamed down, bathing it in a pool of warm light, setting off the brilliance of the simple architecture.

They drove through an arched entrance and into the courtyard, which the monastery wrapped around in a square.

No sooner had they stopped when the heavy oak front door flew open and a petite, raven-haired woman appeared.

Donatella. Luca's mother.

Throughout the journey back to Sicily, Grace had thought with varying degrees of emotion about her mother-in-law.

Donatella had never conformed to the stereotype of the traditional fire-breathing monster-in-law. If a little distant, she had treated Grace with nothing but courtesy and respect. All the same, Grace had never been that comfortable in her company, had always felt if Donatella had been able to choose a wife for her son, she would have chosen someone with traditional Sicilian values. The kind of woman Luca had sworn he never wanted her to be because he loved her exactly as she was. The type of woman he now wanted her to become.

She had no idea what kind of welcome she could expect from her.

Impeccably dressed as always in a smart skirt, blouse and elegant scarf, Donatella stepped into the courtyard.

Luca undid his seat belt before turning to face Grace. 'Remember my warning, *bella*. Now would be a good time to start channelling your inner Sicilian wife.'

Grace clenched her teeth together and glared at him.

With a flare of his nostrils he turned back and exited the car.

Her husband did not make empty promises. If she didn't live up to his expectations she would be torn from Lily's life without preamble or ceremony, and without any hope of appeal.

The situation was hopeless.

She hadn't called the police for assistance in England because they would have arrested her for possession of an illegal firearm, grievous bodily harm and God knew what other charges.

She could forget about assistance here in Sicily. This was Luca's territory and all the important people were in his pocket.

Grace tried to open her door but the child lock had been activated.

She crossed her arms and pursed her lips together.

As Luca and his mother conversed, both kept darting glances at the car. No guesses what they were talking about.

Taking a deep, steadying breath, she gazed down at Lily, who was fast asleep in the baby seat next to her. The poor thing was worn out, having spent the entire flight screaming, her ears no doubt affected by the air pressure. Grace had wanted to wail along with her. At that moment she would love nothing more than a chance to open her lungs and scream every ounce of frustration out of her.

Luca had defeated her. Despite all her efforts, he had won and now, unless she thought of an escape route, she was consigned to live in this medieval prison for the next eighteen years.

'I'll think of a way to get us out of here,' she promised quietly, rubbing a finger over Lily's tiny hand. 'And this time we'll go somewhere he'll never find us.' Outer Mongolia sounded nice.

His conversation over, Luca walked back to the car, opened her door, then strolled round and opened the door on Lily's side.

'I'll get her out,' she said, unclipping the seat belt.

His eyes were cool. 'I will.'

'You've only got one arm.'

'But I still have all my faculties.' He had the baby seat out before Grace had shut her door.

He carried the seat over to his mother, whose hands flew to her cheeks, a purr of pleasure escaping from her throat.

Grace could hardly bear to look. Donatella took the baby seat from him and carried her granddaughter inside.

Luca reached the front door and paused, staring at Grace impassively. 'Are you coming in or do you plan to spend the evening outside?'

Nodding sharply, she clutched Lily's baby bag to her and followed him inside.

It had been only ten months since she had last been in the converted monastery but as she took in the surroundings it felt as if she had been away for a lifetime.

With an enormous sense of déjà vu twisting in her stomach, she walked a step behind him down the wide main corridor, her boots crunching on the redbrick floor.

Luca was about to step into the large family room, one of the only communal rooms in the entire building, when he came to an abrupt stop. Tension emanating from him, he rolled his head back to stare at the ceiling before taking a long, deep breath. He swallowed. 'I have things to do.'

She caught a flash of eyes that burned before he turned and walked away.

For the beat of a moment, her lips parted to call him back. Being alone with his mother for the first time since running away from her son was infinitely more frightening than handling his gorilla-like lackeys.

Steeling herself, she stepped over the threshold.

All the decoration, paintings, furnishings…everything was exactly as she remembered it. As if time had stood still.

But of course, time had not stood still. Her own life had simply accelerated. She had lived a decade in less than a year.

The first time she had been in this room she'd been on top of the world, the happiest woman in existence. At the time she could never have foreseen that the beautiful walls would start to suffocate her. She certainly could not have foretold that the man she would marry would change with such speed, and that the gun she assumed he carried around for personal protection would take on a completely different meaning.

And now she was little more than his prisoner.

Donatella had removed Lily from her car seat and was

cradling her, a look of pure bliss on her perfectly made-up face.

Lily's eyes were open. If she was perturbed to be held in the arms of a stranger, she made no show of it.

Donatella's shrewd eyes flickered to Grace. 'She is beautiful.'

'Thank you.'

'And Lily; such a beautiful name.'

'Thank you,' she repeated, wondering if there had been a more excruciating, incongruous experience in the history of the world.

Luca's warning played over and over in her mind. Under no circumstances could she intimate she was there for any reason other than devotion. But it would help if she knew exactly what he had told his mother about her sudden reappearance in their lives and about the fact of Lily.

'It's getting late. I need to get Lily settled and into bed,' Grace said, not wanting to be stuck in an interrogation that was surely forthcoming and for which she didn't know the correct answers.

Her mother-in-law's eyes flashed before the lines around her mouth softened. 'Please, Grace, let me enjoy my first grandchild for a little longer. I have only just learned of her existence.'

A big stab of guilt twisted in her stomach. Reluctantly, she nodded. 'How about if I go and get our stuff unpacked and then come back for her?'

Donatella's grateful smile twisted the guilt a little more. 'That sounds perfect.'

Traipsing back up the corridor, Grace opened the door that led into the wing she had shared with Luca and took another step into the past.

This time all traces of the past really had been eradicated.

The only familiar item was a large family portrait on the wall, the last photo of the Mastrangelos taken before Pietro, Luca's father, had so tragically died. It had been taken at Luca's graduation. The pride shining on Pietro Mastrangelo's face was palpable. And who, she reflected, would not be proud of such a family? There was Luca, the eldest son, whose serious expression was countered by the amusement in his eyes. Next to him was Pepe, Luca's younger brother, whose air of mischief was not countered by anything. Then there was the composed, elegant Donatella. There was no pride on her face. Donatella radiated serenity. These men were her pride.

A mere two months after the picture had been taken, Pietro had died of a heart attack. The mantle of head-of-family had passed to his eldest son, Luca, a role he had now held for sixteen years.

Slowly she walked through the reception room and began opening the doors of all the rooms that made up their quarters. The vivid colours and delicate murals she had painted in each of the rooms had been painted over in drab, muted tones; the furniture they had chosen together replaced with bland, masculine replicas.

It was not until she opened the door to the master bedroom that her throat closed.

The walls she had spent literally scores of hours painting to create an erotic woodland, filled with beautiful cupids and lovers entwined, had been painted over. The walls she had been so proud of and conceived with such love and hope were now covered in a drab cream. They might never have existed.

Out of everything that had happened that day, this was the one thing that brought her closest to tears.

'You appear shocked.'

She hadn't heard Luca approach.

Her chest rose and she blinked rapidly, fighting the burn in her eyes before turning to face him. 'Not shocked,' she lied. 'More surprised.'

'You are surprised I would paint over the reminders of you?'

She went to tuck her hair behind her ear, an old habit she still couldn't break even though her hair had been cropped for months.

'I had no wish to sleep surrounded by lovers when my own wife had run away.'

'So you didn't change it because your new lover didn't approve?' Where that question came from, she was not quite sure, but the scent of his new cologne had wafted back under her nose.

Had he found a lover who had bought him this new scent?

Had this lover lain in his arms, in this very room, happy to drift into sleep with this scent imprinting on *her* senses?

Her belly churned at the images playing in her head.

Luca's eyes narrowed. 'I do not think you are in a position to ask me anything like that.'

She shrugged to display fake nonchalance at the subject. 'I couldn't care less who you've been screwing. As far as I'm concerned, the day I left we both became free agents.'

A large, warm hand reached out and cupped her shoulder. Even with one arm out of order, he trapped her against the wall with such efficiency she had no time to think, let alone resist. 'I do hope you're not implying that you've been with other men since you left me?'

'It would be none of your business if I had. Now let go of me.' Apart from his hand, none of his body touched her. But she could feel him. That heat that radiated from him; she could feel it. It warmed her, penetrating her skin, heating her veins. The way it always had.

The moment she had met him she had experienced the most incredible charge. It was as if she had been hit by a bolt of lightning. Whenever she was with him the charge would glow red-hot. While their marriage deteriorated, the bedroom had remained the one area in which they remained wholly compatible.

In all the time they had been apart she had not thought about sex. Not once. Protecting herself and her baby had consumed her. In the cold of night she had missed sleeping next to his warm, solid presence, but the actual sex was something she never thought about. Never allowed herself to think about. Assumed it had all been extinguished.

She couldn't breathe.

The extinguished charge that had flickered as if awakening from a deep sleep since he broke into her house came roaring back to life, and for the maddest of moments she longed to be taken into his arms, feel the firm warmth of his lips upon hers and his body harden…

'It is my business,' he contradicted silkily, his face square in front of her, forcing her to look into the fire spitting from his eyes. 'You are still my wife and Lily is my daughter. I have a right to know if you have allowed another man to act as her father.'

His breath was hot on her face, all her senses responding like a sweet-deprived child handed a bag of chocolate.

She twisted her head to the side. How she wished she could tell him tales of scores of lovers she had enjoyed in their time apart. 'There hasn't been anyone else.'

'Good.' He traced a finger down her turned cheek. 'And so there is no room for doubt, know that if you screw another man I will throw you onto the street. You won't even have time to forget to write a note.'

CHAPTER FOUR

LUCA RELEASED HIS hold and took a step back, taking in Grace's heightened colour and the indignation ringing out from her eyes.

He had touched her soft cheek, inhaled her clean, feminine scent, and for the shortest of moments he had experienced a softening in his chest and a hardening in his groin.

Of all the women in all the world, what the hell had possessed him to marry this one? At that moment, he could not recall a single rational reason.

Fantastic sex and an unwillingness to let her out of his sight had been the primary reasons. If he had slowed down a little and comprehended that marrying a free-thinking artist might not be compatible to his way of life, he would surely have kept their relationship to that of lovers. His mother and brother had both warned him of the dangers. He had curtly told them to mind their own business.

He had been smitten. He had fallen head over heels in love, unable to imagine his life without her. Only when she had his ring on her finger had he been able to relax and thank God for bringing her to him. But only after they had signed on the dotted line did he fully comprehend how difficult it would be keeping safe a woman who refused his protection and refused to take his entreaties to be careful seriously.

Well, now she would be given no choice. All that mattered was the well-being of his daughter, and Grace would damn well have to put up with the rules he laid down.

Her breaths were coming in short, shallow bursts. Her eyes were fixed on him, an odd combination of hate and desire pouring out of them. He understood the combination.

Once he had loved her.

Now he despised her.

And after everything she had done, he still desired her.

His sling dug into his collarbone and he welcomed the distraction it provided. She was like poison, an intoxication that had embedded into his bloodstream for which an antidote had yet to be found. 'Would you like me to tell you something amusing?'

'Not particularly.'

'You will like this. You see, *bella*, my search for you was just that—a search. All I wanted was to hear in your own words the reason you left me. You took the coward's way out and I wanted an explanation. Nothing more. I would have left you alone to live your life.'

'Yeah, right,' she stated flatly.

'Yes, that is right.' He shook his head with more savagery than intended. 'You should have told me about the pregnancy. I am a reasonable man. We could have come to an agreement.'

'You? Reasonable? The only agreement would have been on your terms and would have meant me moving back to Sicily.'

'If that is what you choose to believe then go ahead. As you did not take that route the outcome is something you will never know.' He would not give her the satisfaction of knowing she was right but not for the reasons she thought. He'd imagined that all he'd need was five minutes alone with her before she begged to return to Sicily, to return to him. Any other outcome had been incomprehensible.

Such foolish imaginings.

Not that it mattered. Grace was his wife. She belonged to him.

He turned to the door, ready to open it and escort her out of the room. This was all too much. It hurt to even look at her.

Grace spotted a faint glimmer of opportunity. 'Let me and Lily go,' she blurted out before he could open the door. 'If you never intended to bring me home, why put either of us through this?'

Luca had learned he was a father only that morning, she reasoned. Shock could lead to irrational actions, as she knew well. It had been the shock of seeing that poor man's battered face and body, and the *fear* on his face when he recognised her. That, along with the aftershocks of her and Luca's ferocious argument still reverberating through her, had provided the spur she needed to leave. She had spent the drive back from her shopping trip mute with shock. Her brain frozen, she had walked into the bedroom she shared with the man she loved. She had gazed at the cherubs and lovers on the walls and had felt nothing. All the happiness and feeling had been sucked out of her.

The man she had married with such hope and such all-encompassing love was nothing but a criminal. And a dangerous one at that. Whether he'd been a criminal or not when they'd first married had been moot. It made no difference to the man he had become.

'It won't be any good for Lily,' she continued, resolve spurring her on. 'Can you imagine how awful it will be for her growing up knowing her parents hate each other?

Because she will feel it. She will. Children are like emotional sponges.'

'Lily will not suffer because I will not allow it,' he bit back. 'And if you want to remain in her life then you will not allow it either. If I think at any time that you are trying to poison her against me, you will be gone. Now, if you will excuse me, it has been a long day and I would like to shower. You have been put in the blue room.'

Yanking the door open, he held it for her. She couldn't help notice the wince of pain he gave and the tight, queasy feeling in her belly rippled.

She stalked past, flinching when he slammed it shut behind her. Only when she was safely in her new room did she start to shake.

She sank onto the bed and held Lily's bag to her chest, blinking rapidly, trying to catch her thoughts.

The blue room was exactly as it had been when she left. Blue. Blue walls, blue curtains, blue furnishings…even the en suite was the blasted colour. It was the one room of their wing she had never got around to personalising. It had been next on her to-do list, before the discovery of the truth had sent her fleeing.

She hated this room, had deliberately left it until last because she had known this room above all others would give her the greatest fulfilment.

Unzipping a compartment of the bag, she pulled out her fated phone. If there was one silver lining to this imprisonment it was that she could now speak to her mum and Cara. It would be the first time she had spoken to either of them in ten months.

It had been safer all round that no one knew where she was hiding, something she had found especially hard in England. She had known moving to Cornwall was pushing her luck to its limit, but the closer she had come to giving birth, the lonelier and more frightened she had become. There she was, about to go through the most terrifying, life-changing experience of her life and she had no one to share it with. Knowing her mother was only three hundred miles away had at least brought some comfort, but in all honesty her mum would have been a useless birth partner.

Billie Holden was an artist too—a sculptor—but reality rarely intruded in her life. Grace laughed sourly as she acknowledged it was a trait she had inherited—after all, hadn't she refused to allow reality to intrude on her love for Luca?

She remembered her call to Billie from Schiphol Airport with a smile. Typical of her mum, she'd been unfazed when Grace had explained the situation, merely relieved her only child was alive. Even when Grace had said she might not be able to contact her for a very long time, Billie had reacted with a cheery, 'Never mind, my darling, you're the best-equipped person I know to fend for yourself.' She'd probably envisaged Grace's situation as a great adventure rather than confront the reality of the situation.

Grace's childhood had been different from those of her friends. Her mother had treated her like a best friend rather than a daughter. Not for her rigid bedtimes or mealtimes—it was a rare day when Billie even remembered to cook a meal—or the relentless nagging all her friends received. Instead, Grace had been encouraged to embrace life and given all the freedom she desired. Her father was of the same mindset and every bit as much of a dreamer as her mum, but where Billie poured all her energy into her art, Graham devoted his to worthy causes in the developing world, disappearing for months, sometimes years, on end.

For all her parents' benign neglect, Grace had never doubted their love for her. It was just a different love from that which most other parents gave. And if there had been moments—many moments—when she had yearned to test them and ask how deep their love for her ran, she wouldn't swap them for anyone or change a single day of her childhood.

At least she could now make proper contact without worrying that Luca had tapped Billie's phone or could trace her IP address.

For better or for worse, she would no longer have to look over her shoulder. At least, not until she found a way to escape again.

Luca lay in his bed, listening as Lily's cries lessened. The door to the makeshift nursery opened and he heard soft footsteps go past his room.

He willed his eyes to shut but they refused, just as they had refused since he had come to bed five hours ago.

There was too much going on in his head to sleep. This was the first time he had been alone with his thoughts since he had learned of Grace's location. Not even the sedatives in his painkillers could switch his brain off.

He had found her. After ten long months he had really found her. It had all happened so quickly the day held a dream-like quality to it. Or was it a nightmare?

He was a father. That was his daughter crying in the dark. That was his wife comforting her. She was here, back under his roof. Unwillingly back under his roof.

There were no words to describe the loathing he felt towards Grace, as if an angry nest of vipers were festering in his guts, stabbing their fangs into him.

Nothing would give him greater pleasure than to pack her stuff and tell her to leave, to get out and never come back. But he could not. Even after everything she had put him through, he retained enough rationality to know it would be Lily who would suffer the most.

No, Grace's punishment would be of an entirely different nature.

From now on, when they entertained guests or left the estate, she would damn well be deferential towards him. No longer would he tolerate having his business activities probed, his opinions contradicted or his word questioned. No longer would he tolerate a wife who neglected her appearance because her mind was too full of whatever she was currently creating on a canvas to run a brush through her hair or wear clothes that matched. No longer would he find these particular quirks endearing.

He'd never met anyone like her before: someone who saw all the colour the world had to offer. Before Grace, the women he'd dated had always been perfectly turned out with opinions that were in line with his own. They could have been identikit. Until Grace appeared, as if by magic, casting him under her spell, he'd never realised how boring he found them all, or how predictable his life had been.

He'd taken such pride in her talents and the freshness she'd brought to his life that the last thing he'd wanted to do was change her in any way.

He'd loved her exactly as she was.

Well, more fool him.

Grace would learn to be a proper Sicilian wife.

Sleep was not going to come any time soon. Throwing the sheets off, he climbed out of bed and pulled on his dressing gown, carefully navigating the sling.

All the lights were off.

Grace and Lily were nowhere to be found.

He opened every door in the wing, his chest tightening with every empty room.

He returned to Grace's room. Her suitcases lay on the floor, seemingly unpacked. Her toothbrush and toothpaste had been laid on the sink of the en suite, a bulging bag of toiletries placed on the cabinet.

Entering the adjoining room, he flipped on the light. His heart twisted at the empty cot. A pile of nappies and baby accessories he did not recognise had been neatly placed on the dresser.

Where the hell had they gone?

Just as he was debating waking the household and conducting a thorough search for them, Grace walked into the room, her dressing gown covering her tall, slender frame, carrying Lily and a bottle of formula.

Immediately she switched the light off but not before he caught the glare she directed at him.

She walked soundlessly past him and settled in the old rocking chair, curling her legs in a ball and placing the teat of the bottle in Lily's tiny mouth. 'I want her to go back to sleep after she's had this,' she whispered, nodding at the light switch.

'Where have you been?' he asked, adopting an identical whisper.

'In the kitchen warming the bottle up.'

The kitchen was on the other side of the monastery. In the early hours of winter it was always freezing down there. 'Why didn't you get a member of staff to do it for you?'

Even in the dusky light he could clearly identify the look of disdain that crossed her face. 'Apart from your security guards, everyone's asleep.'

'Does she always wake so early?' It was five a.m.

She nodded. 'If I'm lucky she might go back down for another couple of hours. I had worried that after all the travelling she might have trouble settling, but she nodded off without any problems.'

'In future I will ensure someone is available to warm the milk for you.'

She rolled her eyes. 'I'll get a kettle and a jug brought up to my room.'

'That's what I pay the staff for.'

'Luca, I'm not going to argue with you about it. I'm not going to have someone else's sleep disrupted for the sake of a kettle and a jug.'

'I think you'll find you are already arguing with me about it.'

The whisper of a smile curved on her cheeks. 'No change there, then.'

Grace had always enjoyed sparring with him but it had always been done in a gentle, amused fashion. She was the only person, aside from his mother and brother, who did not automatically assume his word was on a par with God's. She challenged him, made him look at the world through a different prism. Where he saw things in black or white, she saw the varying shades of grey in between. It was one of the many things he'd loved about her: the context and sense she helped him make of the world.

Having taken over the running of the estate at the age of twenty-one, he'd been so focused on keeping the high standards set by his father and keeping his family safe from those who would snatch everything away from them, he'd never had the time to really think about *his* place in the world.

When, a year into Luca's marriage, Francesco Calvetti, an old childhood acquaintance whose family had been the Mastrangelos' bitter enemies, had suggested going into business together, it had seemed like perfect timing. Luca had already been toying with the idea. Both men were keen to establish themselves away from the long shadows cast over them by their respective fathers and equally keen to end a feud neither had wanted.

Being with Grace and the fresh perspective she had on

life had, for the first time, made him see that the life he had been living was the life expected of him. He was living in his father's footsteps. His own hopes and dreams had been suppressed for the good of the family. For duty.

It was time to strike out in his own name.

Yet, for all the context his wife had given his world, he failed to see the context or sense in why she had run away.

She thought he was a monster. She had wilfully kept their child a secret from him. Where was the context in that? So they'd had an argument? All couples rowed. One proper argument was not good enough reason to rip a marriage apart.

A lump formed in his chest. He swallowed hard to dislodge it. 'Did you find everything you need in the nursery?'

'Pretty much. Thank you. And thank you for putting me next to her.' She adjusted her hold on Lily and looked back at him. The rising sunlight was slowly dispersing the dusky grey, her features becoming clearer by the passing minute. 'I admit, when you said I was to have the blue room, I thought it was deliberate because you knew how much I hated it. It took a while for me to remember it adjoined another room.'

'She is sleeping in my old cot,' he said. 'My mother got the staff to take it out of hibernation.'

'I did wonder.'

He should leave; return to *his* room. Instead he found his eyes transfixed on the feeding baby. *His* feeding baby. *Their* feeding baby. A child he and Grace had created together.

A part of him longed to reach over and touch her, to stroke his baby's face, to hold her to his chest and feel her warmth on his skin, to smell that sweet, innocent scent.

They looked so perfect together. Even Grace could not create a more beautiful picture.

A spike cut through his heart, piercing him, a pain a

thousand times stronger than the ache in his shoulder. It took all his strength not to sway with its force.

And there was another ache too, a much baser ache that should not exist for her, not any more.

His sex drive had always been high but Grace was the only woman who had been able to turn him to lava with nothing more than a seductive smile or the flash of a shoulder. To his body, there was no more desirable a woman. Even the curve of her ankle was erotic.

There were times when he would swear she was a sorceress. How else could he explain the hold she had over him, the unquenchable yet ultimately poisonous desire that lived in his blood? Why else had he not grabbed his freedom when he'd had the chance, as any other red-blooded Sicilian man would have done?

But he'd had no time for such pursuits. What with running the estate and his other, newer, business interests, there had been no time for any kind of affair. On top of all that, the main focus of his energies had been spent on tracing Grace. Sex had never crossed his mind.

To discover his libido had reawoken because of her and that he could still respond when she wore nothing but a tatty old dressing gown sickened him. That his fingers ached to lean over and trace the delicate line of her neck, that his lips tingled to press against her…

He dragged his gaze upwards and found her staring at him, the same pained yearning mirroring back at him, her angular cheeks heightened with colour. Then her eyelids snapped a blink and she turned her face away.

Clenching his hands into fists, Luca looked to the door and willed his thundering heart to slow.

The sooner he found himself a lover, the sooner he could be released from the sexual hold she still held on him.

The sooner he stopped thinking about making love to his wife, the better.

'Write a list of everything you need for you and Lily, and I'll get someone to get it for you tomorrow.'

Closing the door softly behind him, he went back to his room and fired up his laptop.

There was no way he would be able to get any sleep now.

Work would be his salve, as it had been since Grace disappeared. Work would help focus his attention on the matters that truly deserved it, not the deceptive, heartless bitch he had been foolish enough to marry.

As Grace tiptoed back into her bedroom from the adjoining nursery there was a rap on the door.

She hurried over and yanked it open, her fingers already flying to her lips.

'Shh,' she whispered. 'I've only just got her down for a nap.'

'Here's your passport,' Luca said without any preamble, extending it to her, making no move to step over the threshold.

Snatching it from his hand, she flipped through it. 'I did wonder if you would give it back to me.'

'Why would I want to keep it?' he said, his top lip curving. 'You are free to leave whenever you like.'

'And Lily's passport?'

'I will be keeping that.'

She expected nothing less. 'I suppose it's pointless asking where, exactly, you will be keeping it?'

'You presume correctly. Now give me your phone.'

'I'm surprised you didn't take it from me yesterday.' Turning her back to him, she grabbed it off her bedside table where it was charging.

'Today will suffice.'

She passed it to him. 'I take it you're going to put a tracker in it.'

'You're getting good at this—you assume correctly. If you need to make a call before I get it back to you, use the landline.'

How she hated the coldness of his tone. And how she hated that she hated it.

'I'll do that,' she said with a brittle smile. As he had still not stepped over the threshold she took great delight in shutting the door, quietly, in his face.

The smile dropped. She leaned back against the closed door and crossed her hands over her racing heart.

Her phone was returned that afternoon by one of the maids. She took it from her gingerly and threw it onto the bed. It felt tainted. The first chance she got, she would buy herself a new pay-as-you-go one.

Purchasing another phone turned out to be trickier than anticipated.

When she felt ready to take Lily on a Sicilian shopping trip two days later, a Mercedes was brought out for her. Three heavies were sitting in it.

The number of her personal 'guards' had been increased.

Pushing Lily around Palermo, her gorillas surrounding her, she knew she was onto a lost cause.

Their presence only served to remind her of what she had hated most about her marriage. Before she had opened her eyes to her husband's true nature, the biggest blot on the marital landscape had been the lack of privacy. Sure, on the estate she could come and go as she pleased, but she had always been aware of hidden cameras, supposedly there for all the Mastrangelos' protection, watching her every move on the grounds. Outside the estate, she was under constant armed guard. She couldn't even pop off to buy a paintbrush without one of Luca's gorillas accompanying her.

She had hated it.

She still hated it, loathed the thought of her daughter growing up in an environment where freedom meant nothing.

Freedom was precious. It was unrealistic and dangerous to expect Lily to have the same levels of freedom she had enjoyed, but, unless she found an escape route, her daughter would never experience what it meant to be a proper, regular child. She would never be able to explore and get into mischief without her parents knowing her every move. She would always be in her father's eyeline no matter where he was.

All the material advantages Lily would have being a Mastrangelo would be cancelled out by the disadvantages. And that was without considering what it would be like growing up with a father who was a dangerous gangster.

While Grace didn't believe for a second that Luca would lay a finger on either of them, his rages, which in the last six months or so of their marriage had become more frequent, could be terrifying. Especially for a child. She never wanted her daughter to witness that.

When she returned to the monastery, she carried Lily to the private front door of their wing. Before she could unlock it, Donatella materialised. 'I thought you would want to know that Pepe will be returning tomorrow,' she said, referring to Luca's younger brother who had his own, rarely used, separate wing in the monastery. Pepe was the family firebrand, a playboy rebel without any discernible cause. Yet, despite his outward rebelliousness, he was fiercely loyal to his family.

Grace was not looking forward to his return. Pepe would know the truth of what had gone on between her and Luca.

The last time she had seen him, Pepe and Luca had had a massive argument. She still had no idea what the row had been about but it had been heated enough for her to worry that one of them would get hurt. It still made her blood freeze whenever she recalled questioning Luca about it afterwards and their own subsequent row.

'Thanks for the warning.' She placed the key in the lock and as she turned it Donatella placed a bony hand on her arm.

'Why did you return?'

Grace eyed her warily. There was little point in saying it was because of love. The atmosphere between her and Luca was so cold and yet somehow so charged, the entire household had to be aware things were not right between them. 'What has Luca told you?'

'Luca does not confide with me. All he has said is that he found you and you agreed to try again. He still has not told me why you left to begin with, or what happened to his shoulder.'

Grace blanched. She shook her head, trying to clear the fog that clouded it every time she thought of it. She could still smell the gun smoke.

She could also see the poor beaten man whose eyes had widened with terror when he recognised her as Luca's wife.

'I'm sorry, but it's for Luca to tell you what happened.'

Donatella studied her for a moment before digging into her pocket and producing a key.

Grace stared at it.

'It's the key for your studio,' Donatella said, passing it to her. A shadow crossed her face. 'Luca refused to let anyone in there. He said it was yours until you returned, even if you only came back to collect your belongings.'

'He said that?'

A sliver of ice shot out of her mother-in-law's eyes. 'I am

not a stupid woman. I can tell you do not wish to be here.
But you *are* here even if the circumstances are not what
you or my son would wish.'

With those enigmatic words, Donatella walked off.

CHAPTER FIVE

IT TOOK ANOTHER two days before Grace gave in. Leaving Lily with Donatella, who was delighted to be granted her first official babysitting duty, she headed through the thick forest that surrounded the monastery to her cottage.

Her cottage. Given to her by Luca on their wedding day.

She could still recall her excitement when she'd first walked inside and seen the lengths he had gone to to make it into a proper studio for her. The walls of the ground floor had been knocked down to make one enormous room, and painted white to enhance the natural sunlight. Daylight-mimicking light bulbs had been installed for when the muse took her at night. There were easels to accommodate all different sizes of canvas, a hundred different brushes of varying sizes and hair and, best of all, he had bought every shade of paint from the specific brand she favoured. She had been in heaven.

She had not picked up a paintbrush or done anything as basic as a doodle since she had left. All her creative juices had died when she walked out of the estate.

Taking a deep breath, she turned the key and pushed the door open. Immediately she was hit with the trace of turpentine and oil paint, scents that had seeped into every crevice of the cottage.

At first glance it looked exactly as she had left it. The

canvas she had been working on was still on its easel, a fine layer of dust now covering it; her brushes all rammed into varying pots, her tubes of paint still scattered randomly across her workbench. Stacks of blank and completed canvases still lay in neat stacks; half-finished canvases she had left to dry before working on them again still lined the walls.

Someone had been in there during her absence. It was nothing specific she could put her finger on, more of a gut feeling.

Her stomach tying itself in knots, she climbed the open staircase to the first floor. The sense that someone had been there grew stronger, especially when she entered the bedroom. This was the room she had slept in whenever Luca was abroad or tied up with business until the early hours, something that had dramatically increased throughout the second year of their marriage. Although she'd missed him being around so much, she would take the opportunity to work through the witching hours without guilt and then flop into bed shattered.

One thing she had always been able to take heart from was that he would always join her if he was in Sicily. Wherever she slept, he would seek her out. Always. She would wake to find herself wrapped in his arms. Invariably, they would make love and she would tell herself that everything between them was fine.

She was certain she had left the bed unmade.

The bathroom was dusty but clean, relatively tidy, her toothbrush and other toiletries on display where she had left them. A quick peek in the laundry basket revealed the tatty jeans and paint-splattered jumper she had last worked in.

Her bittersweet trip down memory lane was interrupted when she heard the front door shut.

'Hello?' she called, hurrying to the stairs. About to step

down, she paused when she saw Luca leaning against the front door staring up at her.

'What do you want?' They were alone for the first time since he had found her. Now there was no Lily to temper the tone of her voice for, she made no attempt to hide her hostility.

The first thing she noticed was his lack of a sling. Dressed in black jeans and a light blue sweater, his arms folded across his broad chest, his jawline covered in dark stubble, he carried a definite air of menacing weariness.

'We've been invited to Francesco Calvetti's birthday party in Florence next Saturday,' he said without any preamble.

'Why's he holding it in Florence?' Francesco Calvetti was as big a gangster as her husband. It was only after Luca had invested in a couple of casinos and nightclubs with him that the cracks in their marriage had appeared and he had begun to change…

'He bought a hotel there. I've accepted the invitation for us.'

'It's far too short notice.'

'I wasn't asking your opinion on the matter. I was telling you.'

'And what about Lily?'

'I have spoken to my mother and she has agreed to care for her overnight.'

'Absolutely not.' No way was she going to leave her baby to attend *that* man's party.

'I have also seen the local priest about having Lily baptised,' he continued as if she hadn't spoken. 'I have booked her in for the first Sunday of the new year.'

'Well, that's telling me,' she said, stomping down the stairs. 'We can argue about the christening in a minute. I am not leaving Lily to attend a silly party.'

'It is not a silly party. It is an important event that you will attend as my devoted wife.'

The way his eyes burned into her left Grace with no doubt as to the meaning laced in his words.

Devoted wife.

Luca might have abandoned the idea of displaying togetherness in front of his family but this did not extend to the wider world.

She would be expected to accompany him and act the docile, dutiful wife.

She would be expected to play the role of lover to a man she hated with every fibre of her being. The consequences of failure would be harsh. Banishment from her daughter's life.

'Am I at least allowed a say in the christening? Or is Lily's entire future to be decided by you?'

His nostrils flared. 'That all depends.'

'On what?'

'On whether your opinions concur with mine.'

'So that'll be never, then,' she threw at him bitterly.

'Consider yourself lucky to be here and able to voice an opinion,' he said, his tone a low, threatening timbre. 'It's a sight more than you gave me.'

'It's a sight more than you deserved,' she spat. 'Now, unless there's something else you want to tell me, you can leave.'

Luca clenched his fists by his sides at her defiance, at the folded arms crossed over the slender waist, her hair sprouting in all directions. Since they had returned, the red dye had faded, her natural honey blonde coming through.

He didn't know if he wanted to wrap his hands around her throat or kiss the defiance from her face.

She had been home for six days. In all that time he had

tried to block her from his mind but she was still there, festering in his psyche. He didn't want to exchange one solitary word more than was necessary with her. Simply looking at her deceitful face made his stomach clench.

'I am not yet ready to leave. You owe me some answers.'

Her striking features contorted into something feral. 'I don't owe you anything.'

Every sinew in his body tightened. When she turned her back on him and walked to her workbench, he had to fight the urge to wrench her round and force her to look at him.

'You damn well do. One minute you were there, the next you were gone. No letter, no phone call, nothing to let me know if you were dead or alive.'

She turned around, leaned against the bench and rolled her eyes. 'Steady on, Luca—you make it sound as if you were worried about me. Surely a heart is needed to feel worry?'

It was the dripping cynicism that did it for him. The sheer lack of remorse. The implication that her selfish, unrepentant behaviour was somehow *his* fault.

All the rage he had been smothering since he found her exploded out of him, consuming him in a fury that accelerated when he found his tongue to speak.

'Worried about you?' he said, his words coming out in a raging flow. 'Worried about you? I thought you were dead! Do you hear me? Dead! I imagined you lying cold on a verge. I pictured you cold in a mortuary. For two weeks I could not sleep for the nightmares. So no, I wasn't worried about you. It was *much* worse than that.'

For a moment he thought he caught a flicker of distress on her face before her now familiar insouciance replaced it. 'I apologise if I caused you any distress...'

Slam!

Without conscious thought, the desperate need to

purge the storm of emotions acted for him and he punched the wall.

'You haven't got a clue, have you?' he raged. 'I thought we were happy. When you went missing, I thought you'd been kidnapped but when I received no ransom I thought you had been killed. I called your mother, I called Cara— neither of them had heard from you. Or so they said. It never crossed my mind you would do something so wicked as to up and leave without a word.' He threw his arms out, ignoring the pain in his shoulder, ignoring the throb in his fist. 'You didn't just leave me, you left everything, all your work, all your clothes…'

In the midst of his fury he saw how white she had become, how she clung to her workbench as if she depended on it to keep her upright.

Taking a deep, ragged breath, he fought for control and forced his voice to adopt a modicum of calm. 'Two weeks after you went missing, your bank statement arrived. I opened it and found every euro had been transferred into a new account the same day you disappeared. Do you know how I felt then?'

Slowly, she shook her head.

'Elated. Suddenly there existed the possibility you were alive. Until then it hadn't even occurred to me to check the safe for your passport.' When he had discovered it missing, the relief had been so physical he had slumped to the floor and buried his head in his hands, sitting there for minutes that had felt like hours, his usually quick brain taking its time to process the implications. But once he had processed them…

He had dug up all her bank statements and read them in detail. Apart from the odd splurge on painting materials, Grace had hardly touched the allowance he gave her.

Over a two-year period she had accumulated more than two million euros.

Had she been planning her escape from the start?

Whatever the reason, his wife had saved enough money to start over.

From then, it had been a case of following the money trail. Luckily for him, money—his money—was able to lubricate the tightest of lips and within a day he had been in Frankfurt. Unluckily for him, he had been a week too late. She had already gone. It had taken another four months for him to find her latest location but he had been too late then too.

In the meantime, Pepe had come up trumps with Cara's phone, through which they'd determined what they had good reason to believe was Grace's number. That same number had remained inactive until barely a fortnight ago.

'You put me through hell,' he said flatly. 'I would have gladly traded my life for yours and you let me believe you were dead. Now tell me why I don't deserve some answers.'

'I was going to leave you a note,' she said. For the first time he detected a softening in her voice. 'But I couldn't risk you coming home early and finding it before I had a chance to leave Sicily. I knew you would never let me go.'

'What kind of a monster do you think I am?' he asked, throwing his arms back in the air. 'That argument we had before you disappeared? Was that the cause of it?'

'No! That row—as horrible as it was, I would have forgiven it in time…'

'So tell me! When, exactly, did I frighten you so much that you believed I would stop you doing anything?'

'That's just it! You never let me *do* anything.' She threw her own arms in the air. 'You promised I could exhibit my work in Palermo and it came to nothing—every time I found the perfect venue you found the perfect excuse to keep me from buying it. I wasn't allowed to drive my own car, I had to travel everywhere with armed guards—I couldn't even buy a box of tampons without one of your goons hovering over me. I would insist he stay outside the shop door but I couldn't be certain he didn't have his binoculars out spying on me, ready to report back to you.'

'My men were assigned for your own protection, not to spy on you,' he roared. 'They were there to keep you safe. This isn't England. You knew when you married me that you were marrying into—'

'I most certainly did not! I took you at face value. I thought *everyone* in Sicily carried guns for their personal protection. If I had so much as suspected the kind of monster you really were…' Her vicious tongue suddenly stopped, her eyes widening, fixing on his shoulder. 'Luca, you're bleeding.'

Sure enough, when he followed her line of sight down to his shoulder, a dark stain had appeared. Immediately he became aware of the accompanying ache.

Now he was aware of it, his knuckles throbbed too.

Grace stared for a moment longer, then turned and dragged a paint-splattered chair over to him. 'Sit down and take your top off,' she ordered in short, clipped tones. 'I'll get the first-aid kit.'

'Stop trying to change the subject,' he said. With all the bitterness and acrimony flying around, a sour taste had formed in his mouth. 'You were about to explain what you find so abhorrent about me.'

White-lipped, her jaw clenched, she sank to her knees in front of a small cabinet. 'You're hurt,' she said as she rummaged through it. 'My home truths won't mean a thing if you bleed to death. Let's sort your wound out first.'

Yes, he was hurt. Heartsick and nauseated with a chest

so tight it was difficult to draw breath. 'You are the last person I want tending to any of my injuries, now or ever.'

A small green bag with *first aid* written on it whipped over and landed by his feet.

'If you want to bleed to death like a stuck pig, be my guest. Or, if you want to be an adult about it, let me take a look at your wound.'

She stood before him, hands on hips, glaring at him. He had always known she had proper backbone but its strength had only become fully apparent since he found her.

An image flickered in his hammering brain of his wife facing off against their teenage daughter. Would Lily inherit her mother's independent streak? How often would he have to step in as peacemaker when they faced off to each other?

That was if they lasted that long. At the rate he and Grace were going they would be lucky to see the new year in without killing each other. He could feel the fury that resided in her as clearly as he could feel his own.

He inclined his head and then carefully removed his sweater and shirt.

With brisk efficiency, Grace picked up the first-aid kit and brought another chair over to sit opposite him.

She tilted her head and studied him. 'You've torn the stitches.' Unzipping the kit bag, she removed a square foil package and ripped it open with her teeth. 'Keep still.'

Her head bowed in concentration, she used the antiseptic wipe to clean the blood with her right hand, her left hand resting lightly on his thigh to steady herself.

His senses filled with the fragrance of her shampoo tickling his nose. The trace of turpentine that had become more elusive the longer she had been gone was there too, more pronounced than it had been in months.

Being back in her studio with her filled him with emotions he could not begin to comprehend.

How he had loved watching her paint, watching the deep concentration she applied to her art. She would cut out the world from inside her head so all that remained was her and the canvas that became an extension of herself. If he was home, he would bring his laptop to the studio and work while she painted. For the most part she would be oblivious to his presence, but every now and then she would turn her head and bestow him a beaming smile that left him in no doubt how happy she was to have him there with her.

Even before she disappeared he had missed those times, but the running of the casinos and nightclubs had taken him away from home more frequently than he would have liked, especially in the evenings.

'I like what you've done to your hair.'

She stilled and raised her eyes. 'I thought you would hate it.'

'Is that why you cut it so short? To spite me?'

'Partly. Mostly it was to make it harder for you or anyone searching to recognise me. Every time I moved on I would cut a little more off and change the colour.'

'It's just as well I found you when I did or you would have ended up looking like a Tibetan monk.'

She laughed, but it sounded forced. 'Yes. I might have ended up in a proper working monastery. You would never have found me then.'

'Probably not.' He expelled a breath. There was something incredibly soothing about the way she tended him, her fingers gentle and unrushed. He closed his eyes as he felt the now familiar hardening in his groin.

He did not want to want her.

He *shouldn't* want her.

But dear God he did.

'The bleeding's stopped,' she murmured. 'I'll put a clean

bandage on it but I think you should get the doctor to check it out, just in case.'

He didn't want to hear the concern lacing her voice.

Her eyes creased in concentration as she carefully placed the bandage over the wound but there was now something less assured about her movements, a faint tremor in her fingers, a shallowness to her breathing. He recognised the sound. Its familiarity was akin to pouring petrol on a flame.

His hands clenched into fists but this time it was not anger he was fighting. It was desire, the desire to run his fingers through that short crop, to trace her cheekbones and the softness of her skin.

Grace cleared her throat. When she spoke her voice was husky. 'All done. Let's take a look at your knuckles.'

She lifted her eyes to meet his and for an instant he was thrown back in time to a place where nothing had existed for them but each other. There was the light sprinkling of freckles across her long nose, the same freckles he had been determined to count every last one of, the small beauty spot on her left cheekbone and the tiny childhood scar above her top lip that was the result of an accident with barbed wire. A thousand memories filled him and the desire to press his lips to hers and capture a taste of that remembered honey sweetness came on the verge of consuming him.

Only the ring of his phone saved him.

Those memories were from a different life when he had been a different man and Grace had been a different woman.

Now she was poison.

Shoving his chair back, he got to his feet and dug his stinging hand into his pocket. 'Ciao.'

He sighed as he listened to his PA explain about a production problem in the bottling factory.

'I need to go,' he said once he had ended the call. 'We will finish this conversation another time.'

Grace opened her mouth then closed it. Then opened it again. He braced himself for the anticipated insult she was certain to throw at him. The only thing she threw at him was another antiseptic wipe.

'For your knuckles,' she explained tightly. 'And make sure you see your doctor about the wound.'

For the briefest of moments he caught the desolation in her eyes before she straightened and turned her back on him.

Outside in the fresh air he took a moment to compose himself.

If his phone hadn't rung he would have kissed her. And one kiss would never have been enough. He would have wanted all of her.

Swearing under his breath, he strode back to the monastery.

He would not be a slave to his libido. He would master it until he found a mistress who would serve as an outlet for it.

Yet no matter how hard he tried to envisage this mythical woman, the only image that came to his mind was that of his wife.

CHAPTER SIX

GRACE STEPPED INTO the master bedroom with a real sense of trepidation. It was the first time she had been inside it since the day of her return. There was no denying this room was now very much Luca's territory.

Puffing air through her bottom lip, she walked straight to the door that housed her old dressing room and flung it open.

That sense of walking into the past hit her again. The rows of clothing were exactly as she had left them. All that wonderful colour.

She hadn't bought anything colourful since she left Sicily. Part of that had been because she had known his goons would be searching for a woman who wore vivid colours. The main part had been because the lightness in her heart had darkened and she had subconsciously bought clothes that had reflected that darkness. It had been the same darkness that had killed all her creativity.

Would the light ever return?

Had Luca been through her dressing room in her absence, looking for clues as to where she had gone? When he'd finally realised that she'd left him, had he been tempted to throw all her clothes onto a bonfire?

His mother had said he'd kept all her possessions in case she returned to collect them.

No matter how hard she tried to push the image out of her head, all she could see when she closed her eyes was the agony etched across his features when he described the effect her disappearance had had on him.

The raw emotion that had resonated from him had almost sliced her in two.

Surely he didn't really need it spelled out why she had left? Who in their right mind would knowingly bring a child into such a dangerous world? It was different for him. Luca had been born and raised in it. To him, it was normal.

That had been made abundantly clear two days before she'd left.

She'd been in her cottage painting. For the first time ever, the smell of the turpentine she used to clean her brushes and thin her paints had made her queasy. Truth be told, she'd been feeling nauseous for a few days, had assumed she'd picked up a bug. Her usual boundless energy had deserted her too, so she'd decided to call it a day and get an early night.

She hadn't even opened the door to their wing when she heard the shouting.

Luca and Pepe often rowed but this had been a real humdinger of an argument, vicious, their raised voices echoing off the walls of the corridor surrounding Luca's office. A loud smash had made her jump back a foot.

For an age she had stared at the office door wondering whether she should go in and defuse whatever was going on between them or leave them to get on with it. There was always the risk she could walk in to them throwing stuff at each other and inadvertently get caught in the firing line.

Before she could make up her mind, the door had flown open and Pepe had stormed out, almost careering into her.

He'd stopped short. 'Sorry. I didn't know you were there.'

'Don't worry about it,' she'd said. 'Is everything okay?'

A stupid question. Even if she hadn't heard them argue, one look at the thunder on her brother-in-law's face would have answered it.

'Ask your husband,' he had replied curtly.

When he had left their wing, he had slammed the door hard enough for her to feel sorry for its hinges.

She'd entered Luca's office and found him pacing in front of the window, a glass of Scotch in his hand. A large trail of coffee stained one of the white walls, a smashed cup on the carpet below it.

'What's the matter?' she'd asked. 'Who's been throwing inanimate objects at the wall?'

He'd spun around to face her, his features contorted in the same thunderous expression as Pepe's.

'I thought you were in your studio,' he'd snapped.

Unused to having that tone of voice directed at her, she'd flinched.

'I'm sorry,' he'd muttered, shaking his head. 'It's been one of those days.'

'I heard you arguing with Pepe. What was that about?'

'Nothing important.'

'It must have been important that way you two were shouting at each other. And smashing things.' Deliberately, she had kept her tone even, hoping it would be enough to defuse his rage and calm him down enough to talk to her.

'I *said* it was nothing important.' He had downed his Scotch then pulled his jacket from the back of his chair and shrugged his arms into it.

'Where are you going?'

'Out.'

'Out where?'

'I have business to attend to.'

'It's nearly ten o'clock.'

'My business does not conform to office hours.'

'So I've noticed.'

His gaze had snapped to her. 'And what's that supposed to mean?'

'Your long hours used to be here, on the estate, with me. Since you went into partnership with Francesco, I hardly see you, not properly.'

'I'm part owner of two casinos and a handful of night-clubs,' he'd said, speaking through gritted teeth. 'They are nocturnal businesses and need hands-on management.'

'I am well aware of that.'

'Then what are you complaining about?'

'I'm not complaining.' Then her voice had shaken. There had been something so…feral about him at that moment, a wildness that wasn't just due to his unshaven, dishevelled appearance. Luca was usually so perfectly groomed. 'I'm worried about you. You're working too hard. It's not good for you…'

'I shall be the judge of what's good for me,' he had interrupted with a snap. 'You work long hours yourself.'

'And when I'm tired I stop, as I have this evening. You're working yourself into the ground and you're drinking too much. You've been stressed for weeks. Months. Look how you were with me at the casino last night…'

'I've apologised for that.'

'I know, but I still don't know what was going on…'

'Nothing was going on and I would thank you to stop harping on about it!' His voice had risen to a shout. Before she'd had time to blink, he'd swept all the contents of his desk onto the floor where they landed with a clatter.

She had stared at him with wide eyes. Her heart had hammered beneath her ribs. 'What is *wrong* with you?'

'How many times do I have to tell you to stop interfering?' he'd shouted. 'My business dealings are none of your affair.'

'Of course they are—we're married.' She'd always known Luca had a temper on him but it had never been directed at her before; not like this. But she would not back down. Not this time. 'I'm your wife, not a child. You used to talk to me about everything but now you won't confide in me at all, not about anything, not the business, not your argument with your brother, not *anything*.'

He'd thrown his arms in the air. 'I don't have time for this, *bella*. I need to go.'

'Why?' She had backed against the door to block his exit.

'I've already told you. I have work to do.'

She had folded her arms across her chest and said the words she'd longed to say for months. 'No. I want you to stay at home tonight and talk to me. I want you to tell me what the hell's going on in your life that is turning you into a stranger.'

His face a mask of fury, he had stood before her. 'I am not answerable to you, or Pepe, or anyone. I am your husband and my word alone should be good enough to satisfy any curiosity you may have. Now move aside.'

'Or what? You'll manhandle me out of the way?'

He'd raised his eyes to the ceiling and muttered an oath that even Grace with her limited Italian had understood.

Anyone in their right mind would have got out of his way immediately, but no matter how hard her heart had hammered, no matter how frightened she had been, she hadn't been frightened of *him*. No, something else had scared her and however hard she had tried to swat it away, it had loomed closer than ever.

When he'd looked back down at her, his features had regained some form of composure. 'Please, Grace,' he'd said, his voice surprisingly tender. 'You are reading too much into this. All brothers argue. The casinos and nightclubs need hands-on running, that is all.' He had stroked a finger down her cheek. 'How about I promise to stay out no more than a couple of hours? When I get home we'll share a bottle of wine and I'll give you a massage. How does that sound?'

Despite herself, despite knowing she shouldn't just capitulate, she'd nodded and sighed, pressing her forehead against his chest. Luca's heart had been hammering as wildly as her own.

'I worry I don't know you any more,' she'd confessed. 'You're hardly ever home and when you are, you're distant with me. And you're drinking too much—it scares me.'

Wrapping his strong arms tightly around her, he'd buried his face in her hair. 'You have nothing to worry about, *amore*. I swear. You know I love you. That will never change.'

Tears had pricked her eyes, fear gripping her stronger than ever. 'I love you too.'

When he had returned that night, there had been no shared bottle of wine and no massage. Even though her head had ached and her heart had been heavy, she had fallen asleep on the sofa. He'd carried her to their bedroom and helped her undress, then let her sleep, locked in his arms.

In the morning, she had awoken and immediately sat upright, as if she'd been hit by a lightning bolt. He'd already left for work, leaving a sweet note on his pillow for her. He hadn't been there for her to tell of the vivid dream that had awoken her so abruptly. The dream had brought into sharp focus something that had been hovering in the back of her mind for days, like a wispy cloud that refused to be caught.

She'd dreamt she was pregnant.

* * *

'Is there a problem?'

Grace jumped. She'd been so lost in the past, the carpet so thick, she hadn't heard Luca's approach.

She pressed a hand to her chest and managed the faintest of smiles. 'Lily's napping, so I thought I should see if I had anything suitable to wear for the party on Saturday.'

'I'll get a member of staff to move everything to the blue room,' he said, looking past her. 'But I doubt there is anything suitable to wear in there.'

'What do you mean?'

'In the past I was happy to indulge your preference for bright colours but not any more. The party we're attending is a high-society affair and you will dress appropriately.'

'You always liked that I dressed differently. Unless you were lying to me.'

'That was then,' he said coldly. 'I was far too indulgent. I have already stated my desire for a traditional Sicilian wife. In future you shall wear clothes *I* deem appropriate in public.'

'And what does a Sicilian husband deem appropriate wifely apparel for a party with the cream of Florentine society?'

'Something demure, elegant and sedate. And not just in her dress but in her manners too.' He stared at her pointedly.

'You really are full of it,' she said scornfully. 'I would *kill* to see a man try and tell your mother what to wear and how to behave.'

'My father would never have told her how to behave because he loved her for who she was. The simple difference is, I do not love you. Your wants and needs mean nothing to me. When you accompany me as my wife you will wear what I tell you and behave as I tell you or you can pack your bags and leave.'

He meant every word. She could feel it.

If she called his bluff and packed, he would arrange a driver to take her to the edge of the estate. Once at the border, that would be it. She would never be allowed back in.

'In that case, I shall go shopping for the drabbest dress in the world.' She plastered the biggest, fakest smile she could muster to her face. 'I'll do my best to buy a dress that is the epitome of elegance.'

'Rather than rely on your definition of elegance, I will accompany you.' He checked his watch. 'I'll clear my schedule for the next few hours. We can leave now.'

The dress on the mannequin had thin straps and a tight buttercup-yellow bodice that narrowed in a V at the waist. Its skirt fell to the knees at the front, the back flaring down to the ankles like a peacock tail, a riot of reds, yellows and oranges. It was so beautifully designed and cut, so fantastically offbeat that Grace couldn't help but stare wistfully at it.

Luca appeared by her side with a fawning shop assistant. 'I have selected the dresses I wish you to try,' he said in the offhand manner he had adopted since they'd arrived at the exclusive shopping arcade.

Leaving Lily with him, she followed another assistant into the plush changing room.

He'd selected four dresses. Like the others she had already paraded herself in, they were all in varying shades of beige. If there was one colour she loathed, it was beige. She remembered on one of their previous, happier shopping trips she had regaled him for a good twenty minutes about why beige was so nondescript it didn't deserve to be called a colour. Even in her darkest days she would never have contemplated wearing it.

In their marriage's first incarnation, he had made her

feel like a princess whenever they went shopping together, never caring if her preferences were a little offbeat, his only wish for her to feel confident and happy in whatever she chose. This time he dismissed each of her humiliating parades in front of him with a dismissive sweep of his eyes, his attention taken with the fawning shop assistant, who at one point he permitted to hold Lily.

The spike of jealousy that pierced into her chest was so acute she had to fight the urge to rip her child from the assistant's arms.

'Lily will need a bottle soon,' she finally snapped when displaying the fourth dress for him. 'Will this one do?'

He fixed cold eyes on her. 'I think it is highly suitable.'

'Great.' She bestowed him with a saccharine smile and sashayed back into the changing room. Of all the dresses she had tried on, this one was the greatest antithesis to style. It resembled something her grandmother would wear to a wedding.

She had no choice but to suck it up. She would rather die than be parted from her daughter.

Once the dress was packaged and Luca had paid, he led them to a bustling café for a late lunch.

'Can't we go straight home?' Grace asked, in no mood to spend any more time with him. In three days they would be going on an overnight trip to Florence for the blasted party. She was going to be stuck with him for at least twenty-four hours.

'You're the one who said Lily needed another feed.'

Naturally, Lily chose that moment to start grizzling.

Without exchanging another word between them, they ordered. While they waited for their meals, a waiter was dispatched to heat Lily's bottle.

'Why do you not breastfeed?' Luca asked, finally breaking the silence between them.

Rocking Lily on her shoulder, she stared at him. 'Why?'

'It surprises me. I assumed you would want to.'

His accurate assumption turned her stomach. In the early days of their marriage they had agreed that having a baby would be something to embark on in the future. Grace had only been twenty-three. There had been plenty of time. Selfishly, they had wanted to enjoy each other first. Even so, she had become rather slapdash about taking her contraceptive pill.

'Life happens.'

His eyes hardened. 'Considering I have already missed so much of her life, it is only fair that you fill in the blanks.'

She met his gaze. 'You think?'

He leaned forward. 'I want to know everything about our child. Everything. In due course you will tell me, but for now you can start with why you did not breastfeed.'

Grace was interrupted from glaring at him when the waiter returned with Lily's bottle.

'Well?' Luca said, impatient, once the waiter had left them.

'I couldn't breastfeed,' she said flatly, shifting Lily's position and putting the teat in her mouth. 'The midwives wanted to help but they were too busy. Nothing we tried worked. I was exhausted, Lily was hungry...' She shrugged. 'In the end they had to discharge me because they needed the bed, so Lily and I went home and onto formula milk.'

'Just think,' he said, his voice musing but his eyes like a frozen winter night. 'If you'd had your husband there to take the burden off you, the outcome might have been different.'

'You'd love to think that, wouldn't you?' She shook her head with a grimace. 'The big hero riding to the rescue of his wife's underperforming breasts. Tell me,' she continued, ignoring the throbbing pulse in his temple, which always meant danger, 'how exactly would you have helped? Unless biology has advanced to allow you to lactate, I don't see what possible help you could have given me.'

'I would have been there for both of you. I would have taken care of Lily so you could sleep and recover. Who was there for you, Grace? When you gave birth to our child, who was there for you? Who was there to help you recover?'

Cheeks burning, she gazed down at her guzzling baby.

He leaned forward again. 'You can justify it all you want but you made the first three months of Lily's life an unnecessary struggle for you both.'

She turned her head and stared pointedly at their bodyguards who were sitting at the table next to them. 'Our freedom from you and from them made the struggles necessary. And for all your talk about "being there" for us, don't think it's escaped my attention that you haven't held her yet. Not once. While I've spent the morning acting as a prancing clothes horse, you've spent your time flirting with the shop assistants.'

'You sound jealous.'

'Don't change the subject.'

'There is nothing more unattractive than a jealous wife.'

'And there's nothing more unattractive than a married man flirting with another woman in front of his wife and baby.'

'I was not flirting—'

'And you can't expect me to believe Sicilian women don't get jealous,' she continued, deliberately talking over him. 'How would your mother have reacted if your father had flirted with younger women?'

'She would have pulled his testicles off with her fingernails.' He smiled coldly. 'But my father adored her, so he never needed or wanted a mistress.'

The waiter arrived with their steaming plates of pasta, suppressing her urge to punch Luca in the face.

She wanted to hurt him. Right then she wanted to make him suffer for everything he had put her through, was putting her through, and everything she would have to endure for the next eighteen years. Unless she found an escape route. Which she would.

While she finished feeding Lily, Luca ate his pasta and caught up on his emails, effectively blanking her out.

'Have you even spoken to Lily yet?'

He raised his eyes.

'Have you?' She carefully placed the baby on her shoulder and patted her bottom.

'Babies can't talk.'

'Have you tried *any* form of interaction with her?'

His nostrils flared. 'Lily does not yet know me. I have no wish to upset her.'

'You were happy to let the shop assistant—a stranger—hold her.'

He shrugged. 'She asked.'

'On that basis, you would let any random person who wanted to hold our child have her?'

'Only the ones I find attractive enough to consider making my mistress.'

She flinched. 'So you *were* flirting.'

'I wouldn't call it *flirting*. I would call it *auditioning*.'

'You're really enjoying this, aren't you?'

'I take no pleasure from humiliating people. In your case I am prepared to make an exception.' He took a bite of pasta and cast his eyes back down to his tablet.

'That's funny.'

'What is?'

'You saying you get no pleasure from humiliating people. In your line of work I would have thought humiliation was a perk.'

That got his attention. He put his fork down. His narrowed eyes captured hers. 'My line of work?'

'You're a gangster. A criminal.'

CHAPTER SEVEN

GRACE COULD HAVE sworn Luca blanched, but, it was such a fleeting expression, one blink and it had gone.

'I am not a criminal.'

'Really?' She made no attempt to hide her disbelief. 'How would you describe yourself?'

'I'm a businessman.'

'Hmm. So it's normal behaviour for businessmen to live in the Sicilian equivalent of Fort Knox and travel everywhere with armed guards? Is it also normal for businessmen to beat people?'

His eyes had blackened, his nostrils flared. 'What, exactly, do you mean by that?'

'Do you remember a couple of days or so before I left you, I went with you to the casino? Do you remember when I walked into the office and that man was in there with you all? Do you remember him? Because I do. Even though you marched me out straight away, I got a good look at his face. I saw that man a few days later in Palermo. Both of his arms had been broken and his face looked as if he'd been in a boxing match against an opponent twice his size.'

While she had no time for Luca's nightclubs, she'd liked spending time in his casinos, especially the one in Palermo. She'd come to enjoy their nights out there, dining in the à la carte restaurant and playing cards. The night she had been referring to had been their last night out together. She had been playing poker, a game she was good at, but her frequent yawns had got the better of her. She'd wanted to go home and go to bed, preferably with her husband.

Luca had been nowhere to be found on the gaming floor, so she had wandered off to the security offices on the top floor. Being one of the bosses' wives meant she had access to anywhere she desired.

She had found him in the nondescript office used by the duty manager.

The man in question had been sitting in a chair in the middle of the room surrounded by Luca, Francesco and two men she didn't know. Those two men, with their broken noses and cauliflower ears, had given her the heebie-jeebies.

She could still taste the testosterone of that office, could still feel the menacing atmosphere that had greeted her when she walked through the door.

All the men had fixed their eyes on her, their surprise that she'd barged in on them palpable.

'Everything all right?' she had asked with a naivety she looked back on with disgust.

'We're in the middle of a meeting,' Luca had said curtly, striding over to her.

'Are you going to be much longer? Only I'm tired and want to go home.'

'We will not be long.' He'd taken her arm and ushered her to the door. 'Wait for me in the bar. I'll be with you shortly.'

He'd shut her out before she could make a whisper of protest.

She'd stared at the offending door for too long, an uneasiness creeping through her bones to go with the shock of her own husband frogmarching her from the room. There had been something about the man in the chair's expression that kept flashing through her mind.

When she had challenged Luca about it on the drive home, he'd dismissed the matter, refusing to discuss it.

She'd dropped the subject but the man in the chair had haunted her. The more she'd thought about it, the more convinced she'd become that it had been a pleading terror she had seen in his eyes.

A couple of days later she had walked out of a pharmacy in Lebbrossi and come face to face with him. He'd almost fallen into the road in his haste to get away from her.

She'd watched him hurry away, utterly bewildered. Stuffed in the bottom of her handbag, away from the prying eyes of her minders, had been a pregnancy test.

'That man was cheating the casino,' Luca said, finally breaking the silence that had sprung between them.

'And?' She was being deliberately facetious. She wanted him to spell it out to her. She wanted to watch him justify breaking the bones of a fellow human being.

'And here in Sicily we have our own methods for dealing with people who try to cheat us,' he said coolly. 'Lessons need to be learned.'

'That was one hell of a lesson. That poor man recognised me as your wife. I swear he looked as if he'd come face to face with the Medusa.'

'That *poor man* stole over a hundred thousand euros from us.'

'Ooh, yes, I can totally see how that would justify smashing his face in.' Sick to the pit of her stomach, Grace shook her head. Her tortellini had gone cold but she didn't care. Her appetite had deserted her.

'Believe me, he got off lightly.'

'Lightly? *Lightly?* What planet are you on? How can you even try to justify—?'

'Rules are rules, and breaking them merits punishment, as that man knew very well. He didn't just steal from us, he dishonoured us. He's lucky I'm a reasonable man and refused to counter a harsher punishment.'

She stared at him open-mouthed. *A harsher punishment...?*

'That man had a family,' he continued. 'At my insistence we agreed to give him time to repay the money. But we couldn't let him leave without serving a warning, not just to him but to any other man foolish enough to try and steal from us.'

She shook her head again, trying to make sense of it all. 'So what you're saying is, you took me home and made love to me that night, minutes after beating him.'

'No. I never raised a finger to him.' The corners of his mouth lifted slightly. 'I had a wife I wished to take home and make love to.'

'You might not have *raised a finger* to him but your hands are still tainted with his blood.'

The half-smile dropped. 'This isn't a school playground, Grace.'

'Isn't it? From what I remember of school, it was always the bullies who ruled the roost. And you wonder why I ran away from you when I found out I was pregnant? Who in their right mind would bring a child into this life?'

His eyes blackened. It was like looking into an abyss.

Lily had dozed off on her shoulder, for which she would be eternally grateful. This was not a conversation she wanted her daughter to hear even if she was far too young to understand it.

Surprisingly, being in a public place made the whole thing easier. It meant she had to keep a rein on herself. It meant Luca had to keep his control too.

Taking a deep breath, she forced her attention back on

him. At moments like this it pained her heart to look at him, physically hurt to recall how deeply she had loved him.

It hurt even more to know that, despite everything he had done, he still had the power to affect her more than anyone. Deep inside her existed an ache to turn back the clock, to have stayed at home that fateful day, to stick her head back in the sand. To be happy again.

But Pandora's box, once opened, could not be unopened. She had seen that poor man's face and she had *known*.

Luca's secretiveness. The increased security detail that had already been large enough to shame a head of state. His growing reluctance to let her even leave the estate, never mind go anywhere without him. These were all things that had festered but were forgotten about the minute she was with him. When they were together, making love, and she knew she was the centre of his earth, she would forget all her doubts.

She would forget her worries about his drinking and how a glass of Scotch seemed to be permanently welded to his hand. She'd pretend not to see days of unshaven thick black stubble across his strong jawline. She'd pretend not to notice the wildness that resided in his eyes when she caught him in an unguarded moment.

Ironically enough, since he'd found her again, lookswise it was like being back with the Luca she had married rather than the Luca she had left. But that wildness in his eyes remained. That edge to him that had been there from the start—the same edge she had thought *romantic*—was as strong as it had ever been. Stronger. His hate for her sharpening it to a point.

The pink line of the pregnancy test had shone brightly. In that split second it had no longer been just her and Luca. A tiny spark of life had resided within her, depending on *her*.

Denial had no longer been an option.

She'd forced herself to work on autopilot. She'd left without writing a note because trying to say goodbye to the man she loved had ripped her soul into pieces.

She'd run so fast, she'd never had the chance to ask him any of the million and one questions that had pounded in her head. Those questions still pounded.

'Have you ever used *your* fists on another man?'

'Only when it's been absolutely necessary.'

'But what do you consider necessary?'

His voice was hard. 'People who steal and cheat from me. People who would harm my family. People who would try to take my businesses from me.'

'Have you ever killed someone?' The question was out before her brain had even conjured it.

For the briefest of moments, his jaw slackened, before all his muscles bunched. 'How can you ask me such a question?'

'Because I don't know you.' She hugged Lily closer to her. Never had she wished so hard that she'd moved on from Cornwall when she'd had the chance. If that ridiculous apathy hadn't overcome her she'd likely be living on a remote Greek island away from this madness. 'You *changed*, Luca. Once you went into business with that Francesco Calvetti, you changed. The darkness seemed to take you over. I was walking on eggshells all the time, always wondering and worrying over what kind of a mood you were in. I would spend nights in my studio painting and trying to ignore how terrified I was that you wouldn't come home...'

'Why would you have thought that?'

'Because people in your line of work have a habit of not making it home. Except for in a coffin.'

'My line of work?' Anger rose in his voice. 'I am a legitimate businessman.'

'You're nothing but a thug,' she countered flatly. 'Only I was too blind with love or lust to see it properly.'

A snarl flittered across his face, the pulse in his temple pounding. Pulling his wallet out of his back pocket, Luca rose and threw some euros onto the table. 'Put Lily in her pram. We're leaving.'

Luca had been in bed for the best part of two hours. For two nights, sleep had been a joke. It was worse than when he had first brought Grace home. Try as he might, he could not get her out of his head. Or excise the poison that had spilled from her tongue.

In sheer frustration he threw the sheets off and climbed out of bed. Drawing back the curtain, he stared out of the window at the moonlit view of his estate.

At that moment all was peaceful, the dark rolling hills giving the illusion the vines and olive groves were in deep sleep. He could almost believe he was the only person awake in the whole of Sicily.

Except Grace could be awake too. He'd heard her a while ago, tending to their daughter. She might very well be staring out of her own window, sharing the same view.

His chest tightened and he swallowed away the acid burn in the back of his throat.

She was probably plotting her next attempt to escape with Lily.

She would never succeed. But still she would try.

Her bravery had stood out the first moment he met her. She had trespassed on his land with her best friend. As soon as they had crossed the boundary, an alert had gone out. A camera had zoomed in on the area and they had been spotted. It had been sheer fortune—or misfortune, depending on your take—that Luca had been driving through the estate with his head of security, Paolo, and had been first on the scene. The intruders had been sitting on a picnic blanket, looking as if they didn't have a care in the world.

'*Che ci fate qui?*' he had said, asking what they were doing while removing his gun from its holster. He had not sensed any danger from these young women but he would not take chances. While Salvatore Calvetti lived and breathed, the Mastrangelos would never be safe.

One of them, a curvy redhead, had jumped up in terror at the sight of the gun but the other, a slender blonde, had stayed on her bottom and gazed up at him. After a moment's study, she had raised one hand in the sign of peace and then dived into her rucksack from which she had retrieved a battered notebook.

'*Uno minuti per favore,*' she had muttered as she got to her feet, flicking through her book. 'Er...*mi dispiace, ma il mio italiano non è molto buono.*' When she'd finished her garbled apology for not speaking Italian she'd beamed at him.

He'd taken in her tall, lithe frame, her long honey-blonde hair, the bare, dirty feet and the garish multicoloured top over the pair of frayed denim shorts. For all her grubbiness she'd shone brighter than the blazing midday sun.

'Are you English?' he'd asked, putting the gun back in its holster.

She had nodded.

'This is private land. You must leave.'

'I'm sorry,' she had said. 'We didn't realise we were trespassing. There's a gap in your fence we thought was a footpath.'

He had followed the direction she'd pointed at, and had seen a couple of panels had come off.

'Get that fixed,' he'd said to Paolo, who was hovering in the background, before turning his attention back to the striking woman before him. 'You must leave now.'

'Give us a minute to pack our materials away.' She had turned to her cowering friend who was hiding behind her. 'Are you going to stand there like a stuck lemon or are you going to pull your finger out?'

'He's got a gun!' the friend had yelped, pointing a finger at Luca.

'He's also put it away,' she had replied patiently, throwing Luca a discreet wink. That wink had jolted him to his core. 'We are trespassing in Sicily, Cara, not Surrey.'

It was only when they had started packing their stuff away that he'd realised what they had been doing. 'You are artists?'

'I suppose we are,' had said the brave woman, who had not so much as flinched at the sight of his gun. 'We graduated last summer and have been travelling Europe ever since. We're trying to get in as much art appreciation as we can before the real world drags us into its tentacles. That's why we were pitched up here—Cara dabbles in landscapes and the view was spectacular. Honestly, your estate is *beautiful*.'

But Luca had had no interest in Cara. 'Do you paint too?'

'I do. Portraits. I normally work with oil but as we're outdoors I've brought my sketchbook with me.'

'May I see it?'

'Sure.' She had knelt down for another rummage in her rucksack, giving him a perfect view of her pert bottom.

He had blinked in shock as a stab of lust had run through him.

Grubby urchins were usually well off his radar.

This woman though...

She had brought a large sketchbook over to him.

Taking his time, he had flipped through it. Most of the drawings had been of her companion. They had been, without exception, exquisite.

He had looked back up and met her eyes properly for the first time.

The most enormous feeling of warmth had spread through his bones, a thickening in his chest that had made it hard to catch a breath.

'Do you take commissions?' he had asked after too long a pause during which they had simply stared at each other.

Her wide hazel eyes had crinkled at the sides. 'Not from people whose names I don't know.'

He had extended a hand. 'I'm Luca Mastrangelo.'

'Grace Holden.' She had wiped her hand down the side of her shorts before reaching out to accept his.

A shock of heat had zipped through his hand, permeating through him. 'It is a pleasure to meet you, Grace Holden.'

Her answering smile had stolen his remaining breath.

Neither had made any attempt to relinquish the other's hand.

Later, over a romantic meal at his favourite restaurant, he'd asked why she hadn't been scared when he had pulled out the gun.

She'd smiled mischievously. 'You weren't aiming it at us. You looked peed off but not murderous.'

Out of everything, that was the thing that cut in his craw the most. How could the woman who had judged him so accurately with one glance even dream he was capable of murder? Why the hell did she think they had let that man live? It had been at *his* insistence, that was why. That man had been caught cheating from them before, from their casino in Sardinia. Francesco's men had been ready to tow him out to sea and throw him in with weights on his ankles.

Did she think he *enjoyed* hurting people or having people hurt in his name?

He took no more enjoyment from it than his father had.

A lump formed in his throat. Pietro Mastrangelo had been a fine and honourable man who believed in the sanctity of life. Always he would favour the route that left the least physical and emotional damage, a lesson Luca had taken to heart.

The way Grace had looked at him, the words she had said to him...she truly believed him to be a monster. She gave him no credit for saving that man's life. Thanks to him, that man would still be able to live a long life and be a husband to his wife and a father to his children.

She had been happy to leave him, Luca, unable to be a husband *or* a father.

A wave of bitterness ran through him as he recalled her attempts to deflect her deplorable behaviour by turning it onto him.

He made no apologies for restricting her movements and keeping her in the dark on certain matters. He had been doing his best to keep her safe. He would do anything— *would have done anything*, he corrected himself—to keep her safe. He hadn't wanted her to worry about things she could never understand. That was what he'd told himself.

The sound of Lily's cries carried down the corridor and into his room.

Grace's accusation came back to him. *Have you tried any form of interaction with her?*

Before he met Grace, he'd never imagined he would marry a woman and selfishly want to keep her all for himself, even if just for a while. With Grace, he'd wanted to enjoy every minute they had together before they got around to making lots of bouncing *bambini*. When those mythical babies eventually came along he'd known he would want to be involved in everything. Their children would be born of their parents' love and would want for nothing, from either their mother or their father.

Grace had stolen that from him.

If she had her way she would steal it from him again.

He rubbed his eyes, the sound of Lily's cries ripping into his heart.

'Don't think it's escaped my attention that you haven't held her yet. Not once.'

She was right.

The way he was acting around his own flesh and blood, anyone would think he was scared of her.

How could a baby be construed as even vaguely frightening? Especially when that baby was *his* child.

He left his room and moved stealthily down the dark corridor to the nursery.

Grace's eyes widened when he walked through the door. 'What's the matter?' she whispered, pacing the room, rocking Lily on her shoulder.

The breath caught in his throat.

His wife and daughter. Together. Illuminated by the moonlight seeping through a crack in the heavy curtains, Grace wearing her tatty dressing gown, Lily bundled up in blankets, her whimpers lessening.

It was a sight he knew he would never tire of gazing at.

He cleared his throat, taking in the dark rings circling his wife's eyes. 'When did you last have a proper night's sleep?'

Her brow furrowed, a flash of pain contorting her features. 'About eleven months ago.'

When she had left him.

And just like that, he understood what terrible anguish she must have gone through.

Whatever her reasoning had been, and whatever vitriol she might spout now, it hadn't been any easier for Grace to break their union than it had been for him to accept that she had left of her own accord.

She hadn't left because she no longer loved him.

She had left *despite* it.

Dio, but he had no idea how that made him feel.

'Can I hold her?' He hadn't meant to ask. He'd intended to simply take Lily from her. After all, he was the father. It was his right.

She didn't say anything, her tired eyes simply gazing at him with more than a hint of apprehension. Eventually she inclined her head.

'Aren't you going to give me any tips about keeping her head supported, or anything?' he could not resist asking as he stood before her.

A faint trace of a smile curved her lips, a smile that did something all squidgy to his chest, before it faded away and he detected sadness in its place. 'You'd never hurt her.'

She delivered it as a whimsical statement of fact. The squidgy feeling became a tight mass.

Between them they transferred Lily into his arms, the tight mass solidifying into a heavy weight, spreading up his throat and down into his guts, enveloping his insides. The softness of Grace pressed against his arm, her clean fragrance filling his senses, all of this merged with the plump delicacy of his daughter and the new baby scent that was all her own.

For a moment he couldn't breathe, the feelings evoked so powerful they threatened to overwhelm him.

Lily stopped grizzling. She stared up at him, her midnight eyes almost curious, as if she were trying to work out who this stranger was who now held her so protectively.

Grace watched them, the ray of moonlight casting her in an ethereal light, emphasising both her beauty and her tiredness.

'You need to sleep,' he said, lowering himself onto the rocking chair next to Lily's cot. 'Go to bed. I'll get her back down.'

She opened her mouth, no doubt to argue with him, but all that came out was an enormous yawn, which she covered with the back of her hand.

'If I have any problems I'll wake you.'

Still she hesitated before giving a short nod. 'Okay. If you're sure?'

'I'm sure.'

She closed the space between them and leaned over, placing her lips to their daughter's cheek, her hair inadvertently tickling his throat. 'Sleep tight, my angel.'

As she made to straighten up she wobbled slightly and placed a hand on his bare thigh to steady herself.

'Sorry,' she murmured, taking a step back.

'Don't be.' His skin heated, and he breathed deeply, willing the completely inappropriate feelings to disperse.

She backed up to the adjoining door. 'Well, goodnight, then.'

'Goodnight, *bella*.'

Alone with his daughter, Luca closed his eyes and breathed in Lily's sweet scent. The heavy weight inside him had become a pulsating ball of steel and it took long moments before he felt ready to properly look at her.

Carefully he laid her on his lap and stared, taking in the long limbs, the skinny fingers, the plump cheeks, the snub nose, everything. The longer he looked, the harder it became to breathe.

His daughter. His flesh and blood.

CHAPTER EIGHT

WHEN GRACE AWOKE, she checked the time on her bedside clock and almost fell out of bed in shock.

Throwing the covers off, she jumped out and raced into the adjoining nursery, completely skipping the blurry-eyed, lots-of-yawning routine the morning usually brought.

The cot was empty.

Pressing a hand to her racing heart, she gnawed at her bottom lip and forced her frantic brain to calm down and think.

She checked in the small fridge she'd had placed in the corner of the room. Instead of the two made-up bottles of Lily's milk she'd put in there before going to bed, there was only one.

Still chewing on her lip, she headed off along the corridor. Was it possible Luca had heard Lily call for her breakfast while she had slept through it? Surely not? Her bedroom adjoined the nursery, and her maternal biology was primed to hear her baby's cries.

The door to the master bedroom was ajar. She tapped on it lightly. Getting no response, she tapped again then pushed it open.

Rooted to the floor, all she could do was stare, wide-eyed.

Luca was asleep on the edge of the ultra-king bed. Lily

lay on her back next to him, bang in the middle, wearing a sleep suit Grace was certain she hadn't been wearing when she'd put her to bed. A pile of pillows had been placed neatly along the other edge, sandwiching Lily between them and Luca. On his bedside table sat an empty baby bottle.

Heart in mouth, she swallowed away the compulsion to climb in with them, stood for an age unable to tear her eyes away.

Her presence must have disturbed him, for Luca raised his head. 'What time is it?'

She cleared her throat. 'Nine o'clock.'

As he sat up she noticed how careful he was not to use any sudden movements that could wake Lily. All the same, the baby stirred and kicked her little feet out.

Now fully upright, his black hair mussed, Luca reached for Lily and cuddled her to his bare chest. From Grace's vantage point she could see the wound on his shoulder— the wound *she* had inflicted—was healing well, now a dark red scar. It made her stomach roll to know every time he looked in a mirror and saw that scar, he would be reminded of the time she had shot him.

At the same time fresh guilt was kicking in, her mouth ran dry as she experienced a pang of envy, not that Lily had evidently accepted him without question, but envy that he held her so tenderly.

How Grace had loved to nestle into that broad chest...

'What time did she wake up for her bottle?' she asked, pushing all thoughts of nibbling at his nipples and running her fingers through his black silky hair from her mind.

'A couple of hours ago.' He yawned widely.

'I never heard her.'

'She fell asleep not long after you went back to bed, but as soon as I put her down she woke up and started crying. I didn't want her to wake you, so I decided the best thing to ensure you got a decent amount of sleep was to bring her to bed with me.' He shrugged nonchalantly. 'The bed is big enough.'

That it certainly was.

'Er, well, thank you.'

'I do not require your gratitude,' he said, a touch frostily. 'I *want* to be involved in her care. Besides, it gave you a chance to catch up on some needed sleep.'

She stared at him, too shocked that he'd done something for her partial benefit to speak.

'Which is why our trip to Florence tomorrow could not come at a more opportune moment,' he continued. 'It will do you good to have some space. I'm guessing you've not spent much time apart from her since she was born?'

'Of course I haven't.' Other than her one visit to her cottage studio, she had never been parted from their daughter. She could only tolerate Lily being in the next room by leaving the adjoining door wide open. Which was why it shocked her that she had been able to sleep so deeply. Was it because she knew Lily was in Luca's care…?

He had cared for her beautifully. That much she had to acknowledge. Though she didn't want to. When she looked at Luca she wanted to know she was looking at a bastard, not at a man with the capacity to tend for a young baby on instinct alone.

And now she needed to take Lily back to the nursery and get her ready for the day. And that meant taking her from him. It meant having to get close to his naked chest—*Please, God, let him at least be wearing a pair of boxer shorts.*

As ridiculous as she knew it to be, she had to practically drag her legs over to his side of the bed. Holding her breath, she leaned down and took Lily from his arms.

'What are your plans for the day?' he asked as she took a step back.

'We'll probably go for a walk.' It was on the tip of her tongue to question why he asked, but she stopped herself in time. The last thing she wanted was for him to invite himself along.

Unsurprisingly, his eyes narrowed with suspicion. The only time in the whole of their marriage she had voluntarily gone for a walk and not been badgered into it had been the day she left him. 'Another walk?'

She shrugged. 'It's not for me, it's for Lily. She needs fresh air and I really can't have a SWAT team accompanying us if we leave the estate. Yesterday was bad enough.' The day before, she had taken Lily into Palermo for some Christmas shopping. She hadn't visited the discreet arcade Luca had taken her to to buy the vile dress, but went to a proper shopping centre and market. It had been so crowded her bodyguards had been tripping over the heels of her feet to keep up with them.

'The minders I have assigned to you are discreet.'

'About as discreet as a herd of cows dressed in pink tutus.'

His lips twitched. 'I'm sorry if you find them an inconvenience,' he said without sounding the slightest bit apologetic, 'but as I have explained to you countless times, they're for your safety.'

'Absolutely.' She nodded with faux sweetness. 'It was much harder to tolerate when I thought you were a legitimate businessman and an overprotective bear. But now I know it's all because you're worried one of your victims will get vengeance by going for me and Lily, it makes your attitude so much easier to sympathise with.'

The humour vanished from his face. He climbed off the bed and stalked towards her, a furrow running down the centre of his brow. He wore nothing but a pair of snug black boxer shorts. All the breath in her lungs expelled in a rush.

Luca, virtually naked, was as stunning a sight as if he had been fully nude. He was the only person for whom she had ever wished she were more proficient in sculpture, his body deserving to be immortalised on something even more substantial than canvas.

'My business activities have nothing to do with my security provisions other than in respect of the scumbags it occasionally forces me to associate with. There are no *victims*.'

She averted her gaze from the wonder that was his body and forced herself to meet his eyes. That was no safer place to look, his eyes holding her like a magnet. No matter how hard she tried to look away, she could not.

This physical weakness for him enraged her and she could feel angry colour stain her cheeks. 'You can tell me this until you're blue in the face, but nothing is going to convince me you are anything but a gangster.'

Luca's rage was like a tight coil. She could see it in the way his muscles bunched under his smooth skin.

Her breath hitched.

'You are lucky you can use Lily as a shield,' he said, his silky voice menacing, 'or I would be forced to silence your vicious tongue.'

'That sounds like a threat.'

'Not at all, *bella*. As you should know, I never make useless threats, only promises. If you keep challenging me I will have no option but to shut you up the only way I know that works with you.'

'Oh, yes? And how's that, Gangster Boy?' Why was she antagonising him so? Why could she not simply keep her mouth shut and walk away?

He studied her for an age, the fury in his eyes dispersing and being replaced by a gleam that frightened her a whole lot more than mere anger. Suddenly she was all too aware of the shortness of her nightdress—in her rush to find Lily she'd forgotten to put on her dressing gown.

His olive throat moved; his magnificent chest rose.

She could hear the heaviness of her own breathing, knew he was close enough to hear it too. He was too close. She could smell the musky scent of his skin…

'By kissing you.'

'Now you're being ridiculous.'

He took another step towards her, stopping just short of touching her. But it was enough. The heat of his naked skin so close to hers was enough to make her traitorous body, already wholly aware with her skin tingling and her blood thick and warm, spring alive.

'Ridiculous?' His voice dropped to a murmur. 'Do you not remember how good it used to be between us?'

She shivered, unwanted yet, oh, so potent images of just how good they had been together flittering in her head. 'I thought you were on the hunt for a mistress.'

'So did I.' His eyes were stark with a desire she recognised from old, his voice barely audible. 'But you are the only woman who can make me hard with a single look. And you want me too—I can see it in your eyes. I *know* you, Grace. And I know when you want me. If Lily wasn't in your arms we would already be on that bed screwing each other's brains out.'

The air thickened with the same tightening as in her core. Struggling for oxygen, she fought to make her vocal cords work. 'Don't say another word. You can keep hunting because there is no way I'm *ever* sharing a bed with you again. I don't want you—I *hate* you.'

She turned on her heel and fled, hurrying all the way back to the hateful blue room, a room she loathed almost as much as she loathed her husband. She let the door shut with a slam.

Holding Lily to her, she sat on the bed and waited for her thundering heart to slow to at least near normal levels, berating herself for her stupidity.

Thank God she'd had Lily in her arms. There had been a moment when her fingers had itched to slap him while her lips had tingled to kiss him.

To do more than kiss him.

Why had she not had the good sense to take Lily back to her room immediately, without striking up a conversation with him, without antagonising him?

Deep down, she knew why.

Seeing Luca and Lily together had disturbed her on so many levels she'd had to fight, lest the softening in her bones became a permanent thing.

They had looked so…so…perfect together. Seeing them like that… The guilt had almost split her in two.

Then, when Luca had woken, his defences against her down, his hatred still sleeping, he had looked exactly like the man she had married.

She didn't want to remember anything good about him. She didn't want to remember how convinced she had once been that he would make a fantastic father, even if his offspring would be unable to breathe without his knowledge.

He had been more of a father to Lily in one night than her own father had been to Grace in her entire lifetime.

It had been hard enough to leave Luca the first time. How easy would it be to leave if Lily fell in love with him too? She had to remember the man he had become by the end of their marriage. The man she had run away from.

She cast her mind to the cheap phone currently stuffed in a pair of boots in her wardrobe.

She didn't know how it could help in her escape plan

but just having something that was hers and untraceable felt precious.

If Luca found it, she would be thrown out on the streets. It made no difference that he still wanted her. That was just chemistry. He didn't love her. He would cast her out as if she were nothing more than uneaten food.

She couldn't quite believe she'd been able to acquire it. She hadn't gone shopping with the intention of buying a phone—her only intention had been to buy her mum and Cara a Christmas present each; something to let them know how special they were to her. To make amends.

Not that Billie thought there was anything to make amends for. When she'd spoken to her mum, it was as if she'd never been away—Billie had made some appropriate-sounding noises of relief and appropriate squeals at being a grandmother before discussing, in great detail, her latest commission. By all accounts Grace's dad was somewhere in Africa with no plans to return any time soon. If he knew or cared that she'd been missing, she didn't know. And she didn't ask. Some questions were better left unasked.

Cara's reaction to Grace's reappearance had been some-what different. Other than a couple of vague text messages, her best friend was being decidedly elusive. She couldn't blame her, not after she'd been so flippant about Cara's fright the day they'd first met Luca. Cara had been the one with the sense to be frightened of a man with a gun. And somehow Cara had been the one tricked into giving up her phone so the secrets contained within it could be revealed.

Her three bodyguards had been glued to her side for the whole trip until she had come to a bustling market. One stall had sold scarves. Out of the corner of her eye she had noticed a row of cheap phones behind the busy seller's table.

Snatching the opportunity, she had grabbed a scarf, given the pram to her bodyguards and dived into the throng.

When she had reached the front of the table, the crowd thick behind her, she could only hope her guards didn't have X-ray vision. She'd quickly wrapped the phone inside the scarf and, acting as casual as a woman whose heart rate had quadrupled could, placed her purchases in Lily's large baby bag.

She could only pray Luca never found it.

Luca knocked on the door to the blue room. He was confident that, given a little more time, he would start thinking of it as Grace's room. He was also confident that, given a little more time, he would stop thinking of the master bedroom as *their* room.

He ignored the thought that he'd had well over ten months to stop thinking of it as theirs.

When there was still no response, he pushed the door open. Neither Grace nor Lily were anywhere to be found. A small suitcase lay closed on the bed, the dress he had bought her draped over it as if it had been thrown there without any thought. The fancy box it had been perfectly folded into at the boutique had been thrown in the waste bin.

She hated that dress. Really hated it. It had given him a perverse pleasure buying it for her, knowing she would have to obey his wishes and wear it. He had seen it as a fitting punishment for a woman who thrived on colour and light, one of many punishments she would have to endure.

Turning to leave, he caught sight of his reflection in the full-length mirror and stopped short, suddenly certain he had seen a pair of horns sprouting from his head. He blinked to clear the image.

It was just him. Luca.

Not the monster Grace was adamant he had become.

For a moment though…

What did she see when she looked at him?

Did she really see a man with horns on his head?

An image of his tiny, defenceless daughter floated into his head. Lily was an innocent, dependent on the adults who cared for her. She had no voice.

But one day she would. One day she would be old enough to form her own opinions. If she was anything like her mother, those opinions would be contrary to his. Would his daughter look at him and see a monster, an ogre…?

Another, equally powerful thought occurred to him.

What would his father say if he could see him now?

His father. The man who had gone to such great lengths to leave the old life—indeed had taken the final necessary steps mere months before his great heart had failed.

Would his father see a monster too? Would his father understand the route he, Luca, had taken? Would he understand his need to strike out on his own, to step out from under Pietro Mastrangelo's shadow and do something for *him*, to form partnerships and invest in businesses that were nothing to do with family, or vineyards, or olive groves?

When his father had died, all of Luca's dreams of founding his own business empire had died a death with him. He'd had to step into the breach. There had been no other choice, unless you considered letting the estate fall to ruins a choice.

His mother had fallen to pieces. His brother had been about to head off to university. None of the uncles or aunts in his family had been in a position to help, not for any substantial length of time.

That had left him, Luca, to bury his own grief and step into the breach. With one hand he'd learned the ropes while the other hand had been busy keeping at bay the vultures, led by Salvatore Calvetti, who would snatch the estate from them.

For thirteen years he had done nothing but push the estate onwards, investing surplus profits into new vineyards and olive groves across Southern Europe and beyond, new bottling plants, new everything, in the process making the Mastrangelos billionaires.

For thirteen years he'd done his duty.

It was only seeing the world through Grace's enchanted eyes that had propelled him to get out of the rut he hadn't even known he was in.

Francesco Calvetti had been as relieved at the death of his father, a man who would as soon slit your throat as give you the time of day, as Luca had been. Salvatore's death had freed them both, and it had allowed them to rekindle their old friendship. Like Luca, Francesco was ready to take a different path and strike out on his own.

Along with a chain of international restaurants Luca had bought out in his own right, he and Francesco had invested in a couple of casinos and a handful of high-end nightclubs together. That these particular investments required a management technique that differed from his usual management style had not been something Luca had considered before laying his cash on the table.

Once he had understood it, however, he'd gone along with it with little more than a shrug. And if Francesco had embraced these techniques with an enthusiasm that proved more than a little of Salvatore lived on in him, then so be it. This was the way of the world here. It was how his own father had once been forced to conduct business. It was a method Luca understood. He was not averse to using his fists and other weapons to protect himself and his property, had employed numerous tactics throughout the years to keep Salvatore and his henchmen at bay. This situation was no different: you did what was needed to be done to protect your investments and if that meant sending a physical warning to thieves and swindlers, then so be it.

He would never pretend to like it. There were days when, if he was being honest with himself, he would admit that he despised it. He would never pretend it didn't require a strong stomach, but Scotch was a good settler. Especially a couple of large Scotches.

His father might not be happy with his eldest son's choice of investment and even less happy with his choice of business partner, but surely he would understand. Wouldn't he…?

The acidic churning in his guts answered that question for him.

And what would Pietro say if he knew his firstborn son was forcing his own wife to wear a dress she hated out of a perverse sense of punishment and revenge? Would he understand that…?

'What do you want?'

Grace stood in the doorway, Lily in her arms, glaring at him.

'I wanted to remind you that you'll need to be ready to leave after breakfast tomorrow.'

She rolled her eyes and walked past him, placing Lily on the centre of the bed. Immediately their daughter stuffed a foot in her mouth.

'Where have you been?'

'Running through some stuff with your mum about Lily's routine.' She sat on the bed and placed a hand on the baby's belly.

'Any problems?'

'No. She's all good to go.'

Which is more than you are, he thought. Grace looked wan. 'Are you feeling all right?'

'Me?' She smiled tightly. 'I'm absolutely fine. On top of the world. Leaving my daughter for the first time fills me with nothing but joy.'

He raised a brow at her sarcasm.

'What?' she demanded. 'That's what you want to hear, isn't it? Take some of the guilt away.'

'I don't feel any guilt about leaving her with my mother.' It was one of the only things he *could* think about without feeling as if a heavy weight were slowly crushing his insides.

'Well, you should.'

If he hadn't recognised her belligerence as a mask, he would have left her to stew. Except her hands were trembling and she was blinking too rapidly to be doing anything other than fighting tears.

As much as he hated her, witnessing her trying so hard not to cry tore something in him.

Stepping over, he sat on the bed next to her and took her hand. It was cold.

'I don't feel any guilt because I know my mother will take the utmost care of her. Lily will be spoiled rotten—if she wants caviar in her milk I promise my mother will provide it.'

The tiniest hint of a smile played on the corners of her lips. 'I know. I know. It's just…'

He waited for her to continue. 'It's just what?'

She pulled her hand away and gazed at Lily. It hadn't escaped his attention that, apart from her initial glare, she refused to look at him.

'Florence is so far away.' She sighed. 'Maybe it would be easier if the party was in Lebbrossi or Palermo; places we can nip back from quickly if anything were to happen…'

'Nothing is going to happen.'

'It might.'

'Grace, look at me.' When she kept her focus on Lily he repeated his command, catching her chin with a finger and forcing her attention. Her hazel eyes were bright with unshed tears. 'I'll arrange things with the aviation authorities in Florence so that, in the case of an emergency, we can take the jet back to Palermo at any time necessary.'

'Can you do that?'

'Yes.'

'But if we're flying from the main airport, aren't we supposed to select an advance time slot and—?'

'I'll fix it. It will not be a problem.'

She continued to look at him dubiously.

'Does this solution not ease your mind?'

'Only if you promise not to use intimidation or violence to get your own way.'

He should be affronted that she would think such a thing of him. Yet he could not blame her. Grace was the sort of person who would rather rescue a bug than kill it. Any form of violence was alien to her way of thinking—even if he went through everything about his business ventures and partnership in detail, and explained why things were the way they were, she would never understand. He'd known that from the start, within days of buying into that first casino, when the first man had been foolish enough to steal from it and Francesco's men had been set upon him. He'd known Grace would never accept it or understand the necessity behind it.

There were times he struggled to accept and understand it himself. There had been many a time when only the stiffest of Scotches had allowed him to blur the images that played behind his retinas and dulled the nausea that lined his stomach.

Rubbing his thumb along her soft cheek, he said, 'The only asset I will use to get my own way will be of a monetary value.'

'You can afford it,' she said with what could almost be called a smile.

There was nothing he could say to that. He could afford anything his heart desired. *Apart from Grace's heart*, the sly voice came back at him.

In the beat of a second his head began to pound with the sound of a thousand drums.

Her eyes held his, a softness in them he hadn't seen for so long he had forgotten how amazing it felt to be on the receiving end of it. The hazel in them melted and darkened while her lips parted. Her chest rose and fell sharply, colour heightening her complexion as she held the gaze binding them together.

Dio, but if she wasn't the most beautiful woman on the planet. Was it any wonder he was having such trouble finding another woman to hold his interest for longer than the blink of an eye when he had married the most desirable of them all? Her small breasts jutted through the tight green cashmere sweater she wore. Unthinking, he raised the hand not stroking her cheek and cupped one, sucking in a breath as an enormous jolt surged through him.

Her eyes widened, her own shallow breaths hitching. She raised a hand in turn and brought it to his face where it hovered, not quite touching him, before a pained, almost desperate look crossed her features.

She blinked and shook her head, the softness and desire gone, replaced with the hard wariness he was becoming far too accustomed to. Her full lips, which for a few brief moments he had been about to shape his mouth against and plunder the hot sweetness within, tightened.

She turned away and got to her feet. 'Can you leave us now? Lily needs a bath and I need to write a list for your mum.'

He stared from his wife to his daughter, his head pounding, his heart aching with as much force as the throbbing between his legs. 'Can I bathe her?'

She twisted her head to look back at him. 'You?'

'I've missed so much of her life.' For once there was no accusation in either his tone or his meaning. 'I meant what I said before. I want to be a proper father to her.'

He was certain she would refuse. And when she did? Then he would accept her decision. Grace was Lily's mother. He'd made half her DNA but he would have to earn the right to be her father.

To his surprise, she inclined her head, a wry smile forming on her lips. 'If I were you, I would change into something more waterproof. She has a tendency to splash.'

'I'm sure I'll be fine.'

Twenty minutes later, he regretted not taking Grace's advice. He would never have believed someone so small could make so much mess. Lily's plump legs had kicked most of the water out of the baby bath. The floor was soaked. He was drenched, his bespoke trousers ruined.

When Grace poked her head round the bathroom door she did nothing to hide her smirk before disappearing again.

Unlike the night before, when he'd had Lily sleep with him and a lack of proper winding on his part—or so he had learned from his mother when he confessed the incident to her earlier—had made her throw up, he had little trouble putting her nappy on and dressing her. This time it only took three attempts before he was satisfied the fiddly poppers of the romper suit were properly done up.

Only when Lily was settled in her cot, her belly full and properly winded by Grace, did he leave them.

He shut the door and expelled a long breath, taken aback at the physical wrench leaving them caused.

Putting his daughter to bed, his wife by his side…something inside him had shifted. He couldn't pinpoint what, exactly, but he knew he needed to speak to Pepe before he and Grace flew to Florence the next day. He also knew his scheduled meeting with Francesco Calvetti before the party would have a different agenda from the one Francesco was expecting.

CHAPTER NINE

THE HOTEL THEY checked into dated back to the Renaissance and was as grand as any they had stayed in before. With its high frescoed ceilings and intricate architecture, it was the sort of place Grace loved to explore in detail.

Today, though, the last thing on her mind was exploration of any kind. Being such a distance from Lily felt as if her heart had been ripped out. For twelve long weeks it had been just the two of them, but, while the bond between them had been strong from the word go, she had always been aware of something missing, something she hadn't dared put a name to. She still wouldn't put a name to it, too mindful of the danger it could bring if voiced, even if only in her own head.

That missing something…it had vanished the day they had been forced to move back to Sicily and back into Luca's world.

She tried to tell herself the nausea within her belly was due to separation anxiety and nothing else.

It had nothing to do with being alone with Luca—properly alone—for the first time in so, so long.

But something had changed. She could feel it. Loathing was no longer the chief emotion binding them together. It was more than just desire too, although yesterday, sitting on that bed with him cupping her breast, the heat from his hand permeating the fabric of her top…

They had both been fighting to contain the desire that leaped from one to the other, almost as if the charge that lived within her plugged into a charge within him.

She'd had to fight with everything in her not to press her chest into his palm. She'd had to fight not to touch his face, not to rub her cheek against his, not to simply jump onto his lap, smother him with craven kisses and…

She shuddered and closed her eyes.

If Lily hadn't been in the room with them, she had no idea if she would have been strong enough to keep the war within herself going.

However much she wanted to deny it, anticipation brewed within her too. That treacherous charge in her stomach flamed brightly.

It was at times like this she could punch herself. *She* was in control of her body and its reactions. She and she alone.

To take her mind off her strangely melancholic mood and thoughts, she opened the wardrobe door and stared, not for the first time, at the hideous dress. If there were a bottle of red wine to hand she would happily tip it all over the vile creation. For good measure she would splosh the dregs all over the foul beige shoes Luca had selected for her to wear with it. Her dowdy old primary school teacher had worn similar shoes. However, looking at them cheered her up a little; right then she needed physical evidence of her husband's bastard tendencies.

Checking her watch for the umpteenth time, she saw she still had well over an hour to kill before they were due to leave. Luca had disappeared to a meeting within minutes of their arrival saying only that he would be back in time to shower and change. She hadn't asked who the meeting was with—who else could it be but Francesco? Still, for all she knew, he could be overseeing the beating of another hapless fool stupid enough to try to cheat Luca Mastrangelo and associates.

He hadn't always been like this. The first year of their marriage—although restrictive in terms of freedom—had in all other respects been perfect. Luca had been perfect.

The change had been so subtle she had hardly noticed it, not at first. As his evenings away from her had increased from the odd one here and there to almost every other, she'd comforted herself knowing that more often than not he would join her in the early hours, whether in the master bedroom or the smaller bedroom in her studio. By the last few months of their marriage, those evenings when he was around, instead of the coffee they usually used as fuel, he would have a Scotch in hand. His temper had shortened too—not against her, apart from that one time in his office, but she had been acutely aware of how tense he was, the sharpness of his tone. She'd been desperate for him to confide his troubles in her. But he'd refused. He'd refused to even acknowledge there was anything wrong.

Looking back, she could see she'd never pushed him that hard for answers. Apart from the row they'd had the day before she left him, she'd never *really* pushed him, and even then she'd backed down.

It had been far easier to bury her head in the sand and pretend everything was all right.

And was that what Luca had been doing—*was* doing—too? Burying his head in the sand?

The more she thought about it, the more confused she felt. His abhorrence at being labelled a gangster was real. He genuinely didn't see himself with those eyes.

Closing the wardrobe door, she debated calling Donatella again and checking that Lily was okay. Before she could dial the number, a message pinged into her phone. Opening it, she felt her heart lighten to see a photo of Lily lying on the sofa in her usual starfish position, beaming her new gummy smile. The picture had also been sent to Luca.

The accompanying message read:

Lily sends you both big kisses and says she wants you both to stop worrying and enjoy your night away.

Grace bit her lip and brushed away a relieved tear.

God, she was being such a sap. She wasn't the first woman to leave her baby and she wouldn't be the last. Lily was being cared for by someone who loved her deeply and wouldn't harm a hair on her head.

She reread the message. The *both* part of it jumped out. Did that mean Luca had been calling his mum too?

Watching him bathe and dress their daughter had been so funny and so very touching. When she had got up that morning to give Lily her early bottle, he had appeared within minutes and chivvied Grace back to bed, insisting on feeding Lily himself.

Dear Lord, but he had fallen in love with Lily. She could see it in the softness of his eyes and the gentle tone of his voice, the tender way he held her. Their little daughter had crawled into his heart.

Donatella was smitten too.

If she found a way to escape, how could she, in all conscience, take Lily and disappear? It would be kinder to rip their hearts out and stamp on them.

But she could not allow herself to think of these things. She needed to concentrate on shoring up her mental defences against her husband. She had a whole evening to get through, during which she would be expected to act as Luca's good Sicilian wife and pretend to be some obedient creature whose only objective in life was to please her husband. She would have to pretend she still loved him, pretend she enjoyed having her hand held in his.

Most of all she would have to convince herself he meant nothing to her, that her blood didn't heat or her pulse rocket when he touched her.

Her fingers began to itch, a feeling that startled her. It wasn't the same itch as when she'd wanted to slap him. This was an itch from old.

For the first time in almost a year she felt a desperate urge to paint, to draw, to sketch.

Before she could begin tearing the suite apart looking for some paper and a pen or pencil—when, she wondered, had she stopped carrying a sketch pad with her everywhere she went?—there was a light rap on the suite door.

She checked the spyhole, only opening the door when satisfied her visitor was a member of the hotel staff.

'Signora Mastrangelo?' the severe-looking woman asked, a large package in her hands.

'*Sì*,' Grace replied, showing off a little of her Italian.

'This has just arrived for you,' the woman said in perfect English.

'Who's it from?'

'I do not know, *signora*. Maybe there is a note inside for you?' she added helpfully.

'Thank you. I mean, *grazie*.'

'*Prego*.'

Grace closed the door and took the box to the dining table, intrigued and a little wary of what could be inside and who could have sent it.

Clenching her teeth together, she took a deep breath and ripped off the brown packaging. Inside was a long cream box with a familiar motif.

Her heart suddenly wedged in her throat, she opened

the lid as if she were expecting a load of cobras and rattle-snakes to be inside.

Her hands flew to her mouth. No note accompanied it. No note needed to accompany it.

Inside was the peacock-skirted dress she had fallen in love with before Luca had forced the beige monstrosity on her.

He must have noticed her staring at it on the mannequin. Not only had he noticed but he had remembered.

If her belly wasn't already a mass of noodles and butterflies before, it was now a riot to match the beautiful colours of her dress.

When had he bought it? And why? Why now? So many confused thoughts were flying through her head that at first she didn't hear the new rap on the suite door.

Opening it, she found the same employee standing at the threshold, this time holding another, smaller package.

'My apologies, *signora*. I had not been informed that this too was delivered by the courier.'

Less than a minute later, Grace opened the package and discovered the most amazing pair of high, strappy gold sandals.

Grace was applying her make-up when she heard Luca enter the suite. Immediately her steady hand began to shake, violently enough for her to stab herself in the eye with her mascara wand.

'Grace?' he called out.

'I'm in my room,' she replied, putting a palm to her smarting eye.

'Are you ready?'

'Nearly.'

'Will you be ready to leave in fifteen minutes?'

'Yes.'

Ready in fifteen minutes? Never mind that she needed to reapply her make-up and change from the hotel robe into the dress, she could have fifteen years and she doubted she would be ready.

'Are you all right in there?' He must have heard something in her voice because his tone was concerned.

'I'm fine.'

Removing her palm, she almost laughed out loud at her reflection. One eye was still perfectly made up. The other, the one she had stabbed, had all the make-up running, the eye itself bright red and weeping.

'Brilliant,' she muttered under her breath.

Her door opened.

'You're not fine,' Luca accused, strolling over and peering closely at her. 'What have you done?'

'Stabbed myself with my mascara. Don't worry. I'll give it a couple of minutes to stop weeping and then I'll redo it.'

A slow grin spread over his face. 'You look like Morticia Addams.'

'Very funny.'

'Or that clown. What's its name? Poirot?'

'Pierrot,' she corrected with a snigger.

'That's the one. You painted your friend Cara as Pierrot once.'

'So I did.' She grinned, remembering. Luca had belly-laughed when he'd seen the finished product. 'It was revenge after she trashed one of my dresses when she'd drunk too much wine.'

'Was that when we'd been out to that party in Palermo and she tripped over a tree?'

'Yep.' Taking a quick peek in the mirror, she grimaced. 'I look a mess.'

'How did you come to assault yourself with your make-up?'

'It's all your fault,' she said, fixing him with a stern look. 'You startled me when you started barging around the suite like a jumbo elephant.'

'I'm nothing like a jumbo elephant.' He raised a brow. 'Apart from one particular part of my anatomy.'

She raised a brow in turn and indicated the door. 'Shouldn't you be going for a shower?'

'Wouldn't you prefer to discuss my jumbo-sized appendage?'

A warm, bubbly feeling spread through her veins. She slapped his arm lightly. 'Your modesty never fails to astound me. Now go and have a shower before you stink the whole suite out.'

'I'm going, I'm going,' he said with mock surrender. When he reached the door, he turned back to her. 'Did you receive any packages while I was at my meeting?'

And just like that, she remembered where she was, and all the good feelings inside her vanished.

Consternation hit.

For a few brief seconds, time had turned and transplanted her—them—into the past.

The here and now had disappeared. For that brief moment in time when they had teased each other she had forgotten that she hated him.

'Yes. I received them. Thank you.' And shortly she would have to put on the dress and shoes. Call her contrary but part of her would prefer to wear the hideous beige creation. At least then she would be able to seethe at him all night, would be in no danger of further softening.

When he left, she went straight to the bathroom and washed her face. She was patting it dry when Luca came back into her room.

'Here, take this,' he said, handing her a small tube. 'Put

a couple of drops in your eye and it should get rid of the redness.'

Don't be touched at his thoughtfulness, she warned herself. *Keep your guard up.*

He stood, watching her, waiting for her to say something. 'Thanks.'

He nodded. 'No problem. I've told the driver we'll be a few minutes late, so don't rush.'

'I wouldn't dream of it. I'm sure the last thing you want is for your perfect wife to look as if she was thrown together.'

His mouth tightened. 'That's not what I meant and you know it. I was thinking of you. If you want to twist it then that's your problem.'

Grace stared at his retreating figure wishing she could take it back.

But take what back? Luca had been very clear in his expectation that she be a good Sicilian wife and nothing had been said to alter that.

They couldn't live in a permanent state of angst. It was natural some of the good feeling from their previous marital incarnation should seep into the fabric of this new form. She just had to be alert and ready for it.

She could not afford to drop her guard. Not for a second.

When Luca left his room twenty minutes later, he found Grace sitting on the sofa with her back to him, a glass of red wine on the table in front of her.

'You were quick,' he commented, helping himself to the glass and opened bottle she had left out for him.

She got to her feet and reached for her wine. Taking a sip of it, she turned to face him.

He took her in slowly, studying every inch.

That his wife had never been one for spending hours

on her appearance was somewhat of an understatement. Considering she spent—or *had* spent—most of her natural state splattered with paint, she always used to joke it was pointless. However, she had adored dressing up for nights out, could transform her fresh-faced beauty into gorgeous, quirky sophistication with nothing more than a tiny make-up bag of tricks.

Tonight, in fifteen short minutes, she had outdone herself.

'You're beautiful,' he said hoarsely, unable to take his eyes off her. The sunny colours were perfect on her, the buttercup bodice enhancing her small cleavage and the litheness of her stature. The front of the dress rested above her knees, displaying her long, slender legs to perfection, the back of it mere inches from the floor. Her hair, which had grown into a very short bob, had been spiked in all directions, her make-up bold, her eyes painted a smoky brown that darkened the hazel of her eyes. A splash of orange lipstick, that on any other woman would look crass, completed the look to perfection.

He watched as she swallowed and moved towards him, the peacock skirt swaying as she walked.

'Could you do the zip up for me, please?' Her voice was terse, her features hard.

'Of course.'

In her room, for all of a minute, he'd thought he had found his old Grace, the woman whose mocking was never malicious, intended only to amuse, never to sting.

This woman before him was not that Grace.

He wanted to find his old Grace again. She was in there, somewhere. He wanted to reach in and pull her out permanently.

She turned her back to him. She'd managed to zip it three quarters of the way up. He imagined her fighting it, contorting herself into all different positions in an attempt to zip it fully, anything rather than have to ask him for help.

Standing closer than was necessary, close enough to hear the shallowness of her breaths, he placed a hand on her shoulder, bare except for the thin strap of her dress. Her skin held none of the ruddiness her compatriots were famed for. Grace's skin was a light honey tone and satin to the touch.

He pulled the zip up to where it ended just below her shoulder blades. Instead of stopping and stepping back, he trailed his fingers along that soft skin to the base of her neck.

She stood rigid, like the very mannequin that had worn this same dress, no longer breathing. He brushed his hands down her long, supple arms then snaked them around her waist and pressed against her. She would have to be a corpse not to feel the length of his hardness.

'What are you doing?' she rasped, stepping out of his hold.

'Enjoying my wife.'

'You buy me a dress you know I like and think you can *enjoy* me?'

'Stop twisting things.' He raked his fingers through his freshly styled hair, uncaring that he mussed it. Every time he took a step forward she jumped a mile back.

'Then why did you buy it? What happened to me wearing the punishment dress? Did you buy this as a way of softening me up so I'd fall into bed with you? Or was it an attack of the guilts?'

'I do not need to soften you up to get you back into my bed.' Ignoring her mention of guilt, he took in her heightened colour, the anger in her eyes that fought with the desire also residing there. 'All I would have to do is kiss you and you would be begging for me to take you.'

'Bull—'

'Would you like to put it to the test?' he interrupted. 'One kiss and see where it leads, see whether it leads to you begging for more?'

She fixed her hazel eyes on him, her throat working frantically. 'It'll be a cold day in hell before I kiss you or go anywhere near a bed with you in it.'

'If being in hell means sharing a bed with you, I'll take that over heaven.'

Her mouth formed a perfect 'O' before she snapped it shut and grabbed her clutch bag from the bureau. 'Shouldn't we be making a move?'

'Yes, my good Sicilian wife,' he agreed, fighting to keep his tone amiable. Tonight would likely be awkward enough for them both—he wanted her to at least relax enough to enjoy some of it, but, by God, she was making it hard.

He extended his arm to her. 'It is time for us to be sociable and party with Florence's finest.'

'If they're friends of yours, I expect the party will be full of gangsters with guns.'

The good humour he had been clinging on to by the skin of his teeth vanished, her testiness clearly contagious. 'You push my tolerance too far. I might want you back in my bed, *bella*, but do not think it means I am disregarding our agreement. If you want to stay in Lily's life you had damn well better behave yourself tonight.'

As they were in Florence, in Grace's eyes the art capital of the world, she expected the party to be a refined affair with soft background music and plenty of canapés. And a few machine guns discreetly tucked away in full view.

Francesco Calvetti's party was located in his new hotel, which was as opulent and plush as the hotel she and Luca were staying in, and seeped with as much architectural history. Yet she could give it only cursory appreciation, her exchange with Luca leaving her feeling all wrung out. It was so *hard* having to keep up the fight of her responses towards him. When it came to Luca, her head and her body were poles apart. It was a fight she feared her body was winning.

The drive to the hotel had been a game in ignoring each other: Grace looking out of her window, Luca emailing and conducting whatever cyber business was necessary on a Saturday evening.

However hard she ignored him, her body remained painfully aware.

They entered the lobby flanked by four bodyguards. Luca hooked a muscular arm around her waist. 'Smile and act happy,' he said into her ear, the menacing undertow audible.

She responded with a smile of such saccharine goodness she hoped the sweetness made him puke. Anything had to be better than him knowing her whole body vibrated with excitement at his closeness.

It was somewhat of a shock when they entered the ballroom and found it transformed into a nightclub. Or that was what she assumed it had been turned into with the heavy velvet drapes that covered the walls and the dark mood lighting. Loud music pumped, not the quaint string group she had envisaged but a DJ in a booth high up on a stage, already surrounded by a throng of beautiful women. She recognised him as the house DJ employed at Luca and Francesco's nightclub in Palermo. She had visited it twice and loathed it. Luca had holed himself up in the offices, leaving her bored out of her skull. At least when she accompanied him to one of the casinos there was always something to do that didn't involve gyrating into strangers' groins.

She could feel the vibrations through her fantastic gold sandals. Next to the DJ's booth were two caged podiums in which semi-naked lap dancers writhed. Much as it made her feminist hackles rise, even she could see the professional pride they took in their performances.

For the second time that evening she wished she had her sketchbook with her.

The ballroom was packed, not with shady men in black—although there were a fair number of them around—but men and women from the height of Sicilian and Italian society, minor British royalty and American film and rock stars. She even recognised a few patrons of the arts. Dotted around the enormous room were enough armed guards—unobtrusive but to her trained eye obvious—to overthrow a government.

It seemed as if Luca knew all the guests. Forced to stick to his side, she was introduced to dozens of both new and familiar faces, all of whom studied her with great interest. It was the familiar faces she found the hardest to endure, the curiosity in their eyes at the return of the prodigal wife.

She'd had no idea anyone would be interested about the state of their marriage, not at a birthday party in Florence.

Luca must have picked up on the curiosity too, for he kept her hand tightly clasped in his. Or was he simply marking his territory?

Glasses of champagne were thrust into her free hand, which she took cautious sips of, careful not to drink too much. Alcohol had a terrible habit of loosening her inhibitions and she needed to keep them tightly squashed away.

Her hackles rose again when a tall, lithe man approached them, two women walking to heel as if especially trained.

Francesco Calvetti. The party boy. Luca's main business associate.

CHAPTER TEN

DRESSED IN A dapper silver suit and open-necked black shirt, and looking as if he had just stepped off a catwalk, Francesco was sinisterly handsome. Grace would have bet every penny she owned he winked at his own reflection whenever he looked in a mirror. She had met him half a dozen times and he never failed to make her skin crawl. If she were to paint him she would cast him as a vulture.

'Luca!' He opened his arms wide and pulled him into an embrace that involved lots of back-slapping.

Grace watched Luca carefully, certain she had felt him tense at Francesco's approach. He responded with the same masculine enthusiasm, but as they conversed she could hear the tension in his voice, even if she couldn't understand the words.

Finally, Luca switched to English. 'Do you remember my wife, Grace?'

'But of course.' Francesco's English was faultless. He took her hand and pressed a kiss to it. There was nothing seedy in his manner but, for reasons she could not even begin to quantify, she wanted to snatch her hand away and disinfect it.

'I trust you have fully recovered from the ailment that kept you away for so long?' From the tone of his voice, he seemed to be speaking in code. Unfortunately she did not have the faintest idea what the code stood for.

'Yes, she is fully recovered,' Luca interjected smoothly.

'Excellent news. Please, both of you, accept my congratulations on the birth of your first child together. I hope your family is blessed with many more *bambini*.'

'That's what we hope for too,' said Luca.

The conversation ended with the men exchanging another back-breaking embrace before Francesco disappeared into a melee of beautiful women.

'What the hell was that about?' Grace demanded. 'What am I supposed to have recovered from?'

'Pre-natal depression.'

'What?'

'I told him you'd been in England.' Here he shrugged. 'His own mother suffered from severe pre-natal depression. He assumed you had suffered from it too and had gone to England to be cared for by your mother.'

'Why didn't you set him straight?' she seethed. 'Why couldn't you say I left you but that we had decided to try again for Lily's sake?'

He quelled her with a stare. 'Absolutely not.'

'Of course not,' she said sarcastically. She could feel her skin heating, his implacability heightening her anger. 'It would never do for people to think there was something wrong with *you* that made me leave, would there?'

'There is *nothing* wrong with me.' His eyes bored into her. If Grace's temperature had risen, his had lifted in conjunction. 'All that's wrong is how you interpreted matters to suit your own notions of how a businessman is supposed to conduct his affairs.'

If only she had been born with Medusa-like powers she could turn him into stone to match his heart.

'Where are you going?' he snapped as she stepped away.

'To the ladies', before I give in to temptation and cause a scene. Why? Are you going to follow me to make sure I don't escape?'

A pulse in his jaw throbbed as he leaned into her, his breath hot against her ear. 'If you want to leave, then I promise you one thing: I will not stop you and I will not look for you.'

'I think you'll find that was two things.'

Leaving him to stew in a pit of his own self-righteous anger, Grace proceeded to the ladies' cloakroom, concentrating only on putting one foot in front of another.

In the sanctuary of the opulent bathroom, she took stock of her appearance. As she retouched her eyeliner and re-applied her lipstick all she could think was her own husband had let Francesco think she suffered from depression.

The worst of it was, she could actually understand why a man with Luca's ferocious pride would allow such a thing. In a mad kind of way, it made a heck of a lot of sense. His wife had vanished from the face of the earth. She hadn't just left him, she'd disappeared without a trace. When eventually he found her and discovered she'd had his child, what was he supposed to tell people? That his own wife thought him so evil she would hide his flesh and blood from him? Honour and pride were everything, and she had wounded both.

By letting people believe she had left out of something beyond either of their control he could save face. For both of them.

Jeez, she was actually making excuses for him.

Only when she was satisfied her emotions were sufficiently masked did she leave the bathroom.

The ballroom had become so crowded she had trouble finding him. Snaking her way through the mass of bodies, she finally spotted him on a stool at the bar, nursing a glass of champagne.

As she neared him a warm hand grabbed her wrist. 'There you are. I thought you'd run away again.'

Twisting round, she met the contempt that was in her brother-in-law's eyes. 'Pepe! I didn't know you were here.'

'Well, I am.'

She attempted a smile. She had always adored Pepe, a man who gave the air that life was just one big party. Apart from when arguing with his brother, of course. Not tonight though. Tonight he looked darkly serious.

'Your mother said you would be home a few days ago. Have you been avoiding me?'

He sighed, checked over his shoulder to where Luca was sitting and tugged her into an alcove, away from the throng of people moving like a river around them. 'I thought it best to keep my distance until I could be certain I wouldn't throttle you for what you put my brother through. I didn't think he would appreciate that.'

'He would have cheered you on.'

His eyes became mocking. 'Why would that be?'

'He hates me.' Whatever Luca might say to strangers to explain her absence, his brother would get the truth. However divergent their lives and personalities, however ferocious their arguments, they were close.

'You stole his baby from him.' He made it sound so simple.

She sighed. 'I wish it were as straightforward as that.'

'It is. You ran away and stole his baby, ergo he hated you.'

It was Grace's turn to look over her shoulder, barely registering the past tense Pepe had just used. A woman had joined Luca at the bar. Whatever he'd said to her must have been the funniest thing in the world, for she threw her head back and laughed.

Pepe followed her line of sight. 'Worried he's searching for your replacement?'

She rolled her eyes, masking the stabbing pain piercing her heart. 'I have no control over what Luca does.'

'You have *no idea*.' He shook his head with a scowl of incredulity. 'Do you have any idea why I'm here at this scumbag's party?'

Her brow furrowed. 'Do you mean Francesco?'

'Who else? I'm here because I don't trust the bastard. Now that Luca is cutting all ties with him—'

Certain she had misheard, she cut him off. 'He's what?'

'Luca is ending their association. He told him at their meeting earlier.' His eyes narrowed as he took in her shock. 'I assumed he'd told you.'

She shook her head, hundreds of thoughts fighting for space in her head. 'Luca stopped discussing business with me a long time ago. Were you never part of their business dealings?'

His face contorted into something ugly. 'Francesco Calvetti is scum. I would sooner have made a deal with the devil. The terms would have been friendlier.'

'So you're only here to watch Luca's back?'

'Why else?'

Luca had cut his ties with Francesco...?

She remembered the look on Francesco's face at the casino, when he and Luca had been interrogating that poor man. What she remembered from that brief moment she had been in the office, before Luca had frogmarched her out, had been the cold cruelty she'd observed in Francesco's eyes. It had been in marked contrast to the thoughtfulness she had seen in her husband's.

Francesco enjoyed using threats and violence, whereas

Luca used them only because he felt it necessary. There was a big difference.

It shouldn't make any difference to how she felt about him, but it did.

'I need to get back to Luca,' she murmured, her eyes fixed on her husband and the buxom woman jabbering away in his ear.

As she made to walk off, Pepe called after her, 'Have you seen your friend since you returned?'

'Who? Cara?'

He nodded. His position and the angle of the light above him highlighted the silvery scar that ran across his left cheek.

'Not yet.' Cara's continued elusiveness concerned her. It was unlike her tender-hearted friend to be so evasive...

A thought occurred to her.

'Was it you who stole the data from her phone?'

He cast his eyes about, looking anywhere but at her.

Jaw clenched, she shook her head. It was inconceivable Cara would have let Luca within ten miles of her, but Pepe...

'Cara is the sweetest, nicest person in the world. If you've hurt her, I swear I'll make you live to regret it.'

With a parting 'You don't know what you're talking about,' Pepe disappeared into the crowd of revellers.

Grace took a deep breath to clear her head. Right now, she would have to put her friend to the back of her mind. As selfish as she knew it to be, she had more pressing worries to deal with.

She headed back into the throng and wove her way towards Luca. She could not quite hide the fear that Pepe's analysis was accurate. Was Luca still holding interviews for the role of his mistress?

Judging by the way the woman at the bar was leaning into him, it appeared so.

As she closed in on him her stomach roiled.

Watching her husband flirt with other women was surreal. First the assistant in the boutique and now this tanned, pneumatically boobed creature.

When they had been married—properly married, that was—she had often noticed women eye him up but that had been the extent of their interest. She and Luca had been practically glued at the hip. If another woman had tried to garner his attention he wouldn't have noticed or cared.

As she drew closer she realised any flirting was one-sided, a feeling confirmed when he looked up and she saw the dullness in his eyes.

That look made her heart lighten and relief spread its tentacles through her. The woman could be flirting with a brick wall for all the attention Luca was paying her.

Deliberately, she stepped between them.

'Excuse me!' The woman spoke with a broad cockney accent. Able to look closely at her, Grace recognised her as a glamour model, a favourite of the British press.

'I'm sorry,' she said lightly. 'That was incredibly rude of me. I'm Grace, Luca's wife.' A glass of champagne had been placed on the bar. Without missing a beat, she picked it up and downed it.

'Oi. That was mine.'

'Really?' She feigned ignorance. 'I do apologise. I thought Luca had ordered it for me. Please, let me get you another one.'

'No, don't bother.' The model pursed her lips together and stuck her clutch bag under her arm.

'Lovely to meet you,' Grace called as the model sashayed off to the dance floor, where a whole heap of rich men were congregated.

Luca stared at her, his lips twitching, before raising his chin and taking a swig of his champagne. 'Marking your territory?'

'You should be thanking me for getting rid of her.' Her fake bonhomie faded away. She had to ask, 'Unless you were auditioning her for the role of your mistress?'

His gaze didn't waver. 'I don't want a mistress.'

Something hot flooded her veins and seeped through her bones and into every inch of her flesh. Her lips parted, but no sound came out.

The icy darkness in his eyes melted. It took everything she had to wrench her eyes from his heated gaze.

She swallowed and stared at his champagne flute before being drawn back to meet his eyes. 'I thought you only drank Scotch nowadays?'

He didn't so much as flicker. 'When I realised that you weren't dead and had simply run away, I stopped drinking. I needed every wit I had trying to find you.'

'So my leaving did *some* good.' She smiled to cover the sting that lashed across her chest. As much as she knew he'd deserved every second of worry, it hurt her heart to think of the pain she had put him through. 'I was starting to worry for your liver.'

'You had nothing to worry about.'

'Didn't I?' she asked pointedly.

From the flicker in his eyes, he knew as well as she that she was not just referring to his drinking habits.

'I saw you talking with Pepe,' he said, blatantly changing the subject. 'I'm pleased he didn't give in to his impulse of strangling you.'

'So am I. I think he's saving all his hatred for when he gets the opportunity to dismember Francesco.'

Mirth played on his firm lips. Turning his head, Luca

caught the bartender's eye and indicated for more champagne.

'Francesco is not the demon Pepe would have you believe.' He paused. 'Well, maybe a little.'

'He told me you were cutting your business ties with him.'

'That is correct.'

'Why?'

'That is not a conversation for now.'

'Then when? Tonight? Tomorrow? Next year?'

He turned back to her. 'Tonight.'

'Promise?'

'I give you my word.'

She bit her lip, wishing she could read his mind.

A strange flicker crossed his face. 'I'm sorry I let Francesco believe you had pre-natal depression.'

An apology? From Luca? That had to be a first.

'It was the truth,' she admitted, expelling a huge lungful of air.

He raised an eyebrow, a furrow running down his forehead.

She smiled wryly. 'Oh, it wasn't serious like you told him. More a constant lethargy. Motivating myself to keep moving on kept getting harder.' As if her tongue had a mind of its own, she confided the darkness she had, at the time, been too scared to properly acknowledge to herself. 'It got worse after Lily was born. That's why I bought all the exercise equipment—I was terrified of being put on anti-depressants, terrified of failing Lily. I'd read exercise was a good method of combating it.'

'Did it work?'

'A little.' She shrugged, realising for the first time that her return to Sicily—to Luca—had coincided with the return of her old energy levels. For sure, she was still tired—

having a small baby who rarely slept through the night ensured that—but the cold fog that had enveloped her bones had vanished. 'I definitely feel better in myself now.'

'That's good.' He paused. 'I'm sorry I wasn't there to support you.'

It was on the tip of her tongue to say the same in return, but this time, by the slightest of threads, she managed to keep her mouth shut. To utter another word would be madness. She was in enough danger as it was.

Fresh flutes of champagne were placed before them. Luca handed one to Grace and held his own aloft. His eyes flashed. *'Salute.'*

'Salute,' she echoed, chinking her flute to his. She took a long sip and closed her eyes, enjoying the taste and the sensation of bubbles fizzing in her mouth. It was much the same way she used to fizz at Luca's touch. The way she still did...

'We should dance,' he said.

She took a deep breath and opened her eyes to meet his gaze. 'Why? So we can convince everyone here that we're happy together?'

'Because I want to dance with the sexiest woman here and show them she's mine.'

She swallowed away the dryness of her throat. 'I'm not yours. Only in name.' Even as she spoke the words she knew them to be a lie. Luca had imprinted himself indelibly into every one of her senses.

He leaned into her and spoke into her neck. 'You will *always* be mine.'

The warmth of his breath sent tiny pulsations darting through her. She swayed, her heels no protection against the dizziness evoked by his touch.

He covered her hand, lacing his fingers through hers.

He felt so warm, his touch penetrating her skin and dancing into the very fabric of her being.

As if acting of its own accord, her other hand came to rest on his shoulder.

His muscles bunched beneath her touch. She felt the potent strength that ran through his being, a strength she had always taken such comfort from.

The stars that resided in the midnight of his eyes gleamed, holding her gaze, trapping her into their depths. He had shaved before they left their hotel yet dark stubble had already broken out along his jawline. If there was a sexier man in the world she had yet to meet him.

He brushed his lips against her neck, nipping at the sensitive skin. 'Dance with me.'

She wanted to, badly. She wanted to say to hell with the past and to hell with the future, to simply take the moment for what it was.

His hand sidled down her chest, tracing the outline of her breast, coming to rest on her hip. He dug his fingers through the soft fabric and into her flesh, and pulled her so she was flat against him. 'Dance with me,' he repeated.

For the first time since she'd left Sicily, Grace felt as if the essence of herself had slipped out of the recess in which it had been hiding.

Luca was like a drug to her. She could survive without him but it was like breathing air with only a fraction of the usual oxygen.

She hated him.

She loved him.

The two sides were interchangeable.

The only constant she felt was desire. And she was sick of fighting it and pushing it away. There could only ever be one outcome.

Bending her head, she caught the top of his ear between her teeth. 'Yes,' she breathed, tracing her tongue across the contours. 'I'll dance with you.'

CHAPTER ELEVEN

THE DANCE FLOOR heaved with bodies, the music blasting out an R & B mix with a sensuous beat that throbbed through the wooden floorboards. The model who had flirted with Luca and whose name already escaped him was grinding with a member of the British aristocracy.

And he was dancing with his wife, a leg pressed between hers as they swayed together in time to the pulsating music, her face buried in his neck, her breath warm on his skin.

She moulded into him perfectly. Just as she always had.

This was an event he had looked at as a necessary evil, even before he had decided to cut all business association with Francesco Calvetti. After their meeting that day, attendance had been a requirement to show the world they were parting on good terms. The last thing either man needed was any usurper sniffing around trying to detect weakness.

The subtle politics of his business life was enough to give anyone a headache.

Grace eased his headache. Holding her in his arms drove away the demons that resided within him, just as it always had. No matter how out of control he had felt at times, one embrace from his wife had always been enough to temper it, if only a fraction.

For the moment he could almost forget the demons she had placed in there.

If he closed his eyes, he could almost believe the past year or so had never occurred. Physically they were as in tune as if they had never been apart.

Slowly he ran his hands down the length of her back until he reached her bottom. Cupping her buttocks, he pressed her ever closer. She could be left in no doubt of his arousal. And why would either of them doubt it? Physically, they were made for each other.

His quest to find a mistress had ended before it started. He had to get used to the fact there was not a woman alive, other than his wife, who did anything for him.

Before Grace had exploded into his life with all the subtlety of a flying brick, he'd never been so selective. His body had never been so stubborn to respond.

He shivered as her fingers brushed the nape of his neck. Such clever, talented fingers.

When had she last painted? In the Cornish cottage where he had found her, there had been none of the usual paraphernalia that used to accompany her everywhere. There had been no sign she had picked up a paintbrush or even a simple pencil since she had left him. The thought saddened him. The thought that he could be responsible for it made his chest tighten.

She raised her thigh slightly and ground against him, nipping at his neck. All his thoughts turned to fog, her soft lips sending darts of pleasure pulsing through his blood.

Turning his head, he captured her mouth in his and closed his eyes. Her hot sweetness engulfed his senses.

He forgot to breathe.

There it was, the taste that filled his mouth with moisture, the heat that turned his bones to liquid and his groin to steel, all so familiar and yet all so powerfully new.

Gently, he coaxed her lips apart and deepened the kiss,

deepened the craving that had never left him, had been banished to a dark recess until she came back into his life.

She moaned softly and parted her lips, digging her nails into his scalp.

For an age they stood there, swaying to the music, their mouths fused together, breathing each other in. The swaying bodies surrounding them disappeared into a haze; there but out of sight, the music reduced to a distant beat.

He wanted to consume her. He *needed* to consume her.

However much she might hate him, Grace belonged to him.

And he belonged to her.

A dancing couple inadvertently knocked into them.

Luca broke away with a muttered oath.

The room came swimming back into focus. Grace came swimming back into focus. She looked dazed, her eyes blinking furiously, her outward features exactly mirroring what he felt inside.

'Let's get out of here,' he said, taking her hand and tugging her off the dance floor.

She didn't resist. Indeed, she didn't say a word as they wove through the increasingly drunken revellers and out of the ballroom. Keeping a firm hold on her hand, he texted his driver to meet them at the front of the hotel.

Minutes later the driver opened the back door and they got inside.

'Take us back to our hotel,' Luca commanded.

Only when the limousine was moving and the privacy window had been erected did he turn to face her.

Her small chest heaved with short, ragged breaths. There was a wildness in her eyes, something feral seeping out of her pores.

'Come here.' His voice thick, he snaked a hand around her neck and pulled her to him.

She didn't need to be told twice. She pounced onto his lap and threw her arms around him.

Their lips came back together and he leaned back into the plush leather upholstery, cradling her head tenderly as he did so.

He had no idea what the nectar of myths and fables tasted like but knew it could never be sweeter than his wife's kisses. The most potent aphrodisiac could never evoke the desire one kiss from her could unleash.

Grace was the most openly sensuous woman he had ever known with a sex drive that perfectly matched his own. She'd never feigned coyness and what she initially lacked in experience she had more than made up for in enthusiasm. He had loved that raw honesty about her. The first time she had taken him into her mouth she'd knelt before him and fixed those hazel eyes on him. 'I've never done this before,' she'd said matter-of-factly. 'So sorry if I do it all wrong.'

It had ended up being one of the most incredible experiences of his life.

Now, as she straddled him with the earthy hunger he had always adored, he wondered how he had ever managed without her, without making love to her. Whether their couplings were short and frantic or long and luxurious, they would always end sated and content, locked in each other's arms.

Finally he broke away for air and razed his teeth down her neck, darting his tongue on the lobe of her ear. She moaned lightly and rubbed her cheek against his, her hands creeping down the plane of his chest and tugging his shirt loose so she could burrow under it.

It suddenly dawned on him that they were making out in the back of a car like a pair of adolescent teenagers.

He shifted slightly, then immediately wished he hadn't as his straining erection rubbed against the apex of her thighs.

'Enough,' he said roughly. He grabbed her hips and ma-
noeuvred her so only her legs lay draped over his lap. It did
absolutely nothing to ease the ache in his groin. 'I am not
going to make love to you in the back of a car.'

She looked at him with eyes that were wickedly dazed.
'Why not?'

A bubble of laughter rose in his throat. Grace had per-
fected mock innocence into a fine art. 'Because we're not
teenagers and there are two perfectly good beds waiting
for us just minutes away.'

She pouted. 'Spoilsport.'

'Have I not taught you anything? Anticipation height-
ens pleasure.' He reached over and pulled the straps of her
dress back up. 'You can choose the bed.'

'You're letting me choose something?'

'Don't start,' he warned, before deciding it was easier
to cut an argument off at the bud rather than let it bloom
into something bigger by kissing her again.

'I thought we weren't going to make out in the back of
a car,' she murmured between kisses.

'I make the rules.' He covered her mouth again in another long, delicious kiss.

Without his being fully aware of it, her hand had burrowed back up his shirt. She pinched a nipple. 'That's what
you think.'

Before he could respond she had twisted her body to
climb back on top of him.

Just as he was starting to think there was something
to be said for acting like a lust-driven teenager, the limo
came to a stop.

She lifted her head and peered through the window.
'Oh…. We're back at the hotel.'

Wrapping an arm around her neck, he pulled her down
for one last kiss. 'What did I tell you about anticipation?'

When the driver opened the door to let them out, they were sitting respectably, side by side, thighs pressed together, hands clasped.

Hand in hand, they strode through the hotel lobby, their minders, who had been in the car behind them, having to hurry to keep pace. Luca could only hope no one was paying enough attention to notice the enormous erection straining through his trousers, or spotted that more of Grace's orange lipstick covered her face than her lips.

For Grace, the journey up in the private elevator was little more than torture, the presence of the lift's concierge preventing her from doing anything more than cling to Luca's hand. If she had any doubts about what they were about to do, it was too late. The charge had become an inferno.

The second they were in the privacy of their suite, she was in his arms, her hands wrapped round his neck, drinking kisses that scorched, firing her blood.

Luca pushed her against the wall by the door and pressed against her, a hand tracing up her thigh and bunching the skirt of her dress up to her waist.

'Grace,' he groaned huskily, nipping at her bottom lip before reclaiming her mouth, his fingers playing at the rim of her knickers.

She slipped a hand down the front of his shirt, all the way down to his trousers, lower, until she reached the hardness of his erection. A noise came from his throat, almost a groan, a husky sound that speared her skin. Quickly, she undid the button and pulled the zip down, tugging his trousers and snug boxers down past his hips, allowing him to spring free. With fervoured hands, she held his length and rubbed a thumb over the head, rediscovering the hard, velvet smoothness. If ever an erection was beautiful, Luca's was it. Once she had made him lie on their bed naked, cajoled him with her mouth and tongue until he was as solid as rock then, with a wicked grin, had backed away and sketched him.

Now she had no intention of backing away.

Forget a bed. Forget foreplay. Forget everything. *It had been so long.*

She gasped as her knickers were ripped off and discarded, and when he inserted a finger into her sodden warmth she moaned and ground herself against him, wanting more, *needing* more.

All she wanted was to feel him deep inside her, filling her and fulfilling her as only Luca could, and she almost screamed in frustration when he moved his hand away and reached round to clench her buttocks, lifting her off her feet.

Immediately she released her hold on him and grabbed his shirt, pulling him so he was flush against her.

He broke their kiss and stared at her with a hungry, animalistic look, his eyes devouring her. 'You are the sexiest woman on the planet,' he said, the words coming out as a growl before he smothered her mouth.

Gripping one of her thighs, he raised it, giving her the extra lift she needed to wrap her legs around his waist, his strength supporting them both.

In one sure move he was inside her.

She cried out his name, tearing her mouth from his, biting his earlobe. There was no time to savour the feeling because it wasn't enough. Not nearly enough. All the cells inside her felt ready to explode.

Clinging to him, she buried her face in his shoulder and breathed in his musky scent, nipping at the salty flesh.

It was as if they'd never been apart, their bodies perfectly in tune to the other's needs. And what they both needed was release.

She met every carnal thrust as if it were the last, could

feel the pulsations within her core thicken. Luca's groans deepened and she knew his control was hanging by a thread, something she had always revelled in, the knowledge that this sexy bear of a man wanted her so badly. He knew her body as well as if it were an extension of his own. By pushing her thighs apart just a little and raising her slightly higher against the wall, he deepened the penetrations.

And then she was there. Closing her eyes tightly, she ground into him, her climax careering through her like a cresting wave, the ripples spreading out into every cell from the ends of her toes to the tips of her fingers and up to the strands of her hair.

He plunged into her with one final thrust, before losing his control with a cry, breathing heavily into her hair as together they wrung out every last millimetre of pleasure.

For an age they stayed that way, holding on to each other tightly until the spasms subsided and clarity broke through the haze.

Reluctant though she was to break the union, Grace's legs became limp and unfurled from around him.

Luca laughed lightly and withdrew from inside her, holding her waist securely while she found her feet.

'Okay?' he asked, brushing his lips to her neck.

'I think so.' She wrapped her arms more tightly around him and swayed into his chest, nestling her head into his shoulder. She could feel the thud of his heart reverberating through him, and gave a wistful sigh at the familiarity.

His hands brushed the length of her back. 'Your bed or mine?'

Tilting her head, she met his midnight stare, her heart catching at the warmth in it, and the gleaming heat that was of a very different nature.

As dangerous as she knew it would be to actually spend

a night sharing a bed, sharing even more intimacy with him, she didn't care. At least not then. If she regretted it in the morning, then…well, then she would deal with it in the morning.

'Mine.'

Taking great care not to disturb him, Grace disentangled her limbs from Luca's and crept out of bed.

After making love again, he had pulled her into his arms and fallen asleep. Usually the sound of his deep, steady breathing was enough to pull her into slumber too but tonight her brain refused to switch off. Which was hardly surprising under the circumstances.

Padding out of the bedroom, she headed into the main room of the suite and began rummaging through the bureau. There, she found an A4-sized notepad and an expensive-looking fountain pen with a variety of nibs and ink cartridges. She hardly cared. Her fingers were itching worse than any itch she could recall. She would have been satisfied with a lip liner.

Back in the bedroom she turned the small light of the dressing table down to its dimmest setting, quietly dragged the armchair to the side of the bed and nestled into it.

She had no idea how long she had been drawing when Luca's deep voice broke through the silence. 'Have you given me horns?'

She raised her eyes from the pad on her lap and threw a sheepish smile. Shoving her hand down her side, she pulled out a crumpled piece of paper and threw it at him.

He sat up, unfurled the paper and smoothed it out. He looked from the paper to her and back again. There was no anger in his expression, more a sad acceptance. But that could easily have been a trick of the light.

She'd sketched him sleeping. The more detail she'd put

into it, the tighter her chest had become. The longer she had drawn, the more the hate inside her had continued to squeeze out, and so, in desperation, she had drawn a thick, narrow goatee on his chin, quickly followed by a set of intricate horns above his ears. She'd even popped a red cartridge into the pen to tint the eyes, the only colour on the page. When she'd finished, her gaze had flittered between the devil on the page and the devil on the bed. Except her eyes no longer recognised the devil on the bed for what it was. All she could see was the man, sleeping, strangely innocent in his slumber. Her heart had clenched so tightly her eyes had brimmed. And she'd looked back down on that page and it had felt all wrong.

Screwing it into a tight ball, she'd started again, using nothing but her eyes to dictate what her hands drew. This picture felt cleaner somehow.

'If it's any consolation, the picture I'm drawing now is definitely *sans* horns.' Despite her best efforts she couldn't hide the catch in her throat.

'It is,' he said, his voice thick.

She looked up.

'It is a consolation,' he clarified, a wry smile playing on his lips.

She dropped her gaze back to the pad on her lap and added some strokes to thicken the hair. 'Are you ready to tell me about the breakup of your partnership with Francesco Calvetti?'

Her question seemed to surprise him, catching him mid yawn. 'There's not much to say. I have decided now is the right time to break it.'

Dropping a tiny splodge of ink along the jaw, she rubbed it with her middle finger to represent the dark stubble of his jawline. 'But why now?'

'There are many reasons.'

Silence hung in the air.

'How did you come to work with him in the first place? You never did tell me.' She kept her voice calm and non-accusatory. The soft lighting in the dark room had created a peaceful ambiance and she wanted to keep it that way, reluctant to spoil the harmony they had created, however fleeting that harmony might be.

Expelling a deep breath, Luca swung his legs off the bed and strode to the window, drawing back the curtains.

With his back to her, his naked torso had never looked more magnificent.

Quickly she turned the page of her pad over and started on a fresh sheet.

She waited for him to speak.

'Our fathers were great friends as well as associates. Francesco and I went to school together, spent time on holiday together, that kind of thing.'

'Really? I vaguely remember him from our wedding, but until you went into business with him when you bought the first casino, I didn't even know his name.' And then they had bought another casino and then the nightclubs. It hadn't taken long before she had grown to hate the name Francesco Calvetti.

'Francesco's father was a bastard.'

She paused, saying nothing, letting him fill the silence.

'If you wanted to know what a proper gangster looked like, you would have looked no further than Salvatore Calvetti. He made the de' Medici look like pussy-cats.'

She could hear the disgust in his voice.

The frozen pen on the page had blotted and she whipped it away, rubbing her thumb over the blot, transforming it into shading down the arch of his back.

'The older Salvatore got, the more vicious he became. My father was very different. Age mellowed him. It was no surprise to any of us when he decided to break the association. He wanted to take what *you* would call a more… legitimate path, especially with Pepe and I at an age to follow in his footsteps. The estate had been in the family for generations and had always been a good source of income. My father decided it was time to realise its full potential and turn the vineyard into the pride of the country.'

'And Salvatore was happy to break their…association?'

'No. Only the fact they had been close friends since childhood allowed him to break away without any repercussions.' He placed his hands on the window-sill and stretched a leg back, peering out. 'My father died barely a year later. Pepe and I agreed we would follow his wishes and run the estate free from Salvatore's influence.'

'Did Salvatore try and muscle in?'

'Naturally. He felt it was his right.' His tone became menacing. 'But we set him straight.'

'Is that why the estate is protected like Fort Knox?'

He nodded. 'It had always been highly guarded, but after my father's death I thought it prudent to add extra security measures. I was not prepared to let that bastard anywhere near my family or our home and business. And God knows, he tried.'

'So, when you took over the estate, the business consisted of just that—the estate?'

'We already had the vineyards and olive groves.'

'But only on the Mastrangelo estate.'

He nodded.

Her mind reeled as she considered what her husband had accomplished in the thirteen years before she met him. It wasn't just the expansion, although, considering they now owned dozens of estates in eight European countries and a couple in South America, the expansion was no small feat.

Mastrangelo wine was world famous and had won every

prestigious award going. Mastrangelo olive oil came at a premium and was the oil of choice for discerning chefs in all corners of the globe.

Yes, Pepe had come on board once he had graduated, but Luca had been the driving force behind it all.

'If you hate Salvatore so much, how come you ended up in business with his son?'

'He died a few weeks after our first wedding anniversary.'

'Ah.' Hazily she recalled him mentioning an old family acquaintance passing away, remembered the way his lips had curved in a manner she had been unable to discern.

'You didn't want me at the funeral.' When she'd offered to go with him, Luca had rebuffed her; the first time in the whole of their marriage he had attended anything that could be classed as even vaguely social without her.

'I didn't want you anywhere near that bastard even if he was in a coffin. Pepe and I only went to assure ourselves he really was dead.'

'Is that when you and Francesco reconnected?'

'Yes. Francesco's relationship with Salvatore was difficult to say the least, but he showed his father great loyalty. Salvatore's death freed him to take his own path.'

'And his own path included working with you.'

'Only in certain areas. In some businesses it is good to spread the risk.' He sighed. 'I was only twenty-one when I took over the running of the Mastrangelo estate. This gave me a chance to spread my wings too.'

'Pepe didn't agree?'

'Pepe and Francesco have loathed each other for years— they fell out over a woman. I was at university when it happened. I forget the details.' Luca raised his broad shoulders. 'I am my own man. I do not need my brother's permission or blessing to do anything. Francesco is his own man too. He is not his father. What he proposed made a great deal of financial sense and earned us both a lot of money.'

'If it earned you so much money, why break the association?'

'It is the right time. I shall keep the restaurants—they practically run themselves—but the casinos and nightclubs are nocturnal activities and require a lot of hands-on involvement. I have a child now who is deserving of my time and attention. I want to be there for her bath times, I want to read her stories. I want to be a proper father to her.'

Lucky Lily, she thought, as an unexpected wave of desolation streamed through her.

There was a truism in the saying that you couldn't miss what you'd never had. And Grace hadn't missed her father during his long absences—even when he was at home, Graham's mind was always on worthier causes. She'd known he loved her and that had been enough. She'd known her mother loved her and that had been enough.

Or so she'd told herself.

She'd never pushed either of them on it. She'd simply accepted the situation with her parents for what it was, never allowing herself to consider it in any real depth, too fearful of what the answers might be—that her mother's art and her father's good causes were more important to them than their only child.

She'd never properly pushed Luca about what was *really* going on in his life either, too fearful to probe too deeply— she hadn't wanted to know the truth, only confronting the reality when her pregnancy had left her no choice.

She hadn't stuck around to confront him with the undeniable truth, which had scared and horrified her. Instead, she had run away without even giving him the basic opportunity to defend himself...

'And is that the only reason you're breaking the associ-ation?' she asked him softly. 'Because you want to spend time with Lily?'

He turned his head to look at her, his spine straightening. 'What other reason could there be?'

She shrugged. 'I guess I thought—hoped—it was because you realised what you had become.'

His eyes hardened. 'And what might that be?'

'Everything your father never wanted you to be.'

She regretted the words the moment they left her lips.

Luca barely flinched but that small movement was enough for her to know she'd hit a nerve.

He sucked in a breath and turned his back to her.

Feeling like the worst person in the world, she got up from the chair and joined him at the window. In silence they looked out at the *Piazza del Duomo*. Under normal circumstances, the starlit cathedral would fill her with joy and contentment. But not tonight. Even though she knew she had been right in what she had said, it had been cruel.

How incongruous was that? Just twenty-four hours ago she would have snatched at an opportunity to hurt him.

'I'm sorry, Luca,' she said quietly, placing a hand on his shoulder. 'That wasn't fair of me.'

When he didn't answer, just gazed out of the window, his jaw clenched, she pressed on. 'I don't want another argument. I know my thoughts and opinions don't mean jack to you, but I'll say it anyway—I'm pleased you've broken your association with that man. It makes me feel safer knowing he's no longer in your life.'

It seemed to take for ever for him to break out of his trance.

Slipping away from her, he said, 'It's late. We have an early flight to catch. I'll get some sleep in my own room.'

Biting her lip, she let him go.

Her heart heavy, she turned out the light and got into bed. The thick duvet felt cold without him.

CHAPTER TWELVE

LUCA UNLOCKED THE door of the cottage and switched on the light. Immediately the studio went from darkness to bright, bright light.

Closing the door behind him, his head aching, his chest tight, he paced to the far end of the room where Grace kept her paintings neatly stacked.

This was something he had done on many occasions during her absence, especially in the lonely nights when his bones had always felt cold whatever the outside temperature. He'd examined every one of her paintings, like a detective trying to find clues, seeing if there was anything in them that would even hint at why she had left him.

But it had been more than a mere forensic examination. He'd felt closer to her in there, her personality and spirit etched in her work. If he closed his eyes he could imagine her standing before her easel, her head tilted, her face screwed in concentration.

He sank to his knees to look through the paintings for what had to be the hundredth time and now, finally, he began to see.

Her early paintings had been vivid. She'd painted him, his family and many of the estate workers individually; beautiful, colourful pictures with personality and gusto. There were plenty of celebrity pieces too. He remembered how she would scour magazines, her excitement when she found a picture that 'jumped out' at her. She would cut it out and hurry to her easel, her mind already working overtime. The finished article would be nothing like the original photo but the person in question would never be in doubt.

As the length of their marriage increased, he could see a difference. Nothing obvious, not at first, but if you placed the pictures in chronological order... The later paintings were more muted, as if the vibrancy that lived inside her and extended into her artwork had dimmed.

It was the very last painting he had struggled the most to comprehend, the one left on her easel. The oil had still been wet when she vanished. Unlike her other portraits, which were always human, she had painted a black bird in flight, surrounded by a thin mist. He didn't recognise the breed, guessed she had created it from her own imagination.

For almost a year he had studied that bird, his mind ticking with increased desperation to see what, if anything, it represented. No matter how hard he looked, all he could see was a bird in flight.

Now, for the first time, he could see what he had been missing.

What he had assumed to be a thin mist he could now see was a dome. The bird was trying to fly out of the dome. The bird could see the freedom of the big wide world but was trapped within its cage.

The painting *was* a portrait. It was a self-portrait.

Grace had represented herself as the bird. Luca was the dome.

He staggered back to his feet, disconcerted to find the room swimming before his eyes.

It felt as if the walls were closing in on him.

Resting a hand against the wall, he took deep breaths to steady himself but found his airway restricted.

Dear God, what had he done?

He'd captured a beautiful, vibrant bird and taken away its freedoms and the very vivacity that had made it so special.

And then he had recaptured it and, instead of learning his lesson and nurturing it, he had tethered it ever closer, giving it no chance to spread its wings.

Was this really what he wanted? For Grace's wings to become so clipped she forgot what it even felt like to fly?

And was this what he wanted for Lily, his beautiful fledgling? A life of restriction? Of fear?

An image of his father came into his head, an image that had been fighting for space within him for days.

Grace had been right in her assessment. His father *would* be appalled to see the man his son had become. He had been fooling himself to ever think otherwise. Never minding his treatment of Grace, his father would be saddened that his eldest son seemed to have embraced the very things he had spent the last years of his life rejecting, the very things he had tried to steer his sons away from.

How had he sleepwalked into such a situation? The worst of it all was, deep down, he had known almost from the beginning that he had made a mistake. Instead of holding his hands up and bowing out, he had let his stupid pride take over, allowed the glamour of the establishments to seduce him, and invested in the nightclubs too.

Francesco might have despised Salvatore and abhorred anything to do with drugs or arms trafficking, but he had learned more than a few of his father's old tricks.

Luca remembered the first person they had caught trying to steal from their casino. Francesco's men had half killed him, and for what? All that man had tried to steal was a couple of hundred euros.

Why had he not put a stop to the beating?

It was a question he had asked himself hundreds of times.

He was not averse to violence when absolutely necessary—it was the only language many of the men he dealt with knew—but for two hundred euros? A swift kick in the ribs would have sent just as clear a message.

That night, he'd got home in the early hours and downed a long shot of Scotch before seeking Grace out in her studio. He remembered, clearly, finding her fast asleep in the bedroom, clambering under the sheets and pulling her to him.

His mind had still been reeling, his heart still racing from the assault he had witnessed. In his wife's loving arms he'd found some respite and oblivion.

After that first time, he'd left the security side of things in Francesco's hands with the assertion that his partner's men were to keep all physical damage proportionate and never to the point of no return. Ensuring his wishes were respected meant keeping a very close eye on proceedings.

Knowing no person would be killed in his name allowed him to sleep a little easier.

But as time had gone on, his sleep had become worse. It seemed as if every week someone was caught stealing from them or harassing their female staff. Then there were the drug dealers to contend with, always there, wanting to set up shop in their establishments. These scumbags he had no problem with being dealt with physically. They were nasty, malevolent creatures who deserved everything they got and he would happily throw the odd punch in himself.

These people had to be dealt with, to be taught a lesson that everyone else would understand. Even the petty thieves.

He had let it happen. He had let blood be spilled and bones broken, and told himself he was the force for good within the partnership. Usually he would tell himself that with a large glass of Scotch in hand.

If he thought it was so good, then why had he never shared any of it with Grace? It wasn't simply to do with protecting her or because she wouldn't understand. It was because he had known damn well she would be horrified, had known deep down that her happiness was becoming muted, the constraints of their life wearing her down.

He hadn't wanted to see the horror and disapproval that would have been sure to follow in her eyes.

He hadn't wanted to admit to his wife—even less to himself—that he had taken a wrong turn and was in so deep he could see no way out.

He hadn't wanted to give her any more of an excuse to leave because, out of everything, that was what he'd feared the most—that if he confided the truth of what was bearing down on his conscience, she would turn around and leave him.

And she had. Grace had learned the truth and left him.

Three years ago he'd had everything: a vivacious, beautiful wife who loved and understood him, a flourishing business, more money than he could ever spend in a lifetime...

The business and the money were still there but he'd thrown the rest away.

Grace was the best thing that had happened to him and he'd ruined it with his pride and selfishness. He had brought a danger and violence into their lives that were far more potent than any threat Salvatore had brought.

He staggered over to the large mirror she kept on a stand close to her easel, which she used for looking at her paintings with a different perspective.

His own perspective had altered too.

That sketch she had drawn of him was as close to real life as it was possible to get.

She had been right all along.

He really was the devil. An evil monster.

The weight of reality pushed down hard on his chest, its tentacles spreading out and pulling at him, making his skin tight and his stomach cramp.

He couldn't bear to look at his reflection for a second longer.

With a guttural roar, he ripped the mirror off the stand and threw it onto the terracotta floor, where it landed with a deafening crash.

With deep, ragged breaths he gazed at the shards of mirror scattered around him. His distorted image now reflected off thousands of tiny fragments.

The act was not enough to silence the demons screaming in his head or quell the sickness inside.

There were not enough mirrors in the world to purge him.

He didn't deserve to be purged.

In desperation he spun around, helpless for the first time since his father had died when he'd felt so hollow, as if the heart of him had been ripped out. This felt so much worse.

A sound behind him made him whip around again.

For the blink of an eye he was certain he had conjured her.

'Luca?' Grace said, approaching him with soft footsteps. 'What are you doing in here?'

He tried to move his throat but no words would form.

Her winter boots crunched on the scattered fragments and she froze, her eyes moving from him to the mess surrounding her. She looked back at him, her face creased with concern. 'I've been looking everywhere for you. Whatever is the matter?'

How could she even stomach looking at him, never mind looking at him as if she were *worried* about him?

He was not worthy of her compassion.

How could he have ever thought he hated her?

'Please, Luca,' she begged, crunching slowly towards him. 'Talk to me.'

How many times had she said those words?

How many times had he fobbed her off, refusing to admit to either of them that there was a problem?

What could he say now? Mere words could never convey the deluge of emotions raging through him or make up for everything he had put her through.

In a trice he closed the gap between them and cupped her cheeks in his palms. Her hazel eyes glittered and swirled but she made no attempt to break away, simply stared back as if trying to read his innermost thoughts.

He knew right there and then that he would have to let her and Lily go. He could not force the misery of this life and this unwanted marriage on her for a moment longer. But...

Before he set her free, he had the means to at least make partial atonement.

Closing his eyes, he brought his lips down on hers and held them there, breathing in the heady sweetness of her breath. He waited for a heartbeat, half expecting her to resist. Instead, her hands rose up his arms, bunching his sweater in her fists, and she swayed into him.

It was the sign he'd been waiting for.

Pulling her tightly into his arms, he kissed her hard, his heart expanding when she released her hold on his sweater and looped her arms around his neck, her responsive kisses as ardent as his own. Her fingers slipped into the neck of his shirt and scraped his skin, the warmth of her touch sending shivery tingles down his spine and lower into his groin.

'Upstairs,' he said, speaking into her mouth and sweeping her into his arms.

They had made love in her studio more times than he could ever hope to count, against the wall, on the worktop, on the sofa; pretty much everywhere.

When they had first married he had tried to carry her up the stairs of the cottage. Halfway up, they had collapsed in a fit of giggles and ended up making love right there, never making it to the bedroom.

This time, he carried her all the way. There was not the faintest trace of humour on her face, instead an almost fervoured seriousness he had rarely seen expressed by her.

The bedroom was cold.

He laid her down on the bed then crossed to the window and closed the curtains before flicking the heater on. Until it kicked into life and provided some warmth he would use his own body to warm her.

Her eyes didn't leave him. 'Luca,' she began, but he placed a finger to her lips to silence her.

'Not yet,' he whispered, kicking his shoes off and lying down next to her, replacing his finger with his mouth. She wrapped her arms around him and responded with the passion that was just one of the many things he had always loved about her. Their mouths merged into one, their tongues combining, their clad bodies clinging together, arms and hands stroking wherever they could reach.

Soon he broke away but only with his mouth, tracing his lips over her face, seeking every millimetre of silken skin from the lids of her eyes to the lobes of her ears. The soft moans escaping from her throat were like balm on a wound.

Only when he judged the room had warmed sufficiently that she would not freeze did he move away.

'Stay there,' he ordered, sealing his command with another kiss.

Her eyes had a dazed look about them, but she acquiesced with what could almost be called a contented sigh, stretching an arm over her head and staring at him.

In one swift movement he removed his sweater and threw it to the floor. Not taking his eyes off her, he quickly divested himself of his shirt, trousers and underwear until he was standing before her as naked as the day he had been born but with an erection that ached more than any he had ever known.

The powerful heater was already working its magic but he doubted he would have felt the cold.

Kneeling at the foot of the bed, he unlaced her boots and pulled them off along with her thick socks. Her feet were cold and he rubbed them in turn before dropping a gentle kiss on each toe.

Taking his time, he stripped her clothes, refusing all of her attempts to help. Soon, her jeans and bulky jumper were bundled in a pile on the floor like his own.

Aware this would be the last time he would see her naked, he let his eyes rake over her before following with his lips, determined to kiss and taste every last inch of her. Starting with her delectable mouth, his lips trailed down her neck and over her shoulders, his hands roaming free, exploring her smooth flesh.

Last night, when they had made love in Florence, their passion had been too frenzied to do anything more than touch, both too desperate for him to possess her to care much about foreplay.

Tonight, he could see all he had missed. The longer he kissed and explored, the more changes he found in her body, subtle differences from how he remembered her. Her nipples had darkened and her breasts, judging by the way she sucked in a breath and writhed beneath him when he took them in his mouth, had become even more sensitive.

She had always been naturally toned but now he could

see and feel a softness around her abdomen, as if a small cushion had been placed under her skin. Tiny red slivers ran under her belly button, more signs that she had recently carried a child—his child—inside her. He kissed every red mark reverently, fighting back an unexpected burn in the backs of his eyelids that threatened to break out when he thought of her going through pregnancy and birth alone.

How could he have ever judged her harshly for that, for protecting their child?

Tiny whimpers were coming from her throat. When he moved lower, down to her pelvis and the soft downy hair surrounding her pubis, she reached out and grabbed his hair, her fingers digging into his scalp.

He gently spread her legs. The moment he pressed his lips to her clitoris she gasped and tried to sit up. Holding her down with one hand on her belly, he buried his face there, his tongue rhythmically pressing against the nub of her pleasure, inhaling the musky scent he adored.

Her whimpers lengthened, deepening into groans. He opened his eyes and watched as her head rolled from side to side. Keeping his eyes fixed on her, he increased the pressure, moving the hand that had been holding her down upwards until he reached her breast and covered it.

Her back became rigid, almost lifting off the mattress as she climaxed. He kept his mouth and tongue exactly where they were until he was certain he had coaxed every ounce of pleasure from her. Then and only then did he snake his way back up, covering her belly and breasts with more kisses, his enormous erection rubbing against her thighs until he reached her mouth.

Her cheeks were flushed, her eyes aglow. Hooking an arm around his neck, she almost wrenched him down to kiss her mouth, her free hand trailing down his back to his buttocks.

And then he was inside her, deep within the hot moistness, the relief so great he almost came on the spot.

Closing his eyes, he took a deep breath and steadied himself. This, their last time together, was a moment to be cherished.

Grace had other ideas, raising her thighs for even deeper penetration, clinging to him, her mouth demanding ever more from his kisses.

It took everything he had to slow her down. He wanted—needed—to savour every minute. He wanted her to savour every minute too, to look back on this, their last time together, and think of him, if not with love, then something kinder than hate.

He withdrew, right to the tip, holding it there for as long as he could bear before pushing back inside. He let the motions increase a little with every thrust, until he established a steady tempo that had her whimpering anew, moaning his name, her hand clasping his buttocks, the fingers of her other hand scraping his scalp.

Only when he felt the muscles within her contract and her body go rigid did he finally allow himself to let go too, his cry of relief sounding like a roar as he made one final thrust, holding on to the moment for as long as he could before collapsing on top of her.

For what seemed an age, he lay there, buried inside her and on her, reluctant to move, desperate to hold on to the moment for as long as he could.

Eventually the chill on his back forced him to move.

It hadn't been the power of the heater that had warmed him earlier but the heat Grace created within him.

He covered them in the duvet and pulled her to him, his head already thickening with the need to sleep. One more sleep with her and then…

Grace sat bolt upright, jerking him awake.

'Your mum must be doing her nut!' she cried.

Before she could escape from the bed he trapped her wrist. 'What's the problem?'

'I put Lily to bed and then got your mum to watch over her so I could come and find you—I didn't think I'd be this long!'

'My mother will be fine,' he soothed, pulling her back to him.

'No, she won't. She's shattered.' She wriggled out from his hold and climbed off the bed. 'I think Lily must have kept her awake all night. I promised I wouldn't be long.'

'Why were you looking for me?'

'You missed Lily's bedtime. You haven't seen her since we got back. I knew you were home but I couldn't find you anywhere and you weren't answering your phone.' She looked up from the pile of clothes she was sorting through and threw him a wry smile. 'Maybe I should get a tracker put on it so I can keep tabs on *you.*'

He winced. Knowing he deserved it did not take away the sting.

His heart felt weighted as he watched her dress.

She must have felt him staring, pausing from yanking her jeans up. 'What's the matter?'

There was one question he needed to know the answer to before he let her go. 'Why did you stop painting?'

'I…' She hesitated. 'I'm not sure. I guess I was too busy running.'

'I'm sorry I never bought you a gallery.'

Her eyes widened a fraction.

'You were right—I didn't think it was safe enough outside the estate for you.'

Eyes still wide, she hooked her jumper over her head. When she came up for air she said, 'I was going to buy it for myself.'

'Really?' He was about to ask what money she would have used when it came to him in a flash. 'Your allowance.'

She nodded, smoothing the jumper down over her belly. 'It was just sitting in the bank doing nothing.'

'I wondered why you hadn't touched it.'

'I wasn't going to touch the allowance, not at first. I never wanted it in the first place.'

'So why accept it?'

'When I agreed to it we were in that soppy honeymoon phase. I knew refusing would hurt your feelings and I didn't want to do that. But then a few months before I left I got to thinking—why shouldn't I buy it? That money was mine to do as I wished.'

'But you knew buying it would go against my wishes?'

She slipped her feet into her boots and looked up at him. Her smile was sad. 'Actually, I didn't know that. You never said it in so many words; just evaded the topic every time I brought the subject up. But yes, I had a good idea you wouldn't approve.'

'Yet you were still prepared to go ahead and do it.'

'I like to think I would have. It was either that or hate you for your pig-headedness. I loved you. You were my world. But you were not my life. You knew when we married I had a mind of my own and that I'm not some insipid flower who wilts at the first sign of confrontation...' Her voice trailed off, her eyes becoming glazed.

'Grace?'

She blinked and gave a short shake of her head before continuing where she had left off. 'I knew opening my own gallery without your input would cause conflict between us but I thought—hoped—we were strong enough to overcome it.' She finished tying her laces and looked at her watch again. 'I really need to get back to your mum. Are you coming with me?'

'No. I'll get the mirror cleared up and then I have things I need to do.'

'Okay.' She bit her bottom lip, looking as if she was about to say something. Instead, she shook her head as if to shake an errant thought away. 'I'll see you later, then.'

Only when he was certain she had left the cottage did he slump forward and grip his head in his hands.

CHAPTER THIRTEEN

GRACE LISTENED OUT for Luca's return but the door to their wing remained resolutely closed all night. Lily hardly slept either. If she didn't know better, Grace could swear she was waiting for him to come home too.

Something was troubling him and her heart ached to reach out.

The way he had made love to her…it wasn't just the tenderness, it was the expression in his eyes, so much emotion.

As ridiculous as she knew it to be, it had felt as if he were saying goodbye.

Once Lily was up, fed and dressed, she decided to take her out for a walk. Maybe the crisp air could clear her head of the melancholy that had set in.

Just as she was about to push the pram into the woodland surrounding the monastery, a black Jeep came up the drive. Her heart jumped into her mouth but when it drove slowly past she saw it was one of the guards of the estate. Nonetheless, she waved politely, scolding herself for her irrational reaction. She shouldn't get all skittish at the thought she might see her husband. And her heart certainly should not be pounding because of it.

After an hour of traipsing through the woods and skirting round the vineyards, she headed back feeling every bit as jumbled as she had when she'd left.

At least the fresh air had done Lily some good. She'd fallen fast asleep.

Grace lifted her out of the pram and carried her into their wing. Even when she stripped her out of the thick snowsuit, Lily didn't make a murmur.

After settling her in the cot, Grace wandered back into her own room and saw she'd left her passport on her pillow.

'I must be cracking up,' she muttered under her breath, snatching it up, dislodging an envelope resting under it which she couldn't remember seeing before. She really was going bonkers. She could have sworn she'd put the passport in the top drawer of her dresser when they'd returned from Florence. Except, when she opened the said drawer she found her passport in the exact place she had left it.

She opened the new passport, took one look at the picture and dropped it as if scalded.

It belonged to Lily.

Hands shaking, she retrieved it from the floor and took another look. What the heck was it doing in her room…?

Clutching it to her chest, she wandered out into the corridor.

The master bedroom was empty.

The office door was closed. She nudged it open.

Luca was sitting behind his desk, dressed in the same clothes he'd been wearing when she'd found him in her studio.

He looked a mess, his hair sticking out all over the place, the stubble around his jaw thick.

He raised bloodshot eyes.

She held the passport out. 'I found this in my room.'

He groaned. 'I put it there.'

'You did? But why?'

'Isn't it obvious?'

'Not really.'

He dragged a hand down his face and exhaled slowly. 'You are free to take Lily and leave.'

Fearing her legs would give way beneath her, she leaned back against the door. 'Just like that?'

'Please, Grace, don't make this any harder than it is. Pack your things. I'll arrange for a driver to take you wherever you want to go. When you're ready, call me and we'll sort out the finances.'

She could not respond. She opened her mouth but nothing came out.

'I assume the cheque is adequate to get you started?'

When she continued to stare at him blankly, his forehead creased. 'I wrote a cheque out for you and left it with Lily's passport.'

'I never opened the envelope.'

He scratched his head, breathing deeply. 'If you find it isn't enough, just say and I'll write you another. Or you can give me your bank details and I'll transfer the money straight into it. Not that I would blame you if you didn't trust me with those details.'

Unexpected freedom was within her grasp. She could almost reach out and touch it but her brain was having trouble processing it. This was such an about-face it was hard to comprehend. 'Why are you doing this?'

'Because you don't belong here.'

His answer felt like a slap in the face.

He must have read her shock. 'You have never belonged here,' he said, utter dejection ringing from his eyes. 'The restrictions of my life, the security, my business dealings, all it did was stifle you.'

'You tried,' she said, feeling a strange compulsion to defend him from himself. 'You tried so hard to make me happy.'

He might have got cold feet about her having a proper

gallery away from the estate, but that did not take away from the wonderful studio he had created for her or the hours he had spent in there with her, bringing his work into her world so they could be together. She doubted there were many men who would be so tolerant of a wife prone to disappearing from the marital bed in the middle of the night to paint.

'Please, do not make excuses for me.' His hands balled into fists. 'I deserve nothing but your contempt. We both know you would have left me eventually, even if you hadn't become pregnant.'

'We don't know that.'

'*I do.* Being here was killing the essence of *you.* Sooner or later you would have had enough. Tell me the truth. Given a choice, would you want to live here? Would you want Lily to be brought up here?'

She shook her head, wishing with all her heart that she could lie to him.

Why wasn't she jumping up and down with glee?

Luca was handing her everything she wanted. Her and Lily's freedom.

He closed his eyes but not before she caught the bleakness that had flittered into them. 'You and Lily will be happier away from Sicily. You need somewhere with freedom, a thriving art community, sunlight and people. The only thing I can provide for you here is the sunlight.'

'But…'

'Grace, I should never have forced you back. I have many regrets—so numerous I'm going to spend the rest of my life doing good deeds if I'm to have any chance of avoiding hell—but my biggest regret is my treatment of you. I brought danger into our lives. I kept you a virtual prisoner…' His eyes snapped open to stare at the ceiling. 'Everything I have done has caused you harm. I've behaved like a monster and I do not blame you for wanting to raise our child away from my influence. I will leave it to you to decide if I am to be allowed any contact with her. Whatever you decide, know I will support both of you financially and know I am more sorry than I could ever express.'

She should turn around and go before he changed his mind.

'So that's it?' She needed to make sure. 'Lily and I can leave, right now, and never come back and never set foot in Sicily again and never see you again?'

He rubbed the back of his neck. When he answered it was full of weariness. 'If that is your wish, then yes.'

She believed him. She could grab her daughter and slam the door on Sicily and Luca for ever.

'Please, Grace.' His voice caught before he blew a puff of air out of his mouth. 'Please, leave now. Looking at you hurts my heart.'

'Okay,' she said uncertainly. 'I guess this is goodbye, then.'

He gave a curt nod, no longer looking at her. 'Goodbye, Grace.'

Taking a shuddering breath, she stepped over the threshold.

'If you or Lily need anything—anything at all—I'll always be here for you,' he spoke quietly after her.

Unexpected hot tears burned her eyes. She tried to walk to her room but every step felt as if ten-tonne slabs of concrete had been placed inside her limbs.

For an age she stood there, unable to move, the utter misery and dejection on Luca's face the only thing she could see when she closed her eyes.

He had fallen in love with Lily and he was still letting them go.

And he loved her, Grace, too. She could feel it in her

heart. Since he had come to her bedroom and spent the evening bathing and dressing their daughter, it was as if the old Luca had slipped back into his skin and slowly reclaimed his body.

He was giving her everything she wanted. Except for one thing...

Hadn't she realised that last night, after they'd made love? She would have been happy to buy a gallery knowing it would be against his wishes, but confrontation involving anything *real*, she backed away from.

Unless she put her heart on the line and fought for the one thing she wanted above all else, she would lose it for ever.

She hurried back into his office, her legs suddenly working just fine in her haste.

Luca was slumped over his desk, his face buried in a pile of papers.

'You said I could leave Sicily and never return if that were my wish. Well, what if my wish is for you to come with us?'

He slowly raised his head, a deep groove indented in his forehead.

She took a step towards him. 'What if Lily and I loved you so much we didn't want to be parted from you again?'

His mouth formed a tight line, his eyes not moving from her.

She moved closer. 'What if I were to tell you I stuck it out in Cornwall for longer than I knew was safe because a tiny part of me missed you so badly it wanted you to find me?' As she spoke the words she knew them to be true. That strange lethargy that had overcome her, that hollow feeling that something was missing...

The rational, protective part of her had been terrified of Luca discovering them.

Her irrational heart had ached for him.

'What if I were to tell you I couldn't paint because being without you made me so miserable, the creative part of me died?' Reaching him, she leaned against his desk and took one of his trembling hands. 'What if,' she continued, turning it palm up and pressing a kiss to it, 'what if I were to ask you to start again, somewhere new? Would you do it? Would you be prepared to move and run the estate from a different country if it meant we could be together as a family?'

He reached out to palm her cheek with his free hand, gazing intently into her eyes. The groove on his forehead had vanished. '*Mio Dio*, you're serious.'

The tears she had been holding back spilled over. She wiped them away. Right at that moment tears were a nuisance; she didn't want to cry when she was about to say the most important words of her life. 'You're right. I don't belong here but I do belong with *you*. I've told you about my childhood and what it was like—I was wanted and loved but I never felt that, that…' She struggled to find the right words. 'I guess I always felt separate from my parents. I have *never* felt separate from you, even when we were apart—you were with me for every second of it. I love you, Luca, and I don't think I could bear to be parted from you again.'

He had her on his lap and wrapped in his arms so quickly she had no time to even blink.

Her head pressed against his chest, he held her tightly, breathing deeply into her hair. '*Dio*, I never thought I would ever hear you say that again.'

'Nor did I.' She tilted her head and raised a hand to stroke his cheek. 'I love you.'

'I don't deserve your love.'

Another tear rolled down her cheek and she gave an

impish smile. 'I know. But what can you do?' She straightened so she was face to face with him. 'And you can't put everything on yourself.'

The furrow on his forehead reappeared. 'What do you mean?'

'I'm your wife. I *knew* something was wrong and I should have pushed harder to make you talk to me.'

'Grace, it would have made no difference. I couldn't confide in you. Not then. I was in too deep and too frightened of losing you to think straight.'

'I should have at least tried. But I was too scared.'

Consternation crossed his face. 'Of me? I would *never* raise a—'

'No!' She cut him off sharply. 'I know you would never so much as lift a finger against me. No. I was scared to confront the truth. I was scared that if my suspicions were proven correct then I would have to ask you to choose between me and your association with Francesco. I could never have condoned what you two were doing, whatever the reasoning behind it. I couldn't have lived with it—I just couldn't.' Her voice dropped to a whisper. 'I didn't believe you would choose me.'

She had trusted his love but she hadn't trusted that it was strong enough to put her first. She could see that now. She had spent her entire life feeling that her parents' love for her was secondary to their lives. To her, that kind of love had been normal.

'Ah, *amore*,' he groaned before pressing his head against hers and breathing in deeply. 'I would never choose anyone or anything over you.'

'And maybe if I'd believed that, I would have forced you to confide in me as soon as the warning signs were there that something was wrong. We don't know if things would have turned out differently, and that's what I mean when I say you can't put it all on yourself.'

Luca expelled a breath slowly, the warm air from his lungs tickling her hair.

Grace took her own deep breath. 'So what would you say? If I asked you to abandon your life here and come with us, would you?'

He kissed her forehead almost reverentially. 'I would follow you to the ends of the earth if I thought that was what you wanted.'

She closed her eyes at the suffusion of warmth his words provided.

'But is it what *you* want?' Doubts suddenly crowded her as she thought of what she was really asking of him—to give up the only life he had ever known.

'All I want is you and Lily. Being without you…Grace, I cannot begin to tell you how lost I felt. And you're right. This life here is no kind of life. Not for you.'

'It's your life though.' Now she thought about it, she could see the total abandonment of Sicily would never work. 'There's so much to think about.' She sighed. 'Too much of your life and business is tied up here.'

'The majority of the wine and olive business is in Europe,' he mused. 'Francesco's buying out my share of the casinos and nightclubs, which will free me up to base myself anywhere I choose, like Pepe.'

'But this is your home. How would your mum feel if we moved away? She'd be heartbroken.'

'My mum is as tough as old Parma ham.'

She sniggered. 'I know, but she adores Lily. She can always come with us.'

He pulled away and stared at her quizzically. 'Seriously? You would want my mother to come with us?'

'I know she's never approved of me but she is your mother and she does love Lily.'

'She *does* approve of you,' he insisted. 'She's always thought you were wonderful but she could see from the beginning that the restrictions of living here would wear you down. And she was right.'

She snuggled back into his chest, a warm feeling of contentment seeping through her bones ridding her of the final vestiges of poison.

'We'll work it out,' he promised, stroking her hair. 'As long as we're together, and as long as we're talking to each other about the things that matter, we'll figure it out.'

'Did you know I managed to escape your goons' X-ray vision for all of two minutes and buy a new untracked phone?'

He laughed and rubbed his chin on her hair. 'Now why doesn't that surprise me?'

Snickering, she buried her face in his chest, catching a whiff of stale alcohol. 'Have you been drinking?'

His voice became rueful. 'I stayed the night in your studio nursing the best part of a bottle of Scotch.'

'Were you very drunk?'

'No. Believe me, I tried very hard to find oblivion. I knew what I had to do but I was delaying the inevitable.'

'I can't believe you were prepared to let me go.'

'And I can't believe what a bastard I was in forcing you to stay, and I can't believe you're prepared to give me another chance. I swear, I'll never give you cause to regret it.'

'As long as you promise to stay away from any business venture involving Francesco Calvetti.'

'You can't blame Francesco. I am my own man and I make my own choices. But I promise from now on all my business ventures will be legitimate in the sense that *you* recognise.'

'Good. You must also swear there will be no more secrets between us.'

'No more secrets.'

She rubbed her nose into his neck, catching another scent, a very faint trace of his new cologne. 'Why did you change your aftershave? I thought another woman had bought it for you.'

His laugh was savage. 'There has been no one else. I changed it because every time I smelt the old one it reminded me of you and made me miss you so much it hurt.'

'Good. Because you must also swear to never, ever, *ever* even think about taking a mistress.'

'As long as I'm breathing you are the only woman for me. You. Just you.'

'Good. Because if you went with another woman I swear to God I'd rip your heart out.'

'My heart would have to be ripped out for me to stop loving and wanting you.' He bent his head and brushed his lips to hers. 'I never stopped loving you, even when you shot me.'

Her laugh was shaky. 'And I never stopped loving you, even when I hated you.'

'No more hate.' His lips parted and he pulled her into a kiss of such tender sweetness that the last hollow patch inside her belly filled and made her whole.

EPILOGUE

THE MONASTERY WAS filled with friends and family, the Mastrangelo contingent of aunts, uncles and cousins far outweighing the handful that had flown over for the occasion from England. Lily Elizabeth Mastrangelo had been baptised earlier in the same church in Lebbrossi where Grace and Luca had married. The beaming congregation had all agreed she was the most beautiful baby to bless the earth—although Grace could have sworn one of the small Mastrangelo cousins had likened Lily to a pig, but her language skills were so pathetic it was likely a mistranslation.

Donatella approached her, a glass of red wine in hand. 'Aunt Carlotta has kidnapped Lily,' she said, looking more relaxed than Grace had ever seen her.

'I don't think I've seen her since we got back from the church.' Grace laughed. 'The relatives have been too busy playing Pass the Baby.'

'I'm going to miss her,' Donatella admitted with a rueful smile.

'I know. It's not too late—you can still come with us.'

'Thank you for the offer but my home is in Sicily.'

'It's not as if Rome's the other side of the world. You can visit whenever you like and of course we'll make plenty of trips back here.' She and Luca had found the ideal compromise—half the year in Sicily and half the year in Rome.

She could live with that and so could Luca. Six months of hyper-security and six months of freedom and anonymity. It was a good compromise. Their new home in Rome now beckoned, waiting for their small family to move into it. Her fingers were already itching to get decorating.

Scanning the room for Luca, who had earlier disappeared to their personal wine cellar with a couple of uncles demanding a tour, she spotted Cara and Pepe having what looked to her eyes like a heated discussion. She'd already had a good chat with her friend but had found her distinctly cagey about how Pepe had got hold of her phone. So cagey, in fact, that she had refused to discuss it.

When Luca reemerged a short while later, she pulled him to one side. 'Do you know what's going on between those two?'

He looked over and shrugged. 'Pepe refuses to talk about it with me.'

As Lily's godparents, Cara and Pepe had been required to stand together during the baptism. Grace had noticed the way Cara had refused to even look at him. Now her sweet-natured friend looked as if she wanted to rip his throat out.

'Leave them to get on with it,' Luca advised, clearly reading her mind. Standing behind her, he wrapped his arms around her waist and rested his chin on the top of her head. 'We have guests to mingle with, Signora Mastrangelo, before we can slope off for an early night.'

She didn't have to be a mind-reader to know what was on his mind. She could feel the bulge in his trousers resting in the small of her back.

'The day has worn me out,' she said with faux innocence, pressing back into him so they were completely flush. 'An early night is just what I need.'

'Seeing as it's our last night here, we should get my mum to look after Lily.'

'That would be the nice thing to do. After all, she won't get woken up in the middle of the night by a teething baby for *ages*.'

'We'll be doing her a favour really.'

'Absolutely,' she agreed, heat already bubbling in her veins at the thought of what the night would bring.

* * * * *

THE SICILIAN'S
UNEXPECTED DUTY
MICHELLE SMART

This book is dedicated to Adam, Joe and Zak,
my gorgeous Smarties.

CHAPTER ONE

PEPE MASTRANGELO HELPED himself to another glass of red wine from a passing maid and downed it in one. His aunt Carlotta, who had taken it upon herself to shadow him since they'd arrived back at his family home, was blathering on in his ear about something or other. Probably parroting her favourite inanities about when he, Pepe, was going to follow in his older brother's footsteps and settle down. Namely, when was he planning to get married and have babies?

Aunt Carlotta was not the only guilty party in this matter. The entire Mastrangelo clan, along with the Lombardis from his mother's side, all thought his private life was a matter of public consumption. Usually he took their nosiness in good part, knowing they meant well. He would deflect their questions with a cheeky grin, a wink and a quip about how there were so many beautiful women in the world he couldn't possibly choose just one. Or words to that effect. Anything but admit he would rather swim in a pool of electric eels than marry.

Marriage was for martyrs and fools, and he was neither.

He'd almost married once, when he'd been young and foolish. His childhood sweetheart. The woman who'd ripped his heart out, torn it into shreds and left an empty shell.

Now he considered that he'd had a lucky escape. Once bitten, twice shy. Only complete idiots went back for a second helping of pain if it could be avoided.

Not that he ever shared that little titbit of information with people. Heaven forbid. They'd probably try to talk him into something ridiculous like therapy.

Today though, his usually quick repartee had deserted him. But then, he wasn't usually fielding these questions with a pair of almond-shaped green eyes following his every move. To make it even harder to concentrate, those same eyes were drilling into him with pure loathing.

Cara Delaney.

He and Cara had been appointed his niece's godparents. He'd been forced to sit next to her in the church. He'd been forced to stand by her side at the font.

He'd forgotten how pretty she was—with her large eyes, tiny nose and small heart-shaped lips, she looked like a ginger geisha. Although *ginger* was the wrong word to describe the red flame of hair that fell down her back. Today, wearing a red crushed-velvet dress that showcased her curvy figure yet barely displayed an inch of flesh, she looked more than pretty. She looked incredibly sexy. Under normal circumstances he'd have no hesitation in spending the day in her company, flirting with her, plying her with drinks, maybe seeing if a repeat performance could be on the cards.

Being in the presence of his ex-lovers was not usually a problem, especially as his 'emotionally needy' detector was so acute. As a rule, he could spot a 'looking for marriage and babies' woman at ten paces and avoid her at all costs. As such, meeting up with an ex-lover was usually no big deal.

This time was different. Under normal circumstances he hadn't last seen them when he'd sneaked out of the hotel suite, leaving them sleeping in the very bed they'd just made love in. And usually he hadn't stolen their phone.

As soon as the date for the christening had been set a month ago, he'd known he would have to see Cara again. It was inconceivable that she wouldn't be there. She was his sister-in-law's best friend.

He'd expected the loathing that would be pointed his way. He really couldn't blame her for that. What he hadn't expected was to feel so... The word that would explain the strange sickness churning in his stomach wouldn't come. Whatever the word, he did not like it at all.

A quick glance at his watch confirmed he would have to endure her laser glare for another hour before he could leave for the airport. Tomorrow he'd be taking a tour of a profitable vineyard in the Loire Valley that he'd heard through the grapevine—pun intended—was being considered for sale. He wanted to get in there and, if viable, make an offer before any competitor started digging around.

'I *said*, she's beautiful, isn't she?' Aunt Carlotta's voice had taken a distinctly frosty tone. Somehow, in between her non-stop nattering, she had managed to acquire Lily without him noticing. She held the baby aloft for his perusal.

He peered down at the chubby face with the black eyes staring up at him, and all he could think was how like a little dark-haired piglet she looked. 'Yes, beautiful,' he lied, forcing a wide smile.

Seriously, how could anyone think babies were beautiful? Cute at a push maybe, but beautiful? Why anyone raved about them was beyond him. They were the most boring of creatures. He quite liked toddlers though. Especially when they were getting up to mischief.

He was saved from having to fake any more enthusiasm by a great-aunt barging him out of the way so she too could coo at the poor child.

Using this momentary lapse of Aunt Carlotta's attention, he sidled away.

Was this the way people acted at all christenings? From the way his relatives were behaving, anyone would think Lily had been conceived from a virgin birth. Having not attended a christening in nearly fifteen years, he wouldn't know. Given a chance, he would have got out of this one too. But there'd been no way, not when he'd been made godfather. Luca, his brother, would have strung him up if he'd tried to avoid it.

He wondered how long it would take for Luca and Grace to try again. No doubt they would keep trying until a boy was born. His own parents had struck gold from the outset, the need for an heir immediately satisfied with Luca's birth. Pepe's own conception was more along the 'spare' lines and to give Luca a playmate.

Was he being unfair to his parents? He didn't know or care. He'd been feeling out of sorts all day, and having the red-headed geisha glaring at him as if he were the Antichrist was not helping his mood.

Forget it, he thought, reaching for another glass of red from a passing maid. No one would notice if he left earlier than was deemed polite...

'You look stressed, Pepe.'

He muttered an expletive under his breath.

He should have known he wouldn't be able to escape without her collaring him. There had been something too determined in that expression of hers.

Plastering another fake smile on his face, he turned

around and faced her. 'Cara!' he exclaimed with bonhomie so fake even Lily would see through it. Grabbing her shoulder with his free hand, he pulled her into him and leaned down to kiss both her cheeks. She was so short he almost had to double over. 'How are you? Enjoying the party?'

Her dark coppery eyebrows knotted together into a glare. 'Oh, yes. I'm having a marvellous time.'

Pretending not to notice the definite edge to her voice, he nodded and raised the wattage of his grin. 'Fabulous. Now, if you'll excuse me, I have—'

'Running away again, are you?' Her Irish lilt had thickened since he'd last seen her. When they'd first met, here in Sicily three years ago, her voice had contained only the lightest of traces; by all accounts she'd left Ireland for England when she was a teenager. When he'd seduced her in Dublin four months ago, he'd noticed her accent had become more pronounced. Now there was no doubting her heritage.

'I have to be somewhere.'

'Really?' If an inflection could cut glass, that one word would have done the trick. She nodded her head in his sister-in-law's direction. 'She's the reason you stole my phone, isn't she?' It wasn't a question.

He drew in a breath before meeting Cara's stony glare. The last time he'd been with her, those eyes had been brimful of desire. 'Yes. She's the reason.'

Cara's geisha lips always drew a second glance—her bottom lip was beautifully plump, as if it had been stung by a bee. Now she drew it tightly under her teeth and bit into it. When she released it, the lip was a darker, even more kissable red. Her eyes had become a laser death stare.

'And was it my phone that led Luca to find her?'

There was no point in lying. She already knew the answers. Lying would demean them both. '*Sì.*'

'You came all the way to Dublin, to the auction house where I work, spent two million euros on a painting, and all to get hold of my phone?'

'*Sì.*'

She shook her head, her long copper locks whipping over her shoulders. 'I take it the whole "I've always wanted to visit Dublin, please show me around" thing was also deliberate?'

'Yes.' He held her icy gaze and allowed the tiniest of softening into his tone. 'I really did have a great weekend—you're an excellent tour guide.'

'And you're an unmitigated…' She buried the curse beneath a deep breath. 'But that's by the by. You seduced me for one reason and one reason only—so you could steal my phone the minute I fell asleep.'

'That was the main reason,' he agreed, experiencing the strangest tightening in his chest. 'But I can assure you, I enjoyed every minute. And I *know* you enjoyed it too.'

Cara had come undone in his arms. It had been an experience that still lingered in his memories and his senses, but an experience he ruthlessly dispatched from his head now.

All he wanted was to get away from her, get away from this claustrophobic party with all the talk of *babies* and *marriage*, and find himself a few hours of oblivion.

Her cheeks coloured but her jaw hardened. 'What's *enjoyment* got to do with anything? You lied to me. You spent a whole weekend lying to me, pretending to enjoy my company…'

He flashed his most winning smile. 'I did enjoy your company.' He certainly wasn't enjoying it now though.

This conversation was worse than the frequent visits to the headmaster he'd endured as a schoolboy. Just because he deserved someone's censure didn't mean he had to enjoy it.

'Do I look like I was born yesterday?' she shot back. 'The *only* reason you hooked up with me was because your brother was so desperate to find Grace.'

'My brother deserved to know where his wife had gone.'

'No, he did not. She's not his possession.'

'A lesson I can assure you he has learned. Look at them.' He nodded over to where Luca had joined his wife, his arms locked around her waist. Fools, the pair of them. 'They're happy to be back together. Everything has worked out for the best.'

'I was a virgin.'

He winced. He'd been trying his best to forget that little nugget. 'If it's an apology you're after then I apologise, but, as I explained at the time, I didn't know.'

'I told you...'

'You told me you'd never had a serious boyfriend before.'

'Exactly!'

'And as I told you before, not having a serious boyfriend does not equate to being a virgin.'

'It does—did—for me.'

'How was I supposed to know that? You're a twenty-six-year-old woman.' He'd thought virgins of that age were extinct, a thought he kept to himself. Cara's skin had gone as red as her hair. He didn't particularly fancy being on the receiving end of a punch in the face in front of his entire family, even if she would need a stepladder to reach him. There was something of a ferocious Jack Russell about her at that moment.

'You used me,' she said, almost snarling. 'You let me believe you were serious, and that we would see each other again.'

'When? Tell me, when did I say we would see each other again?'

'You said you wanted me to come to your new house in Paris so I could advise you where to place the Canaletto painting you bought in the auction.'

He shrugged. 'That was business talk. You know about art and I needed an expert's eye.' He still needed one; he'd bought his Parisian home to showcase his art collection, but the entire lot was still in storage.

'You said it while dipping your finger in champagne and then placing it in my mouth so I could suck it off.'

A flare of heat stirred in his groin. That particular moment had been during their last meal together, shortly before she'd agreed to join him in his hotel room and spend the night with him.

He cut his thoughts off the direction they were headed. The last thing he needed at that moment was to remember anything further about that night. It was becoming uncomfortable enough in his underwear as it was.

'Why didn't you steal my phone from the outset? Why string me along for a whole weekend?' Her eyes were no longer firing hostility at him. All he saw in them was bewilderment.

It had been easier dealing with Aunt Carlotta's jabbering mouth than with *this*. Okay, he got that Cara felt humiliated—he hardly recalled his actions that weekend with pride—but surely it was time for her to get over it?

'I couldn't steal your phone because you keep your handbag pressed so tightly to you I knew it would be impossible to steal.' Even now, she had the long strap placed diagonally over her neck and across her chest, the bag itself tucked securely under her arm.

'I'm surprised you didn't arrange for someone to mug me. I'm sure between you and your brother you know enough shady people to do the job. It would have saved you wasting a weekend of your precious time.'

'But you could have got hurt,' he argued silkily. A strange shiver rippled through his belly at the thought, a feeling dismissed before it was properly acknowledged.

He'd had enough. He'd behaved atrociously but it had been necessary. He wasn't prepared to spend the rest of the evening apologising for it. He'd never told her an actual lie—how she'd interpreted his words was nothing to do with him. 'You share a house with three other women, which made breaking into your home too risky, and you keep your phone on you when you're working. If you'd left your handbag unattended just once throughout that weekend, I would have taken it, but you didn't—you didn't let it out of your sight.'

'So now it's *my* fault?' she demanded, hands on hips.

Cara had to be one of the shortest people he'd ever met, certainly on a par with his great-aunt Magdalena. In the four months since he'd last seen her, she'd lost weight, making her seem more doll-like than he remembered. Yet, whether it was the long flaming hair or the ferocity blazing from her eyes, she stood tall and unapologetic before him, as if a tank would not be enough to knock her down.

He bit back another oath. 'What's done is done. I've apologised and as far as I'm concerned that's the end of the matter. It's been four months. I suggest you forget about it and move on.'

With that, he stalked away, striding towards Luca and Grace, ready to tell them he was leaving.

'Actually, it's not the end of the matter.'

Something in the tone of her voice made him pause.

'It's impossible for me to *"forget about it and move on"*.'

A shiver of something that could be interpreted as fear crawled up his spine...

Cara watched Pepe's back tense and all the muscles beneath his crisp pink shirt bunch together.

Only Pepe could get away with a pink linen shirt, unbuttoned at the neck, and snug-fitting navy chinos for his own niece's christening. The shirt wasn't even tucked in! Yet he still oozed masculinity. If she could, she'd rip all the testosterone from him—and there must be buckets of it—and flush it down the toilet. Standing next to him in the church, she had been acutely aware of how overdressed she looked in comparison, and had fumed at the unfairness of it all—*he* was the one underdressed for the occasion. With his long Roman nose, high cheekbones, trim black goatee covering his strong chin and his ebony hair quiffed at the front, Pepe looked as if he'd stepped off a catwalk.

She'd truly thought she'd been prepared. In her head she'd had everything planned out. She would be calm. She would politely ask for five minutes of his time, explain the situation and tell him what she wanted. Above all else, she would be calm.

Under no circumstances would she let him know of her devastation when she'd awoken alone in his hotel suite, or her terror when the stick in her hand had turned pink.

She would be calm.

All her good intentions had been thrown by the wayside when she'd taken one look at his handsome face and wanted to knock his perfect white teeth out.

The whole time she'd been next to him at the christening, even while they were making their respective promises as Lily's godparents, all she could think was how much she wanted to cause him bodily harm. She'd even found herself gazing at the silver scar that ran down his cheek, wishing she could track the culprit down and shake his hand. Or her hand. She'd asked Pepe about the scar during their weekend together but he'd evaded the question with his customary ease. She hadn't pushed the matter but it had tugged at her. All she'd wanted to do was trace a finger down it and make it magically disappear.

Who, she'd wondered, could have hated him enough to do such a thing? Pepe was charm personified. Everyone adored him. Or so she'd thought.

Now it wouldn't surprise her in the least to discover a queue of people wishing to perform bodily harm on him.

The violence of her thoughts and emotions shocked her. She was a pacifist. She'd attended anti-war demos, for cripes' sake!

She'd spent the past four months castigating herself for being stupid enough to fall for Pepe Mastrangelo's seduction. She should have known it wasn't her he was interested in. After all, he'd never displayed the slightest interest in her before. Not once.

On her frequent trips to Sicily to visit Grace, they would often make a foursome for evenings out. Luca had terrified her, had done from the moment she'd met him. Pepe, on the other hand, had been fun and charming. After a few dates she'd been able to converse with him as easily as she could with Grace. Tall and utterly gorgeous, he was the type of man females from all generations and all persuasions would pause to take a second look at.

However much she'd liked his irreverent company, she'd always known he tagged along on their evenings out as a favour to his big brother's wife. He would flirt with Cara as much as the next woman, fix his gorgeous dark blue eyes on her and make her feel as if she were the only woman in the world—until he fixed those same eyes on another woman and made her feel exactly the same way. His blatancy had made her laugh. It had also made her feel safe. He was not a man any woman with a sane mind could take seriously.

Well, more fool her for falling for it. She would *never* make the same mistake again, not for him, not for anyone.

Hadn't she always known that sex was nothing but a weapon? Hadn't she witnessed it with her own eyes, the devastation that occurred when grown men and women allowed their hormones to dictate their actions? It ripped lives and families apart.

Pepe was a man who positively revelled in allowing his hormones to lead the way. He thrived on it. To him, she, Cara, had been nothing but a means to an end, the sex between them a perk of the task he had undertaken. His brother had wanted his wife back and Cara's phone had contained the data with which to find her. The fact that she was a human being with real human feelings had meant nothing. When it came to his family, Pepe was a man without limits.

And that lack of limits had come at a price.

'I can't *"forget about it and move on"*, you feckless, irresponsible playboy, because I'm pregnant.'

CHAPTER TWO

CARA DIDN'T KNOW exactly how Pepe would react to her little statement, but when he finally turned to face her, his wide smile was still firmly in place.

'Is this your idea of a joke?'

'No. I'm sixteen weeks pregnant. Congratulations. You're going to be a daddy.'

His eyes bored into hers but his smile didn't dim, not by a single wattage. All around them gathered his family. She could feel their curious gazes resting on them. Resting on *her*.

It was too late to wish she could hide behind Grace as she had done so many times since her teenage years. Whenever she was in a new social situation she would let Grace hold court until her nerves were silenced and she felt capable of speaking without choking on her own tongue. Grace had understood. Grace had protected her.

But Grace had married and moved countries. Grace had also disappeared for the best part of a year, forcing Cara to get her own life in order. She couldn't keep living her life through her best friend. She needed a life that was her own.

And she'd been getting there. She'd moved back to Ireland, landed a job she loved, albeit at the lowest rung, but it was a start, and even made some new friends. She had truly thought she'd found her own path to some kind of fulfilling life.

Pepe hadn't just blocked the path, he'd driven a ruddy great bulldozer through it and churned it into rubble.

He'd left her alone, scared and pregnant, with a future that loomed terrifyingly opaque.

Eventually he inclined his head and nodded at the door. 'Come with me.'

Relieved to get away from all the prying eyes, relieved to have a moment to gather her wits together, she followed him out and into the wide corridor.

Pepe leaned against the stone wall and ran a hand through his thick black hair.

A maid appeared carrying a fresh tray of canapés, which she took into the vast living room.

No sooner had the maid gone when a couple of elderly uncles came out of the same door, laughing between themselves. When they saw Pepe, they pulled him in for some back-breaking hugs and fired a load of questions, all of which Pepe answered with gusto and laughter, as if he hadn't a single care in the world.

The minute they were alone though, the smile dropped. 'Let's get out of here before any more of my relatives try and talk to me.' He set off in a direction within the converted monastery she'd never been in before.

'Where are we going?'

'To my wing.'

He made no allowances for her legs being half the length of his, and she struggled to keep up. 'What for?'

He flashed her a black look over his shoulder, not slowing his pace for a moment. 'You really wish to have this conversation in front of fifty Mastrangelos and Lombardis?'

'Of course not, but I really don't want to have it in your personal space. Can't we go somewhere neutral?'

'No.' He stopped at a door, unlocked it and held it open. He extended an arm. 'I'm getting on a flight to Paris in exactly two hours. This is a one-off opportunity to convince me that I have impregnated you.'

She stared at him. She couldn't read his face. If anything, he looked bored. 'You think I'm lying?'

'You wouldn't be the first woman to lie over a pregnancy.'

Throwing him the most disdainful look she could muster, Cara slipped past him and into his inner sanctum.

Thank God she had no hankering for any sort of future for them. He was a despicable excuse for a human being.

Pepe's wing, although rarely used, what with him having at least three other places he called home, was exactly what she expected. Unlike the rest of the converted monastery, which remained faithful and sympathetic to the original architecture, this was a proper bachelor pad. It opened straight into a large living space decked with the largest flat-screen television she had seen outside a cinema, and was filled with more gizmos and gadgets than she'd known existed. She doubted she would know how to work a quarter of them.

She stood there, in the midst of all this high-tech luxury, and suddenly felt the first seed of doubt that she was doing the right thing.

'Can I get you a drink?'

'No. Let's just get this over with.' Of course she was doing the right thing, she castigated herself. Her unborn child deserved nothing less.

'Well, I need one.' He picked up a remote control from a glass table in the centre of the room and pressed a button.

Eyes wide, she watched as the oak panelling on the wall behind him separated and a fully stocked bar emerged.

Pepe mixed himself some concoction she didn't recognise. 'Are you sure I can't get you anything?'

'Yes.'

He tipped it down his neck and then fixed his deep blue eyes back to her. 'Go on, then. Convince me.'

Pursing her lips, she shook her head in distaste. 'I'm pregnant.'

'So you've already said.'

'That's because I am.'

'How much?'

'How much what?'

'Money. How much money are you going to try and extort from me?'

She glared at him. 'I'm not trying to extort anything from you.'

'So you don't want my money?' he said, his tone mocking.

'Of course I do.' It gave great satisfaction to watch his ebony brows shoot up. 'You have lots of money. I have nothing. I am broke. Boracic. Poor. Whatever you want to call it, I am skint. I'm also carrying a child whose father can afford to pay for a decent cot and wardrobe and a decent place for him or her to live.'

He sucked in air through his teeth. 'So you *are* trying to extort money from me.'

'No!' Clamping her lips together, Cara opened her handbag and took out a brown envelope, from which she pulled a square piece of paper. She handed it to him. 'There,' she said tightly. 'There's your proof. I'm not trying to extort anything from you. I'm sixteen weeks pregnant. You *are* going to be a father.'

For a moment Pepe feared he would be sick. His stomach was certainly churning enough for it to happen. And his skin…his skin had gone all cold and clammy; his heart rate tripled.

And no wonder.

If this were a forgery, Cara had done an excellent job.

The square piece of paper clearly showed a kidney bean. Or was it that alien thing he had watched as a child? E.T.? Either way, this was clearly an early-stage foetus. He studied it carefully. There was the name of the Dublin hospital on it, her name, Cara Mary Delaney, her date of birth and the due date of the foetus. He did the maths. Yes. This put her at sixteen weeks pregnant.

It had been sixteen weeks since he'd been to Dublin…

'You don't look very pregnant.' She looked thinner than he had ever seen her. She'd never been fat as such, more cuddly. While she hadn't transformed into a rake, she'd lost some of her, for want of a better word, *squishiness*.

'I've been under a lot of stress.' She gave him a tight smile. 'Unexpected pregnancy can do that to a woman. But the baby's perfectly healthy and I'm sure I'll start showing soon.'

He looked again at the scan picture. Cara was a smart woman but he doubted even she could forge something of this standard. The resolution on this picture was more clearly defined than the one he had held and gazed at for hours on end over a decade ago, but everything else was the same.

Cara was pregnant.

He looked back at her, realising for the first time that she was shaking. It took all his control to keep his own body still.

Dragging air into his lungs, he considered the situation as dispassionately as he could, which was hard. Very hard. His brain felt as if someone had thrown antifreeze into it. 'Congratulations. You're going to be a mother. Now tell me, what makes you so certain I'm the father?'

She opened her mouth, then closed it, then opened it again. 'What kind of stupid question is that? Of course you're the father. You're the only man I've been stupid enough to have sex with.'

'And I'm supposed to take your word on that, am I?'

'You know damn well I was a virgin.'

'I am not disputing that you were a virgin. What I am questioning is my paternity. I have no way of knowing what you got up to after I left. How do I know that after discovering all you'd been missing, you didn't go trawling for sex—?'

Her hand flew out from nowhere. *Crack.* Right across his cheek, the force enough to jerk his face to the side.

'Don't you dare pull me down to your own pathetically low standards,' she hissed, her face contorted with anger.

His cheek stung, smarted right where her hand and fingers had made contact. She might be small but she packed a proper punch. He could feel her imprint burrowing under his skin. He raised a hand to it. Her finger marks lay on the long scar that had been inflicted on him when he'd been eighteen. There were still times when he could feel the blade of the knife burn into his skin.

'I will let you do that this one time,' he said, speaking carefully, controlling his tone. 'But if you ever raise a hand to me again you will never see me or my money again.'

Her breaths were shallow. 'You deserved it.'

'Why? Because I pointed out that you are expecting me to take you at your word? Trust me, I take *no one* at their word, especially a woman purporting to be carrying my child.'

'I *am* carrying your child.'

'No—you are carrying *a* child. Until the child is born and we can get a paternity test done, I do not want to hear any reference to it being mine.' After what Luisa had done to him, he would never take anything to do with paternity at face value again. Never.

Only fools rushed in twice.

Cara itched to slap the arrogance off his face again, so much so that she dug her nails into the palms of her hands to find some relief.

If she could, she would leave. But she couldn't. She hadn't been exaggerating about the state of her bank balance. Paying for the return flight to Sicily had left her with the grand total of forty-eight euros to last her until payday, which was still a fortnight away. It was one thing living on baked beans on toast when she had only herself to support, but it was quite another when she would soon have a tiny mouth to feed and clothe. And she needed to find a new home, one that allowed children.

When she'd first discovered she was pregnant, her fear had been primitive, a cold, terrifying realisation that within her grew a life, a baby.

Jeez. A baby. She couldn't remember ever even *holding* a baby.

That real terror had morphed when the freeze in her brain had abated and the reality of everything that having a child meant had hit her.

A child would depend on her for *everything*. Love. Stability. Nourishment. Of the three, came the sharp knowledge that she would only be able to provide the first.

At that precise moment, even more so than when

she'd taken the pregnancy test, her life had changed irrevocably.

What stability did she have living in a shared rented home that banned children? What nourishment could she provide when she barely earned enough to feed herself? Nappies alone cost a fortune on her salary. Maybe if this had all happened a few years down the line, when she'd scaled the career ladder a little higher and was earning more, things would have been more manageable. But they weren't. At that moment she had nothing.

'So that's it, is it?' she demanded, fighting with everything she had to keep her tone moderate, to fight the hysteria threatening to take control. 'What do you want me to do? Give you a ring in five months and tell you if it's a boy or a girl?'

He speared her with a look. 'Not at all, *cucciola mia.*'

Cucciola mia: the endearment that had appropriated itself as his pet name for her during their weekend together. Curiosity had driven her to translate it on the same phone he had stolen from her. She had been more than a little chagrined to learn it meant something along the lines of *my puppy.* The way he said it though…in Pepe's thick Sicilian tongue it sounded tantalisingly sexy.

Momentarily distracted at the throwaway endearment, it took a second before she realised he was studying the scan picture.

'I notice this was taken a month ago,' he said, referring to the date of the scan shown clearly on the corner.

'And?'

'And it's taken you all this time to tell me. Why is that?'

How she hated his mocking scepticism, as if he were looking for a conspiracy in every little thing.

'I didn't tell you any sooner because I don't trust you

an inch—I wanted to be sure I was too far gone for you to force an abortion on me.'

Pepe's firm, sensuous lips tightened and his eyes narrowed, lines appearing on his forehead. After too long a pause, he said, 'Why would you think that?'

She almost laughed aloud. 'You have loved and left so many women it's become a second career for you. What do you, Playboy of the Year, want with a child?'

His features darkened for the split of a second before his usual laconic grin replaced it. 'It might make a nice accessory for pulling more women.'

She would have believed he was serious if the granite in his eyes hadn't said otherwise. She gave an involuntary shiver.

'Do you think I was oblivious to the disparaging comments you made about babies?' she demanded. 'Do you think I didn't notice you rolling your eyes whenever Grace and Luca discussed having kids?'

'So that's proof I would demand an abortion, is it?'

'You made it perfectly clear that kids are not and never will be on your agenda.'

A tiny pulse pounded on his jawline. After a loaded pause, he said, 'Say a paternity test proves it is mine. What do you expect from me? Marriage?'

'No!' She practically shouted her denial. 'No. I do not want to marry you. I don't want to marry anyone.'

'That's a relief,' he drawled, heading back to his bar to pour himself another glass of his concoction. 'But in case you're only saying what you think I want to hear, know marriage will never be on the cards, whatever the outcome of the paternity test.'

Had he drugged her? For a moment she actually considered the possibility. She could hardly credit she had allowed him to seduce her so thoroughly.

She looked back on their weekend together. It was as if she had been under some kind of drug that allowed the hormones so prevalent in the rest of society to actually work in her. For the first time in her life she had experienced desire. It had been the headiest feeling imaginable.

She had *wanted* to believe he was serious about her.

She had *wanted* to believe they could have a future together.

An image of her parents flashed in her head. Was this what it had been like for them? Especially her father, who'd hooked up with a new woman on a seemingly weekly basis. With all the affairs he'd had and all her parents' fights and making up, had they constantly experienced that same headiness? Was that what had caused their monstrous selfishness?

She blinked the image away. She would *not* be like her mother and think only of her own needs. Her unborn child's needs would always take priority, whatever the personal sacrifice.

'I'm glad you think that way because, believe me, I have no intention of marrying you.' She'd rather marry an orang-utan.

'Good. People who marry for the sake of the baby are fools. And I am not a fool.'

She glared at him. 'I can think of many a choice word to describe you but *fool* isn't one of them.'

'Then we are on the same page,' he mocked.

'About marriage, then yes, but, Pepe, I need help. Financially, I am in no position to support a child.'

'So you thought you would come to me.' He tipped his drink down his neck in one swallow.

'If you think for a second I like the idea of having to beg you for money then you have a very twisted view of me. I've come to you for help because this is your responsibility…'

'You're going to pin the blame for this on me?'

'I'm not the one who got carried away,' she countered pointedly. Warmth spread inside her as she recalled lying in his arms after they'd made love for the first time. Pepe's usual languidness had gone. A more serious, reflective side of his nature had come to the fore, a side she'd never seen before. As they'd talked and his face had come closer to hers, she'd found herself staring at his lips. And he'd been staring at hers. And even though they had made love barely ten minutes before, the heat he had created inside her and she in him had flared back to life, and he'd rolled on top of her and kissed her—devoured her—and before either of them had been fully aware of it, he'd been inside her. If she'd thought having him inside her the first time had been something special…this had been indescribable. For what had felt an age, they had simply lain there, gazing into each other's eyes, before he had reluctantly withdrawn to get a condom.

That one stolen moment had been enough to create a life.

'I hardly think that was enough to make a baby,' he said, his tone becoming grim.

'Well, it was. You used me, Pepe. Whether you like it or not, you are responsible.'

It sickened him to know she could be right.

You are responsible.

Despite the playboy image he had cultivated—an image he exulted in—Pepe couldn't remember the last time he'd been so reckless.

Actually, he could remember. The last time he'd made love to a woman without using a condom he'd been eighteen. Young and believing himself to be in love. A lethal combination.

It hadn't been a conscious decision to enter Cara unsheathed. At the time it had felt like the most natural thing in the world. Not that he'd been thinking properly. He'd been reeling from the discovery that she was—had been—a virgin. He'd also been struggling to understand everything going on inside *him*.

Usually he would make love to a woman and get back into bed, have a fun conversation, drink a glass of wine or whatever, maybe make love again and then leave without a second thought or a backward glance. He'd never got back into bed with a churning stomach and a tight chest before. He could only assume it was guilt he'd been feeling. Guilt at her virginity or guilt at what he'd had to do, he did not know.

Guilt or not, he'd *never* got back into bed with a woman and needed to make love to her all over again. Not straight away. For all his reputation, Pepe thought with his brain, not the appendage between his legs. At least he had until that night with Cara.

But he hadn't been inside her for long enough to make a baby. It had been a minute at the most. But *caro Dio*, he'd had to force himself to withdraw and get that condom. Being inside her without a barrier…

His groin twitched as more sweet memories filled him.

For that one minute inside her, he'd felt a sense of sheer wonderment and belonging…

'I need a coffee,' he muttered. He wanted another drink—a proper drink—but knew it was time to stop. A plan was formulating and he needed to think clearly. 'Can I get you anything?'

Cara shook her head. She was leaning against the wall, arms folded, chin jutted up, looking ready for a fight.

By the time he'd made a quick call to the kitchen, his plan was fully developed. Cara could like it or lump it. If she wanted a fight, she had to learn it was one she would never win.

CHAPTER THREE

'SIT DOWN.'

It was a definite command.

Cara tightened her arms around her chest and pressed harder into the wall, which was the only thing keeping her upright—her legs were shot. Not that she could trust the wall. For all she knew, it might be hiding a secret bathroom. The only saving grace was that her dress was long enough to hide her knocking knees.

But even if her legs could be trusted to behave, there was no way she would obey. She didn't care how rich and powerful Pepe was in his world, she would not grant him power over her, no matter how petty. Not without a fight.

'Suit yourself.' He lowered himself onto one of the oversized chocolate leather sofas, stretched out his long legs, kicked off his shoes and flashed a grin.

Her knees shook even harder.

How she hated that bloody grin. It was so…fake. And it did something ridiculous to the beat of her heart, which was hammering so hard she wouldn't be in the least surprised if it burst through her chest.

'I can see you are in a difficult predicament,' he said, hooking an arm behind his head and mussing his hair.

She inhaled slowly, getting as much oxygen into her lungs as she could. 'That's one way to describe it.'

'I have a solution that will suit us both.'

Her eyes narrowed.

'It involves sacrifice on both our parts.' He shot her a warning glance before displaying his white teeth. 'But I can assure you that if I am the father of your child as you say, the sacrifice will be worth it.'

What the heck did Pepe Mastrangelo know about sacrifice? His whole life revolved around nothing but his pleasure.

She nodded tightly. 'Go on.'

'You will live with me until the child is born. Then we shall have a paternity test. If it proves positive, as you say it will, then I will buy you a home of your choice. And, of course, support you both financially.'

'You want me to live with you until the baby's born?' she asked, certain she had misheard him.

'*Sì.*'

'Why?' She couldn't think of a single reason. 'All I need from you at the moment is enough money to rent a decent flat in a nice area, and buy some essentials for the baby. Obviously you'll have to pay child support when the baby's born.'

'Only if the baby proves to be mine. If it isn't, I won't have to pay you a single euro.'

Cara spoke through gritted teeth. 'The baby is yours. But seeing as you're proving to be such a disbeliever, I'm happy to sign a contract stating I have to repay any monies in the event the paternity test proves the Invisible Man is the father.'

He gave a quick shake of his head and turned his mouth down in a regretful fashion. 'If only it were that simple. The problem, for me, is that there exists the possibility that the child you carry inside you *is* mine. I cannot take the risk of anything happening to it.'

'I told you I delayed telling you about the baby so you couldn't force me into an abortion. I'm four weeks too late for one in Sicily and it's completely illegal in Ireland.' She blinked rapidly, fighting with everything she had not to burst into angry tears. She would not give him the satisfaction of seeing her cry. She would not give him the power her mother had given her father.

She might have no choice but to throw her pride at his feet but she had to retain some kind of dignity.

'I never said anything about an abortion,' he pointed out. 'What does concern me is your health. You're clearly not taking care of yourself if your weight loss is anything to go by, and by your own admittance you don't have enough money to support a child. Or so you say. For all I know, you could be on the make, using this pregnancy as a means to help yourself to my bank account.'

It was Cara's turn to swear under her breath. 'Do you have any idea how offensive you are?'

He shrugged, utterly nonchalant. He clearly couldn't care less. 'Finances aside, if that *is* my child growing inside you then I want to make damned sure you're taking care of it properly.'

'I am taking care of myself as best I can under the circumstances, but, I can promise you, our child's welfare means more to me than anything.' Her unborn child meant *everything* to her. Everything. Its well-being was the only reason she was here.

Did Pepe think she *wanted* to throw herself at his financial mercy?

He shook his head in a chiding fashion and stretched his arms out. 'My conditions are non-negotiable. If you want me to support you during the rest of the pregnancy then I will. But I will not give you cash. All you have to do is move in with me, travel where I travel, and I will feed and clothe you, and buy anything else you may need. If paternity is established after the birth, then I will buy you a house in your name, anywhere you choose, and give you an allowance so large you will be set up for life.'

He made it sound so reasonable. He made it sound as if it were such a no-brainer she wouldn't even need to think about it.

And there she'd been, worrying for months against telling him because she'd convinced herself he would demand an abortion.

'You see, *cucciola mia*, I am not the baby-aborting monster you thought I would be,' he said chidingly, reading her mind.

A sharp rap on the main door to the wing provided a moment's relief for her poor, addled brain.

At Pepe's invitation, a maid entered the room carrying a tray with a pot of coffee, a pot of tea covered by a tea cosy and two cups.

'It's decaf,' he explained when it had been placed on the glass table and the maid left.

'I told you I didn't want anything.'

'You need to keep your fluid levels up.'

'Oh, so you're a doctor now? Or have you an army of illegitimates scattered around the world that's made you a pregnancy expert?'

He quelled her with a glance.

She refused to bow to its latent warning. 'Sorry. Am I supposed to believe this is the first time you've had a paternity suit thrown at you?'

His eyes were unreadable. 'I always use protection.'

'And you're expecting me to take you at your word for that?'

His features darkened before his lips gave a slight twitch and he bowed his head. 'A fair comeback.'

He really was ridiculously handsome.

She castigated herself. As far as she was concerned, Pepe's looks and masculinity were void. She would *not* let her hormones create any more havoc.

It was unfair that she was the one standing yet it still felt as if he, all chilled and relaxed on the sofa, had all the advantage.

A whorl of black hair poked through the top of his shirt. She remembered how that same hair covered his chest, thickening across his tightly defined pecs and down the middle towards his navel, and further down... She'd always assumed chest hair would be bristly, had been thrilled to find it as soft as silk. It was the only thing soft about him; everything else was hard...

She swallowed and pressed the tops of her thighs together to try to quash the heat bubbling within her.

Her throat had gone dry.

Damn him, she needed a drink.

Lips clamped together, she moved away from the wall and poured herself a cup of the steaming tea before carrying it to the sofa opposite him. She only intended to perch there but it was so soft and squidgy it almost swallowed her whole. She sank straight into it, her legs shooting out, the motion causing her to spill the tea all over her lap.

Cara cried out, kicking her legs as if the movement would stop the hot fluid seeping through her dress.

Immediately Pepe jumped to his feet and hurried over, snatching the cup from her hand. 'Are you okay?'

In too much pain to do anything more than whimper, Cara grabbed the hem of her dress and bunched it up to her thighs, flapping it to cool her heated skin. Making sure to keep the dress up and away from the scald, she yanked the tops of her black hold-ups down.

'Are you okay?' he repeated. For some silly reason,

the genuine concern she heard in his voice bothered her far more than the scald.

The milky white of her left thigh had turned a deep pink, as had a couple of patches on her right thigh. She took a deep breath. 'It hurts.'

'I'll bet. Can you walk?'

'Why?'

'Because we should run cold water over it.'

Her thighs—especially her left one—were stinging something rotten, so much so she didn't even think of arguing with him.

'Come, we'll run the shower on it.'

Wincing, she let him help her to her feet.

Her legs shook frantically enough that she almost fell back onto the sofa, only Pepe's grip on her hand keeping her upright.

He frowned and shook his head, then, before she knew what he was doing, lifted her into his arms, taking great care not to touch her thighs.

'This is unnecessary,' she complained. She might be in pain but she didn't need *this*. Besides, she was vain enough to know she must look ridiculous with her dress bunched around the tops of her thighs, her modesty barely preserved. Her stupid black hold-ups had fallen down to her knees like the socks of a scatty schoolgirl.

'Probably,' he agreed, heading through the living area and into a narrow corridor, carrying her as if she weighed little more than a child. 'But it's quicker and safer than you trying to walk.'

The position he held her in meant her face was right in the crook of his strong, bronzed neck. A compulsion to press her face into it almost overcame her. Almost. Luckily she still retained some control. But she'd forgotten how delicious he smelt, like sun-ripened fruit. Her position meant her senses were filled with it and she had to use even more restraint not to lick him.

Pepe's bathroom was twice the size of her bedroom and resembled a miniature black, white and gold palace. She had no time to appreciate its splendour.

'You're going to have to take your dress off,' he said as he carried her down some marble steps and carefully sat her on the edge of the sunken bath.

'I jolly well am not.'

'It will get wet.'

'It's already wet.'

'Suit yourself.' He knelt before her and placed a hand on her knee.

She tried not to yelp. 'What are you doing?'

'Taking your stockings off.' He tugged the first one down to the ankle. While she hated herself for her vanity, Cara could not help feel relief that she'd remembered to wax her legs a few days ago.

'They're hold-ups,' she corrected, breathing deeply. The trail of his fingers on her skin burned almost as much as the scald.

'They're sexy.'

'That's inappropriate.'

His lips twitched. 'Sorry.'

'Liar.'

Hold-ups removed and thrown onto the floor, Pepe helped manoeuvre her into the empty bath before reaching for the shower head that rested on the gold taps.

He held it over his hand then turned it on. Water gushed out, spraying over them both.

Adjusting the pressure, he smiled with a hint of smugness. 'Still happy to keep your dress on?'

'Yes.' She would rather suffer third-degree burns than strip off to her underwear in front of him.

'I've seen you naked before,' he reminded her wickedly, turning the shower onto her thighs.

'Not under bright light, you haven't.'

The cold water felt like the greatest relief in the world. Cara closed her eyes, rested her head back and savoured the feeling, uncaring that the cold water spraying off her thighs was pooling in the base of the bath, sloshing all around her bottom. It was worth it. Slowly, wonderfully, her tender skin numbed.

It was only when she opened her eyes a few minutes later that she realised her dress had risen higher and that her black knickers were fully exposed.

One look at the gleam in Pepe's eyes and she knew he'd noticed.

'I think that's enough now,' she said, leaning up and yanking her sodden dress down to cover herself.

Pepe screwed his eyes shut to rid himself of the image. It didn't work.

The image of Cara's soaking knickers and the memories of what they hid burned brightly, almost as brightly as her flushing cheeks.

His trousers felt so tight and uncomfortable it was hard to breathe.

He gritted his teeth and willed his erection to abate.

He turned the tap off, replaced the shower head and crouched back next to her, making sure to look at her face and only her face. 'Your thighs should be okay—it doesn't look as if they're going to blister—but to play safe I've got some salve in the medicine cabinet you can put on them. I'll get it for you and then you can get changed— where's your change of clothes?'

'I didn't bring any.'

'Why not?' Whenever Cara came to Sicily she always came for at least a week.

'I only came for the day.'

'Really?' He'd arrived from Paris with barely twenty minutes to spare before the christening started, avoiding the inevitable for as long as humanly possible. He hadn't imagined Cara had done the same.

'I didn't want to risk spilling the beans to Grace before I'd had a chance to speak to you.'

'That was good of you,' he acknowledged.

'Not really.' Her face tightened. 'I was worried she'd be unable to keep it from Luca and that Luca in turn would tell you.'

Upon reflection, Pepe was certain that if his sister-in-law had known she would have tracked him down at the earliest opportunity and given him hell. 'I'll ask Grace if she has any clothes you can borrow...'

'You jolly well won't.' Cara glared at him.

'You're right. Bad idea.' If he sought Grace out he'd have to explain why her best friend was sitting with scalded thighs in his bath, and then everything about the baby would become common knowledge... 'Have you told *anyone* about the baby?'

'Only my mother, but she doesn't count.'

'Good,' he said, ignoring the tightening of her lips as she mentioned her mother. He had enough to think about as it was.

'Why's that, then? Worried all those doting Mastrangelo aunts and uncles will try and marry us off?'

'They can try all they like,' he answered with a shrug. Given a chance, they'd have him and Cara up the aisle quicker than it had taken to impregnate her.

That was if he *had* impregnated her.

He didn't care that she'd been a virgin, he didn't care that the dates tallied—until he saw cast-iron proof of his paternity he would not allow himself to believe anything. 'I bow to no one.'

'Well, neither do I. Your suggestion that I move in with you is ridiculous. How the heck would I be able to get to and from work if I have to travel all over the place with you? You work all over Europe.'

'And South America,' he pointed out. 'You'll have to give up your job.'

He noticed her shiver and remembered she'd just had a cold shower pressed against her for the best part of ten minutes.

'Let's get you out of the bath. We can finish this argument when you're dry and warm.'

'I'm not giving up my job and I'm not moving in with you.'

'I said we can argue the toss when you're dry.'

He could see how much she hated having to use him for support. Not looking at him, she allowed him to help her to her feet. He held her arms and kept her steady while she climbed out of the bath.

She looked like a drowned rat. Even her face was soaked.

Too late, he realised it was tears rolling down her cheeks.

'You're crying?'

'I'm crying because I'm angry,' she sobbed. 'You've ruined my life and now you want to ruin my future too. I *hate* you.'

He took a large, warm towel off the rack and wrapped it around her shaking frame before taking a deliberate step back. 'If you're telling me the truth then your future is made. I'll give you and the baby more money than you could ever hope to spend.'

'I don't want to be a kept woman. I just want what *our* child is entitled to.'

'You won't have to be a kept woman. The option will be there for you, that's all. If your child is mine, you'll have enough money to do whatever you want. You can hire a nanny—hell, you'll be able to hire an army of them—and return to work.'

Her teeth clattered together. 'But I won't have a job to go back to.'

'There are other jobs.'

'Not like this one. Do you have any idea how hard it is getting a foot on the ladder in the art world without *any* contacts?'

'There are other jobs,' he repeated. Deep inside his chest, a part of him had twisted into a tight ball, but he ignored it. He had to. He could not allow any softening towards her, no matter how vulnerable she looked at that particular moment.

Luisa had shown her vulnerable side numerous times. It had all been a big fat lie and he had been the sucker who had fallen for it. Every day he looked in the mirror and saw the evidence of her lies reflecting back at him. He could have had surgery to remove his scar. Instead he had chosen to keep it as a reminder not to trust and, more especially, not to love.

'You don't have to move in with me,' he said. He drew the towel together so it covered her more thoroughly and forced himself to stare into her damp eyes. He refused to break the hold, no matter the misery reflecting back at him. 'You can catch your flight back to Ireland and carry on eking out an existence. Or you can stay. If you stay, I will support you and we can take the paternity test as soon as the child is born. But if you leave now, you will not receive a single euro from me until my paternity—or lack of it—has been proven. And if you choose to leave, you'll have to go through the courts to get a DNA sample from me. That's if you can find me. As you know, I have homes in four different countries. I can make it extremely difficult for you to get that sample.'

He knew how unreasonable he must sound but he didn't care.

He could not afford to allow himself to care.

If Cara really was carrying his child then he must make every effort to protect its innocent form, and the only way he could do that was by forcing her into a corner from which the only means of escape was his way. Short of tying her up and locking her in a windowless room, this was his best chance of keeping her by his side until the birth.

He would not risk losing another child.

CHAPTER FOUR

CARA DIDN'T THINK she'd ever felt as self-conscious as she did at that moment, and she'd had plenty of experience of feeling awkward and insecure.

Pepe's blue shirt came to her knees and she'd rolled his trousers over so many times to get them to fit length-ways that it looked as if she had two wedges around her ankles. All she needed was a pair of extra-long shoes and she'd make the perfect clown.

Following him up the metal steps and into his jet, she forced herself to return the smiles and friendly greetings given by the glamorous cabin crew. Not one of them batted an eyelid at her presence. Most likely because strange women accompanying Pepe on his travels was par for the course, she thought snidely.

The jet was a proper flying bachelor pad, all leather and dark hardwood panelling. A steward showed her to a seat for take-off. She was nonplussed when Pepe took the seat next to her.

'You have ten seats to choose from,' she said, glaring at him.

'So do you,' he pointed out in return, strapping himself in and stretching his long legs out. He looked at the cheap mobile phone in her hand. 'Who are you contacting?'

'Grace.'

'What are you going to say to her?'

'That her brother-in-law is a feckless scumbag with the morals of an amoeba.'

He cocked an eyebrow.

She sighed. 'I wanted to write that but until we've got the finances sorted I'm not prepared to risk her ripping your head off.'

'That's decent of you,' he said drily.

She speared him with another poisonous glare then hit send. 'I've apologised for leaving the christening without saying goodbye. I've also told her I cadged a lift off you to the airport. Someone was bound to have seen us leave together.'

'Are you worried people will talk?' Pepe didn't sound worried. If anything, he sounded bored.

'Nope.' Let them think what they liked. The truth would come out. It always did. And when the truth came out, people would see that, beneath the charming, affable exterior, Pepe Mastrangelo was a horrid specimen of a man. 'I don't want Grace worrying, that's all.'

It crossed her mind, not for the first time, that she should have gone to Grace for help. In normal circumstances Cara *would* have gone to Grace, but when she'd found out she was pregnant, Grace had been in hiding, going through her own troubles. So, she'd told her mother, but her mam was going through yet another of her new husband's infidelities and so hadn't been particularly interested other than on a superficial level. Not that Cara had expected anything else from the woman who had given birth to her.

But then Luca had tracked Grace down and now the pair of them were madly in love and in a bubble of happiness. It would have been the perfect opportunity to ask for help.

Grace would have given her money and anything else she needed, no questions asked. But Cara wouldn't have been able to keep it contained and the whole sordid story would have come out, and then God knew what would have happened.

In any case, her child was not her friend's responsibility. It was Pepe's.

And this mess was not of Grace's making. This was all on her, Cara. And the feckless playboy, of course.

It was too late to go to Grace for help now. Pepe would undoubtedly turn to Luca, who in turn would put pressure on his wife not to give Cara any financial help. Grace was so loved up at the moment she would probably comply. At the very least it would cause friction between them.

Thanks to Pepe, she couldn't turn to the one person she needed.

The steward, who was still making checks and pretending not to listen to their conversation, finally disappeared into a separate cabin.

'How are your thighs?' Pepe asked. If he was fazed about anything, he had yet to show it.

'Not too bad.' The salve he had given her had been bliss to apply. He'd also given her a wrap that resembled cling film to place on it too. He'd been so... *Concerned* was the wrong word but it was the closest for the way he'd treated her wounds. Not that he'd treated *her* with the same consideration.

How could someone be so gentle and at the same time be so horribly uncaring? That was part of what had tipped her over the edge and set the waterworks off.

'You should take the trousers off. I'm sure it can't help with the material rubbing against it.'

'They're fine.' No way was she taking any of her clothes off within a ten-mile radius of him ever again.

The plane began to taxi down the runway. Cara turned to look out of the window, a lump forming in her throat.

This was utter madness.

'Pepe, please, let me return to Dublin, just for a couple of days to get things in order.' It was an argument they'd had three times in the past hour.

'Impossible. I have a full day of business tomorrow and a business dinner in the evening.'

'Yes, but I don't. I'm supposed to be at work!'

'You will attend my meeting with me.'

She took a deep breath. Her blood pressure really didn't need any more aggravation.

'As I have made you more than aware, the week ahead is filled with appointments.'

'I have to wait until the weekend to go back home?' she said, horror-struck.

'I'm afraid a trip back to Dublin is not on the schedule for the foreseeable future.'

'You're kidding me?'

'You can make any necessary arrangements via other means.'

'So I have to hand in my notice by text or email?'

He shrugged. 'It's entirely up to you how you want to handle it.'

'I'd like to handle it by *not* giving up my job,' she stated angrily. 'But seeing as I *do* have to quit, I'd prefer to tell my boss in person.'

He almost looked sympathetic. 'I appreciate this is an inconvenience but if, as you say, the baby is mine, you will be well recompensed for any aggravation.'

'And my housemates? Will they be *recompensed* too?'

His brow furrowed.

'I'm leaving them in the lurch. If you won't let me go

to Dublin, I can't clear my room out and they can't find another housemate to take my place.'

'That is not a problem. I can send someone over to clear your room for you.'

'You will not!' There was no way she wanted some stranger rifling through her knicker drawer. Closing her eyes, she slowly expelled a lungful of air. They had been so busy arguing she'd barely noticed the jet increase in speed. Suddenly her stomach lurched and she was leaning back.

The jet became airborne.

She took another deep breath. 'If I contact my housemates and ask them to get all my stuff together, can you send someone to collect it?'

'Of course.'

'Can they get it to me for tomorrow morning?'

'Why so soon?'

'Because I have nothing on me apart from my handbag and a stick of mascara. I need my stuff.'

'I've already made arrangements for new clothing to be delivered to the house first thing for you.'

Of course he had. For such a languid person Pepe was proving surprisingly efficient.

'I want *my* stuff.'

'And you will have it. Soon.'

'How soon?'

'Soon. And I will ensure your housemates get adequate compensation from your missed rent.'

'Good.' She would not say thank you.

Her stomach rolled again and she breathed in deeply through her nose.

'Are you okay?'

She did *not* want to hear any concern from him. 'I'm pregnant. My child's father is refusing to acknowledge paternity without a blood test yet still thinks it's accept-able to make me give up my job—a job I love—and leave my housemates in the doodle to follow him around the world like some sort of concubine. Plus I have no cloth-ing or toiletries on me. So, yes. Everything is dandy.'

His gorgeous blue eyes darkened further and crinkled with amusement. 'My concubine, eh? Do you know what a concubine is?'

She felt her cheeks go scarlet. 'It was a statement of my unhappiness not a statement of fact.'

'A concubine is, in essence, a man's mistress.'

'I'm well aware of that.'

'A man pays for all his concubine's bills, buys prop-erty for her—'

'Basically a concubine is there for a man's pleasure when he's bored of his wife's company,' she interrupted. 'But seeing as you have no wife, I can't be your concu-bine.'

A gleam came into his eyes. 'Ah, so as I have no wife, does that mean you are going to be the main source of my pleasure?'

'I'd rather eat worms.'

'I'm sure I can think of something better for you to e—'

'Don't go there. I feel sick enough as it is.'

He laughed. 'That's not how I remember things.'

'Watch it or I will vomit.' But not through the memo-ries of their night together.

Those memories moved her in wholly different ways.

Nope, the queasiness in her belly was solely due to motion sickness. She scrunched her eyes closed and took a long deep breath.

Pepe twisted onto his side to stare at her. Cara really

was incredibly sexy, even with her face contorted into a grimace.

But he would not go there again. Flirting with her was just asking for trouble. They had enough problems to get through.

She opened one eye. 'What?'

'Sorry?'

'You're staring at me.'

'Can't a man stare at a gorgeous woman?' Okay, so flirting was asking for trouble, but Cara really did look beautiful when she was angry, as clichéd as he knew that was.

'I'm pregnant,' she spat.

'You're also incredibly sexy. A man would have to be dead from the waist down not to desire you. But have no fear—I'm not going to make any unwanted passes at you.' All the same, he felt a tightening in his groin and almost groaned aloud at the incongruity of it all.

Cara despised him. No matter how much he might still desire her and, he suspected, she still desired him, he preferred his women to not loathe the very sound of his name.

And sex between them…nothing good could come of it. It had got him into enough trouble as it was, just as he'd always suspected sex with Cara would—why else had he kept such a distance from her sexually before?

In the world in which he mixed, sex was freely given with no real commitment assumed by anyone. Pepe liked it that way. It saved messy entanglements and even messier goodbyes. Everyone knew where they stood, no one got hurt, and everyone was happy.

'Well, that's good to know,' Cara said sarcastically. 'Let me guess—now that you don't need anything from me, there's no need to pretend any more.'

'What do you mean?'

'You never desired me before you needed to get hold of my phone.'

'On the contrary, *cucciola mia*, I've always found you incredibly attractive.'

'I'm pretty sure you find any woman with a pulse attractive. I'm saying you never desired *me* in particular.'

'I did, but I'm terrified of my sister-in-law. She would have tied me naked to a tree if I'd tried anything on with you.'

Despite herself, Cara snickered. Pepe was the cause of all her stress yet somehow he was able to soothe much of it away. The git. 'I would have loved to have seen that.'

'Don't worry—if the baby does turn out to be mine then I'm sure you'll get your chance when Grace finds out.'

'There's no *if* about it. This baby is yours.'

'Time will tell.' A black eyebrow shot up, a quizzical groove appearing in his forehead. 'If it *is* my child, will I also have to worry about your angry father beating at my door?'

'Seeing as he's not around, that's the last thing you'll have to worry about.'

He straightened in his seat, consternation replacing his amusement. 'Oh. I'm sorry. I didn't realise you'd lost your father too.'

It occurred to her that this was the closest Pepe had come to showing genuine contrition all day.

'My father isn't dead,' she quickly clarified, recalling being told his own father had died over a decade ago.

He looked confused. 'Then surely he will want to rip my head off and play football with it?'

She couldn't help the wry smile that formed on her lips, although she experienced the usual sickening churn in her belly she felt whenever she thought of her father. 'I'm sure there's a lot of fathers out there who would love nothing more than to cause you actual bodily harm, but I can assure you my dad's not one of them.'

'Why not? A father's job is to look out for his child.'

'My dad never bothered to read the job description.' Only years of faux nonchalance on the subject kept the bitterness from her voice, yet the churning increased, a situation not helped by the roils in her belly from the motion of the jet. Talking about her father always made her feel so *raw*. 'Believe me, if he were to meet you, the closest he would come to touching you is putting a hand on your shoulder and insisting on buying you a beer.'

For all of Pepe's antics and reputation, he knew damn well that if he had a daughter and some man lied to her and impregnated her, then he would certainly want to rip that man's head off.

Not that he was admitting to having impregnated Cara. Not yet. Not until the DNA test proved it beyond any doubt. And until that DNA test proved it, he would not allow himself to think of that child as being anything but a foetus. After what Luisa had put him through, this was an essential act of self-preservation.

He thought back to a time over a decade before when he had been looking at a scan of a foetus, trying to discern a head and tiny limbs from what was little more than a kidney bean. The emotions provoked by looking at that scan were the strongest he had ever experienced. Totally overwhelming. He had felt fit to burst. He could only imagine the strength of his feelings if that little life had been allowed to develop and allowed to be born.

But that little life had *not* been allowed to develop and be born, a fact that resided inside his guts like a vat of poison...

All the same, he could not imagine having a child and being so disassociated from their feelings that he didn't care if they were used and hurt. He might only be the 'spare' of the family, but he had never doubted his parents' love for him.

It was their respect he'd always failed to achieve.

He could well imagine how his brother would react if anyone were to hurt Lily. That person would likely never walk again.

Cara must have seen the way his thoughts were going because her features contorted into a grimace. 'Do you know, now I think about it, you and my father are incredibly alike. He's a charmer, just like you. Maybe I should introduce you to him—you can exchange shagging tips.'

It took every muscle in his face to keep his smile fixed there. 'Why do I feel I have just been insulted?'

'Because you're not as stupid as you look?' Before he could react to this latest insult, she stood up. 'If it's all the same to you, I'm going to curl up on that sofa and get some sleep. I assume one of the stewards will wake me before we land?'

She *did* look tired. So tired he bit back any further retort and any further questions about her father. Like it or not, she was pregnant and, now that he'd admitted her into his life, her health was his responsibility. Her already pale face was drained of colour.

He experienced a twinge that could be interpreted as concern. 'Are you feeling all right? Physically, I mean,' he added before she could bombard him with another long list of all the wrongs he had done.

'I'm feeling a little icky. But don't worry—it's not bad enough that you have to worry for your upholstery.'

He watched as she made her way to the sofa, holding on to something fixed for stability with every step.

A tap on the door broke through Cara's slumber.

There was none of that 'where am I' malarkey often

experienced when awaking under a new roof. Before she even opened her eyes she knew exactly where she was.

Pepe's house. Or, to be more precise, in a guest room in Pepe's Parisian house.

She'd pretended to sleep for the rest of the flight back to Charles de Gaulle airport. It certainly beat talking to him.

She'd ignored him as they'd gone through Customs, blanked him on the drive back to his house and pretended to be deaf when they arrived at his home, a five-storey town house in an exclusive Parisian suburb. She'd also pretended to be mute. She'd had to clamp her lips so tightly together when she was shown to her room that she'd pretended they'd been superglued. It was either that or have him witness her wonder at its sheer beauty. For a house purported to have been bought to show-case Pepe's art collection—and it was every bit as huge and glamorous as she'd expected—it had a surprisingly homely charm to it.

But she wouldn't tell Pepe that. She didn't want him to think she liked anything about him, not even his beautiful home.

It was talking about her father that had done it.

Her father, the arch charmer, the man who could make a woman forgive him over and over, make a woman believe his faults were in fact *her* faults.

Pepe's charm had always felt different from her father's. He had none of her father's seediness. Or sleaze.

But one thing he did have was the ability to make her *want* to believe in him. She'd wanted to believe Pepe saw her as more than a one-night stand. On his jet she'd felt herself thawing towards him, his gorgeous, easy-going smile slowly melting the edge of her defences. More than that, though, had been the unexpected depths she'd seen in his eyes. For a few moments she could have sworn she'd seen pain in them, something dark, something that hinted there was more to him than what he wore on the surface.

She'd thought she'd seen more to him that weekend in Dublin when he had seduced her so thoroughly. And it had all been a lie. Just as everything that came out of her father's mouth was a lie.

Pepe was of the same mould. Something she would do well to remember.

She sat up and rubbed her eyes.

Another knock at the door.

'Mademoiselle Delaney?' came a muffled female voice.

'I'm awake,' she called back, slipping out of the bed. Much as she hated to admit it, that had to qualify as *the* most comfortable bed she had ever slept on.

The handle turned and a middle-aged woman carrying a tray of coffee and croissants walked in.

Cara remembered her from their arrival, was certain Pepe had introduced her as Monique, his housekeeper.

'Good morning,' said Monique, heading straight for a small round table in the corner of the room and placing the tray on it. 'Did you sleep well?'

'Yes, thank you,' she answered in a small voice, forcing a smile. She always felt so...*noodley* when with strangers, as if her tongue had loosened, then tied itself into knots.

'Your deliveries have arrived,' Monique told her, drawing back the heavy full-length curtains to reveal a small balcony.

Morning sunshine filled the room.

Cara cleared her throat. 'What deliveries?'

'From the boutiques. I will bring them to you now.

Monsieur Mastrangelo has requested that you be ready to leave in an hour.'

Her heart sinking, Cara remembered a trip to the Loire Valley was on the day's agenda.

Her spirits lifted a fraction when Monique, assisted by a young woman, brought the boxes of clothes in to her, and a hand-case of toiletries.

'If there is anything else you require, please let me know,' Monique said before leaving the room.

Putting her half-eaten croissant to one side, Cara began going through the boxes, her spirits sinking all over again as she fingered the beautiful fabrics and accessories.

Why couldn't Pepe have ensured the clothing he'd ordered for her was inappropriate and gross? Here was an entire wardrobe for her and there was not a single item she wouldn't have selected herself if money had not been an object. Simple, elegant, casual clothing with an innate vibrancy. Even the nightdresses he'd ordered were beautiful.

When she opened the hand-case she wanted to scream with both joy and despair. Enclosed was every lotion and potion a woman could want, and make-up selected especially for her colouring. Worst of all was that it was all brands she coveted. She would walk past their counters in department stores and gaze at the beautiful items, promising herself that she would buy them when she earned enough money.

Shouldn't she be pleased she had them roughly five years ahead of schedule? Maybe she should but she couldn't muster up the necessary sparkly feelings. She didn't want to feel any gratitude towards Pepe. Wasn't that how Stockholm syndrome started? Not that she'd been kidnapped, not in the traditional sense of the word.

In the 'really not been given any other option' sense of the word then she had been.

She gathered all the toiletries together and took them into the en suite. Before stepping into the shower, she examined her thighs. Pepe's ointment was a marvel. The only discernible sign of injury was a slight pink mark. No pain *at all*.

The shower itself invigorated her. The gel smelt so utterly gorgeous and the water pressure and heat were so marvellous that she washed herself twice.

Well, that certainly beat the pathetic excuse for a shower she had in her shared bathroom in Dublin.

Wrapping a large fluffy white towel securely around her, she wandered back into her bedroom. She needed to select something to wear, which in theory shouldn't be a problem, but when one was confronted with a dozen beautiful outfits it became one.

For the first time in her life she had a problem selecting what to wear.

Just as she'd decided on a pair of designer black jeans and a cherry-red cashmere jumper, there was another knock on her door.

'Come in,' she called, expecting to see Monique standing there.

Her welcoming smile turned into a scowl when she found Pepe there instead.

CHAPTER FIVE

'WHAT DO YOU WANT?'

'Good morning to you too, *cucciola mia*,' he replied with a flash of his straight white teeth. He was wearing a grey suit with a white shirt and a black cravat. Yes. A cravat. Pepe wore a cravat that should look ridiculous but instead…

He looked far too gorgeous for sensibility.

'We need to leave shortly.'

Cara shrugged. 'If you want me to come with you, then you'll have to wait. I'm not ready.'

'Monique told you to be ready in an hour. That was an hour ago.'

'I don't wear a watch and my phone's out of battery, so I have no way of knowing what the time is. I would charge my phone but the charger's in Dublin,' she added pointedly.

'Is no problem,' he said, brushing his way past her and perching on her bed. 'As you suggested, I will wait for you.'

'Not in here, you won't.'

'And you are going to stop me how?' he asked in a chiding fashion.

She speared him with the nastiest glare she could muster.

He laughed softly, which made her scowl all the more.

Still laughing, he rummaged through one of the boxes and held up a pair of skimpy black lace knickers. 'Are you going to wear these?'

She snatched them from him, knowing her cheeks had turned a deep red to match her hair. 'Get out and let me get changed.'

'I would but I have a feeling you will get ready quicker if I'm in here with you.'

Calling him every nasty word she knew under her breath but loud enough for him to hear, Cara gathered her selected outfit and swept off back into the en suite, letting the door shut with a bang.

For a moment she was reluctant to take the towel off. She had no fear he would barge in on her—where that certainty came from, she could not say—but it wouldn't surprise her in the least to learn he had X-ray vision.

The thought made her feel distinctly off-kilter, in a way that was completely inappropriate.

The thought of Pepe staring at her naked body while she was oblivious should *not* make her breasts feel heavy…

Swallowing away moisture that had suddenly filled her mouth, she pulled her knickers on, too late recalling them being the same pair Pepe had just fingered.

This was how he'd been able to seduce her so easily.

For some reason her testosterone-immune body re-acted to Pepe and became pathetic and weak-willed around him.

By the end of their weekend together she had been like a lust-filled nympho.

What was it about him?

And what was so wrong with her that she still reacted to him, even after everything he had done? Not forgetting that she was pregnant—shouldn't pregnancy act as a natural form of anti-aphrodisiac? If it didn't, it jolly well should.

Pathetic. That's what she was.

Dressed, she went back into the room. Pepe had moved to an armchair in the corner, his long legs stretched out, doing something on his phone.

His eyebrows rose when he saw her. 'Are you going to be much longer?'

'I'm good to go.'

'Your hair's still wet.'

'It's a bit damp, that's all.' She'd towel-dried it as well as she could.

'It's cold outside.'

'My hairdryer's in Dublin.'

Pepe was fast beginning to recognise the look Cara threw at him as her 'if you'd let me get my stuff as I've asked you repeatedly, I wouldn't have this problem, ergo, this problem is *your* fault' look.

'I will ensure a hairdryer is here for you when we return from the vineyard.'

'I'm hoping my hair will be dry by then.'

'Hmm.' He gazed at her musingly. 'I would say sarcasm doesn't suit you but it actually does.'

She scowled. 'Funnily enough, it's only when I'm around you that my sarcastic gene comes out.'

'I will have to work hard to eradicate it,' he said, getting to his feet and leaning over to swipe her nose. She did have the cutest nose. 'And I'll work hard to eradicate the evil looks you keep throwing at me.'

'The only way that's going to happen is if you find *your* reasonable gene and let me return to Dublin.'

'You're welcome to return to Dublin any time you

like,' he said, smiling to disguise his irritation. 'I have made it clear what the consequences will be if you do so.'

'Like I said, you need to find your reasonable gene. Find it and I might lose my sarcastic gene.'

'I have already found my reasonable gene. It is unfortunate it differs from your definition of *reasonable* but there you go—you can't please everyone.' He expanded his hands and mocked a bow. 'Now, my fiery little geisha, it is time for us to leave.'

'What did you call me?' The look she gave him was no mere scowl. If looks could turn a man to stone he would now be made of granite.

'So touchy.'

'Calling me a geisha is pretty much on a par with calling me a concubine.'

'Not at all—a concubine is a permanent fixture in a man's life, there to give pleasure. A geisha is a hostess and an artiste. It is rare for a geisha to have sex with a male client.'

She didn't look in the slightest bit mollified. If anything, her scowl deepened.

'I can see I have my work cut out with you,' he said with a theatrical sigh. 'Maybe it is a good thing you will be with me for five months—I fear it will take me that long to get a smile out of you.'

Cara sat upright as they drove into a heliport, or whatever the name was for a field with a great big white helicopter with red Mastrangelo livery on it, and an enormous hangar right behind it.

Her stomach turned over at the sight of it. 'Please tell me we are not travelling in that thing?'

'It's either an eight-hour round trip to the vineyard by car, or we can do it in a quarter of the time in this beauty.'

'I vote for the car.'

'Sorry, *cucciola mia*, but I vote for the chopper. An hour there, an hour back.'

'It's a split vote.'

'It's my time and money.'

'Do I *have* to come? Can't I just wait here?'

'Yes, you do have to come.' For the first time she detected an edge to his voice. 'I'm not arguing with you again. I assure you, the ride will be perfectly safe and comfortable.' To prove his non-arguing point, he opened his door and got out.

She stuck her tongue out at his retreating form, watching as he joined a trio of men standing by the helicopter, all wearing black overalls. She guessed they were the flight crew.

The interior of the helicopter settled her nerves a touch. It was much less tinny than she had thought a helicopter would be. If anything, it was rather plush. She climbed aboard and sat down on a reclining white leather seat. Pepe showed her where all the big-boy-with-too-much-money gadgets were located on the seat, including a foldaway laptop.

'Aren't you sitting with me?' she asked, perturbed when he went to climb back out.

He grinned. 'One of us has to fly the thing.'

Before she could react, he'd jumped out and slid the door closed. In less than a minute he had opened the door at the front and made himself at home with the controls.

'Very funny, Mastrangelo,' she said, speaking over the low partition dividing them. If she wanted she could lean over and prod him. Which she was seriously considering doing if he didn't stop buggering about…

'Where's the pilot?' she asked, desperation suddenly lacing her voice.

He didn't look back, simply continued doing whatever he was doing with the range of knobs and buttons and thingies before him. 'Ladies and gentlemen, this is your captain speaking,' he said, amusement lacing his deep voice. 'For your own safety, Air Mastrangelo asks that you keep your seat belt fastened at all times and refrain from smoking for the duration of the flight.'

'You are having a laugh.'

He put some headphones on then turned his head back to look at her. 'Put your belt on, Cara—I promise you are in safe hands.'

'What about the men you were talking to? Aren't they going to fly it?'

'They were the maintenance crew.'

It was only when he turned the engine on that she truly believed Pepe was going to pilot it.

'Please,' she shouted over the noise of the propellers—who would have known it would be so *loud*?—'tell me you're only joking.'

'Belt on.' He started speaking into the mouthpiece of the headphone, talking in fluent French, his whole demeanour altering, adopting a serious hue.

'You can really fly this thing?' she asked when he'd stopped speaking and was doing stuff on the dashboard—was it even called a dashboard?

'I really can.'

'You're really qualified?'

'I really am. Have you got your seat belt on?'

'Yes.'

'Then we are good to go.'

And just like that, they were airborne.

And just like that, Cara's stomach lurched. She actually felt her half-eaten croissant and decaf coffee move inside her.

Slowly, the helicopter rose. At least it seemed slow, their ascent high above the heliport gradual.

Nothing was rushed. Everything in the cockpit was calm. And, as she watched him concentrate, watched him fly the beast they were in, her fears and nerves began to subside.

She'd ridden on planes many times, was used to the smoothness and almost hypnotic hum of the engines. This was different on so many levels.

There were so many things she wanted to ask him, not least of which was how did playboy extraordinaire Pepe Mastrangelo have the discipline to get his pilot's licence? His intelligence was not in doubt, but this was a man with the attention span of a goldfish—at least with women. She might know next to nothing about flying a helicopter but she knew for certain there was a lot more involved than learning to drive a car.

Surely it was something he would be proud to tell people? Never mind all the double dates they'd shared with Luca and Grace; they'd spent practically a whole weekend together, discussed all the vineyards he owned with his brother, discussed all the travelling he did between those vineyards as his brother liked to base himself on the family estate in Sicily, and not once had he mentioned flying his own helicopter. He hadn't even hinted at it.

As she looked at him now, relaxed but alert, clearly in his element…it was as if he'd been born to fly.

She wanted to bombard him with questions but, despite the unexpected smoothness of the flight—a smoothness she knew without having to be told came from the skill of his piloting—the nausea in her stomach was spreading, reaching the stage where all her concentration had to be devoted purely to breathing and swallowing the saliva that had filled her mouth.

'Everything okay in the back?' he called out to her.

'All dandy. Thank you.' She inhaled deeply and closed her eyes.

'There are sick bags in the side pocket of your chair,' he said after a few moments of silence had passed.

All she could manage was a grunt.

It was Cara's *thank you* that alerted Pepe to something being wrong. He'd guessed on the jet to Paris from Sicily that she was suffering from motion sickness, had kept a close eye on her sleeping form in case she awoke and needed attention, but nothing had come of it.

He'd piloted enough people in the past decade to know when someone was suffering from it. Right then, he could hear in the deepness of her breathing that she was one of the unfortunate ones. He didn't imagine she would extend politeness towards him under any other circumstance.

'There's a neck pillow in the side pocket too,' he called out over his shoulder, pressing the button to turn the air conditioning on. 'If you put it on it'll help keep your head stable. Find a fixed point in the horizon to focus on. I promise I will make the ride as smooth as I can. The conditions out there are good.'

He received another grunt in return.

If there was one thing he had learned it was that those afflicted by motion sickness were never in the mood for idle chit-chat. All he could do to help on any practical level was concentrate on the job in hand and do his best to keep the craft in as straight a motion as he could. He regretted not taking the 'doors off' approach, but at the time had thought it would probably terrify her if she was alone in the back.

Every now and then he would ask if she was okay and

get a grunt in return. He didn't hear any sound of retching or vomiting, so that was a plus.

By the time he landed on the field a few miles from the vineyard he was thinking of purchasing, all was silent.

When he climbed over the partition to help her out, he almost did a double take. He had never seen anyone turn that particular shade of green before. Except, maybe, the Incredible Hulk.

She'd taken his advice with the neck rest, but apart from that she'd clearly dealt with her malady in her own way, reclining her seat as far back as it would go and keeping her eyes scrunched closed. Her hands gripped an empty sick bag, her knuckles white.

He slid the door open to let the air in then went back to her. He crouched down and placed a hand lightly on her shoulder. 'We're here.'

Cara opened one eye and peered at him. Or was it a glare? He couldn't quite tell. 'I know. We've stopped moving.'

'Can you stand?'

'I'll try in a minute.' She snapped her eye shut again then sucked in a breath and swallowed loudly. 'By the way, if you try and carry me out of here, I will sock you one.'

'Just breathe.'

She filled her lungs.

'That's it. In through the nose and out through the mouth.'

'I do know how to breathe. I've been doing it all my life.' Her snappy retort was said with teeth that weren't so much gritted as sucked.

'That's a very clever trait to have,' he said gravely. He had to admit that, despite her green hue, there was something incredibly sexy about the way she sparred with him. 'I will give you five minutes for your body to right itself and if you're still not capable of walking I *will* carry you to the car.'

His threat did the trick as when he returned exactly five minutes later Cara was sitting upright with her eyes open.

She looked at him. 'I think I need your help getting to my feet.'

'You must be bad.' If he hadn't already seen with his eyes that she was unwell, her clammy skin would have definitely given the game away. Her hand gripped his wrist so tightly her neat but short nails dug into his flesh.

She leaned into him, allowing him to half drag her to the open door.

'It'll be easier for you to get out if you sit down—it's a bit of a gap at the best of times.' Not waiting for an argument, he helped her sit her shaky frame to the floor and dangle her legs out of the overhang.

Then he jumped down.

'Can you get down or do you need my help?' If it was anyone else he'd just pull them down the last few inches.

Her green eyes pierced into him. He could see how much it pained her to have to say, 'I need your help.'

He placed his hands on her waist. 'Put your arms around me.'

'Do I have to?'

'No. It'll probably be safer for you though.'

This time she gritted her teeth for real.

Tilting her head to the side and away from his gaze, she looped her arms around his neck, taking care not to touch him in anything but the loosest of fashions.

Deliberately, he closed the small gap between them, felt her heavy breasts crush against his chest. Not for the first time that day he felt a flicker of excitement stir inside him. It was nice to know he wasn't dead from the waist down as he'd been fearing in recent months.

As it was such a short distance for her feet to reach— although if she'd been a few inches taller she would probably have reached the ground from the sitting position—it was a simple matter of tugging her down onto terra firma.

She swayed into him, her cheek coming to rest against his chest, her arms dropping from his neck like deadened weights.

'I'm sorry,' she muttered.

'I'm not.' He slipped his arms around her waist to support her limp form, and enjoyed the feel of her soft curves pressing against the contrasting hardness of his body. She really was incredibly cuddly. She was also clearly unwell. 'Can you walk?'

'Yes.' There was a definite air of defiance in her affirmation, a defiance aimed at her own legs rather than him. 'Do *not* carry me.'

'Come. The car is waiting for us.'

Half dragging her, Pepe somehow managed to manoeuvre Cara the ten metres or so to the Land Rover.

Christophe Beauquet, the vineyard's current owner, was behind the wheel waiting for them. He made no effort to get out and welcome them and made only the briefest of grunts when Pepe helped Cara sit down in the front.

Pepe leaned over to strap her seat belt on, trying to ignore, again, her gorgeous scent. He could hear her furious swallowing, knew she was doing her best to keep back what her body was so desperate to expel. Her hand still clutched the sick bag.

'She needs to look forwards,' he explained before jumping into the back of the four-wheel drive.

Christophe didn't even try to hide his disgust. 'All this fuss for a short air ride?'

The hairs on Pepe's arms lifted. It took him a moment to realise it was his hackles rising. 'She's pregnant,' he answered shortly, leaning back into his seat and clamping his mouth into a firm line. He did not like the Frenchman's tone. He didn't like it *at all*.

CHAPTER SIX

WHEN CARA AWOKE it was dusky. Unlike when she'd awoken that morning, she didn't have the faintest idea where she was. The last thing she remembered was pulling up alongside a pretty farmhouse. Oh, and she remembered Pepe practically yanking her door open so she could vomit. How he knew she was waiting until the car stopped moving before giving in to it, she didn't have a clue. But he did know. And as she'd vomited out of the car and into the paper bag, he was by her side, rubbing her back and drawing her hair away from the danger zone.

It was support of a kind she'd never expected from him, and remembering it made her belly do a funny skip.

She patted her body, relieved to find herself fully dressed. She felt better. A little woozy, but on the whole much better.

When she sat up, she found her shoes, a gorgeous pair of flats from a designer brand she had coveted for years, laid neatly by the double bed she had been placed in.

She guessed she should get up and find Pepe. He was around somewhere, in this picture-book home.

It didn't take long to find him.

She shuffled out of the room and into an open landing. Below, she could hear voices. Walking carefully, she made her way down the stairs and followed the murmurs into a large kitchen.

Sitting around a sturdy oak table was Pepe, the man she remembered as Christophe and a tiny, birdlike woman. So small, the woman was inches shorter than Cara. It was like looking at Mrs Pepperpot come to life.

Mrs Pepperpot spotted her first and bustled over, taking Cara's arm and leading her over to join them, all the while gabbling away in French.

Pepe rose from his chair. 'Cara,' he said, pulling her into an embrace and kissing her on each cheek. 'How are you feeling?'

'Much better,' she mumbled.

'Good.' He stepped back and appraised her thoughtfully. A half-filled glass of wine lay before him. 'You are still a little too pale but you no longer look like the Incredible Hulk.'

'That's a bonus.' She sat on the chair he'd pulled out for her and budged it close to his. No sooner had she sat down when Mrs Pepperpot put a steaming bowl of what looked like a clear broth in front of her and a basket of baguettes.

'*Mangez,*' she ordered, putting her hands to her mouth in what looked like an imitation of eating.

'Cara, this is Christophe's wife, Simone,' Pepe said by way of introduction. 'She doesn't speak any English but she makes an excellent consommé.'

Cara gave Simone a quick smile. 'Thank you—*merci.*'

The consommé smelt delicious. Her starved belly rumbled. Loudly.

'*Mangez,*' Simone repeated.

'She's been waiting for you to wake up,' Pepe said. 'It's also thanks to her that the doctor made an impromptu home visit.'

Vaguely she remembered a heavily scented woman sitting on her bedside and prodding her with things. 'I thought I'd dreamt that.'

He laughed softly. 'You're four months pregnant. It seemed prudent to get you checked over in case you were suffering from something more serious than motion sickness.'

For all his jovial nonchalance, she knew she hadn't dreamt his concern. A strange warmth swept into her chest, suffusing her blood and skin with heat.

She turned her face away. 'I've suffered from motion sickness since I was a little girl. Pregnancy has just made it worse.'

'Even so, I've made arrangements for my family doctor to fly to Paris tomorrow to check you over. The doctor you saw here had concerns about your blood pressure being too low.'

'It's always been low,' she dismissed with a shrug.

'It is better to be safe. You have a child inside you that is dependent on your good health for its survival. I was going to get my doctor to check you over anyway, so I've just brought it forward by a few days.'

'Steady on, Pepe. You almost sound like a concerned father.'

His eyes flickered but the easy smile didn't leave his face.

Luckily any awkwardness was interrupted by Simone placing a jug of iced water in front of her and pouring Cara a glass.

'Why does she keep staring at me?' Cara muttered under her breath a few minutes later so only Pepe could hear. Simone kept nodding and beaming at her, unlike her surly husband, who did nothing but cradle his glass of wine. The Frenchwoman might not speak English but

Cara would bet Christophe knew more than enough to get by.

'Because you're pregnant and she wants to make sure you're getting the nutrition you need. You need to eat.'

'How can I eat when everyone's staring at me?'

For a moment she thought Pepe was going to make a wisecrack. Instead, he drew Christophe and Simone into conversation and, while the talk between them was of a serious tone, it worked, diverting their attention away from her.

Pepe was right about the consommé. It was delicious. Along with a still-warm bread roll, it filled her belly just enough.

It was at the moment she put her spoon in her empty dish that Christophe laughed at something Pepe said, downed his wine and held out a beefy hand. Pepe rose from his seat to take it and, leaning over the table, the two men shook hands vigorously, Christophe gripping Pepe's biceps.

'Is this a new form of male bonding?' Cara said in an aside to Pepe.

To her surprise, it was Christophe who answered. 'It is always good to formalise a deal with a shake of the hand.'

'You're buying the vineyard?' she asked Pepe.

'I would say it's more that Christophe has agreed to *sell* me the vineyard.' Pepe raised his glass in the Frenchman's direction. 'You drive a hard bargain, my friend.'

'Some bargains deserve to be hard fought.' Christophe lifted the wine bottle and made to refill Pepe's glass.

Pepe held out a hand to stop him. 'Not for me. I will be driving back to Paris shortly.'

'Driving?' Cara asked hopefully.

'*Sì*. I got some staff to bring a car over for us.'

'Where are they?'

'They've taken the helicopter back. Don't worry—
I got the flight crew to come. They left about half an
hour ago.'

For a moment she just stared at him, incredulous. 'Seriously? You got your pilots to drive all this way to drop
off a car and then fly back?' How long had she been
asleep? Five hours? He must have got the wheels in motion the second her head had hit the pillow.

He shrugged as if it were no big deal. 'They weren't
doing anything else. It gave them a day out.'

'Did you do this…for *me*?'

'The helicopter's not long been reupholstered. I didn't
want to risk you ruining it by upchucking everywhere.'

Somehow, she just knew Pepe could not give a flying
monkey about upholstery.

'I thought we were going to a business dinner tonight?'

'I'm sure they can survive without our company for
one night,' he said drily. 'I am not so cruel that I would
force you to spend another hour in a craft that makes you
violently ill for the sake of a dinner party with a handful
of the most boring people in all of Paris.'

A compulsion, a strange, strange desire, tingled through
her fingers to lace themselves through his.

Quickly she fisted her hands into balls.

So what if he'd displayed a hint at humanity?

It didn't mean she had to hold his hand.

It didn't change a thing.

By the time they left the vineyard, the sun had set and
the Loire Valley was in darkness. The roads were clear,
the drive smooth, but still Pepe was aware that Cara's
breathing had deepened.

'Are you feeling all right?' he asked, turning the air
conditioning up a notch.

'I think so.' Her head was back against the rest, her eyes shut.

'Open a window if it helps.' It was too dark to see the colour of her complexion, but he'd bet it had regained the green hue.

Cold air filtered through the small opening she made in the window, and she turned her face towards it, breathing the fresh air in.

'You say you've always suffered from motion sickness?' he said a few minutes later when he was reasonably certain she wasn't going to upchuck everywhere.

'As long as I can remember. Boats are the worst.'

'Have you been on many boats?'

'A couple of ferry crossings from England to Ireland when I was a teenager. I spent most of those hugging the toilet.'

'Sounds like fun.'

'It was—tremendous fun was had by all.'

He laughed softly. If there was one thing he liked about Cara it was her dry sense of humour.

He slowed the car a touch, keeping a keen eye out for any potholes or other potential hazards. The last thing he wanted was to do anything to increase her nausea.

'How long have you flown helicopters?' she asked.

'I got my licence about ten years ago.'

'I had no idea.'

'It's no big deal,' he dismissed.

'Sure it is. I assume it's more involved than passing a driving test?'

'Slightly,' he admitted, recalling the hundreds of flying hours he'd put in and the unrelenting exams. He'd loved every minute of it. And, he had to admit, his mother's pride when he'd received his pilot's licence had been something to cherish. Her pride was generally reserved for Luca.

'Are you going to make me fly in one again?'

'No.' He knew if he insisted, she would—ungraciously—comply. As he was fast learning, keeping Cara Delaney attached to him was proving trickier than first thought.

'So you're going to buy the vineyard, then?' she said, changing the subject.

'I am. It's a good, established business and the soil is of excellent quality.'

'How did you get Christophe to agree to sell it to you? He looked like he'd rather be wrestling bears than dealing with you when we arrived.'

'I think surliness is his default setting,' Pepe mused. 'He's one of those men who feel they have to prove their masculinity by puffing out their chest and pounding on it.'

He heard what sounded like a snigger. For a moment it was on the tip of his tongue to share how he'd been on the verge of telling the Frenchman that he could forget the sale, so incensed had he been by Christophe's attitude to Cara's nausea. If his wife, Simone, hadn't been such a welcome contrast, soothing Pepe's ruffled feathers and chiding her husband's surliness away, he would have refused to even take a tour.

Dealing with ultra-macho men was nothing new—he was Sicilian after all. Most men there drank testosterone for breakfast. Today, for the first time, he hadn't wanted to play the macho games such men demanded. He never gained any gratification from them. His own power was assured. There was no need to beat his chest or play a game of 'mine is bigger than yours'. Without being arrogant, he knew that went without saying—in *all* circumstances. But men like Christophe expected those games to be played. Today, for the first time, Pepe had refused.

He'd wanted to look after Cara.

His fingers tightened on the steering wheel as he recalled the way his stomach had clenched to see her so obviously unwell. Yes. A most peculiar feeling. Maladies did not normally bother him. People became ill, then, as a rule, people recovered. A fact of life.

Pregnancy was also a fact of life. As was motion sickness. Cara's suffering really shouldn't bother him beyond the usual realms of human decency.

Yet it did. It was taking all his self-restraint not to lay a comforting hand on her thigh. Saying that, if he were to lay a hand there, comforting or otherwise, she'd likely slap it.

'Are you going to run the deal by Luca first?' Her soft Irish lilt broke through his musings.

'No.' He spoke more sharply than he would have liked. 'No,' he repeated, moderating his tone. 'This is my domain. *I* run our dealings outside Sicily.'

'I thought Luca was in charge.'

'What made you think that? Is it because he's the older brother?'

'No. It's because he's the more steady and *reliable* brother.'

Even in the dark he knew his knuckles had whitened.

'Your brother might be as scary as the bogeyman but at least he conducts himself with something relatively close to decorum and thinks with more than his penis.'

Any minute and his knuckles would poke through his skin. 'Are you deliberately trying to pick an argument with me?'

'Yes.'

'Why?'

'Because I don't like it when you're nice to me.'

'Does driving you home constitute me being *nice*?'

'As opposed to you flying me back in that tin shack, then yes; yes, it does. And incidentally, you're not driving me *home*. You're driving me back to your house.'

'My home is your home until your baby is born.' Although, at that particular moment, he would take great pleasure in stopping the car, kicking her out and telling her to walk herself back to Paris.

Impossible, ungrateful woman.

Impossible *sexy* woman.

There was no denying it. Cara Delaney was as sexy as sin, and as much as he tried to keep his errant mind on the present, it insisted on going back sixteen weeks to what had been, in hindsight, the best weekend of his life.

'Would you prefer if I spent the next five or so months being horrible to you and having no consideration of your needs?'

'Yes.'

He cocked an eyebrow. 'Really?'

'The only niceness I want from you is my freedom.'

'You have your freedom. You are here under your own free will. You are welcome to leave at any time.'

'But for me to leave would mean a life of poverty for our child. Or at least, the start of its life would be full of poverty unless you do the decent thing and give me money to support him or her.'

'I will give you money to support our child when I have definitive proof that it *is* our child. I will not be played for a fool.'

He heard a sharp inhalation followed by a slow, steady exhalation.

'I really don't get it.'

'Get what?'

'Your cynicism.'

'I am not cynical.'

'You impregnated a virgin yet you refuse to believe your paternity without written proof. If that's not cynical, then I don't know what is. And I don't get why you are that way.'

'There is nothing to get. I do not take anything at face value. That's good business sense, not cynicism.' Much as he tried to hide it, a real edge had crept into his voice. He'd thought she would be grateful he was rearranging his schedule to drive her back to Paris, had assumed a little gratitude would soften her attitude towards him. But no. For all the softness of her curves and her bottom lip, Cara Delaney was as hard as nails.

From the periphery of his vision, he saw her straighten.

'Grace and I used to talk about you,' she said.

'Why doesn't that surprise me?'

'We used to wonder why you were the way you were.'

'I haven't the faintest idea what you're talking about.'

'You come from a loving family. You had two parents who loved and supported you and encouraged you…'

'That is what you used to say about me?' he interrupted with a burst of mocking laughter.

'Your mother dotes on you,' she said coldly. 'By all accounts your father doted on you too. You have a closer relationship with your brother than most siblings can dream of. *That's* what I mean about coming from a loving family.'

'*Sì,*' he conceded. 'My parents loved me. Luca and I are close. It is normal.'

'I have two stepsisters who hate me only fractionally less than they hate each other. I have a bunch of half-siblings scattered around Dublin whom I have never met. I have a mother who doesn't care a fig that I'm pregnant. I have a father who is unaware he's going to be a granddad, but that's because he's had no involvement in my life for over a decade.'

For a moment he didn't know what to say to that unexpected outburst or how to react to the raw emotion behind it. 'You haven't seen your father in ten years?'

'Thirteen years. My parents split when I was eleven. Mam and I moved to England when I was thirteen and I haven't seen him since.'

'My father died thirteen years ago.' Something in his chest moved as he thought of Cara going through her own personal trauma while his own life was shattering, first by the death of his father and then by Luisa's vile and ultimately devastating actions.

'I'm sorry.' Her voice softened. 'I've seen pictures of your dad—you look just like him.'

'*Sì*. He was a very handsome man.'

This time she did laugh. 'Oh, you are so full of yourself.'

'You can be full of me too if you want.'

'Are you trying to make me sick again?'

He chuckled, glancing over at her, certain there was the trace of a smile playing on her lips.

Mind out of the gutter, he chided himself. He needed to keep his attention focused on the road before him, not on memories of burying himself inside her tight sweetness.

All the same, he took a sharp breath in the hope it would loosen the tightness in his groin.

'Did your mother stop your father from seeing you after she left him?'

'No. He stopped himself from seeing me. It was too much hassle for him to go across the Irish channel and see his eldest child. We exchange Christmas cards and that's it.'

For a moment he thought she was going to say something else, but when he glanced at her, he saw her eyes were closed and she was massaging her forehead. For all her bitterness there was a definite vulnerability about her when she spoke of her parents.

'Did you miss him?'

'My father?'

'Yes. It must have been a hard time for you.'

She laughed, a noise that sounded as if it were being done through a sucked lemon. 'If anything, it was a relief. My father is a serial shagger. He cheated on my mum so many times I think even *he* lost count.'

'Were you aware of this at the time?' Surely her father would have been discreet?

'I've always known, even when I was too young to understand. They never bothered keeping it a secret from me. I caught him out twice—once when I was going to the park with my friends and walked past the local pub and saw him through the window draped over some woman.'

'He was with another woman in your local pub?' Even Pepe, who was not easily shocked, was shocked at this.

'You think that's bad?' Her tone rose in pitch. 'The next time I caught him out, which couldn't have been more than six months later, I found him in the marital bed with another woman—a different woman from the woman he was with in the pub.'

'You caught him in the act?'

'No, thank God. They were lying in bed. I remember my dad was smoking a cigarette. I don't know what shocked me the most—I'd no idea he was a smoker.'

And Cara had no idea why she was sharing all this with Pepe of all people.

It had been the same over the weekend they'd shared together. He was such an easy person to talk to and had such an unerring ability to make the person he was with—namely her—believe that every word she uttered was worth listening to, that it was quite possible to spill your guts to him without even realising. He'd done it then, listened to her rabbit on for hours about her love of her job, her hopes for the future.

No one had ever made her feel like that before.

He'd made her believe she was special.

It would be all too easy to believe it again.

She opened the window a little further and practically stuck her nose out of it, inhaling the cold air gratefully. It compressed the anger and pain of those horrible memories back down to a manageable level.

Silence sprang between them, a silence that was on the verge of becoming uncomfortable when Pepe said, 'What did you do? Did you tell your mother?'

She sucked in more cold air before answering. 'Yes. Yes, I did. He didn't even bother to deny it. She threw him out for all of two days before taking him back. She always took him back.'

Her stomach twisted a little more as she recalled hearing them 'make up'. They hadn't cared that their ten-year-old daughter was in the house. They'd never cared.

Her entire childhood had revolved around her father's affairs and her mother's reactions to them. Those reactions had never been about Cara. Their daughter had been secondary to everything in their sick marriage where sex was a weapon used to hurt each other in the most cruel and demeaning ways.

'I always swore I'd never get involved with a man who was like my father, so more fool me.'

'What do you mean by that?'

'You,' she practically spat. 'How else do you think

my dad was able to pull so many women and use them so badly? He's a charmer, just like you are.'

'I am *nothing* like your father.' His vehemence was the most emphatic she had ever heard him.

'You use women for your own gratification with no thoughts of them as real people.'

'That is utter rubbish. I have never cheated on anyone. Ever.' An ugly tone curdled his words. 'I despise cheats.'

'You still use women.'

'I do not use women. I am never anything but honest with my lovers. Do not kid yourself into believing they are in my bed under false pretences.'

'You used me. I thought you wanted me in your bed because you wanted *me*. I had no idea you wanted to get your hands on my stupid phone and not my body.'

It was Pepe's turn to suck in a breath. 'I accept that I used you, Cara. I am not proud of what I did but it had to be done. My brother was a man on the verge of a breakdown. It doesn't change the fact that I found you as sexy as hell. I still do. I wanted to make love to you regardless of the circumstances.'

'You still used me. You can tell me until you're blue in the face that you're nothing like my father but I know better. You're two of a kind. You make love to women and then dump them, leaving them to deal with the emotional fallout. And the unwanted after-effects. Like babies,' she couldn't resist adding.

A screech of brakes and a swerve of the wheels as he brought the Mercedes to a shuddering halt on the verge.

Pepe turned the engine off, his breathing ragged.

Cara took little consolation that she had finally pierced his charming armour.

For long moments the only sound was their breathing.

'I am going to start driving again in a moment,' he

said grimly. 'Unless you want me to leave you to make your own way back to Paris, I suggest you do not speak to me, other than to say if you're feeling ill.'

From the tone of his voice, she knew he meant every word.

CHAPTER SEVEN

IT WAS NO USE. Sleep really had no intention of coming.
She could count as many sheep as she liked but they
might as well be blowing big fat raspberries at her for all
the use they were at getting her off to slumber.

Cara climbed out of bed and reached for her new robe,
which was more of a kimono. However much she might
tell herself that she was itching to get her well-worn flan-
nelette dressing gown back, there was no getting around
the fact this scarlet silk kimono was utterly gorgeous and
felt like liquid on her skin.

After three days in Pepe's Parisian home she still
wasn't as familiar with the layout as she should be, but
she knew her way to the kitchen.

She hadn't seen much of him since their drive back
from the Loire Valley. Instead of keeping her chained
to him, he'd had a change of heart and now insisted she
be chained to Monique the housekeeper instead. Okay,
maybe that was a slight exaggeration. What he had actually said, when they'd arrived back at the house after
almost three hours of ice between them, was that all his
meetings for the rest of the week were in Paris and that
she was free to stay at home if she would prefer. Just
as she'd thought he was becoming a more reasonable
human being, he'd qualified it with, 'Monique is around

during the day. She can accompany you if you need to go anywhere.'

'Where is there for me to go?' she'd shot back. 'I don't speak the language and I don't have any money to do anything. Parisian prices are stupidly high.'

He'd shrugged without looking at her. 'I have a swimming pool and spa—you're welcome to use them whenever you wish. Besides, if the paternity test proves your child is mine then you'll have more money than you know how to spend.'

She'd responded by calling him a name that would have made the nuns from the convent she'd attended before moving to England blush.

The following morning he'd made matters even worse by having a top-of-the-range laptop, smartphone and e-reader delivered to the house for her. The e-reader had, from what she'd been able to ascertain, unlimited credit installed. She'd taken a perverse pleasure in downloading as many books as she could, all featuring the most unheroic, misogynistic protagonists that she could find. Hopefully Pepe would receive an itemised bill with all the titles listed for him.

She hated that he would do something thoughtful. It was the same as when he'd driven her home rather than make her fly back in the helicopter. She didn't want him to be *nice*. She wasn't going to be like her mother and forgive deplorable behaviour because of a stupid gift.

Making her way down the winding staircase, she headed for the kitchen. The house was in darkness but for the dim glow of night lights that were strategically placed throughout.

She switched on the main light of the kitchen, blinking several times as her eyes adjusted to the brightness.

It felt strange being in there, in a kitchen as large as

the house she'd grown up in, feeling as if she were an intruder. She had no idea where anything was but found the fridge easily enough—seeing as it was a whopping American-style fridge large enough to use in a mortuary, it would have been hard to miss.

What she really wanted was some warm milk. Grace's mother, Billie, would make it for them when she went for one of her frequent sleepovers there. It was comforting. Now, if only she knew where to even begin searching for a saucepan…

The whisper of movement froze her to the spot. Her hand gripped the plastic milk carton.

'You're up late, *cucciola mia*,' a deep Sicilian drawl said from behind her.

She spun around to find Pepe striding languorously towards her. 'You scared the life out of me,' she snapped. Or, at least she tried to snap, but her mini-fright had left her a little breathless. Seeing all six feet plus of semi-naked Pepe also did something to her pulse-rate, but there he was, muscle-bound and gorgeous, and wearing nothing but a pair of low-slung jeans that perfectly accentuated his snake hips and showed his taut, olive chest to perfection. The silky hair that ran from his chest and down in a thin line over his toned stomach, thickened where the buttons of his jeans were undone…

His hair was tousled, black stubble breaking out along his jawline, almost as thick as his trimmed goatee.

Sin. That was what he looked like. A walking, talking advertisement for sin. And temptation.

'I didn't mean to scare you,' he said, not looking the least apologetic. 'I heard noise and came to investigate.'

'I couldn't sleep.'

His deep blue eyes held hers, meaning swirling in them. 'Nor could I.'

She broke the lock first, aware of warmth suffusing more than just her face.

'What brings you out of hiding?' he asked, standing a little closer than she would have liked.

She took a step back. 'I've not been in hiding.'

'You've barely left your room in three days. Monique says you've been no further than the dining room.'

'This isn't my home. I don't feel comfortable roaming around as if I belong here.' She felt especially uncomfortable now, but in an entirely different way, in a 'sexy half-naked man in front of me' kind of way.

She must be delirious. Sleep deprivation could do that.

'You *do* belong here. While you are under my roof, this is your home. You are free to treat it as you wish.'

'Except leave it.'

'You are always free to leave.'

She bit back the comment that wanted to break free. What was the point? It would only be a rehash of all their other arguments regarding her freedom.

'I was after some warm milk,' she muttered. 'I thought it would help me sleep.'

'I thought I heard you thrashing about in your bed.' At her quizzical expression, he added, 'My room is next to yours.'

'Oh.'

'You didn't know?' His lips quirked into a smirk.

'No. I didn't.' It shouldn't matter where Pepe slept. He could sleep in a shed for all she cared. But the room next to hers…?

Why the thought should heat her veins, she had no idea.

The playful, sensuous expression in his eyes softened a touch. 'I make a mean hot chocolate.'

It took a moment for her to realise he was offering to make her some. 'Thank you.'

He started busying himself, opening doors and rifling through drawers.

She suppressed a snigger and hoicked herself up on the kitchen table. 'You don't know your way around your kitchen any better than I do.'

'Guilty as charged.' He knelt down and leaned into a cupboard, giving her an excellent view of his tight buttocks straining against the denim. 'I employ housekeepers so I don't have to know my way around my kitchens. When I'm home alone, take-out is my best friend.'

Oh, the blasé way he pluralised *kitchen*! Cara thought of the poky galley kitchen she shared—*had* shared—with three other women. It would probably fit in Pepe's fridge.

When he reappeared he had a milk pan in his hand. 'It would be quicker to microwave it but my mother always taught me it was sacrilege to make a hot chocolate like that.'

'I thought you had a fleet of staff when you were growing up?'

'We did,' he said, matter-of-factly. 'But making our nightly hot chocolate was a job my mother always liked to do herself. She used to sit Luca and I on the kitchen table—much as you're sitting now—while she made it.'

'It sounds wonderful,' she said with more than a touch of envy. Evenings in the Delaney household had normally consisted of her mother fretting about where her father was.

He cocked his head while he thought about it. A glimmer of surprise flittered across his features. 'Yes, it was.'

Pepe added the expensive cocoa powder to the warming milk before spooning some sugar into the mixture, whisking vigorously as he went along.

Looking at his childhood from Cara's perspective, he could see it had been idyllic. His feelings about being spare to Luca's heir were not something that had developed until he'd hit his teenage years, but Luca had always been the good one, whereas he'd always been the naughty one. Looking back, it was as if his parents' expectations of him had been lower from the start.

Or had it been that their expectations of Luca had been set too high? His brother had been groomed to take over the family business. He'd had responsibility thrust upon him from the womb. For Pepe, the only responsibility he'd had—and it was a self-imposed one—was to make his serious big brother laugh.

He whipped the milk pan away from the heat right before it reached boiling point, then poured it into the two waiting mugs.

When he turned to pass Cara her drink, his chest compressed.

Her short legs dangled from the table, hovering inches above the floor, and she was chewing on her bottom lip.

He wondered if she knew the top of her robe had parted a touch, giving him a tantalising glimpse of that wonderful cleavage his senses remembered so well. The first time he'd buried himself in those glorious breasts he'd thought he'd died and gone to heaven.

During the intervening months the wonder of that night was something he had suppressed with a ruthlessness he'd never before had to employ. But it had always been there, hovering in the periphery of his memories, taunting him, tantalising him. Often it would catch him unawares, a visual memory or a familiar scent, always with the same end result, a burst of need that would shoot straight to his groin and clutch at his chest. The same burst of need he was currently experiencing. The same need that had been a semi-permanent ache since he'd stood next to Cara at the font at Lily's christening.

Under normal circumstances, that one night wouldn't have been the end of them. He would have gone back for more. Hell, he might even have brought her here to Paris as he'd insinuated, but not for the sake of his art collection. No, he'd have brought her here so he could devour that delectable body over and over until he was finally spent and there was nothing left for him to discover and enjoy.

As she reached out a hand to take the mug, her kimono strained against her breasts, moulding them for his hungry eyes, and the need in his groin tightened, straining against the denim he wore.

The hem of the kimono barely covered her knees.

Was she wearing *anything* beneath it?

'What are you doing?' Cara's voice was a husky whisper.

Without even realising it, he'd closed the gap between them. One more step and he'd be able to part her creamy thighs and slip between them...

Cara's heart thumped so strongly she could hear it pound against her ribs.

'I asked, what are you doing?' How she managed to drag the words out, she didn't know. Pepe was so close he'd sucked all the air from her lungs.

His large warm hand closed over hers and removed the mug, placing it on the table, out of her reach.

And then he was cupping her cheeks, forcing her to meet his stare. 'I'm going to kiss you.'

'No!' It was more of a whimper than a refusal. She tried to wrench her face free from his clasp but his hold was too strong. And, somehow, too gentle.

'*Sì.*' He brushed a thumb over her bottom lip. 'Yes, *cucciola mia*. I am going to kiss you.'

She didn't want to respond. God alone knew she didn't want to respond.

Yet when his lips slanted onto hers and held there for long moments before prising her mouth apart, and when his thick tongue slipped into her mouth, the only word revolving around and around in her head was *yes*. Yes. Yes. Yes.

The only answer her body gave was yes.

The hands she tried to ball into fists fought back, tracing up his bare biceps and clinging to his shoulders, her nails digging into the smooth flesh.

And still she tried to fight. Desperately she fought against the growing rip tide of need pulsating through her blood, fought against the moisture bubbling in her most intimate area.

But mostly she battled for her head, a fight she was so far from winning she…

His hand was cupping her breast.

When had that happened…?

It felt so…good. Wonderful. His touch…

But it wasn't enough. The silk of the kimono was too restrictive.

Pepe must have read her mind because he slipped a hand beneath the thin material and spread it whole against a breast so sensitive, the relief of him finally touching it—touching her—made her gasp into his hot mouth.

And then she was kissing him back, her lips moving against his with no conscious thought, her tongue dancing against his, her whole body alive to his touch, the heat from his mouth and the taste of *him*.

Roughly he tugged her kimono apart, exposing her

naked flesh. He snaked an arm around her waist and pulled her flush to him, crushing her breasts against his chest, crushing her mouth with an ever deepening kiss, his other hand trailing up her back, up the nape of her neck and then spearing her hair, gently tugging at it, before trailing back and reaching down to take her hand, which he placed on the front of his jeans. His fingers curled into hers as he pressed her hand tight to him. Even through the thick denim she could feel the length and weight of his erection. She could feel the heat emanating from him.

It was a heat her starved body revelled in.

Because it had been starving.

It had been starving for *him*.

He had brought her to life, given her an appetite she hadn't known she had, and then he'd left her. Alone. And pregnant.

'See, *cucciola mia*,' he said, breaking his mouth away and dragging kisses across her cheek and down her neck. 'This is how badly I want you. Enough that I think I might explode if I don't have you.'

His words, the sound of his voice, were things the small part of her shrieking at her treacherous body anchored onto, using them to bring her out of this erotic stupor he had put her in.

Somehow she managed to wedge her hands between their meshed chests—and, God, her body really didn't want her to; her lips ached for just one more kiss, the apex of her thighs begged her to let him continue—and, using all the strength she could muster, pushed him away.

'I said *no*.'

He almost reeled back.

Pepe's chest heaved as he stared at her with eyes that penetrated, almost as if he were reaching into the deepest recess of her mind. 'Your mouth said no. The rest of you said yes.'

Although his words were nothing but the truth, she shook her head, her shaking hands frantically wrapping the kimono back up, tying it as tightly as was physically possible. 'When a woman says no, then the answer is no. No, no, no. You have no right to help yourself to me.'

His face contorted and he took another step back. 'Do *not* imply that I am some sort of rapist. You wanted me as much as I wanted you. You kissed me back. You enjoyed every minute of it.'

The savagery of his words made her flinch.

To compound it all, she felt hot tears sting the backs of her retinas. 'I don't care how much I *enjoyed* it,' she said, forcing the words out, aware her words were hitched. 'This is not going to happen. Unlike you, my brain is in control of my actions.'

His lips curved into something that was supposed to resemble a smile. 'You think? Well, *cucciola mia*, you will learn that my control is second to none. Have no worries—I will not touch you again. Not without a written contract from you saying yes.'

With that parting shot, he strolled out of the kitchen, leaving her rooted to the table she was still sitting upon.

CHAPTER EIGHT

PEPE GROWLED AT the screen before him. The words of the contract could be in gobbledegook for all he cared.

There was no point lying to himself. He was angry. Angry at Cara. Angry at the situation they had been forced into. Angry at himself.

But especially angry at her.

He'd never forced himself on a woman in his life. Never. He despised men who did such things, thought castration too mild a punishment for such deeds.

Had he really misread the situation so badly?

No. Absolutely not.

Cara had the most expressive face of any woman he'd ever known. They said that eyes were windows to the soul. With Cara, her eyes were windows to her emotions. If she was angry, happy, tired or ill, her eyes were the signposts for him to follow.

How had he become an expert on her *emotions*?

He shook his head briskly and rubbed his eyes. He probably wouldn't feel so crummy if he'd managed to get any sleep. But how was a man supposed to sleep when his body ached with unfulfilled desire?

One thing he was not, though, was hurt. His ego might be a touch bruised but, on a personal level, it made no difference if Cara was willing to share a bed with him or not. There were plenty of women out there who were. And in reality, it was probably better that they didn't resume a sexual relationship, especially as she was of a completely different mindset from his usual lovers.

He doubted there would ever come a time he would be able to bump into Cara at a party, sidle over to her, maybe give her bottom a cheeky pinch, and then catch up on old times.

The animosity would always be there.

In any case, if her baby did prove to be his, then he had to concede she would be a huge part of his life...well, for the rest of his life. If the baby was his then they would be for ever united, even in the most cerebral fashion.

An image of a tiny baby with a shock of Cara's flame-red hair came into his head, an image he blinked away along with the nagging voice that kept piping up, asking him if he really wanted nothing more than to be a part-time father.

He clenched his hands into fists.

He didn't want to think that far ahead.

He didn't want to imagine how he would feel if Cara really was carrying his child.

Once, a long time ago, he'd been caught up in the magic of pregnancy, the unmitigated joy and wonder of knowing he had shared in the creation of life and that soon he would be a father. The child had been no more than a foetus but already he had loved it, had thought of the future that child would have with him and Luisa, and the family they would create together.

His child would never have felt second best.

His child never got the chance to feel anything, least of all second best.

Luisa had ripped that chance away from him.

Cara was nothing like Luisa.

Cara was like no one he'd ever met.

But what did he know of her *really*? He'd known Luisa pretty much all of his life but he'd never guessed she was capable of ripping his heart out and stamping on the remnants.

He would never trust another woman. He couldn't. There was only so much pain one man could take and he'd reached that limit before he'd even finished his teenage years.

Only when Cara's baby was born and the paternity test established that he truly was the father would he allow himself to think properly of the future.

Only then would he allow himself to think of what it truly meant to have a child.

Until that time came, his life would continue as it was. Except with a houseguest. A fiery, sexy houseguest.

Suppressing a yawn, he checked his watch. It was time to call it a day. There was a party he had to attend, a party he'd been looking forward to until approximately five days ago, being hosted by a good friend who was celebrating his first wedding anniversary. Not feeling in the mood to drive, he got his driver to take him home, all the while trying to shake himself out of the melancholic mood that had crept under his skin.

By the time he arrived back at his home he felt no better, but, with practised ease, slipped his old faithful smile on and strolled into the house.

'Where is Cara?' he asked Monique, who had hurried out to greet him.

'In her room.'

'Has she left it today?'

'Only for her lunch and a late afternoon snack.'

'Did she eat any breakfast?'

'A croissant and an apple.'

He headed to his room, refusing to reflect on his need to monitor Cara's eating habits. It was simple concern extended towards a pregnant woman, nothing more.

As he passed, Cara's bedroom door opened. Her eyes widened to see him and she took a step back, would no doubt have shut the door in his face if he hadn't stuck a foot in the doorway to prevent her.

'Good evening, *cucciola mia*. How has your day been?'

'Long and boring.'

'Then it must be a source of comfort to know we are going out tonight.'

She pulled a face but opened the door properly and leaned against the door frame, hugging her arms around her chest. 'It's getting late. Do I have to go?'

'Yes.'

'Can't I stay here with Monique?'

'Monique goes home at weekends—aren't you lucky? You can have me all to yourself.'

Her cheeks coloured and she scowled. 'How thrilling. Can't you get another babysitter for me?'

'It's too short notice. Besides, I don't think I could afford to pay anyone else to put up with you.'

'I'm no bother. I just stay in my room. It's like babysitting a five-year-old.'

Anyone listening in on them would be amused at the dryness of their conversation. If they were to scratch a little under the surface it would be a whole different story. The second her door had opened, Pepe's heart had begun to thunder, the weight in his gut twisting and clenching. The half-smile on his face could have been drawn on.

As for Cara...her beautiful lips were pulled in and tight, while her green eyes spat fire at him.

He wanted to touch her. He wanted to pick her up and

carry her across the room, lay her on the bed and make love to every inch of her.

After the way she had reacted in the kitchen in the early hours, it would be a long day in hell before he touched her again. She would have to get down on her knees and beg before he would even consider making love to her.

All the same, he couldn't resist reaching out a hand and tapping her cute little nose. 'We leave in an hour, *cucciola mia*. Cocktail dress. Be ready or I'll come in your room and help you.'

'You wouldn't dare.'

'Is that a challenge?'

'No!'

'In that case, be ready on time. I need to shower—see you in sixty minutes.'

Exactly one hour later, Pepe knocked on Cara's bedroom door. He half hoped she *wasn't* ready.

Forget the good talking-to he'd given himself earlier about not resuming their sexual relationship; just three minutes sparring outside her bedroom had laid waste to those good intentions.

There was something so damn sexy about his red-headed geisha.

If only she really were a geisha. Or better still, his own personal concubine. He was pretty sure bitching at her master wasn't part of either's job description. Geisha or concubine, all the woman concerned herself with was her master's pleasure. Seeing as it was pleasure of a sexual nature he wanted from Cara, he would much rather settle with concubine.

He was certain she did it deliberately, but she made him wait a full sixty seconds before opening her door.

The wait was worth it.

The quip he had ready on his lips blew away as his mouth fell open.

Pepe was used to dating beauties. He shamelessly used his wealth, charm and looks to pick the cream of the crop. Yet Cara outshone all of them.

Dressed in a richly red silk floor-length dress that showed off her curves, the sleeves skimming her shoulders to leave her arms bare, her glorious hair piled into a sleek chignon, she looked stunning. In her ears were heart drop crystals that shimmered under the light, and on her feet were shoes that had the same shimmering effect. Her make-up was subtle bar the lipstick, a rich red that perfectly matched her dress and made her kissable lips infinitely more so.

'*Mio Dio,*' he said appreciatively. 'You are beautiful.'

'It's amazing what money can do,' she said tartly, although her cheeks flamed to match her hair, her dress, her lips…

'You are Hestia come to life,' he breathed.

'That's appropriate seeing as the Vestal Virgins get their name from her Roman counterpart.'

A smile escaped his lips. 'She was also the Roman Goddess of the Hearth—of fire.'

'And I bet you see yourself as Eros—wouldn't you just love to get your hands on the Vestals?'

His smile tightened. 'Actually, no. I've found virgins too needy for my taste.'

It was a low blow and one he wished he could take back as soon as it escaped his lips. There was something about her spiky tongue that he reacted to. Her barbs penetrated him like no one else's.

Cara's eyes narrowed but she raised her chin and pulled the door shut behind her, her movements releasing a cloud of her perfume. 'Then we are better suited than I believed. I've always found lustful men too immature for *my* tastes.'

'How are you going to introduce me to your friends?' Cara asked as they sat in the back of the blacked-out Mercedes through the dark Parisian evening. The city twinkled with what seemed a million lights, giving it a magical quality that enthralled her.

'As my companion.'

'Is that how you introduce all your lovers?'

'I wasn't aware that you were my lover,' he responded easily, the coolness he'd displayed since she'd made the jibe about him being immature having dispersed. She much preferred it when he was cool towards her. It made it much easier to hate him.

'I suppose you can always introduce me as your pregnant one-night stand who you're waiting to give birth so you can get a paternity test to prove that you're the daddy.'

She felt him tense, knew that beneath his tuxedo his frame had tautened.

'Why are you happy to dress in a suit for business and wear a DJ for a party, but refuse to make an effort for your own niece's christening?' she asked, blurting out one of the many questions that played on her mind.

'I wasn't aware I hadn't made an effort for it,' he answered coolly.

She shrugged. Pepe's choice of attire was none of her business. 'So where is this party?'

'In Montmartre.'

Now he mentioned it, the lights of the sprawling hill that comprised Montmartre gleamed before them, the white Basilica of Sacre-Coeur sitting atop, almost surveying all beneath it. As they drove into the bustling arrondissement, she pressed her face to the window to take in the beautiful architecture, ambling tourists and nonchalant locals.

'How are you feeling?' he asked. 'Any nausea?'

'So far so good,' she confirmed.

'That is good.' Not trusting the casual tone to his voice, she looked at him and found him holding a paper bag aloft. He winked. 'Just in case.'

Despite herself, she laughed, the action loosening a little of the angst in her chest.

He moved closer to her and pointed out of the window. 'Through those gardens is the Musée de Montmartre. It is reputed to be the oldest house in Montmartre.'

'Didn't Renoir live in it?' she asked, wholly aware of his thigh now pressed against hers.

'Not quite—there is a mansion behind it that he lived in for a while. Maurice Utrillo lived there though.'

As they snaked their way through the cobbled streets, he pointed out more features of interest, his words breathing life into the ancient buildings, especially from the Impressionist era. He knew so much about the district, had such lively knowledge, his heavy Sicilian accent so lyrical it was a joy to listen to him.

Cara hid her disappointment when the driver came to a stop in a narrow street lined by a terrace of white-washed five-storey homes, cafés and shops. She could have happily continued with their tour.

To her surprise, they went into a packed poky café that smelt strongly of coffee, body odour and illicit cigarettes. Pepe greeted the staff personally with his usual enthusiasm, shaking hands and kissing cheeks, before leading her through the back and out into a small court-yard.

'Ladies first,' he said, waving his hand at a flimsy-looking iron staircase that led all the way to the top floor. 'Don't worry,' he added, clearly reading her mind. 'I assure you it is safe.'

'Aren't there indoor stairs?' She was in no way mollified by his assurance.

'There are, but as you have seen, the café is busy, and if all tonight's guests were to use them, we would get in the way of the staff.'

'So why go through the front entrance? Why not get your driver to drop us off at the back?'

'Because the staff would be most put out if they knew I had been here and hadn't dropped in to say hello.'

'You do have a high opinion of yourself,' she muttered.

His smile dropped a wattage before the teeth flashed. 'Forgive my modesty but I am a good employer.'

Her brow knotted.

'I own the building,' he clarified.

'I thought you owned vineyards.'

'I do. Didn't you know variety is the spice of life?'

She sniffed pointedly, and hugged her wrap closer around her chest, wishing she had worn the thick designer coat Pepe had bought her. 'I'm surprised you haven't turned it into a high-tech hotel.'

He pulled a face. 'And rip it of its charm? This street is old-style Montmartre, unaffected and barely known by the tourists that have infected much of the rest of this glorious place. I intend to keep it that way.'

'You own the entire street?'

He inclined his head in affirmation then looked back to the iron stairs. 'Shall we?'

'I don't know…'

'Do you suffer from vertigo?'

'No.'

'Then where's your sense of adventure?'

'I've never had one.'

'Liar. You spent a year travelling Europe with Grace, so don't tell me you have no sense of adventure.'

'I'm pregnant.'

'Are pregnant women not able to climb stairs?'

'Don't be silly.'

His features softened. 'Cara, I promise I would never allow anything to happen to you or your baby. This staircase is only a couple of years old—I oversaw its construction myself. I'll be right behind you—I promise you'll be safe.'

Much as she knew she must be a fool to believe him, she found herself putting a foot onto the bottom step, half expecting the whole thing to come crashing down on them.

It was a lot sturdier than she anticipated. And, she had to admit, knowing he would be there to catch her if she should trip was…comforting. Pepe's strength and assurance were more than a little comforting.

'Which floor are we going to?' she asked, turning her head to look at him.

The grin that spread across his face made her stomach flip over. 'You and I, *cucciola mia*, are going all the way.'

Her cheeks burning at the suggestion in his tone, she climbed up, slowly at first until she became aware that Pepe, being a couple of paces behind her, had an excellent view of her derrière. Yep, knowing he had a face full of her backside certainly acted as rocket fuel and she reached the top in no time.

She had no idea what she'd been expecting: from the general dilapidation of the café below, she'd half assumed Pepe had made her dress up as a joke, but she certainly hadn't been expecting *this*.

The party was being held in a loft conversion. Except it was nothing like any loft she'd ever been in. Extremely large and airy, simply decorated with what she would refer to as faux shabby chic, it must have covered the length of the entire terrace.

'So do you own this loft too?'

He raised a brow.

'I know; a silly question. But this place…' Her voice trailed off.

'A little different from the café on the ground floor?'

'Yes. Exactly.'

'The café is a fixture in Montmartre. I didn't want to make any changes other than have it fitted with a kitchen that wasn't liable to catch fire at any moment. This loft, on the other hand, was begging to be converted into a proper work and living space.'

'Is it a studio?' There might be so many people crammed into the space that she couldn't see any art paraphernalia, but she'd recognise the smell of turps anywhere—with an artist for best friend, that was a given.

'*Sì.*' He nodded at a diminutive man holding court to a large crowd of glamorous people. 'That is the tenant, Georges Ramirez.'

'I know him,' she said, awed. 'Well, I know *of* him. We've auctioned his work before.'

'He's an old friend. The loft was designed with him in mind.'

As he spoke, Georges looked in their direction and spotted Pepe. His little gang looked too and in the click of a finger two dozen pairs of eyes had widened and two dozen sets of lips had curled into smiles. A few people, including Georges and the pretty woman clutching his hand, broke from the crowd and headed towards them.

In a whirl of French and English, and some Italian and

Spanish, Pepe presented her to people who were clearly his friends, introducing her simply as Cara with no further explanation. Names were thrown at her, hands shaken and embraces exchanged—well, embraces with Pepe were exchanged. All the while she stood there wishing the floor would open up and swallow her, whisk her away to somewhere familiar and calming.

Her hands had gone clammy, her pulse racing. 'I need to use the bathroom,' she whispered for Pepe's ears only, trying to keep any trace of panic from her voice.

He stared at her with a quizzical expression before inclining his head. 'The bathroom is through that door on the left of the bar,' he said, pointing at a long table pushed against a far wall, piled high with all manner of alcohol and soft drinks. 'Go through it and then it's the second door on the right.'

The door by the bar led into another enormous, brightly lit space. Canvases and sculptures were crammed inside, protected by a large stand-up sign that read 'Any Person Found Touching The Work Will Be Chemically Castrated'. An unexpected giggle escaped from her mouth.

Luckily the bathroom was empty and gave her time to collect herself.

She hated crowds. Hated large parties. Especially hated crowds and large parties where she didn't know anyone. It was that *new girl* feeling all over again, the knowledge that everyone was already acquainted with their own little friendship bands. Outsiders were most definitely *not* welcome. Outsiders on the arm of the man who was definitely the alpha male of the pack were as welcome as anthrax.

When she finally left her sanctuary, a tall brunette with the most amazing hazel eyes blocked her way. 'Ah, so *you're* my replacement,' she said with a dazzling smile.

CHAPTER NINE

'SORRY?' CARA DIDN'T have the faintest idea what she was talking about.

'I was Pepe's original date for the evening,' the beauty said without the slightest trace of rancour.

Cara didn't know what to say, could feel herself shrinking from the inside out.

'It is not a problem,' the beauty assured her. 'We used to date but it was over a long time ago. I'm sure we'll hook up again some other time when he's back on the market and in need of a semi-platonic date for the evening. In the meantime, you should enjoy him while you have him.'

Cara searched for signs the woman was having a joke at her expense but saw nothing but open friendliness in those hazel eyes. She swallowed and forced her rooted tongue to work. 'What does *semi-platonic* mean?'

'Oh, you know—what is the English expression?' Her eyes scrunched up as she thought, then another beaming smile broke out on her spectacularly pretty face. 'I know—it means "friends with benefits"!'

'Friends with benefits,' Cara echoed weakly, her stomach roiling at the thought.

That friendliness turned to consternation. 'Have I spoken out of turn?'

'Not at all,' Cara said, knowing as she said the words that they sounded weedy and pathetic.

The woman slapped her own forehead. 'I have a very big mouth—forgive me, I meant no harm. I didn't know you were serious about him.'

'I'm not.' Cara strove to affect nonchalance. From the pity in the other woman's eyes, she failed miserably at it.

'I must use the bathroom now,' the woman said, shuffling to the door. 'Please, forget what I said. I didn't know—'

'I'm not serious about him,' Cara interrupted, her horror at the woman's assumptions trumping her innate shyness. 'I'm well aware Pepe has the attention span of a goldfish.'

'That is a little unfair,' the woman said with a slight crease in her forehead. 'To goldfish.' With a quick wink she entered the bathroom and shut the door behind her.

Taking rapid breaths, Cara rejoined the party, trying desperately to contain the nerves that threatened to overwhelm her.

As she sought out Pepe she could feel people staring at her, feel their curiosity about this stranger in their midst. For this was no social-networking occasion, this was a proper party for friends to mingle, catch up on each other's lives, drink too much alcohol and behave indiscreetly. She couldn't even have a glass of wine to calm her nerves.

Eventually she found him chatting to a couple of women, a tall glass of beer in his hand. Walking towards them, she almost came to a stop when she saw one of the women cup his buttocks and give them a squeeze. How Cara's feet carried on moving, she had no idea, but it felt as if a million hot pins were being poked into her skin.

Pepe laughed and grabbed the wandering hand. He

brought it to his lips. Whatever he said as he kissed it made the wandering-hand woman burst into laughter.

'Cara,' he called, spotting her and beckoning her over. When she reached him, he placed an arm around her waist, his hand gripping her hip. The same hand that just moments earlier had held another woman's hand so he could kiss it.

'I don't think I've introduced you—this is Lena and Francesca. Ladies, this is Cara.'

The two women looked at her with unabashed interest. Wandering-hand lady held her hand out. Much as she wanted to refuse, Cara forced herself to shake it, all the while thinking, *This hand just squeezed Pepe's butt. This is* another *of his ex-lovers.*

How many of them were here?

The hot pins poking her skin were now strong enough to make her brain burn.

'Ladies, look after her for me while I get her a drink.' With that, Pepe disappeared into the crowd.

Francesca, the non-wandering-hand woman, an adorably plump blonde who had squeezed herself into a black dress that gave her a cleavage like two pillows, was the first to speak. 'I don't think we have met before, *non?*'

Cara shook her head.

'How did you come to meet Pepe?'

At least it was a question she could answer. Even so, it took two attempts for the words to form. 'His brother is married to my best friend.'

Francesca's eyes gleamed. 'Ah, Luca. Now that is one fine specimen of man,' she said, turning back to Lena.

The two Frenchwomen spoke in their native language before Lena addressed Cara. *'Je regrette un... non English.'*

'Lena doesn't speak English,' Francesca said apologetically. 'I am translating.'

Even if Cara had actually paid attention in her senior school French classes, there was no way she would have been able to keep up with the speed with which the two women spoke.

As Cara stood there like a spare wheel while the two women conversed loudly before her, that same dreadful outsider feeling doused her all over again.

'I need to find Pepe,' she whispered, backing away, horribly aware her cheeks were flaming.

Slipping back into the crowd, she spotted him easily enough, standing by the bar with what looked like a glass of orange juice in his hand. It came as no surprise to find him talking to a woman. This woman's hand was playing with the lapel of his tuxedo jacket.

If her brain could burn much more it would boil. Everything inside her felt taut, as if it had been wound into a coil. Perspiration broke out on her skin.

'Where are you going?' Pepe caught hold of her wrist as she passed him.

She hadn't even realised her legs were moving.

'To the bathroom.' She said the first thing that came into her mind.

'Again?'

'Yes.'

His eyes narrowed slightly as he studied her. 'You're very pale. Are you all right?'

'Yes.' She tugged her wrist out of his hold. 'Excuse me. I'll be back in a minute.'

The lapel-fingering woman said something to him in French, looking at Cara as she spoke. No doubt she too was asking if Cara was his latest lover. The latest in a long, long line.

Taking advantage of his momentary distraction, Cara slipped out of the door. This time the adjoining room was full of partygoers all talking and laughing loudly. A small queue had formed by the bathroom.

She didn't want the bathroom. She wanted to escape. She wanted to get as far away from Pepe and all the women who had shared his bed as she could.

As she stood there, feeling helpless, not knowing what to do, the opportunity for escape presented itself.

A door in the far corner flew open and a latecomer, dressed in a long coat and carrying a box of champagne, burst into the room. This was clearly someone who hadn't bothered to observe the rule of using the outside entrance.

Screams of laughter greeted the newcomer's entrance. Cara took her advantage and skirted her way past the crowd to the door.

Bingo.

The staircase was dimly lit and narrow, but she easily made her way down the first few flights until she reached the first floor. There, she shrank back to avoid a couple of bustling waitresses exiting large swing doors to the left, expertly carrying plates of steaming food.

Making sure no other member of the café staff was waiting to use the swing doors, she carried on to the ground floor and found herself in the centre of the café, right next to the bar.

A young man pouring a bottle of lager into a glass spotted her. *'Je vous aider?'* he said, openly appraising her.

Not having a clue what he'd just said, she grappled for the right words in a language she hadn't spoken in over a decade. *'Un téléphone, s'il vous plaît?'*

'Un téléphone?'

'Oui. Je voudrais un taxi.' She couldn't hide the desperation from her voice. *'S'il vous plaît.'*

He appraised her a little longer than was necessary before nodding. *'Une minute,'* he said, then left the bar and walked to a table where four middle-aged men were loudly slurping coffee. They all turned to look at her.

'Hey, English,' one of them called to her.

'Irish,' she corrected, inching closer to them.

'Need taxi?'

She hesitated before nodding. She might be desperate to get out of this place but she'd heard every horror story going about single women getting lifts with strange men.

He pulled a wallet out of his back pocket and showed her his ID, proving he wasn't a mad axeman as her hackles feared. He was a taxi driver.

'You have money?' he asked, no doubt referring to her lack of a bag or clutch.

'It's at the house,' she said, thinking of her precious forty-eight euros. She gave him the name of the street where Pepe lived.

He looked her up and down, no doubt estimating the cost of her silk dress before inclining his head and getting to his feet. 'Wait here. I get car.'

She cast a nervous glance over her shoulder to the direction of the staircase. It wouldn't be long before Pepe noticed she was missing.

Actually, with all those women fawning all over him, it was likely he wouldn't notice she'd gone for hours. All the same, she didn't want to take the risk.

If she was to see him now, she had no idea how she would react.

'Is it okay to pay you when we get there?'

He slipped his jacket on and shrugged.

Taking the shrug as assent, she followed him out into

the cold night air, hugging her arms round her chest and wishing she'd had the chance to grab her wrap, which had been whisked away as soon as they'd walked into the loft. The taxi was parked around the corner, but she made no attempt to soak up her surroundings, her entire focus on getting back to Pepe's house, getting her passport and getting the hell out of there.

The journey back passed in a blur. The only thing she saw on the entire journey was those women's hands touching Pepe as if they owned him.

When they arrived on Pepe's street, she got the driver to crawl along until she recognised his distinctive red front door.

'Give me a minute to get my money,' she said, turning the handle. And then God knew what she would do. The fee was thirty euros.

To her disquiet, the driver also got out of the cab and followed her up the steps to the front door.

She rang the bell. And rang it again. Then banged on it. Then rang it again, all the while aware of the driver standing beside her impatiently.

She banged one last time before she remembered— Monique didn't work weekends. Pepe had told her just a few hours ago that she would be returning to her own home.

Despair was almost enough for Cara to hit her head against the unyielding door.

Eejit that she was, she'd run away to an empty house for which she didn't have a key.

Swallowing away the bile that had lodged in her throat, she tried to think. Nothing came. Her mind was a complete blank.

She didn't have a clue what to do.

'I can't get into the house.'

'I want my money.' The driver's tone was amiable enough but she detected the underlying menace in it.

'You'll get it.' She rubbed a hand down her face. 'Give me your address. I'll drop it over to you as soon as Pepe gets home and lets me in. I'll sign anything you want.'

'You don't pay?'

'I will pay. But I can't get into the house, so I can't get my purse.'

'You don't pay, I get police.'

'No, please.' Her voice rose. 'I promise, I will pay it. I promise. I'm not a blaggard.'

A meaty hand grabbed her shoulder. 'You pay or I call police.'

Her fear rising, she tried to shake him off. 'I *will* pay. Please don't call the police.'

His hand didn't budge other than to lock onto her biceps. 'Come, we go see police.'

'Get off me!' she cried. All the heat in her skin had been replaced by cold terror. The thought of being dragged into a police station and being accused of criminality was more than she could bear.

But the driver was clearly furious and had no intention of letting her go. Keeping a tight grip on her, he hauled her back down the steps to the cab.

Before she could open her lungs to scream for help, a large car sped around the corner, coming to a stop before them in a screech of brakes. The engine hadn't been turned off before Pepe jumped out of the passenger side and took long strides towards them.

'Take your hands off her *now*,' he barked, his anger palpable.

'She no pay,' the driver said, refusing to relinquish his hold, even though he'd turned puce at the sight of Pepe.

'I *said*, take your hands off her. *Maintenant!*'

Before Cara knew what was happening, the driver let her go and a slanging match between the two men erupted, all of it conducted in French, so she couldn't keep up. Her hands covering her mouth, she got the gist of it well enough.

If she weren't witnessing it with her own eyes, she would never have believed Pepe was capable of such fury. The menace came off him in waves of pumped-up testosterone, his face a contortion of wrath.

It ended with Pepe pulling a wad of notes from his pocket and throwing them at the driver with a string of words spat at him for good measure. A couple of the said words jumped out at her as she recalled how she and Grace had once made it their mission to learn every possible swear word in French. She was pretty sure Pepe had just used the very choicest of those words.

When he finally looked at her, the rage was still there. 'Get in the house,' he said tightly, sweeping past her and up the steps, unlocking the door.

'What the hell do you think you're playing at?' He slammed the door shut behind her.

'I'd forgotten Monique had the night off. Thanks for coming to my rescue.' Her breaths felt heavy, the words dredged up. She knew she should show proper gratitude towards him—if Pepe hadn't arrived when he did she would likely be bundled in the back of the taxi on her way to the nearest police station. But now they were safely ensconced in his home, her fright had abated a little but blood still pumped through her furiously. Forget the driver, all she could see were those overfamiliar women and Pepe's amused, arrogant self-entitlement as he accepted their attentions.

'I thought he was trying to rape you.'

'Well, he wasn't.' She was barely listening. She kicked

her crystal shoes off. 'He was trying to get me to a police station to have me arrested.'

'What did you run off for? You told me you were going to the bathroom! You humiliated me in front of my friends.'

'Oh, poor diddums,' she said, making no effort to hide her sarcasm. 'I couldn't stomach staying at that party a minute longer.' Turning, she hurried through the reception and up the spiral staircase.

'Are you feeling ill?' He kept pace easily. Too easily.

'Yes. I feel sick. Sick, sick, sick.' She practically ran to her room.

'Why didn't you say something instead of running off and leaving me like a fool waiting for your return?'

'Because *you're* the cause of my sickness. Now get lost.' Thus said, she slammed the door in his face.

Immediately he shoved it back open. 'What the hell do you think you're doing?'

'Leaving.'

Uncaring that he stood mere feet away, and uncaring that the dress she wore cost thousands of euros, she tugged it off and threw it onto the floor, unceremoniously followed by her matching designer bra and knickers. The clothing felt soiled, bought to satisfy his conscience.

'Like hell you are.'

'Like you can stop me.' Storming into the walk-in wardrobe filled with yet more clothing bought to satisfy his conscience, Cara rummaged through until she found the dress she'd worn to the christening. Her dress. Bought with *her* money.

In the back of her mind a voice piped up telling her to clad herself in as much of the designer clothing as she could before leaving. It would be something to sell online.

She ignored it. Sanity could go to hell. These expensive clothes, as beautiful as they were, made her feel cheap.

She found her original underwear, freshly laundered, and stepped into the knickers.

'Where are you going to go?'

'Home.'

'How are you going to get there? You don't have any money.'

She turned on him. 'I don't know!' she screamed. 'I don't know where I'm going to go or how I'm going to get there, but as long as I'm far away from you I don't care!'

'If you walk away you will never see me or my money again. Your child will grow up without a father. Is that what you want?'

'Why would I want our child to know *you* as its father? You'd be a lousy father just as mine was. Selfish.'

'I am *nothing* like your father.'

'So you keep saying and, do you know what, I think you're right. My father might be an utter scumbag but even he wouldn't hold his own baby hostage as you're doing.'

'I'm doing no such thing,' he said, his own voice rising, a scowl forming on his face. 'I'm trying my best under difficult circumstances to protect our child.'

'By holding your bank account and the promise of access to it over my head as a sick method of keeping me prisoner? That'll be a good story to tell the grandkids.'

'I will do whatever is necessary to ensure my child makes it into this world without coming to harm.'

'My child? Our child? So you're admitting paternity now, are you?'

'No!' He swore. At least she assumed he swore, given the word he spurted out in Italian contained real vehemence behind it. 'It was a slip of the tongue.'

'You're good at that,' she spat with as much vehemence as *she* could muster.

'And what do you mean by that?'

'Only that you must have slipped your tongue into half the women at that party tonight. How many of your exes were there? A dozen? More?'

His eyes glittered with fury before the visible anger that had seemed to swell in him dissipated a touch.

He leaned back against the wall and surveyed her. 'You're jealous.'

Her response was immediate and emphatic. 'Don't talk such rot.'

'You are.' He said it with such certainty she tightened her grip on the bra lest she punch him one.

'I am not jealous!' How dared he even suggest such a thing? Jealous because of *him*? 'I was humiliated. All those women acting as if they owned you, all pretty much spelling out what a great lay you are… Is it any wonder it made me feel sick?'

'See?' A half-smile played on his lips. 'I knew you were jealous.'

'For me to be jealous would mean I have to have feelings for you, and the only feelings I have for you are hate. Do you understand that, Pepe? I despise you.'

Turning her back on him, she stormed into her en suite and locked the door behind her.

She absolutely was not jealous.

No way.

For the first time she realised she'd been screaming at him with only her knickers on. Could her humiliation get any greater?

She tried to put the bra on but her hands shook so much she couldn't hook it together. And she'd left her stupid dress in the room.

Pepe banged on the door.

'Go away!' she screamed. 'Just leave me alone.'

'I'm not going anywhere.'

'Well, I'm not coming out until you're gone.'

'Then you'll be in there for a long time. For ever, if necessary. Because I am not going anywhere.' Now there was no amusement to be heard in his voice. Only a determined grimness.

Let him wait. Let him wait for ever. Let him…

Patience was clearly not Pepe's forte. 'You have exactly ten seconds to open this door or I will break it down. Ten.'

The fight began to seep from her. This was all too much. 'Please, Pepe, just leave me alone.'

'Eight.'

He was serious.

'Seven.'

The tears that had been fighting to break free for the past hour suddenly escaped. She could no more contain them than she could prevent him breaking the door down.

'Four.'

With salt water rushing down her cheeks like a mini waterfall and trembling hands, she unlocked the door and pulled it open.

CHAPTER TEN

ALL THE ANGRY emotion raging through Pepe's blood constricted when he saw Cara standing there sobbing, still clutching her bra, only her knickers on to protect her nakedness.

Something hot and sharp pierced through his chest.

Instinct and something deeper, something unquantifiable, made him close the gap between them and wrap his arms around her.

'Shh,' he whispered, resting his chin on her cloud of hair and raising his eyes to the ceiling. 'Please don't cry, *cucciola mia.*'

She didn't even attempt to fight, just clung to him and cried into his chest, sobs racking her frame. Her generous breasts compressed against him but for once he couldn't react to it. Cara's sobs hurt his heart too much for him to care about anything but soothing them away.

He'd spent the past five days doing his best to forget she was pregnant. He'd been so set on blocking it out that he'd completely failed to take *her* feelings into account. Cara was such a feisty woman it was easy to forget her vulnerabilities. But she was vulnerable. Pregnancy made her more so.

He remembered the first time he'd met her. It seemed so long ago that it could have been a different lifetime but in truth it had only been a few years. It was a few weeks before his brother had married Grace. Cara had gone to stay with them in the build-up to the wedding and Luca had talked him into going on a double date, pointing out Cara would feel like a gooseberry otherwise. As she was such an important part of his bride-to-be's life, Luca was determined Cara would find Mastrangelo hospitality second to none.

Pepe hadn't been impressed. He'd been used to strong, confident women; the only bit of vivacity he'd found on Cara had been the colour of her hair. Other than that, she'd been like a wallflower, practically gluing herself to Grace's side, talking to him and Luca only when spoken to and even then in monosyllables. He'd thought her surly and rude.

As the wedding had approached, slowly he'd seen a different side to her unfurl, until, by the day of the nuptials, when he had been best man and she the chief bridesmaid, she was happy to chat with him as easily as she could with Grace.

But no one else.

He'd come to realise she wasn't surly, just painfully shy. It took her a while to overcome her nerves with someone, but when she did, she was excellent company with a dry wit that delighted him. But…she'd been Grace's best friend. She would likely always be a part of his life. There was a vulnerability to her that none of his lovers had. Any attraction to her was quashed.

He would not involve himself with vulnerable women, no matter how sexy they were. All the same, he'd enjoyed her company, would happily return home to Sicily when she stayed there and go out on double dates. They always had the best of times together.

He'd known early on from Grace's disappearance that

Cara would hold the key to finding her. But he'd put it off. And put it off some more, always hoping Grace would turn up of her own accord or that Luca would find another clue to finding her. But as the months had passed with no word, he could not in all conscience stand idly by while his brother turned into an emotional wreck. So he'd swallowed that same conscience and sought Cara out. The one woman he'd sworn he would never seduce…

He'd spent the best weekend of his life with her.

He'd been haunted by memories of it ever since.

And now she was here, back in his arms. Her naked breasts crushed against him. Breasts that tasted like nectar…

His blood thrummed, deep and heavy, his senses reacting to the scent and feel of *her*, a primitive desire that came alive only for her.

He did not want to admit those brief moments of fear when he'd realised she'd gone from the party. Vanished into the night.

He did not want to think of the cold tightness that had clutched at his chest as he'd forced his driver to put his foot down through the dark Montmartre streets.

He did not want to think of his rage when he'd seen that oaf of a taxi driver manhandling her in such a callous manner.

Pepe despised violence. He'd grown up surrounded by it, not in his family, but in the associations his father had had until *he* had allowed his own conscience to lead him away from it.

Growing up, Pepe had vowed he would never allow his fists do the talking for him. Even when he'd felt the hot blade of the knife slice down his cheek he hadn't retaliated. He'd been so numb from the preceding events that it had almost been a relief to feel something.

Yet for all that, it had taken every ounce of restraint not to throw himself onto the taxi driver and pulverise him.

If that driver had hurt her in any way, he doubted he'd have been able to hold on to that restraint.

Cara had stilled. He could feel her breath, hot through the crisp linen of his shirt, tickling his skin.

'I...I need to put some clothes on,' Cara said, trying to break away. It was happening again, that almost liquid feeling in her bones, the slavish desire creeping through her every pore. She tried to pull away but Pepe was too strong.

'You're not going anywhere.'

She hated the thrill that surged through her at his unequivocal declaration.

All she could see were his women. Her head was crowded with them, all lined up and merrily waving at her, happy—proud even—to be used by him and, she had to admit, use him in return. There was no romance. Romance had nothing to do with Pepe's liaisons.

Eejit that she was, she'd once been proud of her immunity to him.

It had been one big fat lie cooked up by her pride because he had never shown the slightest bit of interest in her other than as a friend. He'd flirted with her the same way he'd flirted with every other woman on his radar, but not once had he tried it on. Not until he'd needed something from her.

She'd been *happy* believing his sexual ambivalence towards her was mutual. She'd felt *safe*. Look at the trouble she'd got herself into when she'd allowed herself to believe otherwise.

She didn't feel safe now. Not pressed against his broad frame with his arms wrapped around her so protectively, his hand snaking down her naked spine, marking her, his musky scent filling her senses…

Her tears had left her feeling raw. Exposed and hollow. Except the void inside her was filling with something else that she tried desperately to stop. Heat. Sweet, sweet heat that pushed the tormenting images away, until the only thing that filled her head and the hollow ache inside her was *him*.

'Those women meant nothing to me.' His gravelly tones whispered into her ear, his breath warm, sending tiny darts of pleasure skittling across her skin.

Her breath hitched. 'And I do?'

He clasped her cheeks with his big hands, tilting her head back so she was forced to look at him. His eyes were deep pools of lava.

'I don't know what you mean to me,' he said, his honesty stark. Brutal. 'You've been in my head for four months and I can't shift you from there. If I'd had the choice, I would have wanted more than one night with you. And you would have wanted more than one night with me.'

Before she had the chance to form a lie of denial, his head tilted and his lips moulded on hers.

Her response was stark and utterly shocking. All the sweet heat swirling inside her immediately converged into a pool of need so deep the intensity frightened her. It took all her strength not to react, not to move her lips in time with his.

She wanted to punch at him, but when she moved her hands to his shoulders to push him away, her fingers gripped onto him.

Pepe's lips cajoled and teased and still she resisted, fighting with the last of her will power until his tongue broke through the tight line of her lips and darted into the heat of her mouth.

Something inside her snapped.

Her grip on his shoulders tightened as she responded in kind, exploring his mouth and sensuous lips as if his kisses were the life raft to cling to, to stop her drowning.

His hands caressed away from her cheeks, one snaking round to gather her hair together and spear her scalp— she had no idea when it had escaped the confines of the tight chignon—the other making broad strokes down her back until it reached her bottom. He clasped it and pulled her tight to him so his arousal was stark against her belly.

Pure, undiluted heat rushed through to her core and an unwitting moan escaped from her throat.

'Cucciola mia,' Pepe groaned, breaking away to nip at her delicate earlobe. Unbelievably, he was already fired up enough to explode.

Thank God he was still dressed. If he'd been naked, he would have plunged into her the second that earthy moan had echoed into his senses.

Drums played loudly in his head, his heart thundering to the same rhythm.

The bed was only a few feet away but the distance could be as far as the moon.

Unwilling to break away from her delectable body for more than the fraction of a moment, he shuffled her to the bed then gently pushed her onto it so she was sitting on the edge.

'Don't move,' he ordered, drinking her in, her colour-heightened cheeks, her bottom lip plump and begging to be kissed, her green eyes bright and dilated, her breasts heavy and swollen, the pale nipples ruched.

'Sei bella,' he said thickly. And she was. Beautiful.

Jeez, his hands were trembling, his fingers and thumbs

disconnected from his brain, unable to work the buttons on his shirt.

Abandoning his quest to undress himself, he sank to his knees before her and gripped her hips, pulling her to him so she looked down at him.

There she sat, gazing at him with a heavy desire he recognised and which filled him with something that fizzed in his heated blood. Her fiery hair hung down and he reached for a lock of it, greedily inhaling the sweetness of its scent.

He straightened a little to kiss her again, gratified beyond measure when she responded in kind, kissing him back, her tongue playing with his, mimicking his actions while her small hands gripped his scalp.

He covered one of her breasts with the palm of his hand, thrilling to feel the soft weightiness of it, and rubbed his thumb over the nipple. Cara arched her back in response and dug her nails into his skull, deepening their kiss.

These kisses, no matter how delicious and rousing they were, were not nearly enough.

He wanted to see if she responded with the same wild abandon that had caused him to lose his head four months ago.

But first he wanted to taste *all* of her.

Trailing kisses down her neck, he reached her breasts and hungrily took one puckered nipple into his mouth.

She moaned and cradled his scalp some more, pushing him against her. Lavishing attention on her other breast, he then bent down lower, raining kisses over the softness of her rounded stomach and down to the black lace covering the heart of her.

Hooking the side of her knickers with his fingers, he tugged at them, looking back up at her as he pulled them down to her ankles. He could smell her arousal, a scent that hit him like an aphrodisiac cloud.

'Spread your legs.' Did that thick guttural voice really belong to him?

Colour heightened her cheeks and, for one heart-stopping moment, he thought she would refuse.

'Please,' she said through heavy breaths, 'turn out the light.'

He kissed her. 'It will be good. I promise.'

Understanding her shyness, he did as she requested, turning out the main light so the only illumination came from the landing, then returned to kneel before her.

He placed a hand on a trembling thigh. 'Lie back,' he said thickly.

She swallowed, before leaning back, her eyes not leaving his face until he gently pushed her thigh to one side.

Cara's eyes closed and her head rolled back, her chest rising and falling rapidly.

Moving the other thigh to expose her to his covetous eyes, he held her open to him. Even in the dim light he could see the moisture glistening from her, her arousal there for him to see, and as he pressed his mouth to the heart of her he was suddenly grateful to still be clothed. Unable to relieve his own tension meant there was no danger of embarrassing himself by coming too soon.

Dimly he remembered being on their hotel bed in Dublin and her refusal to let him go properly down on her. He'd placed a simple kiss between her spread legs before she'd pushed him away and clamped her thighs back together.

He hadn't pressed her on it, had simply thought she was as eager as he for him to be inside her. He'd never considered that she could be a virgin who had never been naked in front of a man.

Now he realised he'd got off lightly. If he'd been given a real taste of her arousal then, he doubted he would have slept in four months.

Cara's scent and taste should be bottled as an aphrodisiac.

Her tiny moans deepened and when his tongue found her clitoris she jerked and gasped, tried to move him off her.

'Relax,' he murmured, pressing a hand to her belly while slowly inserting a finger inside her. If he didn't already know how aroused she was, this would have proved it beyond doubt.

Relax? Oh, how desperately she wanted to. How Cara yearned to let herself go and lose herself in the wonders of what Pepe was doing to her, because it felt *so good.*

But she couldn't.

No matter how hard she concentrated on the magic of his tongue and fingers, no matter how much her body ached for release, the switch in her brain refused to turn off and just let go.

'Please, Pepe,' she murmured when she could not take any more. 'Make love to me.'

He looked up at her with hooded eyes, a wolfish grin spreading over his face. 'Say it again.'

'I want…'

He got to his feet. For one fearful moment she thought he was going to leave her there, exposed on so many levels.

Instead he unbuttoned his shirt, his movements deft. He cocked an eyebrow. 'You want…?'

She swallowed moisture away, staring dazedly at the magnificence of his body as he shrugged the shirt off and casually discarded it.

His trousers and underwear quickly followed, and all she could do was gaze at him with a catch in her throat.

Pepe's arousal was all too apparent, his erection jutting out in front of him, large and proud.

'You want?' he repeated, stepping between her still-parted legs. 'I want to hear you say it. I want to hear from your own lips that you want this.'

She understood why he was demanding this from her and in a way she couldn't blame him. Even if she did blame him it would make no difference. If he were to walk away right now the big deep pool she was swimming in would dissolve into a tiny puddle. 'I want this. *I want you.*'

His eyes glittered. 'Then you shall have me.'

He leaned down over her, barely touching her, the dark silky hair on his chest brushing against her sensitised breasts, tickling her. Slanting his lips on hers, he kissed her with a possessiveness that took her breath away, his hands kneading her thighs until he had her exactly where he wanted her.

And then he was inside, joyously, massively, deeply inside her, filling her completely.

'Ahh,' she moaned, pulling him down so his full weight was on her, adjusting herself slightly to accommodate him further, to allow him even deeper penetration.

Her body remembered the heights he'd taken her to before and, like a greedy child, was desperate to feel those same sensations again, to experience the same rippling pleasure that had blown her mind.

In and out he thrust, kissing her, squeezing her breasts, clutching her hips, penetrating to her very core until she felt everything inside her tighten.

As if he could sense that she was on the edge, Pepe

increased the tempo and ground even deeper into her. It was enough.

Her orgasm rippled through her in waves so powerful and beautiful that any form of coherence abandoned her and all she could do was ride it, catching every last swell.

Cara awoke with a jolt.

An arm was curved around her belly. Deep, heavy breathing sounded from the pillow beside her.

Swallowing, she opened her eyes.

Pepe was there beside her, fast asleep. Through the dusky light she gazed at the thick black lashes, the dark stubble across his jawline, the mussed hair, the trimmed goatee.

Her heart constricted then began to hammer. She swallowed again.

After they had made love for a second time, Pepe had gathered her into his arms and fallen asleep with her head resting on his chest. Sleep had come easily for him.

She, on the other hand, had lain awake for an age. She'd disentangled herself from his arms knowing she should wake him and insist he return to his own room. Instead she'd found herself gazing at him, much as she was staring at him now. He was just so beautiful, even in repose with his mouth slightly parted, that firm yet sensuous mouth that had brought her such pleasure.

In this ethereal morning light she couldn't find the energy to rebuke herself for being so stupid as to fall back into his bed.

Recriminations could wait.

All she could focus on at that moment was that sensual mouth.

Slowly she brought her face to his, close enough to feel his breath against her skin. Closing her eyes, she brought her lips to his, breathing him in. She raised a hand to his face and gently traced her fingers down his cheek and down the strength of his neck and over his broad shoulders. It amazed her that a body so hard could be covered with skin so smooth.

Slowly she explored him, dragging her fingers through the silky hair on his chest, circling the dark brown nipples, then tracing down the flat hardness of his belly. Her pale hand contrasted against the darkness of his olive skin. They were a couple full of contrasts, her yin to his yang.

Not that they were a couple, she reminded herself hastily. They were simply two individuals thrown together by circumstances with a chemistry that refused to be denied. If not for the life growing inside her, Cara would not be here. Pepe would likely not be here either, or if he was it would be in the arms of another.

Her stomach curdled at the thought and she squeezed her eyes shut to banish it.

Was that what her mother had done? How many times had *she* squeezed her eyes shut to banish the pictures of her husband with his other women?

Before the images could swamp her, Pepe's eyes opened and fixed on her, bringing her back to the here and now.

'You stopped,' he murmured, his voice thick with sleep. She hadn't realised her hand had stopped its exploration until he enfolded it with his own.

All memories dissolved as he pulled her down for a kiss, breathing in heavily.

Returning it, she closed her eyes and allowed him to guide her hand down to the thick mass of hair on his groin and the erection that had sprung from it.

Tentatively she encircled it, heat surging through her

as she felt its silky weight and length, felt it throb beneath her touch. When she rubbed her thumb over the tip she discovered the bead of moisture already there and felt a thrill like no other that this was for her. Even if it was only for now.

CHAPTER ELEVEN

WINTER SUN SHONE brilliantly through a gap in the heavy drapes right in Cara's eyes, waking her. She turned her head. Pepe had gone.

On legs that felt weighted, she climbed out of bed and padded over to the window, pulling the drapes open.

The room smelt of a familiar scent that she recognised from four months earlier. Sex. Their sex.

Air. That was what she needed. And plenty of it.

Firstly wrapping herself in the kimono, she unlocked the French door and stepped out onto the small balcony overlooking a large park.

The cold air hit her and she accepted it into her lungs, willing the frigid particles to douse her shame.

It did nothing of the sort.

She knew she didn't deserve to have her shame extinguished.

After everything she had been through and all the promises she had made her unborn child, she was no better than her mother.

Every time one of her father's affairs had come to light, which was a regular occurrence, her mother would vow to leave. Every time she changed her mind, too hooked on the highs and lows of her marriage to care about anything as basic as self-respect. Certainly too hooked to care about the effect it was having on her only child.

Her mother had been an addict. Her husband had been her fix. Not even his litter of illegitimates had made any difference.

And now here Cara was, well over a decade after her parents' marriage had finally done them all a favour and disintegrated, and she knew that unless she did something right now she would turn into an addict just as her mother had been.

Movement behind her caused her to turn.

Pepe stepped onto the balcony carrying two steaming mugs and wearing only a pair of faded jeans. There was something about seeing his feet bare that tugged at her in a manner that was entirely different from the effect his bare torso had on her.

'Good morning, *cucciola mia*,' he said with a lazy grin, handing her one of the mugs. Placing his own mug on the small table, he stood behind her and wrapped his arms around her waist, nuzzling into her neck.

'Please, don't,' she murmured, shaking her head. 'One accident with scalding tea is enough for anyone in a lifetime.'

He chuckled. 'In that case, drink up and we can go back to bed.'

She took a deep breath, planning to confess that she didn't want to go back to bed. Or, rather, that she did want to go back to bed with him. But she wanted it too much. That was the problem. She wanted it far too much.

Before she could speak he pressed a kiss into the small of her back then stood beside her at the balustrade.

'I owe you an apology,' he said, his light tone becoming serious. 'I'd forgotten how shy you are around strangers. I shouldn't have left you alone with anyone but me last night, not until I knew you were comfortable with them.'

Cara blinked in shock.

An apology was the last thing she'd expected to hear from Pepe's mouth.

She took a sip of her tea, determinedly looking out to the park, at the distant people walking their dogs, some carrying the morning's newspapers, life going on blithely regardless of her personal torment.

'I also should have warned you that a few of my ex-lovers would be there, but to be honest I never gave it a thought,' he continued. 'It's never been an issue. I should have taken into account that you are made from a different mould from them.'

The mention of his *ex-lovers* pierced like a lance into her skin. She forced herself to breathe, focusing on the park before her, allowing her attention to be captured by a young couple out for a bike ride, a toddler-sized child sitting in a special seat attached to the father's bike.

Pepe would never be a father in the traditional sense. He was too…free. Meeting his friends and the casual, bohemian intimacy they all shared had only confirmed everything she already knew.

And she, Cara, was of a *different mould*.

It hurt to admit it, but he was right. She could never be like those women. The scars of her childhood ran too deep. She could never share the man she loved. Just thinking of Pepe sharing intimacies with another woman made her skin go clammy and nausea swell inside her, and she didn't even love him.

Did she?

No, of course she didn't. Pepe might be able to reduce her to a quivering pulse of sensation but that didn't mean she was falling in actual love with him.

Did it?

'I need to leave,' she said, blurting the words out.

Whatever her feelings for him and whatever they meant, nothing could come of them.

Pepe stilled then cast an unreadable eye on her before getting his coffee. When he rejoined her at the balustrade he stood a good foot away from her.

'I'm going to appeal to your better nature to do the right thing and give me some money now so I can return to Dublin and find a home to raise our child in.'

'And if I don't?'

'Then I guess I'll have no choice but to stay. I know I was going to leave last night but I was so…' she almost said *devastated* '…upset that I wasn't thinking straight. I guess my hormones were playing up too, making every-thing seem ten times worse than it really was.'

Her hormones had had nothing to do with it. The white-hot jealousy she had experienced at the party had been all her own. She would rather chop her own ears off than admit it.

She took a deep breath before continuing. 'Even if I had been able to leave last night I would probably have come back like a dog with its tail between its legs. Noth-ing's changed. I'm still skint. My return ticket from Sicily is worthless here, so I have no way to get home until my wages from the auction house get paid into my account. But, Pepe, I can't stay here, especially not now.'

For the first time since joining Cara on the balcony, Pepe felt the chill of the air. He stared ahead at a young family who had been enjoying a bike ride. The parents had now dismounted and rested their bikes against a large tree, the father in the process of getting the toddler out of its seat.

Once he had dreamt of him and Luisa having such a family, had allowed his hopes and dreams to fill.

'Why are you so keen to get away from me?' he asked bitingly. 'Did I not satisfy you enough last night?'

'No, it was wonderful,' she said wistfully.

'Then what is the problem with staying here and sharing my bed?'

'Because we both know it won't be for ever. Chances are you'll be sharing it with someone else long before our baby is born.'

Imagining someone else in his bed drew a blank. It had drawn a blank since Dublin.

Until he and Cara were able to work through this strange desire that burned between them, he had the most sickening feeling he would never be able to move on.

'And what about you?' he asked more harshly than he would have liked. Something akin to panic was nibbling at his chest. 'How do I know you'll take care of yourself? How do I know you'll do what's right and what's best for the life inside you?'

He heard her take a sharp inhalation, but when she finally spoke her tone was a lot softer than he had been prepared for. 'What happened, Pepe? What happened to turn you into such a cynic that you believe me capable of harming our defenceless child?'

'Because it's happened to me before.'

He could feel Cara's eyes on him, could feel her shock. He kept his own eyes firmly fixed on the family in the distance. He had no idea where the parents had produced a ball from, but they were playing a game of what looked to be catch with their small toddler.

'I've not always been a cynic. I once believed in love and marriage. I was going to marry my childhood sweetheart.' He wasn't aware of the pained sneer that crossed his face. 'Once, just once, we failed to use contraception and Luisa fell pregnant. I was eighteen and she was seventeen.'

He could feel Cara's eyes still resting on him, took a small crumb of comfort that she didn't immediately start peppering him with questions.

His throat felt constricted. This was something he had never discussed before, not with Luca, not with anyone. But he owed Cara the truth, because somewhere, hidden deep inside him, was the knowledge that it *was* his baby she carried, a truth he dared not utter in case, by saying the words, it brought the whole thing crashing down.

'I was delighted at the prospect of becoming a father. I was...' He shook his head at the memory. 'At the time, my head was all over the place. My father had just died from a heart attack and I didn't know how to handle it. But then Luisa told me she was pregnant and suddenly there was proof that life *did* have meaning and that miracles did occur. Luisa and I had spoken of marriage many times and, to me, it made sense to just bring the whole thing forward. I wanted our child to be born a Mastrangelo with parents who shared the same name.'

Trying to collect his thoughts, he finished his now cold and tasteless coffee and finally allowed himself to look at Cara.

She stood with her back to the balustrade, her arms folded across her chest, staring at him.

His heart expanded to see the paleness of her cheeks and the undeniable apprehension ringing in her green eyes.

'I thought Luisa was happy too but as the weeks passed she became more and more withdrawn, refusing to let me tell my family or her family about the baby until the time was right. And then, the morning after the first scan, the day she had agreed we could tell the world of our joy, she confessed that she'd had a one-night stand. She'd slept with someone else while I'd visited Luca at his university for a weekend.' Now he didn't bother hiding his bitterness. 'She and her lover had forgotten to use contraception. She was so terrified I would find out she engineered things so that days later we too got so carried away we forgot to use contraception. That way, if she fell pregnant, she could pass the child off as mine.'

A low whistle escaped from Cara's lips. There was no apprehension in her eyes now. Only compassion. Which somehow made him feel worse.

'The only reason she confessed was because she couldn't live with the guilt.'

'What did you do?' Cara breathed.

He laughed cynically and shook his head. 'I said I didn't care. I told her it didn't matter. I told her I loved her enough that I would raise the child as my own even if there was doubt that it was mine. But that was a lie—it wasn't *her* I loved enough to do that for, it was my unborn child. Because that baby was *mine*. I had already committed my heart to it. I had pictured the boy or girl it would be, the teenager he or she would grow into. I had pictured walking my daughter down the aisle and I had imagined my grown son asking me to be his best man.'

Long-buried unspoken memories threatened to choke him but Pepe forced himself to finish his sordid story. 'At first she agreed. Then, a couple of weeks later, when she was fifteen weeks pregnant, she went away for a weekend to visit an aunt. That too was a lie. She had in fact gone to the UK for an abortion. Her lover—who, it transpired, she was still seeing—had given her the money to pay for it all.'

Silence hung between them, the air thick and heavy.

'Dear God,' Cara whispered. 'I am so sorry.'

'Sorry for what?' he snarled, his attempts to keep a leash on his emotions snapping. 'That I was deceived? That I was stupid enough to want to be cuckolded and by Francesco Calvetti of all people...'

'*He* was her lover?'

'You know him?'

She shook her head and curled her lip in distaste. 'I know *of* him.'

Of course she did. Luca, his brother, had gone into business with the bastard, an association that had recently ended. Grace, his sister-in-law, despised the man. 'When we were kids our parents used to force us to play together. He and my brother were once good friends.'

Cara placed a tentative hand on his arm. He guessed it was supposed to be a comforting gesture, but at that moment comfort was the last thing he needed. He felt too unhinged for that. Spilling his guts for the very first time was not the catharsis people claimed.

He especially didn't want comfort from her, the woman who made him feel more unhinged than he had felt in fifteen years.

Enfolding her hand, he raised it to his cheek and placed it on his scar. 'Luisa gave me this scar. I was so angry at what she'd done, I called her every nasty, vindictive and demeaning name I could think of. In return she slashed me with a knife from her mother's kitchen. I've kept the scar as a reminder never to trust.'

Cara's eyes were huge and filled with something that looked suspiciously like tears.

He dropped her hand. 'So now you know it all. I hope

you can now understand why I do not trust people and why I cannot give you the money you want, not until after our baby is born. It's not personal towards you. Please believe that.'

Cara dressed mechanically in a blue skirt, black roll-neck jumper and a pair of thick black tights, and tied her hair back into a loose ponytail. Her hands shook, her mind filled with him, with Pepe.

After their talk on the balcony he had disappeared, muttering about needing a swim. Wordlessly she had let him go, too shocked and heartsick at his story to even attempt to stop him.

Her heart stopped when she found him in the kitchen eating a *pain au chocolat*. He'd added a black T-shirt to his jeans, his black hair was damp and he'd had a shave.

He lifted his eyes to see her standing hesitantly in the doorway, and got to his feet. 'Please, help yourself,' he said, indicating the plate heaped with pastries in the centre of the table. 'I've made a pot of tea for you.'

Knowing he had gone out of his way to make the tea especially for her kick-started her heart. When he moved with fluid grace to pour a cup out for her and she spotted his bare feet, she had to blink back the sting of hot tears that burned in the backs of her eyes.

She reached for a plain croissant and placed it on the plate he'd laid out for her, then took the seat next to him. She broke a bit of it off and popped it into her mouth, all the while watching as he added milk to her cup before placing it before her.

'Thank you,' she whispered, breaking off another piece of croissant and nibbling at it. She wanted to touch him. She wanted to place her hands on his cheeks and kiss him.

'Do you know what I love the most about Grace?' she asked him when he'd sat back down.

He cocked an eye.

'Nothing. I love *everything* about her. When I moved to England at thirteen and started a new school, I was cold-shouldered by practically everyone. They all had their cliques. I was the outsider. But Grace took me under her wing. She would drag me into the art room at lunch breaks. She would drag me to parties at weekends and stay right by my side, making sure everyone included me. She introduced me to art. Even when it was obvious that I couldn't draw much more than matchstick men, she never put me down. I ended up practically moving into her home. She encouraged me to study History of Art at university because she could see that's where my passion lay. We studied different courses but we lived together and remained inseparable. I would give my life for Grace. She was more than a best friend. She was the one person who believed in me. My parents were so wrapped up in themselves they didn't care about me other than on the level of feeding and clothing me.'

Cara kept her gaze on Pepe as she spoke. If he could lay his soul bare then so could she.

'My father had so many affairs I lost count. Time after time, Mam would say she was leaving but every time she forgave him.' She shuddered. 'I would hear them having make-up sex. It was the most disgusting sound I've ever heard. Do you know what the worst part was?'

He shook his head, his face a mask.

'*He* left *her*. After all the affairs, the lies and the humiliation, one day he went to work and never came back. He'd found a teenage lover who "made him feel like a young man again". My mother was utterly devastated. I don't think she would ever have left him. She held on for two years in the hope that he would come back to her, but when he served her with divorce papers she finally accepted it was over and carted me off to England to start over.'

She popped the last of the croissant into her mouth. Unable to resist any longer, she stroked a hand down his smooth cheek and rubbed her thumb over the thick bristles on his chin. His deep blue eyes, which hadn't left her face, dilated, and his chest rose.

'Not long after we arrived in England, my mam started a new relationship with a man who was just like my dad. An unfaithful charmer. Everyone loves him but he is incapable of keeping his pecker in his trousers. And just like with my dad, she forgives him every time. I've spent my entire life feeling second best to my parents' libidos and hormones, and I'm terrified of turning out like them. Our child will *never* feel second best. Ever. I won't let it happen. Our child is innocent and deserves all the love I—and hopefully you—can heap on him or her.' She bit her lip. 'But, Pepe, I'm so *scared.*'

'Scared of what?'

'You,' she answered starkly. 'Until I met you, sex to me was tawdry and meant nothing but power and humiliation. I wanted none of it. But now I can understand why my mam let my dad treat her like a piece of rubbish and why she lets my stepdad treat her the same way, because I can feel it happening inside me when I'm with you. I woke up this morning and I knew I should leave but I was almost helpless to resist you. I'm scared that if I stay much longer I'll never want to go.'

CHAPTER TWELVE

PEPE COVERED CARA'S HAND, his eyes boring into her. 'Do you think you're falling in love with me?'

'No!' Her denial was immediate. Snatching her hand away, she wrung her fingers together on her lap and looked away.

'Good.'

She flinched.

He placed a finger under her chin and forced her to look up at him. 'I say "good" because there is a way to get through this without screwing either of us up. And without screwing up our child. I have never cheated on anyone in my life. After what Luisa did to me, it is not something I would ever put anyone else through. I like my affairs short and sweet. I admit, there are occasions when I will sleep with an ex, but never if either of us are involved with someone else.'

Pepe watched as she bit into her bottom lip. Learning the full truth of Cara's past explained so many things about her. His complaints about his own childhood seemed unbelievably petty in comparison. He'd never doubted his family's love for him.

'I have a proposal for you,' he said, thinking aloud. 'Will you hear me out?'

With obvious apprehension, she jerked her head.

'Let's see if we can make this work. We don't love each other but we do have a serious case of lust. Eventually it will work its way out of our systems.'

'Do you think?' She looked so hopeful he felt an incomprehensible stab of pain in his chest.

He nodded. 'For as long as we're together I can promise you exclusivity. Your mother lived in a vicious cycle of high emotion and denial, neither of which applies to us. We'll take it all one day at a time. When our desire for each other reaches its natural conclusion, we can go our separate ways—and hopefully we can go our separate ways as friends. We both want what's best for our child and that's for him or her to have parents who respect each other and can work together for their child's happiness. Our child will have two parents who are happy in themselves and have no antagonism towards the other.'

'So you do believe the baby is yours?'

He closed his eyes before inclining his head. 'Yes, *cucciola mia*. I believe the baby is mine.'

Pepe waited for a beat, just in case the world did come crashing down.

'Forgive me. Not trusting people is so hardwired into me that when you told me you were pregnant I went into denial. I think maybe I lost my head a little.'

'Make that a lot,' she said with a smile that lightened her features and lifted his spirits.

Cara was not Luisa. If there was one thing he knew about his flame-haired lover it was that she didn't have a selfish bone in her body. He could not in all good conscience make her continue to pay for Luisa's sins. And nor could he allow his child to pay.

His child.

He really was going to be a father.

His chest swelled with an emotion so pure it pushed all the oxygen from his lungs.

His child.

Their child.

'I think we should both promise to give this…thing a minimum of a fortnight to at least try and make it work.'

'No more being kept as a prisoner?'

'You are free to come and go as you please—I'll even give you your own set of keys. See, I *am* trying.'

'Very,' she agreed with a straight face.

He tapped her snub nose playfully, his spirits lifting even further. This could really work…

'If you give me your bank details I will deposit a sum of money into it which should go some way to recompensing you for your future loss of earnings with the auction house.'

'You do believe I'm not after your money?' she asked, suddenly looking anxious. 'All I want is for our child to be provided for.'

'And it will be,' he promised. Now that he had openly acknowledged his paternity it felt as if a great weight had lifted from him.

Deep inside, he had always known the truth. Cara was too…straight to tell anything but the most innocuous of lies. It was his own damaged pride that had refused to believe it.

A wave of something that felt suspiciously like guilt rolled into his guts.

He'd done the best he could, he told himself defiantly. Anyone who walked in his shoes would have reacted in the same way.

All the same, he knew he would have to go a long way to make it up to her.

And he knew the best way to start.

Reaching for her hips, he pulled her so she was sitting astride him.

'What are you doing?' she asked with a gasp.

'Celebrating our agreement.' Thus said, he tilted his head and kissed her.

'So this is how we celebrate?' she said when they finally came up for air.

He nuzzled into her neck, marvelling at the softness and the oh-so-heady scent. He was reminded of the way she had tasted on his tongue, could almost taste it anew. 'Can you think of a better way?'

She tilted her head back to give him better access and sighed. 'No. Nothing better. This is perfect.'

A fortnight came and went. It didn't even cross Cara's mind to leave.

Now that she was no longer a prisoner, life in general improved considerably. She could come and go as she pleased. She spent hours wandering around Paris's famous museums and galleries, including three days back-to-back at the Louvre, and spent many a happy lunch doing nothing but hanging out in Parisian cafés drinking hot chocolate.

Her personal belongings, including all her beloved art and history books, had finally been shipped over from Dublin and she had a marvellous time going through all her stuff. Most of it was put back in the boxes—she reminded herself on a daily basis that this was only a temporary arrangement and that it would not do to start thinking of it as permanent.

All the same, life with Pepe was good. More than good. Now that they had reached an understanding, all the antagonism had died. She knew that whatever happened between them, their child would not suffer for it.

He treated her like a princess. They'd gone for her twenty-week scan together, and to witness the adoration on his face was almost as thrilling as seeing her baby for herself. The money he'd put into her account—an amount that, if she were a cartoon character, would have made her eyes pop out of her head—had been happily spent that morning on baby furniture and other paraphernalia, with more than a little change left over. It was all now being stored in Pepe's humongous garage alongside his fleet of sports cars.

And now, back at the house, they were having a swim together in Pepe's underground luxury pool. Or, rather, she was lazing in the shallow end watching him swim lengths. He sped through the water like a porpoise, his strokes long and practised. There was something rather hypnotic about watching him, she mused. Who needed a book when one could watch Pepe?

After she'd counted him do approximately fifty lengths, he waded over to her, a large grin on his face. 'You should swim, lazybones.'

'I was admiring the view.'

His grin broadened and he swooped in for a kiss.

'Hmm,' she sighed, greedily kissing him back. It never ceased to amaze her how much Pepe wanted her. Or how much she wanted him. Already she could feel the stir of an erection in his swimming shorts, rubbing against her thigh.

'I've been thinking,' she said as he nuzzled into her neck, 'that I should really look at getting a driver's licence for when the baby's born.'

He stilled a touch. 'I can provide you with a car and a driver.'

'I'm sure you can,' she agreed drily. 'But it would be

nice to have the freedom to just…go, when the mood takes me.'

She had to think practically. She just had to. Thinking in detail about her and their baby's future kept her silly emotions in check. And if ever her stomach rolled at the thought of their future being without Pepe, she quashed it. After all, Pepe would always be an enormous part of their lives; they'd just be living under different roofs.

For the time being, things between them were magical, but she would *not* allow herself to think it could last for ever. Pepe didn't do for ever.

'Have you thought about where you'll want to live with the baby?' he asked, reading her mind.

'I was thinking maybe here in Paris,' she admitted. In the month they'd been together she'd travelled with him to his homes in Portugal and Spain. Of all the places Pepe called home, Paris was her favourite. There was something so wonderful about the city, the bustle, the chic women, the architecture, the art. Wandering the streets always evoked a feeling of contentment that was only surpassed at night when she would lie sated, wrapped in his arms, drifting off to sleep.

'Really? That's a great idea.' And it *was* a great idea, Pepe told himself. His stomach hadn't really cramped at the thought of Cara and their baby living away from him.

'It just makes sense, especially as this house is going to become your main base. It'll make it easier for the baby to be living in the same city as her mam and dad.'

He forced a smile. 'I was thinking of turning your old room into a nursery.'

'An excellent idea. You'll be right next to him or her then.' Her face scrunched. 'You'll have to move my boxes into another room though, at least until I move out.'

'Not a problem.' For practicality, they'd moved her

clothes and toiletries into his room, but all her other stuff was still in her old room, still in boxes from when he'd had it flown over from Dublin.

Cara was saying words that should have been balm to his ears. She'd not developed feelings for him that ran beyond a sexual level, and nor had she dropped any hints, subtle or otherwise, about making things between them permanent. Everything was proceeding exactly as planned. He was positive that any day soon his lust for her would start to abate. Any day.

So why did the thought of her living under a different roof from him make his chest feel so tight? Why did the thought of living without her make it hard to breathe?

After a long weekend in Sicily with Pepe's family, spent hanging out with Grace and deflecting her friend's worries about Cara and Pepe's relationship, Pepe left for a week-long trip to Chile, a distance they'd agreed was too far for her pregnant self to accompany him.

Alone in the house, Cara's mind kept drifting back to the talk she'd had with Grace, when her friend had tentatively voiced her concerns.

'Cara, you do know Pepe isn't a man for the long term? It's just that there's been no mention of marriage or anything—'

'Of course it's not permanent,' Cara had interrupted. 'We're just taking it a day at a time until it runs its course.'

'Do you know what you're doing?' Grace had asked with a furrowed brow.

'Of course I do,' she'd said defiantly. 'I'm getting to know my child's father properly. We're not going to have some fake marriage for the sake of the baby which only ends in misery for everyone. When our relationship runs its course we'll still be friends, which will only benefit our child. We don't want him or her being born into a war zone.'

She'd ignored her friend's worried face, pushed the image away now as she cast her eye around the huge space that was Pepe's living room.

Before leaving for Chile he had taken her to the huge vault storing his infamous art collection. 'I'm putting the hanging and placement of my collection in your hands,' he'd said solemnly.

Cara had been incredibly touched.

Pepe had left his multimillion-euro art collection in *her* hands, giving her carte blanche to hang and place them in his home as she saw fit. Trusting her.

Deciding where to place it all, overseeing the hanging— he'd insisted on getting professionals in because he didn't want her having to climb up and down stepladders when she was six months pregnant—had fulfilled her more than she had thought possible. It had been a project and a half, and one she had embraced with all the Irish enthusiasm that flowed in her blood.

Pepe had such an amazing and eclectic eye for art. Among the Old Masters were more modern pieces, including several by Georges Ramirez, one of which was a nude bronze whose torso she would recognise with her eyes closed using only her hands. The face was a blank but she would bet Pepe had been the model for it.

The only piece she disliked was the Canaletto. It brought back too many bad memories, serving as a reminder that Pepe could be ruthless when it came to getting what he wanted. She'd stuck that particular painting in a small guest room, all two million euros of it.

'Cara?'

Pepe's deep voice rang out from downstairs.

Quashing the urge to skip down the stairs to greet him, Cara forced her legs to move in a more sedate fashion.

'I'm right here,' she said, unable to hide the beam that spread over her face at the sight of him. It was the longest they had been apart and, despite the task he'd set her, she'd missed him dreadfully. Especially at night. The bed had felt empty without him. She would never admit it, lest he read too much into it, but on the second night she had given in and borrowed one of his shirts to sleep in.

After a long, knee-trembling kiss from him, she took his hand to give him the tour.

'Wow,' he said with open admiration as they stood in the main living area. 'You really know your stuff.'

Pepe was the first to admit he didn't know the first thing about art. The pieces he bought were never about investment—although that played a part in it—but were simply pieces that caught his eye and pulled at him.

Cara's own eye had placed them all exactly where they should be, the items selected for each room complementing the feel and décor of that particular room.

He'd smiled to see the portrait his sister-in-law had done of him hanging on the wall of his office. Grace had painted him as a Greek god but with a definite touch of irony and not a little humour.

'Are you happy to have that there, where anyone can see it?' Cara said, indicating the bronze by Georges Ramirez, which she had placed in the corner of the living room.

'You recognise it?' he asked wickedly.

'Of course I do,' she said with a frown.

With a jolt he realised she'd been living with him for two months. She knew him far more intimately than any other living person.

When, he wondered, would her allure no longer affect him?

He'd assumed they'd stay together for a few weeks, maybe a month, before he'd get her out of his system. He'd suggested a minimum of a fortnight, more to convey his sincerity in wanting to make things work between them than in any real hope.

Two months on and they were still together and he wanted her every bit as much as he had at the beginning. More so, if that was possible.

'Have you considered doing this professionally?' he asked, waving his hands around the room. 'I know plenty of people who would pay a small fortune to have their art collections displayed to their very best.'

'Not really,' she said with a shrug. 'Before Grace married Luca we often said we'd like to open our own gallery— she'd do all the art and I'd run it. But life takes over. I was very happy at the auction house.'

'Speaking of galleries, we've got a few hours to kill before we go to the exhibition tonight,' he said, referring to the opening of an up-and-coming new artist's work he'd promised they would attend. 'Shall we go for a swim?'

She pulled a face. 'My bikini line hasn't been done for weeks.'

'So? It's only me who's going to be looking.' He would be doing a lot more than looking. He'd be doing a lot more right now but for Monique bustling around in the kitchen, liable to barge into the living room at any moment.

A whole week without Cara had felt interminably long.

'I'd still feel self-conscious.'

'I can do it for you.'

Cara didn't trust the gleam that came into Pepe's eyes. 'Do what?'

'Your bikini line.'

'No way.'

'Why not?'

'Because…' Because she still wasn't comfortable with him being *down there*. Blame it on her Catholic upbringing—which was an irony in itself—or blame it on her reaching the grand old age of twenty-six before getting naked with a man, but, whatever the reason, she had a hang-up about her nether regions. Not Pepe's though. She adored *his* nether regions.

He arched an eyebrow. 'Because?'

She was stumped for a good answer.

She was still stumped for a good answer fifteen minutes later, sitting naked on a towel on the sofa in Pepe's bedroom.

'Relax, *cucciola mia*,' he purred, kneeling before her, having placed a jug of hot water on the floor beside him. He also carried a couple of razors and a tube of shaving gel. To make her feel less self-conscious he'd stripped off too. Or so he'd said.

'I need you to spread your legs,' he said, pouring some gel onto his palm.

Swallowing, she did as she was bid and parted her thighs.

'Further.'

She took a deep breath and exposed herself to him, resting her head back in a futile attempt to do as he'd suggested and *relax*.

'I won't hurt you,' he said with the utmost sincerity, before planting a kiss on her inner thigh. 'Trust me.'

Mixing the gel on his palm with a couple of droplets of the hot water, he rubbed his hands together to form a lather, then carefully swiped it over her bikini line, taking great care around the delicate area.

She closed her eyes. Happy to wax her legs, she'd always drawn the line at waxing her bikini area, preferring the less painful route of shaving.

Never in a million years would she have believed she'd allow someone else to do it for her.

When she finally dared look, she found his head bowed in concentration.

Trust me, he'd said.

With a jolt of her heart she realised that she *did* trust him.

She trusted him as she'd never trusted anyone other than Grace.

But this was a different form of trust. This was a deeper, more intimate trust, a trust she'd never expected to find with a man, with anyone.

'Okay?' Pepe's dark blue eyes were looking up at her.

She nodded and gave a half-smile. Her legs and torso were no longer tensed; indeed, her entire body had now relaxed.

'What do you think about Charlotte for a girl?' she said.

He looked up briefly, his lips pursing the way they always did when he was considering something. They'd already agreed on Pietro for a boy, in honour of Pepe's father. Choosing a girl's name had proved trickier. At first she'd thought he was being deliberately awkward when he dismissed the names she kept coming up with... until the penny dropped that he was, in his own subtle fashion, trying to avoid naming their child after any of his ex-lovers. Not all the names, thank God. A few he dismissed for other reasons, like thinking a particular name was 'wet'.

She'd now taken to throwing a name at him, watching him purse his lips and then shake his head, all the while hoping she never came across one of his 'friends' who shared that particular name.

This time, there was no shake of the head. Instead, a broad grin spread across his handsome face. 'That is perfect.' He nodded, still grinning. 'Charlotte Mastrangelo-Delaney. *Sì*—perfect.'

When he refocused his attention to his current handiwork, Cara tried to shake away the jealousy coursing through her blood, knowing she was being irrational. So what if Pepe had been prepared to marry Luisa so they and their child could all share the same surname? In those days he'd been little older than a child himself with romantic ideals that had no place in the real world.

Cara and Pepe had reached the perfect compromise when it came to naming their child, both reasoning that it wasn't his baby, or her baby, but *their* baby, and therefore should share both their names.

At least he was capable of compromise. Most of the time. He still had an unerring ability to get his own way on most things. Like now.

Before much more time elapsed, he leaned back and flashed a grin. 'See—that wasn't too bad, was it?'

'It was fine.'

'Stay where you are—I need to get some fresh water to clean you up.'

She watched him stride off to the en suite, not in the least bothered about his nudity, with a lump in her throat. No wonder so many artists clamoured to immortalise him in whatever medium they used. Pepe's strength and poise, mixed with his underlying good humour, were like nectar to a bee.

He returned with a fresh jug of water and a towel.

This time he didn't have to ask her to part her legs.

'Have you done this lots of times?' she asked, then

immediately castigated herself. His answer had the potential to lance her.

His eyes met hers, glittering with something she didn't recognise. 'Never.'

Her heart hitched.

For long moments neither moved. She wished she could read what was swirling in his eyes, but before she could catch it, he broke the hold.

Bowing his head, he placed a kiss on the area he'd just shaved. Then another kiss. And another.

His movements were so gentle and…reverential, that as he made his way to the very heart of her she forgot to feel embarrassed, lying back to rest her head on the back of the sofa and simply *feel*.

Pepe was such a wonderful lover, she thought dreamily. So tender yet so fantastically wild, and always wanting her. She remembered how he'd arrived back from an overnight stay in Germany. Within five minutes of getting home he'd had her bent over on the desk in his study. She'd been so desperate for him too that they'd been like a pair of rutting animals.

Heat from these gorgeous memories pooled into her core right at the moment Pepe found her clitoris. She moaned.

Her mind drifted off, her body a haze of sensation all circling around what this wonderful man was doing to her.

Oh, how she loved him. With every fibre of her being.

And as this realisation filled her, the pulsations that had been building inside filled too, and, with a cry, she felt the pulsations explode, rippling out of her in one long, continuous wave of sensation.

When she opened her eyes, Pepe was gazing up at her, his eyes hooded and glistening.

'That's the most beautiful thing I have ever seen,' he said hoarsely, before rising to kiss her. Pulling her into his arms, he lifted her off the sofa and carried her over to his sprawling bed.

His lips fused to hers, his hands gripping hers above her head, he entered her immediately. But, despite his impatience to be inside her, there was nothing hurried about their coupling. This was tender beyond her imagination.

With her body already fizzing from her earlier climax, she didn't think she was capable of another orgasm, but Pepe knew her so well, knew exactly when to increase the friction to bring her all the way back to the edge.

Clinging to him, she gloried in his fervent control, her heart singing in tune with her body. Pepe might not love her—might never love her—but in this moment he was making love to her as if she meant more to him than just the mother of his child and his lover for the moment. He was making love to her as if she were the most precious thing in his world.

When her climax finally erupted, he was right there with her, his face buried in her shoulder, groaning words in Italian as he drove himself inside her with a final thrust.

'You are crying?' he asked, long minutes later when he eventually lifted his head from her neck.

She hadn't even noticed tears were streaming down her face.

'Did I hurt you?'

She gave a quick shake of her head. 'Hormones' was the most she could utter.

How could she tell him she was crying because she'd done the one thing she'd sworn she would never do?

Far from living together as a couple sating the desire between them, it had shifted it into something deeper.

She had fallen in love with him, and she knew without a shadow of doubt that when the time came for Pepe to call it a day her heart was going to shatter into tiny pieces.

CHAPTER THIRTEEN

'ARE YOU SURE you're okay?' Pepe asked for the third time since they'd left the house. Cara seemed to have lost much of her colour and was much too quiet for his liking.

'I guess I'm a little apprehensive about this exhibition.'

Reaching for her hand, he pulled it over to rest on his thigh. 'I won't leave you alone for a second when we're there, I promise.'

She smiled wanly. 'I know you won't.'

'How did you cope when you worked at the auction house? You had to deal with new people on a daily basis.'

'That was different. It was work and so I could put my professional head on.'

'Maybe you should try that tonight,' he mused. 'If you see all the rich guests as potential clients for when you go back to work—if you go back to work—you might find it easier to cope.'

'It's worth a try,' she agreed non-committally.

Shifting gear, he drove into a street that was officially the beginning of Montmartre. Knowing how much Cara loved to hear about the arrondissement, he began pointing out places of interest, making a mental note to actually take her to them and not just drive past.

She looked so beautiful this evening. But then, she always looked beautiful. Tonight, she'd left her hair down, the red locks spread out over her shoulders like a fan. She was wearing a simple, high-necked, long-sleeved black dress with a wide red belt hanging loosely around the middle, resting on the base of her swollen belly. In the week he'd been away, her bump had grown. For the first time she actually looked pregnant. In his eyes she'd never looked more beautiful.

'Who's the artist exhibiting tonight?' she asked when he turned into the small car park at the back of the exhibition room.

'Sabine Collard. Have you heard of her?'

She shook her head. 'Sabine Collard,' she repeated. He loved the way she tried to pronounce her Rs the French way. It sounded so adorable coming from her Irish lilt.

The gallery was already packed.

Keeping a firm hold on Cara's hand, he guided her through the throng and towards the star of the evening.

When Sabine, a young, angry-looking young lady, spotted Pepe, she embraced him and planted kisses on his cheek.

'Let's stick to English,' Pepe said when Sabine began jabbering in French. He didn't want Cara unable to join in with the conversation.

Sabine gave a Gallic shrug. '*D'accord.* It is very good to see you. I have missed you at the studio.'

Had it been very long? With a jolt, he realised he hadn't visited the studio since Cara had moved in.

'Sabine shares a studio with a few other artists,' Pepe explained to Cara, whose grip on his hand had become vice-like. Casually he rubbed his thumb over her wrist in a wordless show of support.

'So modest!' Sabine exclaimed before addressing Cara directly. 'Your lover owns the studio. It is a *huge* building that was once a hotel. And it is not a "few" artists working and living there—we number fifteen! All living and working rent-free because your lover is one of the few patrons of the art who truly is a patron in all senses of the word.'

'It's not completely selfless,' Pepe hastily explained when Cara's eyes widened. 'I allow them to live and work there rent-free in exchange for a cut of any money they make when they sell their pieces.'

'Five per cent,' Sabine snorted. 'Hardly a big cut, especially when the most of us don't sell anything.'

'I can always raise it,' he warned with a grin.

A beatific expression came over her face. 'Oh, look, there is Sebastien LeGarde. I must socialise.'

Cara watched the chic Frenchwoman sashay away in the direction of a rotund man with the shiniest bald spot she'd ever seen.

Even if she'd been born French she would never have that certain élan Sabine carried off so effortlessly.

'No.'

She looked back at Pepe. 'No what?'

'No, I haven't slept with her.'

'I didn't say you had,' she pointed out primly.

'You were thinking it.' He reached out and gently stroked her cheek. 'There is a chance a couple of my exes will be here though.'

'There's always a chance we'll bump into your exes whenever we step out of the front door,' she said, more tartly than she would have liked.

She had no right to feel jealous. Ever since they'd agreed to make a go of some sort of semblance of a relationship, Pepe had treated her with nothing but respect. Whenever they went out he stuck to her side, his unspoken support worth more than all the money in the world.

He really was nothing like her father and she knew

with as deep a certainty as she'd ever known anything that he would never cheat on her.

All the same, she couldn't help the cloying sickness that unfurled inside her whenever she met his ex-lovers or even made the mistake of thinking about them.

There was a reason jealousy was oft referred to as the green-eyed monster. Thinking of Pepe with anyone else made her go green inside and made the monster within her want to scratch eyes out.

One day soon she would have to find a way to live with it.

She had no idea how she would be able to.

Pepe wanted them to part as friends?

She didn't think she'd even be able to cope with fleeting glances at him. How could *anyone* be strong enough to endure that, to love someone with all their heart and know the recipient would never feel the same way?

All she could do was hold on and hope for a miracle.

Miracles happened. Didn't they?

But even if they didn't, one thing she did know was that she would not behave as her mother had with her father. Whatever happened, Cara was confident her child would never witness the selfish behaviour that Cara had witnessed from *her* parents. Both she and Pepe were committed to that.

Any devastation would take place internally.

'I didn't know you owned a studio,' she said, quickly changing the subject away from something that could easily make her vomit. As she spoke, a sharp stab of pain ran down the side of her belly.

'Are you okay?' Pepe asked, noticing her reflexive wince.

Sucking in a quick blast of air, she nodded.

'You're sure?'

'Yes.' As she reassured him that all was well, it suddenly occurred to her that her back had ached all day. She'd been so excited about Pepe coming home after a week away that she hadn't thought much about it.

'I bought an old hotel a few years back,' Pepe said. 'I had it turned into a home for artists, a place where they could live and work. As you know from Grace, artists often work strange hours. The majority live in poverty.'

'What made you want to do it?' she asked, glad of the conversation to take her mind off irrational thoughts. Besides, she loved hearing anything that helped unlock the mystery that was Pepe Mastrangelo.

His mouth tightened a fraction before he answered. 'There is something incredibly *free* within the art world which I have always felt an affinity with. Growing up in Sicily…it was like living within a straightjacket. It's probably the reason I enjoy flying so much—it gives me a real sense of freedom. Many artists pursue their craft in defiance of their parents' wishes. I wanted to create a space for them to pursue their dream without having to worry about where the rent money was going to come from. Only artists who have been cut off financially from their families are eligible to live there. The only other stipulation is that the artist must have a genuine talent.'

'That's an amazing thing to do,' she said, genuinely touched.

'Not really,' he dismissed. 'It's an investment for me.'

She raised a brow. 'Five per cent?'

He suddenly grinned. 'Georges Ramirez started off in that studio.'

'Really?'

He nodded. 'He was only there for six months before a gallery owner I introduced him to gave him an exhibition and…the rest is history.'

'And does he pay full market rate on the loft?' she asked slyly.

'Near enough,' he said, grinning.

'You never cease to amaze me,' she said with a shake of her head. 'You're always trotting off from country to country on family business, yet you still invest your time as well as your money in the art community.' She gave him a crafty wink. 'How many of your artists have you dropped your kecks for in the name of art?'

His lips twitched. 'Half a dozen. Can I help it if I'm prime model material?'

She sniggered and reached for his hand, lacing her fingers through his. 'Do your family know what you do for the art world?' Somehow, she thought not. Grace would certainly have mentioned it.

He began scanning the room. 'I don't think they would be that interested. My life has never been that much of an interest to them before.' Suddenly he looked back at her with a grin. 'Saying that, they were always interested whenever I got into trouble.'

'Were you a very naughty boy?' she asked, matching his light tone, although she had caught a definite shadow in his eyes.

A gleam now shone in those same eyes. '*Sì.* I was a *very* naughty boy.' He leaned down to whisper into her ear. 'When we get home I'll show you what a naughty boy I can still be.'

Heat filled her from the tips of her toes to the long strands of hair on her head. 'I look forward to it.'

Suddenly filled with the urge to jump onto him and kiss his face off, which, given they were in full view of dozens of people, wouldn't do at *all*, she brought their conversation back to a less suggestive level. 'How come you joined the family business when your heart is clearly elsewhere?'

He shrugged. 'My father died. Luca had been groomed from birth to take over the business but none of us expected my dad to die so young. Luca held the fort on his own while I completed university but I knew he needed me. It wasn't fair for him to shoulder all the burden and pressure on his own. I'd spent my childhood playing the joker and it was time to grow up. Plus it was a good distraction from losing my father and from what Luisa had done to me.'

Her stomach contorted again, although whether this was because he'd mentioned Luisa's name or because of something physical, she didn't know, but it quickly passed.

'I think your father would be very proud if he could see you now, Pepe Mastrangelo.'

His eyes widened a fraction and glistened with something she couldn't discern.

'*I'm* very proud of you. And I know our child will be too.'

Before Pepe could respond, Georges Ramirez joined them, his pretty wife, Belinda, in tow.

Another, sharper pain cut through Cara's stomach.

Blocking out everything around her, she concentrated on breathing through the pain. This was definitely physical.

Cold fear gripped her.

'Not drinking?' Georges asked, looking pointedly at the orange juice in Pepe's hand.

'I'm driving.' Pepe could have used his driver tonight but he enjoyed driving Cara around, especially now she seemed over the worst of her travel sickness. He always made sure to drive her in the car with the sturdiest stabilisers and keep his speed at a steady level—too much heavy braking and up she would chuck. As good as his driver was, Pepe preferred to trust in his own driving ability to keep Cara free from nausea. In any case, it hardly seemed fair for him to be quaffing champagne when she had to stick to soft drinks. If she could make the minor sacrifice of forsaking alcohol for nine months, then he could do his bit too.

'Good—you can drive me and Belinda home. Stay for drinks…'

But Pepe had tuned Georges out.

Cara was *proud* of him?

Such a simple word but one that filled his chest with something so light and wonderful he couldn't begin to find the words to describe it.

Like a thunderbolt came the realisation that Cara had the capacity to bring him more joy than anyone else in the world.

Holding tight to her hand, he scanned the room, looking at some of the women who had once shared his bed and the women who, if Cara hadn't come into his life, he would have considered bedding.

There was no comparison, and it was nothing to do with the physical, although that certainly played its part.

Bedding all these women…

He'd been hiding. Tied up with his feelings of being second best to his brother and after everything Luisa had put him through, he'd sworn *never again*. Never again would he put himself in a position where he could be hurt. Those women had been nothing but a temporary affirmation that he was worth something, a good time, a boost to his ego.

Cara made him feel like a king, as if everything he did was worth something, if only to her.

At some point he'd stopped hiding the essence of himself from her—he didn't know where or when, it had been a gradual process born of their enforced intimacy over the past few months—and, even after seeing the real man behind the mask, she could still stand there and declare her pride in him.

And it came from her. The one woman in the world whose opinion actually mattered.

Because *she* mattered.

She mattered more than he had ever dreamt possible.

'Pepe?'

Even though he'd successfully tuned Georges out, Cara's whispered call of his name brought him back to sharp focus…and with it came the realisation that something was wrong.

Her hand, still clasped in his with a grip tight enough to cut off his circulation, had gone clammy. In the blink of an eye she had gone from being pale to totally devoid of colour.

He placed a hand to her forehead. It was cold. And damp.

'Cara?'

He'd hardly got her name out when she doubled over with an anguished cry and fell to the floor.

Rancid fear clung to Pepe like a cloak. For the first time in his life he felt helpless. Totally helpless.

The ambulance sped through the streets of Montmartre and he had to stop himself from demanding the driver go faster. The sirens blared but it rang like a dim distant noise, drowned out by the drumming in his head.

Cara's huge eyes, so full of pain and terror, didn't leave his. An oxygen mask had been strapped to her face. He wished he could take her hand but the paramedic had ordered him to keep his distance so she could do her work.

Dio.

Under his breath he said a prayer. A long prayer. He prayed for their child. But mostly he prayed for Cara. For the sweetest, most beautiful woman on the planet, who had brought such meaning and happiness to his life.

Caro Dio, please let him have the chance to tell her how much she meant to him.

When she'd collapsed he'd known immediately something bad was happening. And she had known it too. While they'd waited for the ambulance to arrive, she'd clung to him. He hadn't realised he'd been clinging to her too until the paramedic had prised him off her.

And now it was all out of his hands. Cara's fate and their baby's fate were in the hands of someone else. If anything should happen to her...

Caro Dio, but it didn't bear thinking about.

Cara didn't want to open her eyes. Didn't want to face the reality that opening them would bring.

Soft voices surrounded her then a door shut.

Silence.

She knew exactly where she was. In a hospital. The smell was too distinctive to be anywhere else.

She also knew why she was there.

'Cara?' A tender finger wiped away the single tear that had leaked out.

This time she did open her eyes and found Grace sitting beside her, her face drawn.

'Where's Pepe?'

'He's talking to the doctor. He'll be back soon.'

'I want Pepe.' It came out as a whimper.

Grace clasped Cara's hands. 'He won't be long, I promise.'

'I want Pepe.' This time it came out as an anguished howl.

Although it went against all regulations, Grace climbed onto the bed and wrapped her arms tightly around her, letting Cara sob as if there were no tears left to cry.

Pepe staggered along the corridor, the coffee his brother had given him hours ago still clutched in his hand, cold.

When he got to Cara's room, Grace and Luca came out before he could go in.

'Is she awake?'

'She was. She's sleeping again. Probably the best thing for her.'

He nodded mutely, Grace's words sounding distant and tinny to his ears.

Dimly he was aware of them exchanging glances.

Grace took his hand and clasped it in hers.

When he looked he could see she'd been crying.

'Luca and I have been talking and we think Cara should come home with us.'

'No.' He snatched his hand away.

They exchanged another significant glance.

Luca put his hand on his brother's shoulder and drew him away. 'Pepe, I know you're hurting but Cara needs to be with someone who loves her and that person is Grace. You told me yourself you were only together because of the baby.'

Pepe couldn't even find the strength to punch him.

You were only together because of the baby...

Was that really true? Had that *ever* been true?

He didn't know. His brain hurt too much to think.

Everything hurt.

It had all been so sudden.

One minute, everything had been fine. The next...

'Listen to me,' Luca said in a gentle tone he'd never heard him use before. 'It is at times like this a woman needs to be surrounded with love and compassion. Your relationship was only ever temporary. Cara and Grace are closer than sisters. Grace will take care of her. I guarantee it.'

'She's got to stay in hospital for a few more days,' Pepe said dully. 'She's had major surgery. She shouldn't travel.' The obstetricians had delivered their baby via a caesarean section. Cara had been knocked out for it.

He wished he had been knocked out for it too.

'We need to arrange the funeral. She won't want to travel anywhere until we've said goodbye.'

Luca winced at the mention of a funeral.

'What?' Pepe snarled, suddenly springing to life. 'You think I'm not going to give my baby girl a proper goodbye because she was *stillborn*? You think Cara will not want to say goodbye to Charlotte? You think we'll want to forget she ever existed, is that it?'

'No...'

Whatever Luca, who had gone white, was going to say was pushed aside when Grace stepped between them.

'Pepe, please, forgive us. All we want is what's best for Cara, and for you. Nothing more. And you're right— she won't want to go anywhere until after the funeral. When she's ready, she can come to Rome with me. Luca will go back to Sicily to be with Lily.'

'It's what's best for Cara,' Luca added quietly.

Pepe knew his brother was right. Although it ripped his insides to shreds, he knew it.

Cara would want to be with Grace. She wouldn't want to be with him.

He finally jerked a nod. 'Okay,' he said heavily. 'But only if that's what Cara wants. If she wants to stay with me then neither of you are to say anything to change her mind.'

Without waiting for a reply, he strolled into the private room and took the seat by Cara.

She was pale enough to merge into the white sheets.

He was glad she was asleep. At least if she slept she wouldn't have to remember, or, worse, feel.

He would gladly give up every organ in his body if it would take away her pain.

The next time Cara awoke, Pepe was sitting on the private room's windowsill, looking out.

'Hi,' she whispered.

His head snapped round and in a trice he was by her side.

He looked dreadful. Still in the same tuxedo he'd worn to the gallery; what had been an impeccably pressed suit was now rumpled. *He* looked rumpled.

He didn't say anything, just took her hands in his and pressed a kiss to them.

'I'm so sorry,' she croaked.

His brow furrowed, but he didn't speak.

'I keep thinking I should have known something was wrong...'

He placed a gentle finger to her lips and shook his head, his face contorted. 'No,' he croaked vehemently. 'Not your fault. It was a severe placental abruption. Nothing could have been done to prevent it. Nothing.'

She swallowed and turned her head away. Everything inside her felt dry, and so, so heavy, as if a weight were crushing her.

Time passed. It could have been minutes. It could have been hours. She had lost all sense of it.

'Has Grace spoken to you about going back to Rome with her?' Pepe asked quietly.

She looked back at him and mouthed a silent 'no'.

His lips compressed together. 'Grace wants to take care of you. She thinks you will want to be with her.'

More time passed as she looked into his bloodshot eyes. He really did look wretched, and no wonder. Pepe had lost his child too. He was suffering too.

'What about you?' she finally said, dragging the words out. 'What do you think?'

He shrugged, an almost desperate gesture. 'This isn't about me. It's about what's best for you.'

Oh.

Somewhere in the fog that was her brain was the re-membrance that their relationship had only ever been temporary.

Nothing lasted for ever, she thought dully. Nothing.

She had no doubt Pepe would allow her to return home with him if she asked. He'd take care of her as best he could.

But he wasn't asking her to go home with him, was he? He was giving her—them—a way out.

And she knew why.

Every time he looked at her he would be reminded of the loss of yet another child.

And every time she looked at him her loss would double.

He'd loved their baby, not her.

She'd loved them both.

'I need to sleep,' she whispered, disentangling her hand and carefully turning onto her side, not quite turn-ing her back to him.

She could hear his breaths. They sounded heavy. Raspy.

'So you're going to go with Grace?'

She nodded, utterly unable to speak.

It was only when she heard the door shut that the dryness inside her welled to a peak and the tears fell, saturating the pillow.

Incoherent with grief, she was unaware of the needle that was inserted into her arm to sedate her.

CHAPTER FOURTEEN

'ARE YOU SURE you want to do this?' Grace asked as the driver pulled up outside Pepe's Parisian home.

Cara nodded absently, gazing at the place she had called home. The place where she had spent the happiest months of her life. The place where the man she loved was holed up, alone.

'You don't have to do this.'

Cara attempted a smile. 'I know that. I *want* to.' How puny a word *want* sounded when describing the desperate yearning that lived inside her to be with him.

But Grace was right. She didn't have to do this. She could get on the jet that was waiting for them and fly off to Rome. The world would still turn. In time she would heal.

But her heart wouldn't. Without Pepe she doubted she would ever feel whole again.

'Are you sure you don't want me to come in with you?'

Cara shook her head. 'No. I need to do this alone. I want to say goodbye to him properly.' At the graveside Pepe had looked desolate. She'd had Grace on her arm, holding her up. He'd stood apart from them all, shunning even his brother.

She needed to satisfy herself that he was holding up. Who was taking care of *him*? she wondered. His mother was in Sicily taking care of Lily. His brother was already en route back to Sicily, having returned for the funeral. Pepe had rejected his attempts to stay with him, assuring both Luca and Grace that he was perfectly all right, and throwing himself into his work.

But he wasn't all right. He couldn't be. The few conversations they'd had to discuss the funeral arrangements had been almost too painful to recall. He'd sounded empty.

His friends, as lovely as she'd come to accept most of them were, were too wrapped up in their own lives to see beyond the tragedy of what had happened between them on anything but a superficial level. And now that the funeral was over, she suspected those that had been there for him thus far—if he'd even let them be there for him, which she doubted—would fall by the wayside.

She'd held off for a full twenty-four hours before caving in to her need to see him. Her mind was tormented with worries for his state of mind. She'd phoned the house and been assured by Monique that he was working from home. She'd called at the right time—Monique had been put on leave with full pay until further notice. She was only at the house at that time with the ostensible excuse of having to drop some dry-cleaning off. She too was worried for him.

'Make sure you take things easy,' Grace warned kindly.

Two weeks had passed since Cara's baby had been so cruelly taken from her. It would be another four weeks before she'd be allowed to lift anything heavier than a cup of tea. 'I promise. I'll call you when I'm done.'

'No rush. I'll wait at the house.' Since her discharge, Cara and Grace had been staying at the home of a friend of Pepe's who was away on business. 'The jet's ready to leave when we are.'

Swallowing her apprehension, Cara used her key to unlock the front door. The alarms were disabled, so she knew he had to be around somewhere, but only silence greeted her. Heavy, oppressive silence.

Slowly she walked through the ground floor. Everything was just as it had been when she'd last walked through this house, when the future had seemed full of hope, when they'd found a new level of intimacy and she'd believed that maybe miracles could occur.

But there were no miracles to be had.

Nothing had changed but the house felt like a shell of itself.

How could Pepe bear to live here all alone with only his own thoughts for company?

At least she had Grace. She would always have Grace and would for ever be grateful to her best friend for everything she had done for her and continued to do. But all Cara wanted was Pepe. It was his arms she wanted around her, holding her. Just holding her. Sharing their grief.

'Pepe?'

No answer.

'Pepe? It's me. Cara,' she added as an afterthought.

Where was he? Oh, please let him be okay.

There was another reason for her being here.

Taking a deep breath, she entered the garage.

All the stuff was there, exactly where she had left it, still in the boxes. The cot. The dresser. The pram. Even the baby bath. Everything.

The weighty nausea that had lined her stomach for the past two weeks began its familiar roll. She closed her eyes and leaned against the wall for support.

Her baby would never sleep in that cot or ride in that pram.

Her chest heaved as she fought back another fresh wave of tears. So many tears. So much grief. And the man she wanted so desperately to cling to could hardly bring himself to look at her.

Heavy steps came into the garage accompanied by even heavier breathing.

'Sorry, I was on a teleconference,' Pepe said tonelessly.

She opened her mouth to say not to worry. Instead, bile and hysteria rose in her throat. The boxes ripped at her.

'Are you healing well?'

She wanted to say yes, but all she could see were the boxes. 'I don't know what to do with this lot. I just don't know what to do.'

At first he didn't answer. 'I'll keep them here until you decide.'

She jerked a nod, and finally made herself look at him. 'Thank you.'

He raised a shoulder. 'No problem.'

Despite his casual air, she wasn't fooled. Not for a second. Pepe was hurting every bit as much as she.

He looked wretched too, even more so than she'd seen at the graveside, when she'd been too heartbroken and scared to do more than cast him fleeting glances. Scared she would take his hand and offer the support he so clearly didn't want. Scared his grief would make him reject her.

He couldn't have shaved at all since it had happened. The man who took such pride in his trim goatee now had a fully fledged black beard. His eyes were bloodshot and wild. Even his clothes were all wrong. He hadn't dressed. He'd thrown clothes on.

His feet were bare.

She longed to reach out but didn't know…

She didn't know anything. She didn't know how to cross the bridge to him.

What did she think she was doing? Pepe didn't want her there.

He didn't want anyone.

She straightened and inhaled deeply, closing her eyes as she said, 'I need to go.'

She took his lack of an answer as agreement.

Her hand on the door, she turned to face him one last time. 'Be kind to yourself, Pepe.'

Tears blinding her, she walked through the living room, fumbling in her bag for her phone to call Grace, who'd likely not even made it back to the house yet.

'Cara?'

Hastily brushing the tears away with the back of her hand and in the process clonking her nose with her phone, she stopped and slowly turned.

Pepe shuffled towards her, his hand outstretched. 'Don't go.'

Her brow furrowed in confusion.

Her legs too weak to carry her any further, her stomach feeling the strain of being upright for too long, she sank onto the chair right behind her.

When he reached her, he knelt down and placed his hand on her neck. 'I can't bear it,' he said hoarsely. 'I think I could cope if it was just the loss of our baby, but losing you too…'

A sound like a wail echoed in the room. It took the beat of a moment for Cara to realise the sound had come from *her.*

Pepe's face contorted and he looked down to her belly then back up to her face, his eyes searching for…something. 'I know what I'm asking is selfish but, please, *cucciola mia*, please don't go. I'll take care of you. I'll help you heal. Please, just give me the chance to show how much you mean to me and prove how much I love you.'

When Pepe saw the confusion and doubt ringing in Cara's eyes, he almost gave up. It was the tiny spark of hope he also saw that gave him the courage to forge on.

To put his heart on the line. Because if he didn't say it now it would be too late.

'When Luisa aborted our baby—and I believe with all my heart that child was mine—it was the loss of that child so soon after the loss of my father that ruined me. Her lies and deceit were supplementary. I never missed *her*. I'd been in love with a dream that didn't exist—in my own family I'd always felt like a spare part. Luca was the brother who mattered; I was just the spare, and, no matter how much my parents loved me, I always knew that. With Luisa, I dreamt of having my own family where *I* mattered.

'Cara, losing *our* baby has broken my heart. Our child was more than a dream. *You* were more than a dream, and you leaving…it's broken *me*. I don't know how to go on. I'm lost without you. I'm…' His voice went. All the desolation he'd been sitting on for the past two weeks burst through and choked him. He didn't even realise he was crying until Cara wrapped her arms around him and pulled his head to her chest.

She kissed his head, over and over, murmuring sweet words and cradling him with such love and compassion that for the first time in a fortnight a trickle of warmth cut through the ice in his chest.

'Oh, my poor love,' she whispered, her own tears falling into his hair. 'I've been so desperate to be with you.

I thought you wouldn't want me here any more. If I'd known how you felt I would never have gone with Grace.'

He raised his head and found his face being rained upon with her tears. 'I thought you *wanted* to be with her.'

She shook her head. 'I wanted to be with you. Just you. I love you, Pepe.'

'You do?'

What looked like a brave smile broke through her tears. 'How could I not fall in love with you? I always thought love between a man and a woman was about sex and power and humiliation. I had no idea it could be about sex and friendship and support. You're everything to me.'

'I'm so sorry for the way I treated you when you first came to me about the pregnancy. And I'm sorry for the way I treated you in Dublin.'

'I understand. You were helping your brother. While I don't agree with your methods, I can see it was something you felt you had to do for his sake. I would have done the same for Grace.'

'I was terrible,' he stated.

'It's done,' she said gently, 'and if it makes you feel better then know I forgive you. I forgave you a long time ago.'

Pepe hadn't realised how badly he'd needed her forgiveness until another trickle of warmth seeped into his bones. It would be a long time before the cold left him, but with Cara at his side he didn't have to freeze alone. And neither did she. Together they could bring the warmth back.

'A part of me always knew getting involved with you would bring me nothing but trouble,' he confessed.

'Really?'

'*Sì*. And I was right. It wasn't just that you were a virgin or that I felt guilt for what I'd done: I couldn't get you out of my head. The pregnancy came almost as a relief—it meant I had a legitimate reason to keep you in my life without having to acknowledge that my feelings for you ran far further than I could ever admit.'

Her bee-stung lip wobbled. He pressed a finger to it and then the tenderest of kisses. 'I used to tease you about being my concubine or my geisha. I can see now how wide off the mark I was—*I* should be *your* concubine because your needs are all that matter to me. The rest of the world can go to hell. *You* are all that matters to me, and whatever it takes to get us through this whole horrific ordeal I will do. I swear.'

'As long as you're by my side, I know I'll get through it,' she said gently. 'And part of that is you letting *me* help *you*. We can support each other.'

'Do you really mean that?'

'More than anything. I used to think wanting to be with a man meant weakness and that to fall in love would make me lose something of myself. But it hasn't. My mum's life is not mine—and you have shown me that. I know I can survive without you, Pepe. I know I can lead a fulfilling life on my own, but I don't want to. I want to be with you. I want to support you just as you've supported me. I love you. Seeing you alone at the graveside tore me in two.'

'Shall we go on our own tomorrow, to say goodbye together?'

Cara nodded through fresh tears then buried her face into his shoulder. Except these tears didn't feel quite as desolate as all the others had. Pepe's love had given her the hope and desire to see the silver lining on the dark cloud.

Together they would heal each other, and then who

knew where their love would take them? All she knew with bone-deep certainty was that wherever they went, they would always be together, united. As one.

As love.

EPILOGUE

'HAVE I TOLD you how beautiful you look today, Signora Mastrangelo?' Pepe whispered into his wife's ear.

She grinned up at him. 'You're looking pretty spiffing yourself. It's nice to see you've made the effort,' she added with a snigger, referring to the charcoal suit he wore with his salmon cravat.

The priest coughed and they forced their attention back to the proceedings before them. When instructed, Pepe carried baby Benjamin to the font, Cara right by his side.

Of course he'd made the effort today, at their youngest child's christening, just as he had for the christening of their twins. From the corner of his eye he saw a pair of miniature grenades launch themselves up the aisle, quickly followed by his elegant mother, who had been designated babysitter for the day.

A loud voice stage-whispered theatrically, 'Gracie and Rocco are being *very* trying today.'

Titters could be heard throughout the congregation. Luca and Grace were standing at the font with them, their heads bowed, their frames shaking at the precociousness of their eldest daughter, who sat in the front row looking self-important for all her five years of age. Their youngest daughter, two-year-old Georgina, was conspicuous by her absence, no doubt rifling through handbags in the hope of finding sweets. Pepe knew a couple of his artist friends had planned to bring sweets laden with sugar and additives in the hope of watching all the toddlers turn into Scud missiles.

Pepe still felt guilt whenever he recalled turning up at Lily's christening dressed more appropriately for a day out sailing than the baptism welcoming his niece into the world. Looking back, he couldn't believe he'd been so selfish. A child's baptism was one of the most wondrous days for all the family. Instead of appreciating that, he'd deliberately dismissed the event, determined to prove to himself that babies and marriage meant nothing when, in reality, family meant everything.

What a shallow life that had been.

Thank God for Cara.

He would never be able to express the pride he felt in her and the pride she gave in him. He would watch her chatting to clients at the gallery they owned in partnership with his brother and Grace, and which Cara ran, and be awed at her knowledge and the daily battle she fought to unlock her shy tongue and speak coherently. She'd even had another go in his helicopter, a trip that had been aborted after five minutes. Some battles just couldn't be won, and severe motion sickness brought on by helicopter travel was one of them.

Once the ceremony was over, all the guests trickled out and headed to the party being held at their Parisian home.

Pepe, Cara and their children lingered a little longer.

They walked to the altar at the side of the church, which held the memorial candles, Pepe holding a sleeping Benjamin in his arms. Cara gave the three-year-old twins, Gracie and Rocco, some change to put in the donation box, then helped both children light a candle.

'Is this for Charlotte, Mama?' Gracie asked.

Cara's eyes were bright with unshed tears but she nodded and smiled for their daughter.

Then it was their turn. Standing close together, they lit their candles and each whispered private words of love to the child who would for ever live in their hearts.

Once the five candles were lit—Pepe lit one for Benjamin too—he turned to his wife and kissed her, a chaste brush of the lips that sweetened the melancholy of the moment.

Only then did they leave the church, somehow managing to keep a hold of each other as well as their hyperactive toddlers and newborn baby.

In his heart he knew they would always keep hold of each other.

* * * * *

TAMING THE NOTORIOUS SICILIAN

MICHELLE SMART

This book is dedicated to all the staff and volunteers at the John Radcliffe Children's Hospital, with especial thanks to the team on Kamran's Ward. Without their care, compassion and sheer dedication, my beautiful nephew Luke would not be here.

This book is also dedicated to the memory of Henry, Lily and Callum. May you all be playing together with the angels.

CHAPTER ONE

FRANCESCO CALVETTI BROUGHT his MV Agusta F4 CC to a stop and placed his left foot on the road as he was foiled by yet another set of red lights. Barely 7:00 a.m. and the roads were already filling up.

What he wouldn't give to be riding with nothing but the open road before him and green fields surrounding him.

He thought of Sicily with longing. His island had none of the grey dreariness he was fast associating with London. This was supposed to be *spring*? He'd enjoyed better winters in his homeland.

He yawned widely, raising his hand to his visor out of pure habit. After all, no one could see his face with his helmet on.

He should have gotten Mario to bring him home after such a long night, but being driven by anyone irritated him, especially in a car. Francesco was a man for whom *drive* had multiple definitions.

The light changed to green. Before twisting on the throttle and accelerating smoothly, he swiped away the moisture clinging to his visor.

What a country. At the moment it was like driving through a saturated cloud.

As he approached yet another set of lights, a cyclist on a pushbike just ahead caught his attention—or, rather, the fluorescent yellow helmet she wore caught it. She reached the lights at the moment they turned amber. If that had been him, Francesco mused, he would have gone for it. She'd had plenty of time.

But no, this was clearly a law-abiding woman with a healthy dose of self-preservation. She stopped right at the line. The car in front of Francesco, a large four-wheel drive, drew level on her right side.

She had the thickest hair he'd ever seen—a shaggy mass of varying shades of blonde reaching halfway down her back.

The light turned green and off she set, sticking her left arm out and turning down the street in that direction. The car that had been beside her also turned left, forced to hang a little behind her, with Francesco joining the convoy.

The road ahead was clear. The cyclist picked up speed....

It happened so quickly that for a moment Francesco was convinced he had imagined it.

Without any indication, the four-wheel drive in front of him pulled out to overtake the cyclist, accelerating quickly, but with the spatial awareness of a cauliflower, because it clipped the cyclist's wheel, causing her to flip forward off the saddle and land head-first on the kerb.

Francesco brought his bike to an immediate stop and jumped off, clicking the stand down through muscle memory rather than conscious thought.

To his disgust, the driver of the offending car didn't stop, but carried on up the road, took a right and disappeared out of sight.

A passer-by made a tentative approach towards the victim.

'Do not move her,' Francesco barked as he pulled off

his helmet. 'She might have a broken neck. If you want to help, call for an ambulance.'

The passer-by took a step back and dug into his pocket, allowing Francesco to stand over the victim.

The woman lay on her back, half on the pavement and half on the road, her thick hair fanning in all directions. Her helmet, which had shifted forward and covered her forehead, had a crack running through it. Her bike was a crumpled heap of metal.

Dropping to his haunches, Francesco yanked off his leather gloves and placed two fingers on the fallen cyclist's neck.

Her pulse beat faint beneath his touch.

While the passer-by spoke to the emergency services, Francesco deftly removed his leather jacket and placed it over the unconscious woman. She wore smart grey trousers and an untucked black blouse covered with a waterproof khaki jacket. On one of her bare feet was a white ballet shoe. The other was missing.

His chest constricted at the thought of the missing shoe.

He wished he could tuck his jacket under her to create a barrier between her and the cold, damp concrete, but he knew it was imperative to keep her still until the paramedics arrived.

The important thing was she was breathing.

'Give me your coat,' he barked at another spectator, who was hovering like a spare part. A small crowd had gathered around them. Vultures, Francesco thought scornfully. Not one of them had stepped forward to help.

It never occurred to him that his presence was so forbidding, even first thing in the morning, that none of the crowd *dared* offer their assistance.

The spectator he'd addressed, a middle-aged man in

a long lambswool trench coat, shrugged off his coat and passed it to Francesco, who snatched it from his hands. Francesco wrapped it across the woman's legs, making sure to cover her feet.

'Five minutes,' the original passer-by said when he disconnected his call.

Francesco nodded. For the first time he felt the chill of the wind. He palmed the woman's cheek. It felt icy.

Still on his haunches, he studied her face carefully, ostensibly looking for a clue to any unseen injuries. No blood ran from her nose or mouth, which he assumed was a good thing. Her mass of blonde hair covered her ears, so he carefully lifted a section to look. No blood.

As he searched, he noticed what a pretty face she had. Not beautiful. Pretty. Her nose was straight but just a touch longer than the women of his acquaintance would put up with before resorting to surgery. She had quite rounded cheeks, too, something else that would be fixed in the endless quest for perfection. But yes, pretty.

He remembered she'd had something slung around her neck before he'd covered her chest with his jacket. Carefully, he tugged it free.

It was an identity card for one of the hospitals in the capital. Peering closer, he read her name. *Dr H Chapman. Specialist Registrar.*

This woman was a doctor? To his eyes she looked about eighteen. He'd guessed her as a student…

Her eyes opened and fixed on him.

His thoughts disappeared.

Shock rang out from her eyes—and what eyes they were, a moreish hazel ringed with black—before she closed them. When they reopened a few beats later, the shock faded to be replaced by a look of such contentment and serenity that Francesco's heart flipped over.

Her mouth opened. He leaned closer to hear what she had to say.

Her words came out as a whisper. 'So there really is a heaven.'

Hannah Chapman leaned her new bike against the stone building and gazed up at the sparkling silver awning that held one word: *Calvetti's*.

She admired the explicitness of it. This belonged to Francesco Calvetti and no one else.

Even though it was 6:00 p.m. and the club wasn't due to open for another four hours, two hefty-sized men dressed all in black stood beneath the awning, protecting the door. She took this as a good sign—the past three times she'd cycled over, the door hadn't been manned. The club had been empty.

'Excuse me,' she said, standing before them. 'Is Francesco Calvetti in?'

'He's not available.'

'But is he in?'

'He's in but he's not to be disturbed.'

Success! At last she'd managed to track him down. Francesco Calvetti travelled *a lot*. Still, tracking him down was one thing. Getting in to see him was a different matter entirely.

She tried her most winning smile.

Alas, her fake smile wasn't up to par. All it resulted in was the pair of them crossing their arms over their chests. One of them alone would have covered the door. The pair of them standing there was like having a two-man mountain as a barrier.

'I know you don't want to disturb him, but can you please tell him that Hannah Chapman is here to see him?

He'll know who I am. If he says no, then I'll leave, I promise.'

'We can't do that. We have our orders.'

She could be talking to a pair of highly trained SAS soldiers, such was the conviction with which the slightly less stocky of the duo spoke.

Hannah sighed. Oh, well, if it wasn't meant to be, then… so be it.

All the same, she was disappointed. She'd wanted to thank the man personally.

She thrust forward the enormous bunch of flowers and thank-you card. She'd cycled the best part of two miles through London traffic with them precariously balanced in her front basket. 'In that case, could you give these to him, please?'

Neither made a move to take them from her. If anything, their faces became even more suspicious.

'Please? This is the third bunch I've brought for him and I'd hate for them to go to waste. I was in an accident six weeks ago and he came to my rescue and…'

'Wait.' The one on the left cocked his head. 'What kind of accident?'

'I was knocked off my bike by a hit-and-run driver.'

They exchanged glances, then drew back to confer in a language that sounded, to her untrained ear, as if it was Italian. Or she could have imagined it, knowing Francesco Calvetti was Sicilian.

Since she'd discovered the identity of her benefactor, she knew a lot more than she should about Francesco Calvetti. internet searches were wonderful creations. For instance, she knew he was thirty-six, unmarried but with a string of glamorous girlfriends to his name, and that he owned six nightclubs and four casinos across Europe. She also knew his family name was synonymous with the Mafia in Sicily and that his father, Salvatore, had gone by the nickname Sal il Santo—Sal the Saint—a moniker allegedly given due to his penchant for making the sign of the cross over his dead victims.

She wouldn't have cared if his father had been Lucifer himself. It made no difference to what Francesco was—a good man.

The man who'd brought her back to life.

The stockier one looked back to her. 'What did you say your name was?'

'Hannah Chapman.'

'One minute. I will tell him you are here.' He shrugged his hefty shoulders. 'I cannot say if he will speak to you.'

'That's fine. If he's too busy, I'll leave.' She wasn't going to make a scene. She was here to say thank you and nothing else.

He disappeared through the double doors, letting them swing shut behind him.

She hugged the flowers to her chest. She hoped Francesco wouldn't think them pathetic but she hadn't a clue what else she could give him to express her gratitude. Francesco Calvetti had gone above and beyond the call of duty, and he'd done it for a complete stranger.

In less than a minute, the door swung back open, but instead of the bouncer, she was greeted by a man who was—and Lord knew how this was even possible—taller than the guards he employed.

She'd no idea he was so tall.

But then, her only memory of the man was opening her eyes and seeing his beautiful face before her. How clearly she remembered the fleeting certainty that she was dead and her guardian angel had come to take her to heaven, where Beth was waiting for her. She hadn't even been sad about it—after all, who would be upset about being escorted to paradise with the most gorgeous man on either heaven or earth?

The next time she'd opened her eyes she had been in a hospital bed. This time, the fleeting feeling was disappointment she hadn't gone off to paradise with Adonis.

Fleeting feeling? No. It had been more than that. Adonis had come to take her to Beth. To learn she was still alive had been on the verge of devastating. But then, of course, sanity poked through.

As she'd come back to the here and now, and memories of her Adonis kept peppering her thoughts, so, too, came the revelation that she truly was alive.

Alive.

Something she hadn't felt in fifteen years.

Limbo. That was where she'd been. She, hardworking, practical Hannah Chapman, for whom bedtime reading consisted of catching up on medical journals, had been living in limbo.

In the weeks since her accident, she'd convinced herself that her memory of that brief moment was all wrong. No one, surely, could look like he did in her memory and be a mortal? She'd had severe concussion after all. Even the pictures she'd found on the internet didn't do justice to her memory of him.

Turned out her brain hadn't been playing tricks on her.

Francesco Calvetti truly was beautiful…

But in a wholly masculine way.

His tall, lean frame was clothed in tailored dark grey trousers and a white shirt unbuttoned to halfway down his chest, the sleeves rolled up to his elbows. In the exposed V—which she was eye height with—he wore a simple gold cross on a chain, which rested on a dark whorl of hair.

A rush of…*something* coursed through her blood, as if a cloud of heat had been blown through her veins.

Unsettled, Hannah blinked and looked back up at his unsmiling face. Not even the forbidding expression resonating from his deep-set eyes—and what a beautiful colour they were, making her think of hot chocolate-fudge cake—could dent the huge grin that broke out on her face. She extended the flowers and card to him, saying, 'I'm Hannah Chapman and these are for you.'

Francesco looked from the flowers back to her. He made no effort to take them.

'They're a thank you,' she explained, slightly breathless for some reason. 'I know they're a drop in the ocean compared to what you've done for me, but I wanted to get you something to show how grateful I am—I am truly in your debt.'

One of his thick black brows raised and curved. 'My debt?'

A shiver ran up her spine at his deep, accented voice. 'You have done so much for me,' she enthused. 'Even if I had all the money in the world I could never repay you for your kindness, so yes, I am in your debt.'

His eyes narrowed as he studied her a little longer before inclining his head at the door. 'Come in for a minute.'

'That would be great,' she said, not caring in the least that his directive was an order rather than a request.

The two-man mountain that had flanked Francesco up to this point, guarding him as well as they would if she were carrying an Uzi nine-millimetre, parted. She darted between them, following Francesco inside.

After walking through a large reception area, they stepped into the club proper.

Hannah's eyes widened. 'Amazing,' she whispered, turning her head in all directions.

Calvetti's oozed glamour. All deep reds and silver, it was like stepping into old Hollywood. The only club she'd been to was at the age of eighteen when her entire class had descended on The Dell, their sleepy seaside town's only nightclub, to celebrate finishing their A levels. It had been one of the most boring evenings of her life.

Compared to this place, The Dell had been grey and dingy beyond imagination.

And, in fact, compared to Francesco, with his olive skin, short black curly hair and strong jawline, all the men she had ever met in her life were grey and dingy beyond imagination, too.

'You like it?'

Her skin heating under the weight of his scrutiny, she nodded. 'It's beautiful.'

'You should come here one evening.'

'Me? Oh, no, I'm not into clubbing.' Then, fearing she had inadvertently insulted him, quickly added, 'But my sister Melanie would love it here—it's her hen night on Friday so I'll suggest she drops in.'

'You do that.'

It didn't surprise Francesco to learn Hannah Chapman wasn't into clubbing. The women who frequented his clubs were a definite type—partygoers and women looking to hook up with a rich or famous man, preferably both.

Hannah Chapman was a doctor, not a wannabe WAG. He allowed himself to take in her appearance more fully, and noticed that she was dressed professionally, in another variation of the trouser suit she'd been wearing on the day she was knocked off her bike. The lighting in the club had the effect of making her white blouse see-through, illuminating her bra, which, to his trained eye, looked practical rather than sexy. Her thick blonde hair looked as if it hadn't seen a hairbrush in weeks, and he could not detect the slightest trace of make-up on her face.

He'd assumed when he'd seen her at the door that she

had come with an agenda. In his experience, everyone had an agenda.

He slipped behind the bar, watching as she set the flowers and card to one side. He had never been presented with flowers before. The gesture intrigued him. 'What can I get you to drink?'

'I could murder a coffee.'

'Nothing stronger?'

'I don't drink alcohol, thank you. In any case, I've been working since seven and if I don't get an enormous shot of caffeine I might just pass out.' He liked the droll way she spoke, the air of amusement that laced her voice. It made a change from the usual petulant tones he was used to hearing from her sex.

'You're back at work already?'

'I was back within a fortnight, as soon as I'd recovered from the concussion.'

'Any other injuries?'

'A broken clavicle—collarbone—which is fusing back together nicely. Oh, and a broken middle finger, but that seems to be healed now.'

'You don't know if your own finger's healed?'

She shrugged and hopped onto a stool, facing him. 'It doesn't hurt anymore so I assume it's healed.'

'Is that a professional diagnosis?'

She grinned. 'Absolutely.'

'Remind me not to come and see you if I need medical attention,' he commented drily, stepping over to the coffee machine.

'You're about twenty years too old for me.'

He raised a brow.

Her grin widened. 'Sorry, I mean you're twenty years too old for me to treat in a medical capacity, unless you want to be treated on a ward full of babies, toddlers, and kids. I'm specialising in paediatrics.'

It was on the tip of his tongue to ask why she had chosen to specialise in children but he kept his question to himself. He wanted to know why she had sought him out.

He placed a cup in the machine and pressed a button. 'Do you take milk and sugar?'

'No milk but two sugars, please. I might as well overdose on that as well as caffeine.'

His thoughts exactly. He added two heaped spoons to both cups and passed one to her.

His initial assessment of her had been correct. She really was very pretty. Of average height and slender, her practical trousers showcased the most fabulous curvy bottom. It was a shame she was now sitting on it. The more he looked at her, the more he liked what he saw.

And he could tell that she liked what she saw, too.

Yes, this unexpected visit from Dr Chapman could take a nice twist.

A *very* nice twist.

He took a sip of his strong, sweet coffee before placing his cup next to hers, folding his arms across his chest and leaning on the bar before her.

'Why are you here?'

Her eyes never left his face. 'Because I needed to let you know how grateful I am. You kept me warm until the ambulance arrived, then travelled in the ambulance with me, stayed at the hospital for hours until I'd regained consciousness, *and* you tracked down the driver who hit me and forced him to hand himself in to the police. No one has *ever* done anything like that for me before, and you've done it for a complete stranger.'

Her face was so animated, her cheeks so heightened

with colour, that for a moment his fingers itched to reach out and touch her.

How did she know all this? He'd left the hospital as soon as he'd been given word that she'd regained consciousness. He hadn't seen her since.

'How about you let me buy you dinner one night, so I can thank you properly?' Colour tinged her cheeks.

'You want to buy me dinner?' He didn't even attempt to keep the surprise from his voice. Women didn't ask him out on dates. It just didn't happen. For certain, they thought nothing of cajoling him into taking *them* out to expensive restaurants and lavishing them with expensive clothes and jewellery—something he was happy to oblige them in, enjoying having beautiful women on his arm. But taking the initiative and offering *him* a night out…?

In Francesco's world, man was king. Women were very much pretty trinkets adorning the arm and keeping the bed warm. Men did the running, initially at least, following the traps set by the women so the outcome was assured.

She nodded, cradling her coffee. 'It's the least I can do.'

He studied her a touch longer, gazing into soft hazel eyes that didn't waver from his stare.

Was there an agenda to her surprising offer of dinner?

No. He did not believe so. But Francesco was an expert on female body language and there was no doubt in his mind that she was interested in him.

He was tempted. *Very* tempted.

He'd thought about her numerous times since her accident. There had even been occasions when he'd found his hand on the phone ready to call the hospital to see how she was. Each time he had dismissed the notion. The woman was a stranger. All the same, he'd been enraged to learn the police had failed to track down the man who'd so callously knocked her down. The driver had gone into hiding. Unfortunately for the driver, Francesco had a photographic memory.

It had taken Francesco's vast network precisely two hours to track the driver down. It had taken Francesco less than five minutes to convince the man to hand himself in. By the time he'd finished his 'little chat' with him, the man had been begging to be taken to the police station. Francesco had been happy to oblige.

And now she had come to him.

And he was tempted to take her up on her offer of a meal—not that he would let her pay. It went against everything he believed in. Men took care of their women. The end.

If it was any other woman he wouldn't think twice. But this one was different. For a start, she was a doctor. She was a force for good in a world that was cruel and ugly.

Despite her age and profession, Hannah had an air of innocence about her. Or it could just be that she was totally without artifice. Either way, she had no business getting involved with the likes of him.

If he was a lesser man he would take advantage of her obvious interest, just like his father would have done if he'd been alive.

But he would not be that man. This woman was too... *pure* was the word that came to mind. If she were the usual kind of woman who frequented his world, he would have no hesitation in spelling out how she could repay her so-called debt to him. Naked. And horizontal.

'You owe me nothing,' he stated flatly.

'I do...'

'No.' He cut her off. 'What you consider to be your debt is not redeemable. I did what I did without any thought of payback—consider the fact you are alive and healthy and able to do the job you love to be my payment.'

The animation on her face dimmed a little. 'So you won't let me buy you dinner?'

'Look around you. You don't belong in this seedy world, Dr Chapman. I thank you for taking the time to visit me, but now I have business to attend to.'

'That sounds like a dismissal.'

'I am a busy man.'

Those hazel eyes held his for the longest time before she cast him the most beautiful smile he'd ever been the recipient of, lighting her face into something dazzling.

Then, to his utter shock, Hannah levered herself so her torso was on the bar and pressed her lips to his.

They were the softest of lips, a gentle touch that sent tiny darts fizzing through his blood.

He caught a faint whiff of coffee before she pulled away.

'Thank you. For everything,' she said, slipping back down onto her stool then getting to her feet. Her cheeks glowing, she finished her coffee and reached for her bag, her eyes never leaving his. 'I will never forget what you've done for me, Francesco. You have my undying gratitude.'

As she turned to leave, he called out after her, 'Your sister—she has the same family name as you?'

She nodded.

'I'll leave word that Melanie Chapman's hen party is to be given priority at the door on Friday.'

A groove appeared in her forehead. 'Okay,' she said slowly, clearly not having the faintest idea what he was talking about.

'Your sister will know what it means.' A half smile stole over his face. 'Tell her she'll be on the list.'

'Ah—on the list!' The groove disappeared. Somehow the sparkle in her eyes glittered even stronger. 'I know what *that* means. That's incredibly lovely of you.'

'I wouldn't go that far,' he dismissed, already regretting

his impulsive offer, which had come from where he knew not, but which unsettled him almost as much as her kiss.

Francesco never acted on impulse.

That same serene smile that had curved her cheeks when she'd lain on the road spread on her face. 'I would.'

He watched her walk away, his finger absently tracing the mark on his lips where she'd kissed him.

For the first time in his life he'd done an unselfish act. He didn't know if it made him feel good or bad.

CHAPTER TWO

HANNAH STARED AT the queue snaking all the way round the corner from the door of Calvetti's and sighed. Maybe the queue was an omen to stay away.

No. It couldn't be. Even if it was, she would ignore it. Just being this close to his sanctum was enough to send her pulse careering.

Meeting Francesco in the flesh had done something to her…

'Come on, Han,' her sister said, tugging at her wrist and breaking Hannah's reverie. 'We're on the list.'

'But this is the queue,' Hannah pointed out.

'Yes, but we're *on the list*.' Melanie rolled her eyes. 'If you're on the list you don't have to queue.'

'Really? How fabulous.' She'd thought it meant getting in for free—she had no idea it also encompassed queue jumping.

Giggling, the party of twelve women dressed in black leotards over black leggings, bright pink tutus and matching bunny ears hurried past the queue.

Three men in long black trench coats guarded the door.

Melanie went up to them. 'We're on the list,' she said with as much pride as anyone with a pink veil and bunny ears on her head and the words *Mucky Mel* ironed onto the back of her leotard could muster.

Hannah had guessed Calvetti's was popular but, judging by Melanie's reaction, she could have said she'd got VIP backstage passes to Glastonbury. Her sister had squealed with excitement and promptly set about rearranging the entire evening. Apparently Calvetti's was 'the hottest club in the country', with twice as many people being turned away at the door than being admitted.

Luckily, Melanie had been so excited about it all that she'd totally failed to pump Hannah for information on the man himself. The last thing Hannah wanted was for her sister to think she had a crush on him. It was bad enough knowing her entire family thought she was a closet lesbian without giving them proof of her heterosexuality—one sniff and they'd start trying to marry her off to any man with a pulse.

The bouncer scanned his clipboard before taking a step to one side and unclipping the red cordon acting as a barrier.

'Enjoy your evening, ladies,' he said as they filed past, actually smiling at them.

Another doorman led them straight through to the club, which heaved with bodies and pulsated with loud music, leading them up a cordoned-off set of sparkling stairs.

Her heart lifted to see one of the man mountains who'd been guarding the club the other afternoon standing to attention by a door marked 'Private'.

Surely that meant Francesco was here?

A young hunk dressed in black approached them and led them to a large round corner table. Six iced buckets of champagne were already placed on it.

'Oh, wow,' said Melanie. 'Is this for us?'

'It is,' he confirmed, opening the first bottle. 'With the compliments of the management. If you need anything, holler—your night is on the house.'

'Can I have a glass of lemonade, please?' Hannah asked,

her request immediately drowned out by the hens all badgering her to have one glass of champagne.

About to refuse, she remembered the promise she'd made to herself that it was time to start living.

She, more than anyone, knew how precarious life could be, but it had taken an accident on her bike for her to realise that all she had been doing since the age of twelve was existing. Meeting Francesco in the flesh had only made those feelings stronger.

If heaven was real, what stories would she have to tell Beth other than medical anecdotes? She would have nothing of real *life* to share.

That was something she'd felt in Francesco, that sense of vitality and spontaneity, of a life being *lived*.

Settling down at the table, she took a glass of champagne, her eyes widening as the bubbles played on her tongue. All the same, she stopped after a few sips.

To her immense surprise, Hannah soon found she was enjoying herself. Although she didn't know any of them well, Melanie's friends were a nice bunch. Overjoyed to be given the VIP treatment, they made sure to include her in everything, including what they called Talent Spotting.

Alas, no matter how discreetly she craned her neck, Hannah couldn't see Francesco anywhere. She did, however, spot a couple of minor members of the royal family and was reliably informed that a number of Premier League football players and a world-championship boxer were on the table next to theirs, and that the glamorous women and men with shiny white teeth who sat around another table were all Hollywood stars and their beaus.

'Thank you so much for getting knocked off your bike,' Melanie said whilst on a quick champagne break from the dance floor, flinging her arms around Hannah. 'And thank you for coming out with us tonight and for coming here—I was convinced you were going to go home after the meal.'

Hannah hugged her in return, holding back her confession that she *had* originally planned on slipping away after their Chinese, but that the lure of seeing Francesco again had been too great. It had almost made up for the fact Beth wasn't there to share Melanie's hen night. She wouldn't be there to share the wedding, either.

The wedding. An event Hannah dreaded.

She felt a huge rush of affection for her little sister along with an accompanying pang of guilt. Poor Melanie. She deserved better than Hannah. Since Beth's death, Hannah had tried so hard to be the best big sister they both wished she could be, but she simply wasn't up to the job. It was impossible. How could she be anything to anyone when such a huge part of herself was missing? All she had been able to do was throw herself into her studies, something over which she had always had total control.

But now her drive and focus had been compromised.

Never had she experienced anything like this.

Hannah was a woman of practicality, not a woman to be taken in with flights of fancy. Medicine was her life. From the age of twelve she'd known exactly what she wanted to be and had been single-minded in her pursuit of it. She would dedicate her life to medicine and saving children, doing her utmost to keep them alive so she could spare as many families from the gaping hole that lived in her own heart as she could.

At least, she had been single-minded until a car knocked her off her bike and the most beautiful man in the universe had stepped in to save her.

Now the hole in her heart didn't feel so hollow.

Since that fateful cold morning, her mind had not just been full of medicine. It had been full of *him*, her knight in shining armour, and meeting him in the flesh had only compounded this. She wasn't stupid. She knew she would never fit into his world. His reputation preceded him. Francesco Calvetti was a dangerous man to know and an *exceptionally* dangerous man to get on the wrong side of. But knowing this had done nothing to eradicate him from her mind.

That moment when she'd been lying on the cold concrete and opened her eyes, she had looked at him and felt such warmth.... Someone who could evoke that in her couldn't be all bad. He just couldn't.

'Come on, Han,' said Melanie, tugging at her hand. 'Come and dance with me.'

'I can't dance.' What she really wanted to do was search every nook and cranny of Calvetti's until she found him. Because he was there. She just knew it.

Melanie pointed at the dance floor, where a group of twenty-something men with more money than taste were strutting their stuff. 'Nor can they.'

Francesco watched the images from the security cameras on a range of monitors on his office wall. Through them, he could see everything taking place in his club. The same feeds were piped into the office where his security guys sat holed up, watching the same live images—but the only eyes Francesco trusted were his own. Tomorrow he would head back to Palermo to spot-check his nightclub and casino there, and then he would fly on to Madrid for the same.

A couple of men he suspected of being drug dealers had been invited by a group of city money men into the VIP area. He watched them closely, debating whether to have them dealt with now or wait until he had actual proof of their nefarious dealings.

A sweep of thick blonde hair with pink bunny ears

caught his attention in one of the central feeds. He watched Hannah get dragged onto the dance floor by another pink-tutued blonde he assumed was the hen of said hen party, Melanie.

Not for the first time, he asked himself what the hell Hannah was doing there.

She looked more than a little awkward. His lips curved upwards as he watched her try valiantly to move her body in time to the beat of the music. He'd seen more rhythm from the stray cats that congregated round the vast veranda of his Sicilian villa.

The half smile faded and compressed into a tight line when he read the slogan on her back: Horny Hannah.

That all the hen party had similar personalised slogans did nothing to break the compression of his lips.

It bothered him. Hannah was too…*classy* to have something so cheap written about her, even if it was in jest.

He downed his coffee and absently wiped away the residue on the corner of his lips with his thumb.

What was she doing here? And why did she keep craning her neck as if she was on the lookout for someone?

Since he'd dismissed her three days ago, he'd been unnerved to find her taking residence in his mind. Now was not the time for distractions of any sort, not when the casino in Mayfair was on the agenda. This particular casino was reputed to be one of the oldest—if not *the* oldest—in the whole of Europe. It had everything Francesco desired in a casino. Old-school glamour. Wealth. And credibility. This was a casino built by gentlemen for gentlemen, and while the old 'no women' rule had been relaxed in modern times, it retained its old-fashioned gentility. More than anything else, though, it was the one business his father had wanted and failed to get. This failure had been a thorn in

Salvatore's side until his dying day, when a life of overin-dulgence had finally caught up with him.

After almost forty years under the sole ownership of Sir Godfrey Renfrew, a member of the British aristocracy, the casino had been put up for sale.

Francesco wanted it. He coveted it, had spent two months charming Godfrey Renfrew into agreeing the sale of it to him. Such was Godfrey's hatred of Francesco's dead father, it had taken a month to even persuade him to meet.

What was more, if Francesco's spies were correct, Luca Mastrangelo was sniffing around the casino, too.

This news meant he absolutely could not afford to lose focus on the deal, yet still he'd found himself, an hour be-fore opening for the night, giving orders to his hospitality manager to reserve the best table in the club—for a hen party of all things. He'd only ever intended to have Mela-nie Chapman's party on the guest list.

Under ordinary circumstances, free tables were given to the most VIP of all VIPs and only then because of the publicity it generated.

He hadn't expected Hannah to be in attendance, but now she was here he couldn't seem to stop his eyes from flick-ering to whichever monitor happened to be fixed on her.

Hannah tried heroically to get her feet moving in time with the music, aware her dancing was easily the least rhyth-mic of the whole club. Not that this seemed to put any of the men off. To her chagrin, a few seemed to be suffering from what her sister termed Wandering Hand Syndrome. One in particular kept 'accidentally' rubbing against her. When his hand brushed over her bottom the first time she'd been prepared to give him the benefit of the doubt, and had stepped away from him. The second time, when he'd been bolder and tried to cup her buttocks, she'd flashed him a smile and said in her politest voice, 'Please don't do that,' he'd removed his hand. Which had worked for all of ten seconds. The third time he groped her, she'd 'accidentally' trod on his foot. And now the sleaze had 'accidentally' palmed her breast and was grinding into her back as if she were some kind of plaything.

Did people actually *like* this kind of behaviour? Did women really find it *attractive*?

Just as she was wishing she had worn a pair of stilettoes like all the other women there so she could bruise him properly, a figure emerged on the dance floor.

Such was Francesco's presence that the crowd parted like the Red Sea to admit him.

Her sister stopped dancing and gazed up at him with a dropped jaw. The other hens also stared, agog, their feet seeming to move in a manner completely detached from their bodies.

And no wonder. A head taller than anyone else on the dance floor, he would have commanded attention even if he'd looked like the back end of a bus. Wearing an immaculately pressed open-necked black shirt and charcoal trousers, his gorgeous face set in a grim mask, he oozed menace.

Even if Hannah had wanted to hide her delight, she would have been unable to, her face breaking into an enormous grin at the sight of him, an outward display of the fizzing that had erupted in her veins.

She'd hoped with a hope bordering on desperation that he would spot her and seek her out, had prepared herself for the worst, but hoped for the best. She'd also promised herself that if he failed to materialise that evening then she would do everything in her power to forget about him. But if he were to appear…

To her disquiet, other than nodding at her without making proper eye contact, his attention was very much focused on the man who'd been harassing her who, despite trying to retain a nonchalant stance, had beads of sweat popping out on his forehead.

Francesco leaned into his face, his nostrils flaring. 'If you touch this woman again, you will answer to me personally. *Capisce?*'

Not waiting for a response, he turned back into the crowd.

Hannah watched his retreating figure, her heart in her mouth.

Melanie shouted over the music to her, her face animated, yet Hannah didn't hear a single syllable.

It was now or never.

Unlike the regularity of her life, where the only minor change to her schedule came in the form of the monthly weekend-night shift, Francesco's life was full of movement and change, hopping from country to country, always seeing different sunsets. Her life was exactly where she had planned it to be and she didn't want to change the fundamentals of it, but there was something so intoxicating about both Francesco and the freedom of his life. The freedom to wake up in the morning and just *go*.

He could go anywhere *right now*.

Hurrying to catch him, she followed in his wake, weaving through the sweaty bodies and then past the VIP tables.

'Francesco,' she called, panic fluttering in her chest as he placed his hand on the handle of the door marked Private.

He stilled.

She hurried to close the gap.

He turned his head, his features unreadable.

The music was so loud she had to incline right into

him. He was close enough for her to see the individual hairs in the V of his shirt and smell his gorgeous scent, all oaky manliness, everything converging to send her pulse racing.

'Why did you just do that?' she asked.

His eyes narrowed, the pupils ringing with intent, before he turned the handle and held the door open for her.

Hannah stepped into a dimly lit passageway. Francesco closed the door, blocking off the thumping noise of the music.

She shook her head a little to try to clear her ringing ears.

He leaned back against the door, his eyes fixed on her.

'Why did you do that?' she repeated, filling the silence with a question she knew he'd heard perfectly well the first time she'd asked it.

'What? Warn that man off?'

'Threaten him,' she corrected softly.

'I don't deal in threats, Dr Chapman,' he said, his voice like ice. 'Only promises.'

'But why?'

'Because he wouldn't take no for an answer. I will not allow abuse of any form to take place on my premises.'

'So you make a point of personally dealing with all unwanted attention in your clubs, do you?'

His eyes bored into hers, his lips a tight line.

Far from his forbidding expression making her turn and run away, as it would be likely to make any other sane person do, it emboldened her. 'And did I really hear you say *capisce*?'

'It's a word that the man will understand.'

'Very Danny DeVito. And, judging by his reaction to it, very effective.'

Something that could almost pass for amusement curled on his lips. 'Danny DeVito? Do you mean Al Pacino?'

'Probably.' She tried to smile, tried hard to think of a witty remark that would hold his attention for just a little longer, but it was hard to think sensibly when you were caught in a gaze like hot chocolate-fudge cake, especially when it was attached to a man as divine as Francesco Calvetti. If she had to choose, she would say the man was a slightly higher rank on the yummy stakes than the cake. And she liked hot chocolate-fudge cake *a lot*, as her bottom would testify.

'Thank you for rescuing me. Again.'

'You're welcome.' He made to turn the door handle. 'Now, if you'll excuse me...'

'Dismissing me again?'

'I'm a very...'

'Busy man,' she finished for him. God, but her heart was thundering beneath her ribs, her hands all clammy. 'Please. I came along tonight because I wanted to see you again. Five minutes of your time. That's all I ask. If at the end of it you tell me to leave then I will and I promise never to seek you out again.'

She held her breath as she awaited his response.

He eyed her coolly, his features not giving anything away, until, just as she feared she was about to run out of oxygen, he inclined his head and turned the handle of another door, also marked Private.

Hannah followed him into a large room that was perhaps the most orderly office she had ever been in. Along one wall were two dozen monitors, which she gravitated towards. It didn't take long to spot her sister and fellow hens, all back at their table, talking animatedly.

It occurred to her that she had simply walked away without telling Melanie where she was going.

'So, Dr Chapman, you wanted five minutes of my time...'

She turned her head to find Francesco staring pointedly at his chunky, expensive-looking watch.

He might look all forbidding but she could sense his curiosity.

How she regretted allowing Melanie to talk her into wearing the 'hen uniform', but it would have been churlish to refuse. She had denied her sister too much through the years. Dressing in a ridiculous outfit was the least she could do. Still, it made her self-conscious, and right then she needed every ounce of courage to say what she needed to say.

She swallowed but held his gaze, a look that was cold yet made her feel all warm inside. Seriously, how could a man with chocolate-fudge-cake eyes be all bad?

'When I was knocked off my bike I thought I'd died,' she said, clasping her hands together. God, but this was so much harder than she had imagined it would be and she had known it would be hard. 'I honestly thought that was it for me. Since then, everything has changed—*I've* changed. My accident made me realise I've been letting life pass me by.'

'How does this relate to me?'

Her heart hammered so hard her chest hurt. 'Because I can't stop thinking about you.'

His eyes narrowed with suspicion and he folded his arms across his chest.

Hannah's nerves almost failed her. Her tongue rooted to the roof of her mouth.

'What is it you want from me?'

Out of the corner of her eye she spotted the thank-you card she'd given him. Seeing it there, displayed on his desk, settled the nerves in her stomach.

Francesco had kept her card.

He'd sought her out and rescued her *again*.

She wasn't imagining the connection between them.

She sucked her lips in and bit them before blurting out, 'I want you to take my virginity.'

CHAPTER THREE

FRANCESCO SHOOK HIS HEAD. For the first time in his thirty-six years he was at a loss for words.

'God, that came out all wrong.' Hannah covered her face, clearly cringing. When she dropped her hands her face had paled but, to give her credit, she met his gaze with barely a flinch. 'I didn't mean it to come out quite so crudely. Please, say something.'

He shook his head again, trying to clear it. 'Is this some kind of joke?'

'No.'

'You're a virgin?'

'Yes.'

For a moment he seriously considered that he was in some kind of dream.

Had he fallen asleep at his desk?

Since the discovery of his mother's diaries ten months ago, he'd been consumed with rage. This rage fuelled him. Indeed, for the past ten months, his drive had been working at full throttle. Only a month ago his doctor had told him to slow down, that he was at risk of burnout. Naturally, he'd ignored that advice. Francesco would not slow down until he had eradicated every last trace of Salvatore Calvetti's empire.

And to think he'd almost missed those diaries. Had he

not given the family home one last sweep before emptying it for sale, he would never have found them, hidden away in boxes in the cubbyhole of his mother's dressing room. He hadn't even intended to go into his mother's rooms but the compulsion to feel close to her one last time had made him enter them for the first time in two decades.

Reading the diaries had been as close to torture as a man could experience. The respect he'd felt for his father, the respect that had made him a dutiful son while his father was alive, had died a brutal death.

His only regret was that he hadn't learned the truth while his father was alive, would never have the pleasure of punishing him for every hour of misery he'd put his mother through. Duty would have gone to hell. He might just have helped his father into an early grave.

He hoped with every fibre of his being that his father *was* in hell. He deserved nothing less.

Because now he knew the truth. And he would not be satisfied until he'd destroyed everything Salvatore Calvetti had built, crushed his empire and his reputation. Left it for dust.

The truth consumed him. His hate fuelled him.

It was perfectly feasible he had fallen asleep.

Except he'd never had a dream that made his heart beat as if it would hammer through his ribcage.

He rubbed the back of his neck and stared at the woman who had made such a confounding offer.

She looked ridiculous in her hen outfit, with the pink tutu, black leotard and leggings, and black ballet slippers. At least the other hens had made an effort, adorning their outfits with the sky-high heels women usually wore in his clubs. It didn't even look as if Hannah had brushed her hair, never mind put any make-up on. What woman went clubbing without wearing make-up?

Indeed, he could not remember the last time he'd met a woman who *didn't* wear make-up, full stop.

And she still had those ridiculous bunny ears on her head.

Yet there was something incredibly alluring about Hannah's fresh-faced looks. Something different.

He'd thought *she* was different. He'd resisted her offer of a date a few short days ago because of it; because he'd thought she was *too* different, that she didn't belong in his world.

Could he really have judged her so wrong?

What kind of woman offered her so-called virginity to a stranger?

And what the hell had compelled him to warn her groper off and not send one of his men in to resolve the situation? If he'd followed his usual procedures he wouldn't be standing here now on the receiving end of one of the most bizarre offers he'd ever heard.

It had been watching that man paw her—and her dignity when rebuffing his advances—that had made something inside him snap.

The rules were the same in all his establishments, his staff trained to spot customers overstepping the mark in the familiarity stakes. The usual procedure was for one of his doormen to have a polite 'word' with the perpetrator. That polite word was usually enough to get them behaving.

Francesco might have little respect for the type of women who usually littered his clubs but that did not mean he would tolerate them being abused in any form.

In the shadows of his memory rested his mother, a woman who had tolerated far too much abuse. And he, her son, had been oblivious to it.

A rush of blood to his head had seen him off his seat,

out of his office and onto the dance floor before his brain had time to compute what his feet were doing.

'I have no idea what you're playing at,' he said slowly, 'but I will not be a party to such a ridiculous game. I have given you your five minutes. It's time for you to leave.'

This *had* to be a game. Hannah Chapman had discovered his wealth and, like so many others of her gender, decided she would like to access it.

It unnerved him how disappointed he felt.

'This isn't a game.' She took a visibly deep breath. 'Please. Francesco, I am a twenty-seven-year-old woman who has never had sex. I haven't even kissed a man. It's become a noose around my neck. I don't want to stay a virgin all my life. All I want is one night to know what it feels like to be a real woman and you're the only man I can ask.'

'But why me?' he asked, incredulous.

Her beautiful hazel eyes held his. 'Because I trust that you won't hurt me.'

'How can you trust such a thing? I am a stranger to you.'

'The only men I meet are fellow doctors and patients. The patients are a big no-no, and the few single doctors I know...we work too closely together. You might be a stranger but I *know* you'll treat me with respect. I know you would never laugh at me or make fun about me being a twenty-seven-year-old virgin behind my back.'

'That's an awful lot of supposition you're making about me.'

'Maybe.' She raised her shoulders in a helpless gesture. 'I thought I was dead. When I opened my eyes and saw your face I thought you'd come to take me to heaven. All I can think now is *what if...* What if I *had* died? I've done *nothing* with my life.'

'Hardly,' he said harshly. 'You're a doctor. That takes dedication.'

'For me, it's taken everything. I'm not naturally bright—
I had to work hard to get my grades, to learn and to keep
learning. In the process I've been so focused on my career
that I've allowed my personal life to go to ruin.' The same
groove he remembered from the other evening reappeared
on her forehead. 'I don't want to die a virgin.'

Francesco rubbed his neck.

*It seemed s*he was serious.

Of course, she *could* be lying. Having discovered who
he was, this could be a clever, convoluted game to access
his life and wealth.

Yet her explanation made a mad kind of sense.

He remembered the expression of serenity that had
crossed her face at the moment she'd opened her eyes and
looked at him, remembered her words and the fuzzy feelings they had evoked in him.

Something had passed between them—something fleeting but tangible.

There was no way Hannah could have known who he
was at that moment.

One thing he did know was that she had gained a false
impression of him. If she knew who he really was, he would
be the last man she would make such a shameless propo-
sition to.

Regardless, he could hardly credit how tempted he was.

He was a red-blooded male. What man *wouldn't* be
tempted by such an offer?

But Hannah was a virgin, he reminded himself—despite
the fact that he'd thought virgins over the age of eighteen
were from the tales of mythology.

Surely this was every man's basest fantasy? A virgin
begging to be deflowered.

'You have no idea who I am,' he told her flatly.

'Are you talking about the gangster thing?'

'The gangster thing?' His voice took on a hint of menace. How could she be so blasé about it? Was she so naive she didn't understand his life wasn't something watched from the safety of a television set, played by men who likely had manicures between takes?

Scrutinising her properly, her innocence was obvious. She had an air about her—the same air he saw every time he looked through his parents' wedding album. His mother had had that air when she'd married his father, believing it to be a love match, blissfully oblivious to her husband's true nature, and the true nature of his business affairs.

Hannah raised her shoulders again. 'I've read all about you on the internet. I know what it says your family are.'

'And do you believe everything you read on the internet?'

'No.' She shook her head to emphasise her point.

Deliberately, he stepped towards her and into her space. He brought his face down so it was level with hers. 'You *should* believe it. Because it's true. Every word. I am not a good person for you to know. I am the last person a woman like you should get involved with.'

She didn't even flinch. 'A woman like me? What does that mean?'

'You're a doctor. You do not belong in my world.'

'I just want *one night* in your world, that's all. One night. I don't care what's been written about you. I know you would never hurt me.'

'You think?' Where had she got this ludicrous faith in him from? He had to eradicate it, make her see enough of the truth to scare her all the way back to the safety of her hospital.

He straightened to his full height, an act capable of intimidating even the hardest of men. He breached the inches between them to reach into her thick mane of hair and tu the rabbit ears free. They were connected by some kind of plastic horseshoe that he dropped onto the floor and placed a foot on. He pressed down until he heard the tell-tale crunch.

She stared at him with that same serene look in her hazel eyes.

'Tell me,' he said, gently twisting her around so her back was flush against him, 'how, exactly, do you want me to take your virginity?'

He heard an intake of breath.

Good. He'd unnerved her.

Gathering her hair together, he inhaled the sweet scent of her shampoo. Her hair felt surprisingly soft. 'Do you want me to take you here and now?'

He trailed a finger down her exposed slender neck, over the same collarbone that had been broken less than two months before, and down her toned arm before reaching round to cup a breast flattened by the leotard she wore.

'Or do you want me to take you on a bed?' He traced his thumb over a nipple that shot out beneath his touch.

'I...' Her voice came out like a whimper. 'I...'

'You must have some idea of how you would like me to perform the deed,' he murmured, breathing into her ear and nuzzling his nose into a cheek as soft as the finest silk. 'Is foreplay a requirement? Or do you just want to get it over with?'

'I...I know what you're doing.'

'All I'm doing is ascertaining how, exactly, you would like me to relieve you of your virginity. I can do it now if you would like.' He pressed his groin into the small of her back so as to leave her in no doubt how ready he was. 'Right here, over the desk? Up against the wall? On the floor?'

Much as he hated himself for it, his body was responding to her in the basest of fashions.

He would control it, just as he controlled everything else.

He would *not* give in to temptation.

He would make the good doctor see just how wrong she was about him.

Hannah Chapman was one of the few people in the world who made a difference.

He would not be the one to taint her, no matter how much he desired her or how much she wanted it.

He was better than that. He was better than the man who had created him, who would, no doubt, have already relieved Hannah of her virginity if he'd been in Francesco's shoes.

He would not be that man. And if he had to come on heavy to make her run away, then that was what he would do. Reasoning clearly didn't work with her.

'You're trying to scare me off.'

Francesco stilled at her astuteness.

Although her breaths were heavy, he could feel her defiance through the rigidity of her bones.

It was with far too much reluctance that he released his hold and turned her back round to face him.

Hannah's hair tumbled back around her shoulders. Her cheeks were flushed, her eyes wide. Yet there was no fear. Apprehension, yes, but no fear.

'You are playing with fire, Dr Chapman.'

She gave a wry smile. 'I'm trained to treat burns.'

'Not the kind you will get from me. You'll have to find another man to do the job. I'm not for hire.'

His mind flashed to the man who'd been groping Hannah earlier—who, he imagined, would be more than happy to accede to her request. He banished the image. Who she chose was none of his concern.

All the same, the thought of that man pawing at her

again sent a sharp, hot flush racing through him. She was too...*pure*.

A shrewdness came into her eyes, although how such a look could also be gentle totally beat him.

She tilted her head to the side. 'Do I scare you?'

'On the contrary. It is you who should be afraid of me.'

'But I'm not scared of you. I don't care about your reputation. I'm not after a relationship or anything like that— the only thing being with you makes me feel is good. After everything you've done for me, how can I not trust that?'

He shook his head.

This was madness.

He should call his guards and have her escorted out of his club. But he wouldn't.

Francesco had heard stories about people who saved lives being bound to the person they'd saved, and vice versa. And while he hadn't saved her in a technical sense, it was the only explanation he could think of for the strange chemistry that brewed between them. Total strangers yet inexplicably linked.

Something had passed between them, connecting them. It was his duty to sever that link. *His* duty. Not his guards'.

He would make her see.

'You think I'm worthy of your trust?' Unthinkingly, he reached out a hand and captured a lock of her hair.

'I *know* you are.' Reclosing the gap between them, she tilted her head back a little and placed a hand on his cheek. 'Don't you see? A lesser man wouldn't try to scare me off—he would have taken what I offered without a second thought.'

His skin tingled beneath the warmth of her fingers. He wanted to clasp those fingers, interlace his own through them....

'I'm not cut out for any form of relationship—my career matters too much for me to compromise it—but I want to *feel*.' She brought her face closer so her nose skimmed against his throat, her breath a whisper against his sensitised skin. 'I want one night where I can throw caution to the wind. I want to know what it's like to be made love to and I want it to be you because you're the only man I've met who makes me feel alive without even touching me.'

Francesco could hardly breathe. His fingers still held the lock of her hair. The desire that had been swirling in his blood since he'd nuzzled into her neck thickened.

When had he ever felt as if he could explode from arousal?

This was madness.

'If I believed you felt nothing physically for me, I would walk away now,' she continued, her voice a murmur. 'I certainly wouldn't debase myself any further.'

'How can you be so sure I feel anything for you physically?'

'Just because I'm a virgin doesn't mean I'm totally naive.'

In his effort to scare her away, he'd pressed his groin into her back, letting her feel his excitement through the layers of their clothing.

That particular effort had backfired.

Hannah had turned it round on him.

Well, no more.

Clasping the hand still resting against his cheek, he tugged it away and dropped it. He stepped back, glowering down at her. 'You think you can spend one night with me and walk away unscathed? Because that isn't going to happen. Sex isn't a game, and I'm not a toy that can be played with.'

For the first time a hint of doubt stole over her face. 'I

never meant it like that,' she said, her voice low. 'It's not just that I'm wildly attracted to you, it's more than that. I can't explain it, but when I look at you I see a life full of excitement, of travel, of so much more than I could ever hope to experience. All I want is to reach out and touch it, to experience some of it with you.'

'You think you know me but you don't. I'm not the man you think. My life is seedy and violent. You should want nothing to do with it.'

For long, long moments he eyeballed her, waiting for her to drop her eyes. But it didn't happen—her gaze held his, steady and immovable.

'Prove it.' She gave a feeble shrug. 'If you really think you're so bad for me, then *prove* it.'

He almost groaned aloud. 'It's not a case of proving it. You need to understand—once your virginity's gone you will never get it back. It's lost for ever, and who knows what else you might lose with it.'

She swallowed but remained steady. 'There's nothing else for me to lose. I'm not after a love affair. Francesco, all I want is one night.'

It was hearing his name—and the meaning she put into it—on her lips that threw him.

It made him want to find a dragon to slay just to protect her. Yet he knew that the only thing Hannah needed protecting from was herself.

He reminded himself that he did not need this aggravation. His mind should be focused on the Mayfair deal—the deal that would be the crowning glory in his empire. Hannah had compromised his concentration enough these past few days.

Maybe if he gave her some of what she wanted his mind could regain its focus without her there, knocking on his thoughts.

'You want proof of who I really am?' he said roughly. 'Then that's what you shall have. I will give you a sample of my life for one weekend.'

Her eyes sparkled.

'*This* weekend,' he continued. 'You can share a taste of my life and see for yourself why you should keep the hell away from me. By the end of our time together I guarantee you will never want to see my face again, much less waste your virginity on a man like me.'

CHAPTER FOUR

HANNAH HAD BEEN twitching her curtains for a good half hour before Francesco pulled up outside her house on an enormous motorbike, the engine making enough racket to wake the whole street.

It didn't surprise her in the least that he waited for her to come out to him. Once Francesco had agreed to a weekend together, he had wasted no time in dismissing her by saying, 'I will collect you at 7:00 a.m. Have your passport ready.'

He was taking her to Sicily. To his home.

She couldn't remember the last time she'd been this excited about something. Or as nervous.

Her very essence tingling with anticipation, she stepped out into the early-morning sun, noticing that at least he had taken his helmet off to greet her.

'Good morning,' she said, beaming both at him and, with admiration, at the bike. There was something so...*manly* about the way he straddled it, which, coupled with the cut of his tight leather trousers, sent a shock of warmth right through her. 'Are we traveling to Sicily on this?'

He eyed her coldly. 'Only to the airbase. That's if you still want to come?' From the tone of his voice, there was no doubting that he hoped she'd changed her mind.

If she was honest, since leaving his office six short hours

ago, she'd repeatedly asked herself if she was doing the right thing.

But she hadn't allowed herself to even consider backing down. Because all she knew for certain was that if she didn't grab this opportunity with both hands she would regret it for the rest of her life, regardless of the outcome.

'I still want to come,' she said, almost laughing to see his lips tighten in disapproval. Couldn't he see, the more he tried to scare her off, the more she knew she was on the right path, that it proved his integrity?

Francesco desired her.

The feel of his hardness pressed against her had been the most incredible, intoxicating feeling imaginable. She had never dreamed her body capable of such a reaction, had imagined the thickening of the blood and the low pulsations deep inside were from the realms of fiction. It had only served to increase her desire, to confirm she was following the right path.

She'd been his for the taking in his office but he had stepped back, unwilling to take advantage. Again.

Francesco was doing everything in his power to put her off, but she doubted there was anything to be revealed about him that would do that. What, she wondered, had made him so certain he was all bad? Was it because of his blood lineage? Whatever it was, she knew there was good in him—even though he clearly didn't believe it himself.

Face thunderous, he reached into the side case and pulled out some leathers and a black helmet. 'Put these on.'

She took them from him. 'Do you want to come in while I change? Your bike will be perfectly safe—all the local hoodlums are tucked up in bed.'

'I will wait here.'

'I have coffee.'

'I will wait.'

'Suit yourself.'

'You have five minutes.'

In her bedroom, Hannah wrestled herself into the tight leather trousers, and then donned the matching jacket, staggering slightly under the weight of it.

When she caught sight of her reflection in the full-length mirror she paused. Whoever said leathers were sexy was sorely mistaken—although she'd admit to feeling very Sandra Dee in the trousers.

Sandra Dee had been a virgin, too.

Hannah was a virgin in all senses of the word.

But, she reminded herself, with Francesco's help she was going to change that. Just for this one weekend. That was all she wanted. Some memories to share with Beth.

She took a deep breath and studied her reflection one last time. Her stomach felt knotted, but she couldn't tell if excitement or trepidation prevailed.

She checked the back door was locked one last time before grabbing her small case and heading back out to him.

'That will not fit,' Francesco said when he saw her case.

'You're the one whisking me away for a romantic overnight stay on a motorbike,' she pointed out. 'What do you suggest I do?'

'Let me make this clear, I am not whisking you away anywhere.'

'Semantics.'

'And I never said anything about us going away for one night only. We will return to the UK when *I* am ready.'

'As long as you get me back in time for work at nine o'clock Monday morning, that's fine by me.'

His face was impassive. 'We will return when my schedule allows it, not yours.'

'Is this the part when I'm supposed to wave my hands and say, "oh, in that case I can't possibly come with you?"'

'Yes.'

'Bad luck. I'm coming. And you'll get me back in time for work.'

'You sound remarkably sure of yourself.'

'Not at all. I just know you're not the sort of person to allow a ward full of sick children to suffer from a lack of doctors.'

His features contorted, the chocolate fudge of his eyes hardening. 'That is a risk you are willing to take?'

'No.' She shook her head, a rueful smile playing on her lips. 'I know there's no risk.' At least no risk in the respect of getting her to work on time. And as to Francesco's other concerns, Hannah knew there was no risk in the respect of her heart, either; her heart hadn't functioned properly in fifteen years.

More practically, she supposed there were some dangers. She could very well be getting into something way out of her depth, but what was the worst that could happen? Hannah had lived through her own personal hell. The worst thing that could happen had occurred at the age of twelve, and she had survived it. God alone knew how, but she had.

It was only one weekend. One weekend of *life* before she went back to her patients, the children she hoped with all her semi-functioning heart would grow up to lead full lives of their own.

'On your head be it,' said Francesco. 'Now either find a smaller case for your stuff, put it in a rucksack you can strap to you, or leave it behind.'

Her gaze dropped to her case. She didn't have either a smaller case or a rucksack....

'Give me one minute,' she said, speaking over her shoulder as she hurried back into the house. In record time she'd grabbed an oversized handbag and shoved her passport, phone, purse, clean underwear, toothbrush, and a thin sundress into it. The rest of her stuff, including some research papers she'd been reading through for the past week, she left in the case.

This was an adventure after all. Her first adventure in fifteen years.

'Is that all you're taking?' Francesco asked when she rejoined him, taking the bag from her.

'You're the one who said to bring something smaller.'

He made a noise that sounded like a cross between a grunt and a snort.

She grinned. 'You'll have to try harder than that to put me off.'

Nostrils flaring, he shoved her bag into the side case then thrust the helmet back into her hands. 'Put this on.'

'Put this on…?' She waited for a *please*.

'Now.'

How could *anyone* be so cheerful first thing in the morning? Francesco wondered. It wasn't natural.

What would it take to put a chink in that smiley armour?

With great reluctance, he reached over to help her with the helmet straps. Even through the darkened visor he could see her still grinning.

If he had his way, that pretty smile would be dropped from her face before they boarded his plane.

'Have you ridden on one of these before?' he asked, tightening the straps enough so they were secure without cutting off her circulation.

She shook her head.

'Put your arms around me and mimic my actions—lean into the turns.'

Only when he was certain that she was securely seated did Francesco twist the throttle and set off.

Francesco brought the bike to a halt in the airport's private car park.

'That was amazing!' Hannah said, whipping off her helmet to reveal a head of hair even more tangled than a whole forest of birds' nests.

If his body wasn't buzzing from the exhilaration of the ride coupled with the unwanted thrum of desire borne from having her pressed against him for half an hour, he would think she looked endearing.

His original intention had been to take advantage of the clear early-Saturday-morning roads and hit the throttle. What he hadn't accounted for was the distraction of having Hannah pressed so tightly against him.

And no wonder. Those trousers…

Caro Dio…

Behind that sensible, slightly messy exterior lay a pair of the most fantastic legs he had ever seen. He'd noticed how great they looked the night before, but the ridiculous pink tutu had hidden the best part: the thighs.

Not for a second had he been able to forget she was there, attached to him, trusting him to keep her safe.

Where the hell did she get this misplaced trust *from*?

In the end, he'd kept his speed strictly controlled, rarely breaching the legal limits. Not at all the white-knuckle ride he'd had in mind.

His guards were already there waiting for him, forbidden from following him when he was riding in the UK. It was different on the Med, especially in Sicily. The only good thing he could say about England was he never felt the need to have an entourage watching his back at all times.

In as ungracious a manner as he could muster, he pulled

Hannah's bag from the side case, handed it to her, then threw the keys of his bike to one of his men.

'What are you doing?' he asked, spotting Hannah on her phone. It was one of the latest models. For some reason this surprised him. Maybe it was because she was a virgin who dressed in a basic, functional manner that he'd assumed she'd have a basic, functional phone.

'Answering my emails,' she said, peering closely at the screen as she tapped away.

'From who?'

'Work.'

'It is Saturday.'

She peered up at him. She really did look ridiculous, with the heavy jacket clearly weighing her down. Still, those legs... And that bottom...

'Hospitals don't close for weekends.' She flashed him a quick grin. 'I'll be done in a sec.'

Francesco had no idea why it irked him to witness Hannah pay attention to her phone. He didn't want to encourage her into getting any ideas about them but, all the same, he did *not* appreciate being made to feel second best.

'All done,' she said a moment later, dropping the phone back into her bag.

Once the necessary checks were made, they boarded Francesco's plane.

'You own this?' she asked with the same wide-eyed look she'd had when she'd first walked into his club carrying a bunch of flowers for him.

He jerked a nod and took his seat, indicating she should sit opposite him. 'Before I give the order for us to depart, I need to check your bag.'

'Why? It's already been through a scanner.'

'My plane. My rules.' He met her gaze, willing her to

fight back, to leave, to get off the aircraft and walk away before the dangers of his life tainted her.

He thought he saw a spark of anger. A tiny spark, but a spark all the same.

She shrugged and handed it over to him.

He opened the bag. His hand clenched around her underwear. He should pull it out, let her see him handle her most intimate items. The plane hadn't taken off. There was still time to change her mind.

But then he met her gaze again. She studied him with unabashed curiosity.

No. He would not humiliate her.

His fingers relaxed their grip, the cotton folding back into place. He pulled out a threadbare black purse.

Resolve filled him. He opened it to find a few notes, a heap of receipts, credit and debit cards, and a photo, which he tugged out.

Hannah fidgeted before him but he paid her no heed.

She wanted him to prove in actions how bad he was for her? This was only the beginning.

He peered closely at a picture of two identical young girls with long flaxen hair, hazel eyes, and the widest, gappiest grins he had ever seen.

'You are a twin?' he asked in surprise.

Her answer came after a beat too long. 'Yes.'

He looked at her. Hannah's lips were drawn in. Her lightly tanned skin had lost a little of its colour.

'Why was she not out last night with you, celebrating your other sister's hen night?'

Her hands fisted into balls before she flexed them and raised her chin. 'Beth died a long time ago.'

His hand stilled.

'Please be careful with that. It's the last picture taken

of us together.' There was a definite hint of anxiety in her voice.

This was another clear-cut opportunity to convince her of his true self. All he had to do was rip the photo into little pieces and he guaranteed she would leave without a backward glance.

But no matter how much he commanded his hands to do the deed, they refused.

Hannah's voice broke through his conflicted thoughts. 'Can I have my stuff back now?' she asked, now speaking in her more familiar droll manner.

Without saying a word, he carefully slotted the photo back in its place, blinking to rid himself of the image of the happy young girls.

The last picture of them together?

His stomach did a full roll and settled with a heavy weight rammed onto it.

Getting abruptly to his feet, he dropped the bag by Hannah's seat. 'I need to speak with the crew. Put your seat belt on.'

Hannah expelled all the air from her lungs in one long movement, watching as Francesco disappeared through a door.

There had been a moment when she'd been convinced he was going to crush the photo in his giant hands.

If there was one thing she'd be unable to forgive, it was that.

But he hadn't. He'd wanted to, but the basic decency within him had won out. And he hadn't fired a load of questions about Beth at her, either.

It was very rare that she spoke about her twin. Even after fifteen years, it still felt too raw, as if vocalising it turned it back into the real event that had ripped her apart. People treated her differently. As soon as someone learned about it, she just knew that was how they would start referring to her. *That's the girl whose twin sister died.* She'd heard those very whispers at school, felt the curious glances and the eyes just waiting for the telltale sign of her suffering. She knew what her schoolmates had been waiting for—they'd been waiting for her to cry.

She'd cried plenty, but always in the privacy of her bedroom—the room she'd shared with Beth.

She'd learned to repel the curiosity with a bright smile, and ignore the whispers by burying herself in her school-work. It had been the same with her parents. And Melanie. She'd effectively shut them all out, hiding her despair behind a smile and then locking herself away.

When Francesco reappeared a few minutes later, she fixed that same bright smile on him.

'We'll be taking off in five minutes,' he said. 'This is your last chance to change your mind.'

'I'm not changing my mind.'

'Sicily is my turf. If you come, you will be bound under my directive.'

'How very formal. I'm still not changing my mind.'

His eyes glittered with menace. 'As I said earlier—on your head be it.'

'Gosh, it's hot,' Hannah commented as she followed Francesco off the steps of the plane. She breathed in deeply. Yes, there it was. That lovely scent of the sea. Thousands of miles away, and for a moment she had captured the smell of home. Her real home—on the coast of Devon. Not London. London was where she lived.

'It's summer' came the curt reply.

At least she'd had the foresight to change out of the leathers and into her sundress before they'd landed. Not that Francesco had noticed. Or, if he had, he hadn't acknowledged it, keeping his head buried so deep into what he was doing on his laptop she wouldn't have been surprised if he'd disappeared into the screen. The only time he'd moved had been to go into his bedroom—yes, he had a *bedroom on a plane*!—and changed from his own leathers into a pair of black chinos, an untucked white linen shirt, and a blazer.

A sleek grey car was waiting, the driver opening the passenger door as they approached. Another identical car waited behind, and Francesco's guards piled into it—except one, who got into the front of their own car.

The doors had barely closed before the guard twisted round and handed a metallic grey object to Francesco.

'Is that a gun?' Hannah asked in a tone more squeaky than anything a chipmunk could produce.

He tucked the object into what she assumed was an inside pocket of his blazer. 'We are in Sicily.'

'Are guns legal in Sicily?'

He speared her with a look she assumed was supposed to make her quail.

'I hope for your sake it's not loaded,' she said. 'Especially with you keeping it so close to your heart.'

'Then it's just as well I have a doctor travelling with me.'

'See? I have my uses.'

Despite her flippancy, the gun unnerved her. It unnerved her a lot.

Knowing on an intellectual level that Francesco was dangerous was one thing. Witnessing him handle a gun with the nonchalance of one handling a pen was another.

He's doing this for effect, she told herself. *Remember, this is an adventure.*

'Where are we going?' she asked after a few minutes of silence had passed.

'My nightclub.'

It didn't take long before they pulled up outside an enormous Gothic-looking building with pillars at the doors.

'This is a nightclub?'

'That's where I said we were going.'

In a melee of stocky male bodies, she followed him inside.

The Palermo Calvetti's was, she estimated, at least four times the size of its English counterpart. Although decorated in the same glitzy silver and deep reds and exuding glamour, it had a more cosmopolitan feel.

A young woman behind the bar, polishing all the hardwood and optics, practically snapped to attention at the sight of them.

'*Due caffè neri nel mio ufficio,*' Francesco called out as he swept past and through a door marked *Privato*.

Like its English equivalent, his office was spotless. Two of his men entered the room with them—the same two who'd been guarding the English Calvetti's when she had turned up just five short days ago.

Francesco went straight to a small portrait on the wall and pressed his fingers along the edge of the frame until it popped open as if it were the cover of a book.

'Another cliché?' she couldn't resist asking.

'Clichés are called clichés for a reason,' he said with a shrug of a shoulder. 'Why make it easy for thieves?'

Watching him get into his safe, Hannah decided that it would be easier to break into Fort Knox than into Francesco Calvetti's empire. The inner safe door swinging open, her eyes widened to see the sheer size of the space inside, so much larger than she would have guessed from the picture covering it.

Her stare grew wider to see the canvas bags he removed from it and she realised that they were filled with money.

Francesco and his two men conversed rapidly, all the

while weighing wads of notes on a small set of electronic scales and making notes in a battered-looking A4 book. When the young woman came in with two coffees and a bowl of sugar cubes, Francesco added two lumps into both cups, stirred them vigorously, then passed one over to Hannah, who had perched herself on a windowsill.

'Thanks,' she said, ridiculously touched he'd remembered how she liked her coffee.

Not that it would have been hard to remember, she mused, seeing as he took his exactly the same.

The same thought must have run through Francesco's head because his eyes suddenly met hers, a look of consternation running through them before he jerked his head back to what he was doing.

It amazed her that he would allow her in his inner sanctum when such a large amount of money was, literally, on the table. Then she remembered the gun in his jacket, which he had placed over the back of his captain's chair.

Peering less than subtly at his henchmen, she thought she detected a slight bulge in the calf of the black trousers one wore.

Unnerved by the massive amounts of money before her and the fact she was alone in an office with three men, two of whom were definitely armed, she reached for her phone to smother her increasing agitation.

Working through her messages, Hannah's heart sank when she opened an email from an excited Melanie, who had finally, after months of debate, settled on the wedding-breakfast menu. She could only hope the response she fired back sounded suitably enthusiastic, but she couldn't even bring herself to open the attachment with the menu listed on it, instead opening a work-related email.

It was the most significant event in her little sister's life and, much as Hannah wanted to be excited for her, all she felt inside when she thought of the forthcoming day was dread.

'What are you doing?' Francesco asked a while later, breaking through her concentration.

'Going through my messages.'

'Again?'

'I like to keep abreast of certain patients' progress,' she explained, turning her phone off and chucking it back into her bag.

'Even at weekends?'

'*You're* working,' she pointed out.

'This is my business.'

'And the survival and recovery of my patients is *my* business.'

She had no idea what was going on behind those chocolate-fudge eyes but, judging by the set of his jaw and the thinning of his lips, she guessed it was something unpleasant.

A few minutes later and it appeared they were done, the two henchmen having placed all the money into a large suitcase.

'Before you leave for the bank, Mario,' Francesco said, speaking in deliberate English, 'I want you to show the good doctor here your hand.'

The guns hadn't made any overt impression on her, other than what he took to be a healthy shock that he armed himself in his homeland. He felt certain the next minute would change her impression completely.

Mario complied, holding his hand with its disfigured fingers in front of her.

She peered closely before taking it into her own hands and rubbing her fingers over the meaty skin.

A hot stab plunged into Francesco's chest. He inhaled deeply through his nose, clenching his hands into fists.

She was just examining it like the professional she was, he told himself. All the same, even his mental teeth had gritted together.

'What do you see?' he demanded.

'A hand that's been broken in a number of places—the fingers have been individually broken, too, as if something heavy was smashed onto them.'

'An excellent assessment. Now, Mario, I would like you to tell Dr Chapman who broke your hand and smashed your fingers.'

If Mario was capable of showing surprise, he would be displaying it now, his eyes flashing at Francesco, who nodded his go-ahead. This was an incident that hadn't been discussed or even alluded to in nearly two decades.

'Signor Calvetti. He did it.'

Hannah looked up at Francesco. 'Your father?'

Deliberately, he folded his arms across his chest and stretched his legs out. 'No. Not my father.'

Her eyes widened. 'You?'

'*Sì*. I caught him stealing from my father. Take another look at his hand. That is what we do to thieves in my world.'

CHAPTER FIVE

FRANCESCO KEPT HIS gaze fixed on Hannah, waiting for a reaction other than her current open-mouthed horror.

See, he said with his eyes, *you wanted proof? Well, here it is.*

She closed her eyes and shook her head. When she snapped them back open, she gave Mario's hand another close inspection.

'These scars look old,' she said.

'Nearly twenty year,' Mario supplied in his pigeon English. 'Is okay. I ask for it.'

'What—you asked for your hand to be smashed?'

'What he means is that he did the crime knowing what his punishment would be if caught,' said Francesco.

Her eyes shrewd, she nodded. 'And yet, even after what you did to him and his so-called crime, he still works for you, is trusted enough to handle large quantities of money on your behalf, and, if I'm reading this right, carries a gun that he has never turned on you in revenge.'

How did she do it?

She'd turned it round on him *again*.

'Do not think there was any benevolence on my part,' he countered harshly, before nodding a dismissal at Mario, who left the office with his colleague, leaving them alone.

Hannah remained perched on the windowsill, her hair

now turned into a bushy beehive. She'd crossed her legs, her pale blue dress having ridden up her thighs. It was one of the most repulsive articles of clothing he had ever seen: shapeless, buttoned from top to bottom, clearly brought for comfort rather than style. And yet…there was something incredibly alluring about having to guess what lay beneath it.…

'What did he steal?'

'He was a waiter at one of my father's restaurants and made the mistake of helping himself to the takings in the till.'

'How much did he take?' she asked. Her former nonchalance had vanished. It pleased him to hear her troubled tone.

'I don't remember. Something that was the equivalent of around one hundred pounds.'

'So you maimed him for one hundred pounds?'

Francesco drew himself to his full height. 'Mario knew the risks.'

'Fair enough,' she said in a tone that left no doubt she meant the exact opposite. 'Why didn't you just call the police?'

'The police?' A mirthful sound escaped from his throat. 'We have our own ways of handling things here.'

'So if he stole from your father, why did *you* mete out the punishment?'

Francesco remembered that day so clearly.

He'd caught Mario red-handed. There had been no choice but to confront him. He'd made him empty his pockets. His father had walked in and demanded to know what was going on.

How clearly he remembered that sickening feeling in the pit of his stomach when Mario had confessed, looking Salvatore square in the eye as he did so.

And how clearly he remembered feeling as if he would

vomit when Salvatore had turned his laser glare to him, his son, and said, 'You know what must be done.'

Francesco had known. And so had Mario, whose own father had worked for Salvatore, and Salvatore's father before him. They'd both known the score.

It was time for Francesco to prove himself a man in his father's eyes, something his father had been waiting on for years. Something *he'd* been waiting on for years, too. A chance to gain his father's respect.

But how could he explain this to Hannah, explain that it had been an opportunity that hadn't just presented itself to him but come gift-wrapped? Refusal had never been an option.

And why did he even care to explain himself?

Francesco didn't explain himself to anyone.

He hadn't explained himself since he'd vomited in the privacy of his bathroom after the deed had been done, and only when he was certain he was out of earshot.

That was the last time he'd ever allowed himself to react with emotion. Certainly the last time he'd allowed himself to feel any vulnerability.

Overnight he'd put his childhood behind him, not that there had been much left of it after his mother had overdosed.

'I did it because it needed to be done and I was the one who caught him.'

She kept her eyes fixed on him. There was none of the reproach or disgust he expected to find. All that was there was something that looked suspiciously like compassion....

'Twenty years ago you would have been a boy.'

'I was seventeen. I was a man.'

'And how old was he?'

'The same.'

'Little more than children.'

'We both knew what we were doing,' he stated harshly. 'After that night we were no longer children.'

'I'll bet.'

'And how many more hands have you mangled in the intervening years?'

'Enough of them. There are times when examples need to be made.'

Violence had been a part of his life since toddlerhood. His mother had tried to protect him from the worst of his father's excesses but her attempts had not been enough. His first memory was looking out of his bedroom window and witnessing his father beating up a man over a car bonnet. The man had been held down by two of his father's men.

His mother had been horrified to find him looking out and dragged him away, covering his eyes. Francesco had learned only ten months ago that the bruising he often saw on his mother's body was also from the hands of his father, and not the result of clumsiness.

Francesco had spent his entire life idolising his father. Sure, there were things he'd never been comfortable about, but Salvatore was his father. He'd loved and respected him. After his death four years ago, certain truths had been revealed about aspects of his father's business that had taken some of the shine off his memories, like discovering his drug importing. That in itself had been a very bitter blow to bear, had sickened him to the pit of his stomach. But to learn the truth of what he'd done to his mother… It had sent Francesco's world spinning off its axis.

The walls of the spacious office started to close in on him. The air conditioning was on but the humidity had become stifling, perspiration breaking out on his back.

Hannah stared intently into those beautiful chocolate eyes. Only years of practice at reading her patients allowed her to see beneath the hard exterior he projected. There was pain there. A lot of it. 'What is it about me that scares you so much?'

His lips curled into a sneer. Rising from his chair, he strode towards her like a sleek panther. 'You think you scare me?'

'What other reason is there for you to try so hard to frighten me off and go out of your way to try to make me hate you? Because that's what you're doing, isn't it? Trying to make me hate you?'

He stilled, his huge frame right before her, blocking everything else out.

She reached out a hand and placed it on his chest. 'I bet you've never treated a woman like this before.'

'Like what?' he asked harshly, leaning over and placing his face right in hers, close enough for her to feel the warmth of his breath. 'You're the one with the foolish, romanticised notions about me. I warned you from the start that you didn't belong in my world, and yet you thought you knew best.'

'So this is all to make me see the real you?'

'We had a deal, Dr Chapman,' he bit out, grabbing her hand, which still rested against his hard chest, and lacing his fingers through it. He squeezed, a warning that caused no physical pain but was undoubtedly meant to impress upon her that, if he so chose, he *could* hurt her. 'I made you a guarantee that by the end of our time together I would be the last man you would want to give your virginity to.'

Squeezing his fingers in return, her mouth filling with saliva, she tilted her chin a touch. His mouth was almost close enough to press her lips to....

'If you really want to prove it, then hurt me, don't just give me a warning. You're twice my size—it would take no effort for you to hurt me if you really wanted.' Oh, but she was playing with fire. She didn't need Francesco to point that out. But no matter what she had seen in the two hours she'd been in his country, deep in her marrow was the rooted certainty that he would never hurt her, not in any meaningful sense.

If eyes could spit fire, Francesco's would be doing just that. But there was something else there, too, something that darkened as his breathing deepened.

'See?' she whispered. 'You can't hurt me.'

'Where does your faith in me come from?' His voice had become hoarse.

'It comes from *here*,' she answered, pulling their entwined fingers to her chest and pressing his hand right over her heart. 'I've seen the good in you. Why do you have so little faith in yourself?'

'I have no illusions about what I'm like. You have dedicated your life to healing sick children, whereas my life revolves around power and money, and all the seediness they attract.'

'Your power and money mean nothing to me.'

A groan escaped from his lips and he muttered something she didn't understand before snaking his free hand around her neck and pressing his lips to hers.

All the air expelled from her lungs.

She'd had no notion of what kissing Francesco would be like, could never have envisaged the surge of adrenaline that would course through her veins and thicken her blood at the feel of his firm lips hard against hers, not moving, simply breathing her in.

Returning the pressure, she placed a hand to his cheek, kneading her fingers into the smooth skin as she parted her lips and flitted her tongue into the heat of his mouth.

Francesco's breathing became laboured. His hold on her neck tightened then relaxed, the hand held against her chest moving to sweep around her waist and draw her flush against him to deepen the connection. When his own tongue darted into her mouth, she melted into him, two bodies meshed together, kissing with a hunger that bloomed into unimaginable proportions.

He tasted divine, of darkness and coffee and something else Hannah could only assume was *him*, filling her senses.

Deep inside, the pulsations she had first experienced when he had touched her in his London office began to vibrate and hum.

To think she had gone for twenty-seven years without experiencing *this*.

Brushing her hand down his cheek to rest on the sharp crease of his collar, she stroked the tips of her fingers over the strong neck, marvelling at his strength and the power that lay beneath the skin.

It wasn't the power that came from his position in the world that attracted her so much, she thought dimly, it was the latent masculine power within *him*.

Before she could make sense of all the wonderful sensations rising within her, he pulled away—or, rather, wrenched apart the physical connection between them.

His chest rising and falling in rapid motion, Francesco took a step back, wiping his mouth as if to rid himself of her taste.

'I know my power and money mean nothing to you,' he said, virtually spitting the words out. 'That's why getting involved with you is wrong on every level imaginable.'

Trying to clamp down on the humiliation that came hot on the heels of his abrupt rejection, Hannah jumped down from the windowsill. 'I don't know how many times I have to say this, but I do *not* want to become involved with you, not in any real sense. All I want is to experience some of the life every other woman takes for granted but which has passed me by.'

'And you *should* experience it, but it should be with someone who can give you a future.'

'Medicine is my future.'

'And that stops you building a future with a man, does it?'

Not even bothering to hide her exasperation, she shook her head. 'I'm married to my work, and that's the way I like it. I want to make it to consultant level and I've worked too hard and for too long to throw it all away on a relationship that would never fulfil me even a fraction as much as my job does.'

'How can you know that if you've never tried?'

She pursed her lips together. A deep and meaningful debate about her reasons for not wanting a relationship had not been on the agenda. 'I just know, okay?'

'Your job will never keep you warm at night.'

'My hot-water bottle does a perfectly good job of that and, besides, what right do you have to question me on this? I don't see a wedding ring on your finger. If the internet reports on you are true, as you say they are, you seem to have a phobia towards commitment yourself.' Hadn't that been another tick on her mental checklist, the fact Francesco appeared to steer away from anything that could be construed as permanent?

His face darkened. 'I have my reasons for not wanting marriage.'

'Well, I have mine, too. Why can't you respect that?'

Francesco took a deep breath and slowly expelled it. Why could he not just take everything Hannah said at face value? *His* body was telling him to just accept it, to take her back to his villa and take her, just as she'd asked, until she was so sated she would be unable to think.

But even if he did take her words at face value and accepted that she wasn't asking for anything more than one night, it didn't change the fact that making love to her would taint her. She deserved better than Salvatore Calvetti's son, even if she couldn't see it herself.

He would make her see.

'Let's get out of here,' he said, unable to endure the claustrophobia being shut in four walls with Hannah Chapman induced a minute longer. 'I'm taking you shopping.'

'Shopping?'

'You need a dress for tonight.'

'Why? What's happening tonight?'

'We're going to my casino. There's a poker tournament I need to oversee. I'm not having you by my side dressed as some kind of bag lady.'

Her face blanched at his cruel words, but he bit back the apology forming on his tongue.

In truth, there was something unbearably sexy about Hannah's take-me-as-I-am, comfortable-in-my-skin approach to her appearance, and the longer he was in her company, the sexier he found it.

A bag lady.

Francesco looked at her and saw a *bag lady*?

Having been dumped in a designer shop, whereby Francesco had promptly disappeared, leaving at her disposal a driver with the words, 'I'll meet you at my villa in a few hours—buy whatever you want and charge it to me,' Hannah still didn't know whether she wanted to laugh or punch him in the face.

Trying on what was probably her dozenth dress in the plush changing room, she reflected on his words.

Okay, so her appearance had never been a priority, but did she really look like a bag lady?

Her clothes were mostly bought online when the items she already owned started wearing out. She selected clothes based on suitability for work and comfort. Clothes were a means of keeping her body warm.

Her hair… Well, who had the time for regular haircuts? Not hardworking doctors fighting their way up the food chain, that was for sure. And if the rest of her colleagues managed to fit in regular visits to a salon, then good for them. Still, she had to admit her hair had become a little wild in recent years, and racked her brain trying to remember the last time a pair of scissors had been let loose on it. She came up with a blank.

She could remember the first time her mother had let her and Beth go to a proper hairdresser rather than hack at their hair with the kitchen scissors. It had been their twelfth birthday and the pair of them had felt so grown-up. How lovingly they'd attended their hair after that little trip, faithfully conditioning it at regular intervals.

She tried to think of the last time she'd conditioned her hair and came up with another blank.

Was it really possible she'd gone through the past fifteen years without either a haircut or the use of a conditioner? A distant memory floated like a wisp in her memories, of her mother knocking on her bedroom door, calling that it was time for her appointment at the hairdresser's. She remembered the knots that had formed in her throat and belly and her absolute refusal to go.

How could she get a haircut when Beth wouldn't be there to share it with her? Not that she'd vocalised this particular reasoning. She hadn't needed to. Her mother hadn't pressed her on the issue or brought the subject up again. Haircuts, make-up, all the things that went with being a girl on the cusp of womanhood were banished.

How had she let that happen?

After selecting a dress, a pair of shoes and matching clutch, and some sexy underwear which made her blush as she fingered the silken material, she handed the items to the manager, along with her credit card.

'Signor Calvetti has made arrangements to pay,' the manager said.

'I know, but I can pay for my own clothes, thank you.'

'It is very expensive.'

'I can afford it.' And, sadly, she could. She didn't drink and rarely socialised—Melanie's hen do had been Hannah's first proper night out that year. After paying off her mortgage and other household bills every month, her only expenditure was food, which, when you were buying frozen meals for one, didn't amount to much. She didn't drive. Her only trips were her monthly visits to her parents' home in Devon, for which she always got a lift down with Melanie and her soon-to-be brother-in-law.

Her colleagues, especially those around the same age as her, regularly complained of being skint. Hannah, never spending any money, had a comfortable nest egg.

How had she allowed herself to get in this position?

It was one thing putting money aside for a rainy day but, quite frankly, she had enough stashed away that she could handle months of torrential rain without worrying.

Despite her assurance, the store manager still seemed reluctant to take her card.

'Either accept my card or I'll find a dress in another shop,' Hannah said, although not unkindly. She smiled at the flustered woman. 'Honestly, there's enough credit on there to cover it.'

'But Signor Calvetti…'

Ah. The penny dropped. It wasn't that the manager was worried about Hannah's credit; rather, she was worried about what Francesco would do when he learned his wishes had been overruled. 'Don't worry about him—I'll make sure he knows I insisted. He's learning how stubborn I can be in getting my own way.'

With great reluctance, the manager took Hannah's card. Less than a minute later the purchase was complete. Hannah had spent more in one transaction than she'd spent on her entire wardrobe since leaving medical school.

'I don't suppose you know of a decent hairdresser that could fit me in with little notice, do you?'

The manager peered a little too closely at Hannah's hair, a tentative smile forming on her face. 'For Signor Calvetti's lover, any salon in Palermo will fit you in. Would you like me to make the phone call?'

Signor Calvetti's lover... Those words set off a warm feeling through her veins, rather as if she'd been injected with heated treacle. 'That's very kind, thank you—I'll be sure to tell Francesco how helpful you've been.'

Five minutes later Hannah left the boutique with a shop assistant personally escorting her to the selected salon, her driver/bodyguard trailing behind them.

Having her hair cut was one of the most surreal events she could ever recall and, considering the dreamlike quality of the day thus far, that was saying something.

The salon itself was filled with women who were clearly the cream of Sicilian society, yet Hannah was treated like a celebrity in her own right, with stylists and assistants fawning all over her and thrusting numerous cups of strong coffee into her hands.

At the end, when she was given the bill, she made an admirable job of not shrieking in horror.

Oh, well, she told herself as she handed her credit card over for another battering, it would surely be worth it.

She was determined that, after tonight, Francesco would never look at her like a bag lady again.

CHAPTER SIX

HANNAH HAD BEEN shopping in Palermo for such a long time that Francesco started to think she'd had second thoughts and hopped on a plane back to London.

He could have found out for himself by calling the bodyguard he'd left to watch over her, but resisted each time the urge took him. He'd stopped himself making that call for almost two hours.

Thus, when the bulletproof four-by-four pulled up within the villa's gates late afternoon, he fully expected Hannah to get out laden with bags and packages, having gone mad on his credit card. Likely, she would have changed into one of her new purchases.

Instead, she clambered her way out and up the steep steps leading to the main entrance of his villa, still dressed in that ugly shapeless dress. All she carried was her handbag and two other bags and, to top it all off, she wore a navy blue scarf over her hair.

She looked a bigger mess than when he'd left her in the boutique.

Even so, his heart accelerated at the sight of her.

Taking a deep breath to slow his raging pulse, then another when the first had zero effect, Francesco opened his front door.

Hannah stood on the step before him. 'This is your home?' she asked, her eyes sparkling.

'*Sì.*'

'It's fabulous.'

It took every ounce of restraint within him not to allow his lips to curve into the smile they so wanted. 'Thank you.'

He took a step back to admit her. 'You were a long time.' Immediately he cursed himself for voicing his concern.

'The boutique manager—a fabulous woman, by the way—managed to get me into a hairdresser's.'

'You've had your hair cut?' He caught a whiff of that particular scent found only in salons, a kind of fragrant chemical odour. It clung to her.

'Kind of.' Her face lit up with a hint of mischief. 'You'll just have to wait and see—the hairdresser wrapped the scarf round it so it didn't get wind damaged or anything.' She did a full three-sixty rotation. 'I can't believe this is your home. Do you live here alone?'

'I have staff, but they live in separate quarters.'

'It's amazing. Really. Amazing.'

Francesco's home was a matter of pride, his sanctuary away from a life filled with hidden dangers. Hannah's wide-eyed enthusiasm for it filled his chest, making it expand.

'Who would have guessed being a gangster would pay so well?' Her grin negated the sting her words induced. 'I'm just saying.' She laughed, noticing his unimpressed expression. 'You're the one trying to convince me you're a gangster.'

'You really don't believe in beating around the bush, do you?'

Her nose scrunched up a little. 'Erm…I guess not. I've never really thought about it.'

'It's very refreshing,' he surprised himself by admitting.

'Really? And is that a good thing?'

'Most refreshing things are good.'

'In that case…excellent. It's nice to know there's something about me you approve of.' Despite the lightness of her tone, he caught a definite edge to it, an edge he didn't care for and that made him reach over and grab her wrist.

'When are you going to learn, Dr Chapman, that my approval should mean nothing to a woman like you?'

'And when are you going to learn, Signor Calvetti, that I may be a doctor but I am still a human being? I am still a woman.'

He was now certain the edge he had detected was the whiff of reproach.

Surely he should be delighted she was starting to see through the layers to the real man inside. So why did he feel more unsettled than ever?

'Believe me, *Dr* Chapman,' he said, putting deliberate emphasis on her title, 'I am well aware that beneath your haphazard appearance is a woman.'

A smile flitted over her face, not the beaming spark of joy he was becoming accustomed to but a smile that could almost be described as shy. Bright spots of colour stained her cheeks.

Shoving his hands in his pockets lest they did something stupid like reach out for her again, Francesco inclined his head to the left. 'If you head in that direction you will go through several living rooms before you reach the indoor pool, which you are welcome to use, although you might prefer the outside one. If you go through the door on the other side of the pool you'll find the kitchen. If you're hungry my chef will cook something for you, but I would suggest you keep it light as we will be dining in the casino.'

'We're eating out?'

'Yes. I'll show you to the room you will be sleeping in whilst you're here as my guest.'

'Which is only until tomorrow,' Hannah stated amiably, biting back the question of whether it would be *his* room she would be sleeping in, already knowing the answer.

Francesco's villa was a thing of beauty, a huge white palace cleverly cut into the rocks of the hillside. Walking up the steps to his home, the scent of perfumed flowers and lemons had filled her senses so strongly she would have been happy to simply stand there and enjoy. If she hadn't been so keen to see Francesco, she would have done.

She'd been aware he possessed great wealth, but even so...

It felt as if she'd slipped through the looking glass and landed in a parallel universe.

She followed him through huge white arches, over brightly coloured tiled flooring, past exotic furniture, and up a winding stone staircase to a long, uneven corridor.

'Was this once a cave?' she asked.

He laughed. *Francesco actually laughed.* It might not have been a great big boom echoing off the high ceilings, more of a low chuckle, but it was a start and it made her heart flip.

'Its original history is a bit of a mystery,' he said, opening a door at the end of the corridor. 'This is your room.'

Hannah clamped a hand over her mouth to stop the squeal that wanted to make itself heard. Slowly she drank it all in: the four-poster bed, the vibrant colours, the private balcony overlooking the outdoor pool...

'Wow,' she said when she felt capable of speaking without sounding like a giddy schoolgirl. 'If I didn't have to get back to work on Monday, I'd be tempted to claim squatters' rights.'

'You're still trusting I will get you back to London in time?'

She rolled her eyes in answer.

'Let us hope your faith in me is justified.'

'If I turn out to be wrong then no worries—I'll get my own flight back.'

'And what about your passport? You will need that to leave the country.'

'My passport's in my bag.'

'You are sure about that?' At her puzzled expression, Francesco leaned over and whispered into her ear, 'A word of advice, Dr Chapman—when in the company of criminals, never leave your bag open with your passport and phone in it.'

With that, he strolled to the door, patting his back pocket for emphasis. 'Be ready to leave in two hours.'

Hannah watched him close the door before diving into her handbag.

Unbelievable! In the short time she'd been in his home, Francesco had deftly removed her passport and mobile and she hadn't noticed a thing.

She should be furious. She should be a lot of things. He had her passport—effectively had her trapped in his country—but it was her phone she felt a pang of anxiety over.

She had to give him points for continuing to try to make her see the worst in him, but there was no way in the world he would keep hold of her stuff. She had no doubt that, come the morning, he would return the items to her.

The morning...

Before the morning came the night.

And a shiver zipped up her spine at the thought of what that night could bring.

Francesco sat on his sprawling sofa catching up on the day's qualifying event for one of the many motor racing sports he followed, when he heard movement behind the archway dividing the living room from the library.

Sitting upright, he craned his neck to see better.

He caught a flash of blue that vanished before reappearing with a body attached to it. Hannah's body.

Hannah's incredible body.

His jaw dropped open.

There she stood, visibly fighting for composure, until she expanded her arms and said, 'What do you think? Do I still resemble a bag lady?'

A bag lady? He could think of a hundred words to describe her but the adjective that sprang to the forefront of his mind was *stunning*.

Where the blue dress she had changed into on his plane had been a drab, ill-fitting creation, this soft blue dress was a million miles apart. Silk and Eastern in style with swirling oriental flowers printed onto it, it skimmed her figure like a caress, landing midthigh to show off incredibly shapely legs.

Whatever the hairdresser had been paid could never be enough. The thick mop of straw-like hair had gone. Now Hannah's hair was twisted into a sleek knot, pinned in with black chopsticks. There was not a millimetre of frizz in sight. If his eyes were not deceiving him, she'd had colour applied to it, turning her multicoloured locks into more of a honey blonde.

She wore make-up, too, her eyes ringed with dark smokiness that highlighted the moreish hazel, her lips a deep cherry-red...

She looked beautiful.

And yet...

He hated it.

She no longer looked like Hannah.

'No. You no longer resemble a bag lady.'

'Well, that's a relief.' She shuffled into the room on shoes with heels high enough to make her hobble—although not as high as many women liked to wear—and stood before him, her hand outstretched. Her short nails hadn't been touched, a sight he found strangely reassuring. 'Can I have my phone back, please?'

'You can have it back when you leave Sicily.'

'I'd like it back now.'

'For what reason?'

'I've told you—I like to keep abreast of what's going on with my patients.'

'And what can you do for them here?'

'Not worry about them. No news is good news.'

'Then it seems I am doing you a favour.'

'But how am I going to know if there is no news? Now I'll worry that bad news has come and I won't know one way or the other.'

Hiding his irritation, he said, 'Do all doctors go to such lengths for their patients?'

Her lips pressed together. 'I have no idea. It's none of my concern what my colleagues get up to when they're off duty.'

'What happened to professional detachment? I thought you doctors were trained to keep your distance?'

A hint of fire flashed in her eyes. 'Keeping a check on the welfare of my patients is at odds with my professionalism?'

'I'm just asking the question.'

'Well, don't. I will not have my professionalism questioned by you or anyone.'

It was the first time Francesco had heard her sound even remotely riled. He'd clearly hit a nerve.

Studying her carefully, he got to his feet. 'I think it will do you good to spend one evening away from your phone.'

Hannah opened her mouth to argue but he placed a finger to it. 'I did not mean to question your professionalism. However, I am not prepared to spend the evening with someone who has only half a mind on what's going on. Constantly checking your phone is rude.'

Her cheeks heightened with colour, a mutinous expression blazing from her eyes.

'I will make a deal with you,' he continued silkily. 'You say you want to experience all the world has to offer, yet it will be a half-hearted experience if you are preoccupied with worrying about your patients. If you prove that you can let your hair down and enjoy the experience of what the casino has to offer, I will give you your phone back when we return to the villa.'

For the first time since she'd met him, Hannah wanted to slap Francesco. Okay, keep her passport until it was time to leave—that didn't bother her. She knew she would get it back. She knew she would get her phone back eventually, too, but she needed it *now*. She needed to keep the roots the mobile gave her to the ward.

And how dared he imply that she had no detachment? She had it. But she refused to lose her empathy. Her patients were her guiding motive in life. Never would she allow one of her young charges to be on the receiving end of a doctor who had lost basic humanity. She wouldn't. She couldn't. She'd been at the other end and, while it hadn't made the pain of what she went through any worse, a little compassion would have helped endure it that little bit better.

Eventually she took a deep breath and bestowed Francesco with her first fake smile. 'Fine. But if you want me to let my hair down and enjoy myself it's only fair you do the same, too. After all,' she added airily, 'I would say that, of the two of us, you're the greater workaholic. At least I take weekends off.'

Calvetti's casino was a titanic building, baroque in heritage, set over four levels in the heart of Palermo. Hannah followed Francesco up the first sweeping staircase and into an enormous room filled with gambling tables and slot machines as far as the eye could see. It was like stepping into a tasteful version of Vegas.

Flanked by his minders, they continued up the next set of stairs to the third floor. There, a group of men in black parted to admit them into a room that seemed virtually identical to the second floor. It took a few moments for her to realise what the subtle differences were. The lower level was filled with ordinary punters. The third floor, which had around a quarter of the number of customers, was evidently the domain of the filthy rich.

Sticking closely to Francesco, Hannah drank everything in: the gold trimming on all the tables, the beautiful fragrant women, the men in tuxedos—which, she noted, none filled as well as Francesco, who looked even more broodingly gorgeous than usual in his. After a host of conversations, Francesco slipped an arm around her waist and drew her through a set of double doors and into the restaurant.

And what a restaurant it was, somehow managing to be both opulent and elegant.

'Are the customers on the second floor allowed to dine in here?' she asked once they'd been seated by a fawning maître d' at a corner table.

'They have their own restaurant,' he said, opening his leather-bound menu.

'But are they allowed to eat in here?'

'The third floor is for private members only. Anyone can join, providing they can pay the fifty thousand euro joining fee and the ten thousand annual membership.'

She blinked in shock. 'People pay that?'

'People pay for exclusivity—the waiting list is longer than the actual membership list.'

'That's mind-blowing. I feel like a gatecrasher.'

She only realised he'd been avoiding her stare when he raised his eyes to look at her.

'You are with me.'

The possessive authority of his simple statement set her pulse racing, and in that moment she forgot all about being mad at him for refusing to hand back her phone.

'So what do you recommend from the menu?' she asked when she was certain her tongue hadn't rooted to the roof of her mouth.

'All of it.'

She laughed, a noise that sounded more nervous than merry.

A waiter came over to them. *'Posso portarti le bevande?'*

Francesco spoke rapidly back to him.

'He wanted our drink order,' he explained once the waiter had bustled off. 'I've ordered us a bottle of Shiraz.'

'Is that a wine?'

'Yes. The Shiraz we sell here is of the highest quality.'

'I don't drink wine. I'll have a cola instead.'

A shrewdness came into his eyes. 'Have you ever drunk wine?'

'No.'

'Have you ever drunk alcohol?'

'I had a few sips of champagne at Mel's hen do.' Suddenly it occurred to her that Melanie's hen party had been just twenty-four hours ago.

Where had the time gone?

It felt as if she'd experienced a whole different life in that short space of time.

'And that was your first taste of alcohol?'

She stared at him, nodding slowly, her mind racing. After all, wasn't the whole point of her being in Sicily with Francesco to begin her exploration of life? 'Maybe I *should* have a glass of the Shiraz.'

He nodded his approval. 'But only a small glass. Your body has not acquired a tolerance for alcohol.'

'My body hasn't acquired a tolerance for anything.'

The waiter returned with their wine and a jug of water before Francesco could ask what she meant by that comment.

The more time he spent with Hannah, the more intriguing he found her. Nothing seemed to faze her, except having her professionalism cast into doubt. And having her phone taken away.

He watched as she studied the menu, her brow furrowed in concentration. 'Are mussels nice?' she asked.

'They're delicious.'

She beamed. 'I'll have those, then.'

A platter of antipasto was brought out for them to nibble on while they waited for their meals to be cooked.

'Is this like ham?' she asked, holding up a slice of prosciutto.

'Not really. Try some.'

She popped it into her mouth and chewed, then nodded her approval. Swallowing, she reached for a roasted pepper.

'Try some wine,' he commanded.

'Do I sniff it first?'

'If you want.' He smothered a laugh when she practically dunked her nose into the glass.

She took the tiniest of sips. 'Oh, wow. That's really nice.'

'Have you really never drunk wine before?'

'I really haven't.' She popped a plump green olive into her mouth.

'Why not?'

Her nose scrunched. 'My parents aren't drinkers so we never had alcohol in the house. By the time I was old enough to get into experimenting I was focused on my studies. I wasn't prepared to let anything derail my dream of being a doctor. It was easier to just say no.'

'How old were you when you decided to be a doctor?'

'Twelve.'

'That's a young age to make a life-defining choice.'

'Most twelve-year-olds have dreams of what they want to do when they grow up.'

'Agreed, but most change their mind.'

'What did you want to be when *you* were twelve?'

'A racing bike rider.'

'I can see you doing that,' she admitted. 'So what stopped you? Or did you just change your mind?'

'It was only ever a pipe dream,' he said with a dismissive shrug. 'I was Salvatore Calvetti's only child. I was groomed from birth to take over his empire.'

'And how's that going?'

Francesco fixed hard eyes on her. 'I always knew I would build my own empire. I am interested to know, though, what drew you to medicine in the first place—was it the death of your sister?'

A brief hesitation. 'Yes.'

'She was called Beth?'

Another hesitation followed by a nod. When Hannah reached for her glass of water he saw a slight tremor in her hand. She took a long drink before meeting his eyes.

'Beth contracted meningitis when we were twelve. They said it was flu. They didn't get the diagnosis right until it was too late. She was dead within a day.'

She laid the bare facts out to him in a matter-of-fact manner, but there was something in the way she held her poise that sent a pang straight into his heart.

'So you decided to be a doctor so you could save children like Beth?'

'That's a rather simplistic way of looking at it, but yes. I remember walking through the main ward and going past cubicles and private rooms full of ill children and their terrified families, and I was just full of so much… Oh, I was full up of every emotion you could imagine. Why her? Why not me too? Meningitis is so contagious….' She took a deep breath. 'I know you must think it stupid and weak, but when Beth died the only thing that kept me going was the knowledge that one day I would be in a position to heal as many of those children as I could.'

Francesco expelled a breath, the pang in his heart tightening. 'I don't think it's weak or stupid.'

Hannah took another sip of her water. The tremor in her hand had worsened and he suddenly experienced the strangest compulsion to reach over and squeeze it.

'My mother was hospitalised a number of times—drug overdoses,' he surprised himself by saying. 'It was only the dedication of the doctors and nurses that saved her. When she died it was because she overdosed on a weekend when she was alone.'

He still lived with the guilt. On an intellectual level he knew it was misplaced. He'd been fifteen years old, not yet a man. But he'd known how vulnerable his mother was and yet still he and his father had left her alone for the weekend, taking a visit to the Mastrangelo estate without her.

It had ostensibly been for business, his father and Pietro Mastrangelo close friends as well as associates. At least, they had been close friends then, before the friendship between the Calvettis and Mastrangelos had twisted into antipathy. Back then, though, Francesco had been incredibly proud that his father had wanted him to accompany him, had left with barely a second thought for his mother.

While Francesco and Salvatore had spent the Saturday evening eating good food, drinking good wine and playing cards with Pietro and his eldest son, Luca, Elisabetta Calvetti had overdosed in her bed.

To think of his mother dying while he, her son, had been basking in pride because the monster who fed her the drugs had been treating him like a man.... To think that bastard's approval ever meant anything to him made his stomach roil violently and his nails dig deep into his palms.

His mother had been the kindest, most gentle soul he had ever known. Her death had ripped his own soul in half. His vengeance might be two decades too late, but he would have it. Whatever it took, he would avenge her death and throw the carcass of his father's reputation into the ashes.

'I have nothing but the utmost respect for medical professionals,' he said slowly, unfurling the fists his hands had balled into, unsure why he was confiding such personal matters with her. 'When I look at you, Dr Chapman, I see a woman filled with compassion, decency, and integrity. The world I inhabit is driven by money, power, and greed.'

'You have integrity,' she contradicted. 'A whole heap of it.'

'On that we will have to disagree.' He nodded towards the waiter heading cautiously towards them. 'It looks as if our main courses are ready. I suggest we move on from this discussion or both our meals will be spoiled.'

She flashed him a smile of such gratitude his entire chest compressed tightly enough that for a moment he feared his lungs would cease to work.

CHAPTER SEVEN

THANKFULLY, FRANCESCO KEPT the conversation over the rest of their meal light, with mostly impersonal questions about medical school and her job. His interest—and it certainly seemed genuine—was flattering. In turn, he opened up about his love of motorbikes. It didn't surprise her to learn he owned a dozen of them.

When their plates were cleared and Hannah had eaten a dark-chocolate lava cake, which was without doubt the most delicious pudding she'd ever eaten—except hot chocolate-fudge cake, of course—Francesco looked at his watch. 'I need to check in with my head of security before the poker tournament starts. Do you want to come with me or would you like me to get one of my staff to give you a tour of the tables?'

'Are you entering the tournament?'

'No. This one is solely for members. It's the biggest tournament that's held here, though, and the members like to see me—it makes them feel important,' he added, and she noticed a slight flicker of amusement in his eyes, which made her feel as if she'd been let into a private joke. It was an insight that both surprised and warmed her.

'You don't have much time for them?'

'I always make time for them.'

'That's not what I meant.'

'I know what you meant.' His lips, usually set in a fixed line, broke into something that almost resembled a lazy smile. He drained his glass of wine, his eyes holding firm with hers. 'Do you know the rules of poker?'

'Funnily enough, I do. It's often on late at night when I'm too brain-dead to study any longer and need to wind down before bed.'

'You're still studying?'

'Yes. Plus there are always new research papers being published and clinical studies to read through and mug up on.'

'Doesn't sound as if you leave yourself any time for having fun,' he remarked astutely.

'It's fun to me. But you're right—it's why I'm here after all.'

'When you said you'd spent your whole adult life dedicating yourself to medicine, I didn't think you meant it in a literal sense.'

She shrugged and pulled a face. 'It's what I needed.'

'But that's changed?'

'Not in any fundamental way. Medicine and my patients will always be my first priority, but my accident… It made me open my eyes…' Her voice trailed away, unexpected tears burning the back of her eyes. It had been so long since she'd spoken properly about Beth.

Hannah carried her sister with her every minute of every day, yet it had felt in recent weeks as if she were right there with her, as if she could turn her head and find Beth peering over her shoulder.

Blinking back the tears, she spoke quietly. 'I don't know if heaven exists, but if it does, I don't want Beth to be angry with me. She loved life. We both did. I'd forgotten just how much.'

She almost jumped out of her seat when Francesco placed a warm hand on hers, so large it covered it entirely. A sense of calm trickled through her veins, while conversely her skin began to dance.

'Would you like to enter the poker tournament?'

'Oh, no, I couldn't.'

'Think of the experience. Think of the story you'll have to tell Beth.'

With a stab, she realised how carefully he'd been listening. Francesco understood.

The sense of calm increased, settling into her belly. 'Well…how much does it cost?'

'For you, nothing. For everyone else, it's one hundred thousand euros.'

If her jaw could thud onto the table, it would. 'For one game of poker?'

'That's pocket change to the members here. People fly in from all over the world for this one tournament. We allow sixty entrants. We've had a couple drop out, so there is room for you.'

'I don't know. Won't all the other entrants be cross that I'm playing for free?'

'They wouldn't know. In any case, it is none of their business. My casino, my rules. Go on, Hannah. Do it. Enjoy yourself and play the game.'

It was the first time he'd addressed her by her first name. Oh, but it felt so wonderful to hear her name spilling from his tongue in that deep, seductive accent.

Play the game.

It had been fifteen years since she'd played a game of any sort—and school netball most certainly did *not* count when compared to this.

Straightening her spine, she nodded, a swirl of excitement uncoiling in her stomach. 'Go on, then. Sign me up.'

* * *

Francesco watched the tournament unfold from the sprawl-ing security office on the top floor of the casino, manned by two dozen staff twenty-four hours a day. Other than the bathrooms, there wasn't an inch of the casino not moni-tored. Special interest was being taken in a blackjack player on the second floor—a man suspected of swindling casi-nos across the Continent. Of course, there was the option to simply ban the man from the premises, but first Francesco wanted proof. And banning was not enough. Once his guilt was established, a suitable punishment would be wrought.

The first round of the tournament was in full swing. On Hannah's table of six, two players were already out. Her gameplay surprised him—for a novice, she played excep-tionally well, her poker face inscrutable. Of those remain-ing, she had the second-largest number of chips.

The dealer dealt the four players their two cards and turned three over on the table. From his vantage point, Fran-cesco could see Hannah had been dealt an ace and a jack, both diamonds. The player with the largest pile of chips had been dealt a pair of kings. One of the table cards was a king, giving that player three of a kind. The player went all in, meaning that if Hannah wanted to continue playing she would have to put *all* her remaining chips into the pile.

She didn't even flinch, simply pushed her pile forward to show she wanted to play.

There was no way she could win the hand. Lady Luck could be kind, but to overturn a three of a kind… The next table card to be turned over was an ace, quickly followed by another ace.

She'd won the hand!

It seemed that fifteen years of perfecting a poker face,

along with too many late nights half watching the game played out for real on the television had paid off.

Hannah allowed herself a sip of water but kept her face neutral. The game wasn't over yet. No one looking at her would know the thundering rate of her heart.

The look on her defeated opponent's face was a picture. He kept staring from his cards to hers as if expecting a snake to pop out of them. Her two remaining opponents were looking at her with a newfound respect.

If she wasn't in the midst of a poker tournament, she'd be hugging herself with the excitement of it all. It felt as if she were in the middle of a glamorous Hollywood film. All that was needed was for the men to light fat cigars and create a haze of smoke.

As the next hand was dealt she noticed a small crowd forming around their table and much whispering behind hands.

She looked at her two cards and raised the ante. One of her opponents matched her. The other folded, opting to sit out of the hand. The table cards were laid. Again she raised the ante. Again her opponent matched her. And so it went on, her opponent matching her move for move.

She didn't have the best of hands: two low pairs. There was every chance that his cards were much better. All the same, the bubble of recklessness that had been simmering within her since she'd followed Francesco off the dance floor the night before grew within her.

It was her turn to bet. Both she and her opponent had already put a large wedge of chips into the pot.

Where was Francesco? He'd said he would be there socialising with the guests.

He wasn't in the room, but somehow she just *knew* he was watching her.

Her heart hammering, she pushed her remaining chips forward. *Please* let Francesco be watching. 'All in.'

Her opponent stared at her, a twitch forming under his left eye.

She stared back, giving nothing away.

He rubbed his chin.

She knew before he did that he was going to fold, hid her feelings of triumph that she'd successfully bluffed him.

The big pile of poker chips was hers.

It would appear that her long-practised poker face had become a blessing in itself.

Francesco could hardly believe what he was witnessing over the monitors.

Hannah was a card shark. There was no other way to describe the way she played, which, if you were in a position to see the cards she'd been dealt, as he was, at times verged on the reckless. Not that her opponents could see how recklessly she played. All they saw was the cool facade, the face that didn't give away a single hint of emotion.

For a woman who had never played the game before, it was masterful. And yet...

Something deep inside his gut clenched when he considered why she'd been able to develop such a good poker face. Only someone who'd spent years hiding their emotions could produce it so naturally. He should know. He'd been perfecting his own version for years.

When she'd knocked her fourth opponent out... The way she'd pushed her chips forward, the clear *simpatico* way she'd said, 'All in...'

His gut had tightened further. Somehow he'd known those two little words meant more than just the chips before her.

It didn't take long before she'd demolished her final opponent. Only when she'd won that final hand did that beautiful smile finally break on her face, a smile of genuine delight that had all her defeated opponents reaching over to shake her hand and kiss her cheeks. The mostly male crowd surrounding her also muscled in, finding it necessary to embrace her when giving their congratulations.

They wouldn't look twice if they could see her in her usual state, Francesco thought narkily. They would be so blinkered they would never see her for the natural beauty she was.

'I'm going back down,' he said, heading to the reinforced steel door. For some reason, his good mood, induced by dinner with Hannah, had plummeted.

Striding across the main playing area of the third floor, he ignored all attempts from players and staff to meet his eyes.

With play in the tournament temporarily halted so the players who'd made it through to the second round could take a break, he found Hannah sipping coffee, surrounded by a horde of men all impressing their witticisms and manliness upon her.

When she saw him, her eyes lit up, then dimmed as she neared him.

'What's the matter?' she asked.

'Nothing.'

'Ooh, you liar. You look like someone's stolen your granny's false teeth and you've been told to donate your own as a replacement.'

Her good humour had zero effect on his blackening mood. 'And you look like you're having fun,' he said pointedly, unable to contain the ice in his voice.

'Isn't that the whole point of me entering the tournament? Didn't you tell me to enjoy myself?'

Francesco took a deep breath, Hannah's bewilderment

reminding him he had no good reason to be acting like a jealous fool.

Jealousy?

Was that really what the strong compulsion running through him to throw her over his shoulder and carry her out of the casino and away from all these admiring men was?

His father, for all his catting about with other women half his age, had been consumed with it. His mother had suffered more than one beating at his hands for daring to look at another man the wrong way.

Francesco had assumed that, in his own case, jealousy had skipped a generation. The closest he'd come to that particular emotion had been in his early twenties. Then, he'd learned Luisa, a girl he was seeing, was two-timing him with Pepe Mastrangelo, whom she'd sworn she'd finished with. That hadn't been jealousy, though—that had been pure anger, a rage that had heightened when he learned she'd tricked him out of money so she could hightail it to the UK for an abortion. So duplicitous had she been, she'd no idea if he or Pepe was the father.

He'd despised Luisa for her lies, but not once had he wanted to seek Pepe out. Instead, Pepe had sought *him* out, his pain right there on the surface. But the only bruising Francesco had suffered had been to his ego, and the fight between them had been over before it started.

To learn he was as vulnerable to jealousy's clutches as the next man brought him up short, reminding him that he had Calvetti blood running inside him.

Salvatore Calvetti would never have walked away from the Luisa and Pepe debacle as Francesco had done. If Salvatore had walked in his shoes, Luisa would have been scarred for life. Pepe would likely have disappeared, never to be seen again.

But he didn't want to be anything like Salvatore.

He never wanted to treat *anyone* the way his father had treated his mother.

Raking his fingers through his hair, a growl escaped from his throat. Whether he liked it or not, Calvetti blood ran through his veins.

Just one more reason why he should never touch her.

Hannah looked as if she wanted to say something, but the gong sounded for the second round. She was placed on table one. Her chips were passed to her. Francesco watched as she stacked them into neat piles, oblivious to the crowd forming around her table.

The strength of his possessiveness had him clenching his fists. Was she really so ignorant of the admiring glances and lecherous stares?

She raised her eyes to meet his glare and gave a hesitant smile. He looked away.

A discreet cough behind him caught his attention. He turned to find his general manager standing there.

'We have the proof—the blackjack player *is* cheating us,' he said, his lips barely moving.

'Give me a few minutes.' Francesco barely bothered trying to hide his impatience.

Hannah was still looking at him, a puzzled groove in her forehead.

'I can get the ball moving…'

'I *said*, give me a few minutes.' The blackjack cheat could wait. Francesco would not step a foot away from the room until Hannah was done with the tournament. His presence was the only thing stopping the fawning men from trying their luck that bit harder.

She was done much earlier than he'd envisaged. From playing the first round like a pro and with a good dollop of luck, her game fell to pieces and she was the first player out.

She shrugged, smiled gracefully, took a sip of water, and leaned back in her chair.

He was by her side in seconds. 'Come, it is time for us to move elsewhere,' he said, speaking into her ear, ignoring the curious stares of all those surrounding them.

'I want to watch the rest of the tournament.'

'You can watch it from my security office. There are things I need to attend to.'

Hannah turned to face him. 'Go and attend to them, then,' she said with a shrug.

'But I require your company.' Or, rather, he wanted to get her away from this room full of letches.

Swivelling her chair around with exceptionally bad grace, she got to her feet.

'What is the matter with you?' he asked as they swept through the room and out of the door.

'Me?' Incredulous, Hannah stopped walking and placed a hand on her hip. 'I was having a lovely time until you came in looking as if you wanted to kill me.' Seriously, how could anyone concentrate with Francesco's handsome face glowering at them? 'You totally put me off my game, and then you dragged me out before I could enjoy watching the rest of it.'

She glared at him. She'd had such a wonderful meal, had thought he'd enjoyed himself, too, the aloof, arrogant man unbending into something infinitely more human that warmed her from the inside out. But now he'd reverted, and was more aloof and arrogant than ever.

'It wasn't you that angered me.'

She folded her arms and raised a brow in a perfect imitation of him. 'Really?'

'Did you not see the way those men were looking at you? As if you were a piece of meat.'

'They were just being friendly.' Men *never* looked at her

in that way. Not that she ever met men outside the hospital environment, she conceded.

'Take a look in the mirror, Dr Chapman. You're a beautiful woman.'

His unexpected compliment let loose a cluster of fluttering butterflies in her belly.

'And I'm sorry for putting you off your game—you're quite a player.'

'You think?' His compliment—for it was definitely a compliment coming from him—warmed her insides even further, making her forget to be cross with him.

He smiled, an honest-to-goodness smile, and reached out to touch a loose tendril of her hair. 'If you were to give up medicine, you could make a good living on the poker circuit.'

The butterflies in her belly exploded. Heat surged through her veins, her insides liquefying.

Was it her imagination, or was the longing she could feel swirling inside her mirrored in his eyes…?

Dropping his hand from her hair, he traced a finger down her cheek.

She shivered, her skin heating beneath his touch.

'Come. I need to attend to business,' he said before steering her off to the top floor, not quite touching her but keeping her close enough that she was constantly aware of his heat, of *him*.

'What are we going up here for?' she asked once she'd managed to get her tongue working again. But, oh, it was so hard to think straight when the skin on her cheek still tingled from his touch.

'A player from the second floor has been caught cheating. Stealing from us.'

'Have you called the police?'

He looked at her as if she'd asked if the moon was made of chocolate. 'That is not how we do things here.'

'How do you do things…?' The strangest look flitted over her face. 'Oh. You break hands.'

The sadness in Hannah's tone cut through him. Francesco paused to look at her properly. 'The punishment is determined by the crime.'

'But surely if a crime has been committed then the police should be left to deal with it? That's what they're paid for after all.'

'This is Sicily, Dr Chapman. The rules are different here.'

'Because that's what you were taught by your father?'

Her question caught him up short. 'It's nothing to do with my father. It's about respect and following the rules.'

'But who makes the rules? This is *your* empire, Francesco. Your father isn't here anymore. You're an adult. Your actions are your own.'

The air caught in his lungs, an acrid taste forming in his throat. 'Do you have an answer for everything?'

'Not even close.' She looked away, avoiding his gaze. 'If it's all the same to you, I'd like to wait downstairs.' Her tone had become distant.

His stomach rolled over. 'Nothing will happen to the cheating thief on these premises.'

'I don't want anything to happen to him off the premises, either. I'm a doctor, Francesco. I can't be—won't be—a party to anything that harms another person. I know this is your life and what you're used to, but for me…' She shook her head. 'I could never live with myself. Can you get one of your men to take me back to the villa?'

'Wait in the bar for me,' he said. 'I'll be with you in ten minutes.'

Not smiling, she nodded her acquiescence and walked

back down the stairs, gripping onto the gold handrail as she made her descent.

Francesco's chest felt weighted, although he knew not why.

He never made any apologies for his life and the way his world worked. Hannah knew the score—he'd never hidden anything from her. He'd *told* her what it was like. He'd warned her. In fact, it was the only reason he'd brought her here, so she could see for herself that he was not worth wasting her virginity on. It was not his fault she hadn't listened.

So why was the only thing he could see as he pushed the door open the sad disappointment dulling her eyes?

He entered the manager's office. Mario and Roberto, another of his most trusted men, were already there, along with the cheat.

Up close, he could see the cheat was a young man in his early twenties, who looked as if he should be playing computer games with an online community of other awkward young men, not systematically ripping off casinos across the Continent. He sat in the middle of the room. He looked terrified.

There was a tap on the door and the manager walked in, handing Francesco a dossier on the blackjack player's activity. It made for quick reading.

Mario watched him, waiting for the nod.

This was the part of the job Francesco liked the least. When he'd first bought into this, his first casino, three years ago, he'd employed his father's old henchmen, knowing them to be reliable and loyal. Within months, he'd paid the majority of them off when it became clear they expected to continue using the methods enjoyed by Salvatore as punishment. While he had always respected his father, Francesco had always known that when the time came for him to take over, his methods would be different, less extreme.

Mario was Francesco's man and capable of great restraint. Apart from one drug dealer who'd frequented Francesco's Naples nightclub and who they'd discovered was pimping out vulnerable teenage girls, he never made the punishments personal and never caused damage that would not heal.

When he gave the nod, Mario and Roberto would take the young man somewhere private. They would teach him a lesson he would never forget—a lesson that rarely needed to be given, as most people were not stupid enough to try to cheat a Calvetti casino. Francesco's reputation preceded him. And, really, this was the perfect opportunity to rid himself of Hannah. It was clear this whole situation had unsettled her enough to at least consider getting a flight home. If he gave the nod, he could guarantee she would be on the first flight back to England....

Yet her insinuation that he was following in his father's brutish footsteps jabbed him like a spear.

He was *not* his father. If this young cheat had tried any such behaviour in any of Salvatore's businesses, he would have disappeared. For ever.

Rules were rules, even if they were only unwritten. They were there for a reason.

His father would never have dreamed of breaking them....

Hannah nursed her strong coffee, gazing absently at the huge flat-screen television against a wall of the bar showing music videos. She didn't want to think of what was happening on the floor above her. If she thought about it hard enough she might just scream.

But when she tried not to think about it, thoughts of Melanie's wedding filled the space instead.

How could she endure it? Every morning she woke knowing the nuptials were one day closer, the knot in her belly tightening another notch.

She would give anything to get out of going, but even if an excuse came fully presented on a plate she would not be able to take it. Melanie had appointed her maid of honour, a role Hannah knew she did not deserve.

The wedding was something she would have to find a way to cope with. Whatever it took, she would try to keep smiling so her little sister could walk down the aisle without her day being ruined.

'*Due bicchieri di champagne.*'

Francesco's sudden appearance at her side startled her.

'Hi,' she said dully, hating that her heart thumped just to see him.

'*Ciao.*' He nodded. 'I've just ordered us each a glass of champagne.'

'You said you would take me back to the villa.'

'And I will. Five minutes. You look as if you need a drink.'

'I need to get my phone and my passport, and go home. To England,' she added in case her meaning wasn't absolutely clear.

Francesco had been right from the start. She really didn't belong in his world, not even on a temporary basis.

The injuries to Mario had been inflicted a long time ago and were, in effect, history. Mario's loyalty to Francesco only served to reinforce this notion of a long-forgotten event, something that had no bearing on the present.

The person they'd caught stealing tonight... This was now; this *was* the present.

Hannah was a doctor. She had dedicated her life to

saving lives. She could never be a party to someone else's injury.

'Come, Dr Chapman. You are supposed to be living a little. You are here to see something of the world and experience the things that have passed you by. You hardly touched your wine at dinner.'

'I'm really not in the mood.'

Pressing his lips to her ear, he said, 'I called the police.'

Her head whipped round so quickly she almost butted his nose. 'Seriously?'

Two glasses of champagne were placed before them. Francesco picked them up and nodded at a corner sofa. Thoroughly confused, she followed him.

Sitting gingerly next to him, she would have ignored the champagne had he not thrust it into her hand.

'Drink. You need to relax a little—you're far too tense.'

'Did you really call the police?'

'As you implied, I make the rules.' A slight smile played on his lips. 'I thought about the prison system here. When I said I was calling the police, the thief begged for a beating.'

She couldn't contain the smile that spread over her face or the hand that rose to palm his cheek. 'See? I *was* right about you.'

At his quizzical expression, she added, 'I knew there was good within you. You proved it by taking care of me so well after my accident, and now you've reaffirmed it.'

He shook his head. 'It's just for this one time, okay? And only because I respect your profession and the oath you took.'

'If you say so.' A feeling of serenity swept through her. Stroking her fingers down his cheek, she took a sip of her champagne.

'Better?'

She nodded. 'Much. I'll feel even better when I have my phone back.' She felt lost without it.

'Finish your champagne and I will take you back.'

His eyes bored into her, *daring* her to drink it. The sip she'd had still danced on her tongue, tantalising her, just as Francesco tantalised her.

This was why she was here, she reminded herself. Not to involve herself in the intricacies of his life but to experience her *own*.

Putting the flute back to her lips, she tipped the sparkling liquid into her mouth and drank it in three swallows.

A grin spread across his face, somehow making him even more handsome, a feat she hadn't thought possible.

'Good for you.' He downed his own glass before rising to his feet. 'Come. It is time to take you back.'

Hannah grabbed her clutch bag and stood. Her body felt incredibly light.

Surrounded by Francesco's minders, who'd been waiting in the corner of the bar for them, they left. When they reached the stairs, he placed a hand on the small of her back, a protective gesture that lightened her even further.

CHAPTER EIGHT

FRANCESCO'S VILLA WAS in darkness, but as soon as his driver brought the car over the foot of the driveway, light illuminated it, bathing it in a golden hue. With the stars in the moonless night sky twinkling, it was the prettiest sight Hannah had ever seen.

'Can I get you a drink?' Francesco asked once they were alone inside, his minders having left for their own quarters. 'How about a brandy?'

The effects of the champagne had started to abate a little, but did she want to risk putting any more alcohol into her system?

'Only a small one,' he added, clearly reading her mind.

'Yes, please. A small one,' she agreed, hugging herself.

She followed him through the sprawling reception and into the living room, where Francesco swept a small white object from the windowsill. 'Catch,' he said, throwing it at her.

Luckily she caught it. Before she could admonish him for the reckless endangerment of her phone, he'd continued through the huge library, through the dining room, diverted round the indoor swimming pool, stepped through huge French doors and out onto a veranda overhanging the outdoor pool.

It was like stepping into a tropical-party area where the

only thing missing was the guests. A bar—a proper bar, with flashing lights, high stools, and everything—was set up at one end. Tables, chairs, and plump sofas abounded.

'I bet you have some fantastic parties here,' she said. The perfect setting for the playboy Francesco was reputed to be, yet, she reflected, not at all the man who she was learning he was.

'Not for a long time.'

'Why's that?'

'I have different priorities now.' He raised his shoulder, affecting nonchalance, but there was no doubting the 'I'm not prepared to discuss this' timbre in his voice.

That was fine by her. She doubted she wanted to know what his new priorities were anyway.

She spotted a long white board jutting through the trellis. 'Is that a diving board?'

He nodded. 'It beats walking down the steps to reach the swimming pool.'

'You should get a slide—that would be much more fun.'

He chuckled and slipped behind the bar. 'That's not a bad idea. Do you swim?'

'Not for years.'

'I would suggest a dip now but alcohol and swimming pools do not mix well. We will have time for a swim in the morning—that is, if you want to stay the night. Or do you still want to get a flight home?'

There was no mistaking the meaning in his quietly delivered words.

A thrill of excitement speared up her spine, making her shiver despite the warmth of her skin in the balmy night air.

Dimly she recalled saying she wanted to go home. The anger that had made her say those words had gone. All that lay within her now was a longing, wrapped so tightly in her chest it almost made her nauseous.

This was what she'd wanted. It was the whole reason she was here.

She shook her head. 'I don't want to go home. I want to stay.'

His eyes held hers, heat flashing from them before he reached for a bottle and poured them both a drink, topping the smaller measure with a splash of lemonade. He handed it to her. 'I've sweetened it for you, otherwise your untried taste buds might find it a little too harsh.'

Their fingers brushed as she took the glass from him. That same flash of heat sparked in his eyes again.

'*Saluti,*' he said, holding his glass aloft.

'*Saluti,*' she echoed, chinking her glass to his.

Francesco took a swallow of his drink. 'I thought you would have checked your phone by now.'

'Oh.' Disconcerted, she blinked. 'I should, really.' After all the fuss she'd made over it, she'd shoved it into her clutch bag without even checking the screen for messages.

For the first time since she'd gained her permanent place on the children's ward, the compulsion to check her phone had taken second place to something else. And that something else was gazing at Francesco.

The more she looked at him, the more the excited nausea increased. Was it even nausea she felt? She didn't know; she had no name befitting the ache that pulsed so, so low within her.

While she stood there rooted, helpless for the first time to know what to do, all her bravado and certainty from the night before gone, Francesco finished his brandy and laid the glass on the bar. 'Time for bed.'

Bed…

Immediately the butterflies inside her began to thrash about, her heart racing at a gallop.

It was late. She'd been awake the best part of two days

after a night of hardly any sleep, yet she didn't feel the least bit weary.

But sleep wasn't what Francesco was implying with his statement.

She gulped her drink down, completely forgetting it had alcohol in it. It had a bitter aftertaste that somehow soothed her skittering nerves a touch. She felt like grabbing the bottle and pouring herself another, this time without the lemonade.

Francesco must have read what was going on beneath her skin, for he stepped out from behind the bar and stood before her. He reached out a hand and pulled her chopsticks out. After a moment's suspended animation her hair tumbled down.

'That's better,' he murmured. Before she could ask what he meant, he inhaled deeply and took a step back. 'I'm going to my room. I will let you decide if you want to join me in it or if you wish to sleep alone.'

'But…'

'I can see you're nervous. I want you to be sure. I meant what I said last night—I will not take advantage of you. My room is two doors from yours. I leave the ball in your court.' With that, he bowed his head, turned on his heel, and strode away.

After a long pause in which all the blood in her body flooded into her brain and roared around her ears, Hannah expelled a long breath of air.

What had she expected? That Francesco would take charge, sweep her into his arms, and carry her manfully all the way to his bedroom as if she weighed little more than a bag of sugar? That he would lay her on his bed and devour her, taking command of every touch and movement?

Hadn't she known he was far too honourable for that?

How right she had been that he would never do anything

to hurt her—even taking her phone had been, according to Francesco's sense of logic, for her own good. Saying that, if he ever stole it from her again she certainly wouldn't be so forgiving…. Oh, what was she thinking? After tonight he would never have another opportunity to steal her phone. Once this weekend was over she would throw herself back into her work—her life—and Francesco would be nothing but a memory of one weekend when she'd dared embrace life in its entirety.

If she wanted Francesco to make love to her, she would have to go to him….

But could she do that? Could she slip into his room and slide under his bedcovers?

Could she not?

No. She couldn't *not* do it.

She would never meet another man like him—how could she when she'd spent twenty-seven years having never met *anyone* who made her feel anything?

It had all felt so different last night, though, when she'd practically begged him to make love to her. Before she'd spent time with him and discovered the complex man behind the cool facade, the man who could be both cruel and yet full of empathy. A man who was capable of both great brutality and great generosity. He was no longer some mythological dream figure. He was flesh and blood, with all the complexity that came from being human.

Francesco stood under the shower for an age, fixing the temperature to a much lower setting than the steaming-hot he usually favoured. If he kept it cold enough it might just do something to lessen his libido.

He pressed his forehead to the cool tiles.

Hannah was his for the taking. She'd been his for the taking since she'd first strolled into his nightclub carrying a bunch of flowers for him. All he had to do was walk two doors down and she would welcome him into her arms.

It unnerved him how badly he wanted to do that. How badly he wanted her.

Would she come to him?

He honestly could not guess.

She was not one of the worldly women he normally spent time with, for whom sex was a form of currency.

Hannah was a twenty-seven-year-old virgin who'd hidden the essence of herself from the world—from herself, even—for the best part of fifteen years.

He'd seen the hesitation in her eyes when he'd said it was time for bed. All the boldness from the night before had vanished, leaving her vulnerability lying right there on the surface.

He would not be the man to take advantage of that vulnerability, no matter how easy it would be and no matter how much she would welcome it.

Francesco could pinpoint the exact moment when the determination to keep her out of his bed had shifted. It had been when he'd looked at that cheating thief, a man so like all those other men who'd been fawning over her during the poker tournament. Now that Hannah's sexuality had awoken, it wouldn't meekly lie back down when she returned to London and return to its former dormancy. Eventually she would meet another man she wanted enough to make love to. It could be any of those men. It could be any man, not one of whom could be trusted to treat her with the tenderness she deserved.

Hannah wanted *him*.

And, *caro Dio*, he wanted her, too, with a need that burned in the very fabric of his being.

But he knew that this final step had to come from her

and her alone, however agonising the wait for her decision would be.

Stepping out of the shower, he towelled himself dry, brushed his teeth, and wandered naked through the doorway of the en suite bathroom into his bedroom....

While he'd showered, Hannah had crept into his room. She stood before the window, her eyes widening as she took in his nude form.

'You've taken your make-up off,' he said, walking slowly towards her. She'd showered, too, her hair damp, her body wrapped in the thick white bathrobe kept in the guest room.

She raised a hand to a cheek, which, even in the dim light, he could see had flushed with colour.

He covered her hand with his own. 'This is better. You're beautiful as you are.'

She trembled, although whether that was down to the hoarseness of his voice or a reaction to his touch he could not say.

Slowly he trailed a hand down the swan of her neck to the V made by the bathrobe, slipping a finger between the bunched material to loosen it, exposing the cleavage of her creamy breasts. Slower still, he slid down to the sash and, using both hands, untied it before pushing the robe apart, exposing her to him.

Hannah's breaths became shallow. Her chest hitched. She stood as still as a statue, staring at him with a look that somehow managed to be both bold and shy. He pushed the shoulders of the robe so it fell softly to the floor.

His own breath hitched as he drank her in.

Her body was everything he'd imagined and more—her breasts fuller and higher, her belly softly toned, her hips curvier, her legs longer and smoother.

He swallowed, the ache in his groin so deep it was painful.

He forced himself to remember that she was a virgin. No matter how badly he wanted to go ahead and devour her, he needed to keep the reins on himself.

Hannah had never felt so exposed—had never *been* so exposed—as she was at that moment. Her heart thundered, her blood surged, but none of it mattered. The hunger in Francesco's eyes was enough to evaporate the shyness and quell any last-minute fears, although, when she dared cast her eyes down to his jutting erection, she experienced a different, more primitive fear that was accompanied by a wild surge of heat through her loins.

Naked except for the gold cross that rested at the top of his muscular chest, Francesco was truly glorious. For such a tall, powerful man he had a surprising grace about him, an elegance to his raw masculinity that tempered the powerhouse he was.

Moisture filled her mouth. She swallowed it away, her eyes captured by the heat of hot chocolate fudge that gleamed.

She wanted to touch him. She wanted to rake her fingers through the whorls of dark hair covering his chest, to feel his skin beneath her lips.

Except she was rooted to the spot on which she stood, helpless to do anything but receive his study of her naked form.

'We'll take it very slowly,' he said, his words thick.

She couldn't speak, could only jerk a nod, aching for it to start, yearning for it to be over, a whole jumble of thoughts and emotions careering through her. Out of the fear and excitement, though, it was the latter that rose to the top.

This was it....

And then she was aloft, clutched against Francesco's hard torso as he swept her into his arms and carried her over to the enormous four-poster bed, her private fantasy coming to life.

Gently he laid her down on her back before lying beside her. He placed a hand on her collarbone—the same bone that had been broken during the moment that had brought him into her life—before slanting his lips on hers.

The heat from his mouth, the mintiness of his breath, the fresh oaky scent of him...sent her senses reeling. His kiss was light but assured, a tender pressure that slowly deepened until her lips parted and his tongue swept into her mouth.

Finally she touched him, placing a hand on his shoulder, feeling the smoothness of his skin while she revelled in the headiness evoked by his increasingly hungry kisses.

He moved his mouth away, sweeping his lips over her cheek to nibble at her earlobe. 'Are you sure about this?'

'You have to ask?' In response to the low resonance of his voice, her own was a breathless rush.

'Any time you want to stop, say.'

She turned her head to capture his lips. 'I don't want to stop.'

He groaned and muttered something she didn't understand before kissing her with such passion her bones seemed to melt within her.

His large hand swept over her, flattening against her breasts, trailing over her belly, stroking her, moulding her. And then he followed it with his mouth. When his lips closed over a puckered nipple she gasped, her eyes flying open.

Always she had looked at breasts as functional assets, understanding in a basic fashion that men lusted after them. Never had it occurred to her that the pleasure a man took from them could be reciprocated by the woman—by *her*. She reached for him, digging her fingers into his scalp, silently begging him to carry on, almost crying out when he broke away, only to immediately turn his attention to the other.

It was the most wonderful feeling imaginable.

At some point he had rolled on top of her. She could feel his erection prod against her thigh and moaned as she imagined what it would feel like to actually have him inside her, being a part of her...

Oh, but she burned, a delicious heat that seeped into every inch of her being, every part alive and dancing in the flames.

It was as if Francesco was determined to kiss and worship every tiny crevice, his mouth now trailing down over her belly whilst his hands...

Her gasp was loud when he moved a hand between her legs, gently stroking his fingers over her soft hair until he found her—

Dear God...

He knelt between her legs, his tongue *there*, pressed against her tight bud.

What was happening to her?

Never in her wildest imaginings had she dreamed that the very essence of her being could ache with such intensity. Nothing. Nothing could have prepared her.

Oh, but this was incredible—*he* was incredible...

Right in her core the heaviness grew. Francesco stayed exactly where he was, his tongue making tiny circular motions, increasing the pressure until, with a cry that seemed to come from a faraway land, ripples of pure pleasure exploded through her and carried her off to that faraway land in the stars.

Only when all the pulsations had abated did Francesco move, trailing kisses all the way back up her body until he reached her mouth and kissed her with a savagery that stole her remaining breath.

He lifted his head to gaze down at her. The chocolate in his eyes had fully melted, his expression one of wonder. 'I need to get some protection,' he said, sounding pained.

She didn't want him to leave her. She wanted him to stay right there, to keep her body covered with the heat of his own.

He didn't go far, simply rolling off her to reach into his bedside table. Before he could rip the square foil open, she placed her hand on his chest. Francesco's heart thudded as wildly as her own.

Closing her eyes, she twisted onto her side and pressed a kiss to his shoulder. And another. And another, breathing in his musky scent, rubbing her nose against the smoothness of his olive skin.

With trembling fingers she explored him, the hard chest with the soft black hair, the brown nipples that she rubbed a thumb over and heard him catch a breath at, the washboard stomach covered with a fine layer of that same black hair that thickened the lower she went, becoming more wiry...

She hesitated, raising her head from his shoulder to stare at him. How she longed to touch him properly, but there was a painful awareness that she didn't know what she was doing. How could she know what he liked, how he wanted to be touched? It wasn't that she had minimal experience— she had *no* experience. Nothing.

'You can do whatever you want,' he whispered hoarsely, raking his hands through her hair and pressing a kiss to her lips. 'Touch me however you like.'

Could he read her mind?

Tentatively, she encircled her hand around his length, feeling it pulsate beneath her touch. Francesco groaned and lay back, hooking one arm over his head while the other lay buried in her hair, his fingers massaging her scalp.

His erection felt a lot smoother than she'd expected, and as she moved her hand up to the tip, a drop of fluid rubbed in her fingers.

A rush of moist heat flooded between her legs, a sharp pulsation, the same ache she had experienced when Francesco had set her body alight with his mouth. To witness his desire for her was as great an aphrodisiac as anything she had experienced since being in his room.

So quickly she didn't even notice him move, he covered her hand with his. 'No more,' he growled. 'I want to be inside you.'

She couldn't resist wrapping an arm around his neck and kissing him, pressing herself against him as tightly as she could.

Hooking an arm around her waist, Francesco twisted her back down, sliding a knee between her legs to part them.

With expert deftness, he ripped the foil open with his teeth and rolled it on before manoeuvring himself so he was fully on top of her and between her parted thighs, his erection heavy against her.

He pressed his lips to hers and kissed her, his left hand burying back into her hair, his right sliding down her side and slipping between them.

She felt him guide the tip of his erection against her and then into her, and sucked in a breath. Francesco simply deepened the kiss, murmuring words of Sicilian endearment into her mouth. He brought his hand back up to stroke her face and thrust forward a little more, still kissing her, stroking her, nibbling at the sensitive skin of her neck, slowly, slowly inching his way inside her.

There was one moment of real discomfort that made her freeze, but then it was gone, her senses too full of Francesco and all the magical things he was doing to dwell on that one thing.

And then he was there, all the way inside her, stretching her, filling her massively, his groin pressed against her pubis, his chest crushing against her breasts.

'Am I hurting you?' he asked raggedly.

'No. It feels…good.' It felt more than good—it felt heavenly.

'*You* feel so good,' he groaned into her ear, withdrawing a little only to inch forward again.

His movements were slow but assured, allowing her to adjust to all these new feelings and sensations, building the tempo at an unhurried pace, only pulling back a few inches, keeping his groin pressing against her.

The sensations he'd created with his tongue began to bubble within her again but this time felt fuller, deeper, more condensed.

Her arms wrapped around his neck, her breaths shallow, she began to move with him, meeting his thrusts, which steadily lengthened. And all the while he kissed her, his hands roaming over the sides of her body, her face, her neck, her hair…everywhere.

She felt the tension increase within him, his groans deepening—such an erotic sound, confirmation that everything she was experiencing was shared, that it was real and not just a beautiful dream. The bubbling deep in her core thickened and swelled, triggering a mass of pulsations to ripple through her. Crying out, she clung to him, burying her face in his neck at the same moment Francesco gave his own cry and made one final thrust that seemed to last for ever.

CHAPTER NINE

FRANCESCO STRETCHED, LOOKED at his bedside clock, then turned back over to face the wall that was Hannah's back. When they'd fallen into sleep she'd been cuddled into him, their limbs entwined.

The last time he'd had such a deep sleep had been his birthday ten months ago. That had been just two days before he'd discovered his mother's diaries.

For the first time in ten months he'd fallen asleep without the demons that plagued him screwing with his thoughts.

Only the top of Hannah's shoulder blades were uncovered and he resisted the urge to place a kiss on them. After disposing of the condom, he'd longed to make love to her again. He'd put his selfish desires to one side. She'd had a long week at work, little sleep the night before, and her body was bound to ache after making love for the first time. Instead he'd pulled her to him and listened to her fall into slumber. It was the sweetest sound he'd ever heard.

He rubbed his eyes and pinched the bridge of his nose, expelling a long breath.

If someone had told him just twenty-four hours ago that making love to Hannah Chapman would be the best experience of his life, he would have laughed. And not with any humour.

To know he was the first man to have slept with her

made his chest fill. To know that he'd awoken those responses... It had been a revelation, a thing of beauty.

Francesco had never felt humble about anything in his life, yet it was the closest he could come to explaining the gratitude he felt towards her for choosing him.

Hannah hadn't chosen him for his power or his wealth or his lifestyle—she'd chosen and trusted him for *him*.

To think he'd dismissed her when she'd blurted out that she wanted him to make love to her. She could have accepted that dismissal. Eventually she would have found another man she trusted enough...

It didn't bear thinking about.

The thought of another man pawing at her and making clumsy love to her made his brain burn and his heart clench.

Suddenly he became aware that her deep, rhythmic breathing had stopped.

His suspicion that she'd awoken was confirmed when she abruptly turned over to face him, her eyes startled.

'Buongiorno,' he said, a smile already playing on his lips.

Blinking rapidly, Hannah covered a yawn before bestowing him with a sleepy smile. 'What time is it?'

'Nine o'clock.'

She yawned again. 'Wow. I haven't slept in that late for years.'

'You needed it.' Hooking an arm around her waist, he pulled her to him. 'How are you feeling?'

Her face scrunched in thought. 'Strange.'

'Good strange or bad strange?'

That wonderful look of serenity flitted over her face. 'Good strange.'

Already his body ached to make love to her again. Trailing his fingers over her shoulder, enjoying the softness of her skin, he pressed a kiss to her neck. 'Are you hungry?'

His lust levels rose when she whispered huskily into his ear, 'Starving.'

A late breakfast was brought out to them on the bar-side veranda. Their glasses from the previous evening had already been cleared away.

Wrapped in the guest robe, her hair damp from the shower she'd shared with Francesco, Hannah stretched her legs out and took a sip of the deliciously strong yet sweet coffee. Sitting next to her, dressed in his own dark grey robe, his thigh resting against hers, Francesco grinned.

'You are so lucky waking up to this view every morning,' she sighed. With the morning sun rising above them, calm waves swirling onto Francesco's private beach in the distance, it was as if they were in their own private nirvana.

Breakfast usually consisted of a snatched slice of toast. Today she'd been treated to eggs and bacon and enough fresh rolls and fruit to feed a whole ward of patients.

Yes. Nirvana.

'Believe me, this is the best view I've had in a *very* long time,' he said, his eyes gleaming, his deep voice laced with meaning.

Thinking of all the beautiful women she'd seen pictured on his arm, Hannah found that extremely hard to believe.

Her belly twisted.

It was no good thinking of all those women. Comparing herself to them would be akin to comparing a rock to the moon.

For the first time in her life she wished she'd put some make-up on, then immediately scolded herself for such a ridiculous thought. All those women who had the time and inclination to doll themselves up...well, good luck to them. Even after the make-up lesson she'd been given in the salon, painting her face for their night out had felt like wasted time. Looking at her reflection once she was done had been like looking at a stranger. She hadn't felt like *her*.

She supposed she could always look at it as practice for Melanie's wedding, though—a thought that brought a lump to her throat.

'You do realise you're the sexiest woman on the planet, don't you?' Francesco's words broke through the melancholy of her thoughts.

'Hardly,' she spluttered, taking another sip of her coffee.

'I can prove it,' he murmured sensually into her ear, clasping her hand and tugging it down to rest on his thigh. Sliding it up to his groin, he whispered, 'You see, my clever doctor, you are irresistible.' As he spoke, he nibbled into the nape of her neck, keeping a firm grip on her hand, moving it up so she could feel exactly what effect she was having on him.

A thrill of heady power rushed through her. Heat pooled between her legs, her breath deserting her.

They'd already made love twice since she'd awoken. She'd thought she was spent, had assumed Francesco was, too.

With his free hand he tugged her robe open enough to slip a hand through and cup a breast, kneading it gently. 'You also have the most beautiful breasts on the earth,' he murmured into her ear before sliding his lips over to her mouth and kissing her with a ferocity that reignited the remaining embers of her desire.

'What…what if one of your staff comes out?' she gasped, moving him with more assurance as he unclasped her hand and snaked his arm round her waist.

'They won't.' Thus saying, he slid his hand under her bottom and lifted her off the chair and onto the table, ignoring the fact that their breakfast plates and cups were scattered all over it.

Francesco ached to be inside her again, his body fired up beyond belief, and such a short time after their last bout. It was those memories of being in the shower with her, when she'd sunk to her knees and taken him in her mouth for the first time....

Just thinking about it would sustain his fantasies for a lifetime.

Dipping his head to take a perfectly ripe breast into his mouth, he trailed a hand down her belly and slipped a finger inside her, groaning aloud to find her hot and moist and ready for him.

Diving impatiently into his pocket, he grabbed the condom he'd put in there as an afterthought and, with Hannah distracting him by smothering any part of his face and neck she could reach with kisses, he slipped it on, spread her thighs wide, and plunged straight into her tight heat.

Her head lolled back, her eyes widening as if in shock.

Silently he cursed himself. Such was his excitement he'd totally forgotten that until a few short hours ago she'd been a virgin.

'Too much?' he asked, stilling, fighting to keep himself in check.

'Oh, no.' As if to prove it, she grabbed his buttocks and ground herself against him. The shock left her eyes, replaced with the desire he knew swirled in his own. 'I want it all.'

It was all he needed. Sweeping the crockery this way and that to make some space, he pushed her back so she was flat on the table, her thighs parted and raised high, her legs wrapped around his, and thrust into her, withdrawing to the tip and thrusting back in, over and over until she was whimpering beneath him, her hands flailing to grab his chest, her head turning from side to side. Only when he felt her thicken around him and her muscles contract did he let himself go, plunging in as deep as he could with one final groan before collapsing on top of her.

It was only when all the stars had cleared that he realised they were still in their respective robes, Hannah's fingers playing under the Egyptian cotton, tracing up and down his back.

She giggled.

Lifting his chin to rest it on her chest, he stared at her intently.

'That was incredible,' she said, smiling.

He flashed his teeth in return. 'You, *signorina*, are a very quick learner.'

'And you, *signor*, are a very good teacher.'

'There is so much more I can teach you.'

'And is it all depraved?'

'Most of it.'

She laughed softly and lay back on the table, expelling a sigh of contentment as she gazed up at the cobalt sky. He kept his gaze on her face. That serene look was there again. To think he was the cause of it…

A late breakfast turned into a late lunch. Francesco did not think he had ever felt the beat of the sun so strongly on his skin. For the first time in ten months he enjoyed a lazy day—indeed, the thought of working never crossed his mind. The rage he felt for his father, the rage that had boiled within him for so long, had morphed into a mild simmer.

In the back of his mind was the knowledge that at some point soon he would have to arrange for his jet to take Hannah back to London, but it was something he desisted from thinking about too much, content to make love, skinny-dip, then make love again. And she seemed happy, too, her smile serene, radiant.

Kissing her for what could easily be the thousandth time, he tied his robe around his waist and headed back indoors and to his bedroom for more condoms.

The box was almost empty. He shook his head in wonder. He'd never known desire like it. He couldn't get enough of her.

When he returned outside, Hannah had poured them both another cup of coffee from the pot and was curled up on one of the sofas reading something on her phone.

'Everything okay?' he asked, hiding the burst of irritation that poked at him.

This was the third time she'd gone through her messages since they'd awoken.

She's a dedicated professional, he reminded himself. *Her patients are her priority, as they should be.*

For all his sound reasoning, there was no getting around the fact he wanted to rip the phone from her hand and stamp on it. After all, it was the weekend. She was off duty.

She looked up and smiled. 'All's well.'

'Good.' Sitting next to her, he plucked the phone from her hand and slipped it into his pocket.

'Not again,' she groaned.

'Now you have satisfied yourself that your patients are all well, you have no need for it.'

'Francesco, give it back.'

'Later. You need to learn to switch off. Besides, it's rude.'

'Please.' Her voice lowered, all her former humour gone. 'That's my phone. And I wasn't being rude—you'd gone to the bedroom.' She held her hand out, palm side up. 'Now give.'

'What's it worth?' he asked, leaning into her, adopting a sensuous tone.

'Me not kicking you in the ankle.'

'I thought you didn't believe in violence.'

'So did I.' A smile suddenly creased her face and she burst out laughing, her mirth increasing when he shoved her phone back into the pocket of her robe. 'Now I get it—threats of violence really do work.'

He kissed her neck and flattened her onto her back. 'The difference is I knew you didn't mean it.'

Raking her fingers through his hair, she sighed. 'I guess you'll never know.'

'Oh, I know.' Hannah healed people. She didn't hurt them.

But he didn't want to think those thoughts. The time was fast approaching when he'd have to take her home, leaving him limited time left to worship her delectable body.

'I'm going to be in London more frequently for a while,' he mentioned casually, making his way down to a ripe breast. 'I'll give you a call when I'm over. Take you out for dinner.' With all the evidence pointing to Luca Mastrangelo still sniffing around the Mayfair casino, Francesco needed to be on the ball. If that meant spending more time in London, then so be it. The casino would be his, however he had to achieve it. He would secure that deal and nothing would prevent it.

Hannah moaned as he circled his tongue around a puckered nipple.

At least being in London more often meant he could enjoy her for a little longer, too.

It never occurred to him that Hannah might have different ideas.

Hannah opened the curtains and stepped into the cubicle, pulling the curtains shut around her. She smiled at the small girl lying in the bed who'd been brought in a week ago with encephalitis, inflammation of the brain, then smiled at the anxious parents. 'We have the lab results,' she said, not wasting time with pleasantries, 'and it's good news.'

This was her favourite part of the job, she thought a few minutes later as she walked back to her small workspace—telling parents who'd lived through hell that their child would make it, that the worst was over.

Clicking the mouse to get her desktop working, she opened the young girl's file, ready to write her notes up into the database. Her phone vibrated in her pocket.

She pulled it out, her heart skipping when Francesco's name flashed up.

Time seemed to still as she stared at it, her hands frozen.

Should she answer?

Or not?

It went to voicemail before she could decide.

Closing her eyes, she tilted her head back and rolled her neck.

Why, oh, why had she agreed to see him again? Not that she had agreed. At the time she'd been too busy writhing in his arms to think coherently about anything other than the sensations he was inducing in her....

She squeezed her eyes even tighter.

Francesco, in all his arrogance, had simply assumed she'd want to see him again.

An almost hysterical burst of laughter threatened to escape from her throat.

There was no way she could see him again. She just couldn't.

Their time together in Sicily had brought him, her dream man, to life—the good and the bad. Being with him had been the most wonderful, thrilling time imaginable. She had felt alive. She had felt *so much*.

She had felt *too* much.

All she wanted now was to focus on her job and leave Francesco as nothing but a beautiful memory.

She would carry on seeking out new experiences to share with Beth for when the time came that they were together again. But these experiences would be of an entirely different nature, more of a tick box—*I've done that, I've parachuted out of an aeroplane*—experience. Nothing that would clog her head. Nothing that would compromise everything she had spent the majority of her life working towards.

But, dear God, the hollowness that had lived in her chest for so long now felt so *full*, as if her shrivelled heart had been pumped back to life. And that scared her more than anything.

It was easier to shatter a full heart than a shrivelled one.

'Hannah, you should go home,' Alice, the ward sister said, startling her from her thoughts. Alice looked hard at her. 'Are you okay?'

Hannah nodded. Alice was lovely, a woman whose compassion extended from the children to all the staff on the ward. 'I'm fine,' she said, forcing a smile. 'I'll be off as soon as I get these reports finished.'

'It'll be dark soon,' Alice pointed out. 'Anyway, I'm off now. I'll see you in the morning.'

Alone again, Hannah rubbed her temples, willing away the tension headache that was forming.

She really should go home. Her shift had officially finished two hours ago.

The thought of returning to her little home filled her with nothing but dread, just as it had for the past three days since she'd returned from Sicily.

Her home felt so empty.

The silence…how had she never noticed the silence before, when the only noise had been the sound of her own breathing?

For the first time ever, she felt lonely. Not the usual loneliness that had been within her since Beth's death, but a different kind of isolation. Colder, somehow.

Even the sunny yellow walls of her little cubbyhole felt bleak.

Francesco's phone rang. *'Ciao.'*

'That young drug dealer is back. We have him.'

'Bring him to me.'

Francesco knew exactly who Mario was on about. A young lad, barely eighteen, had visited his Palermo nightclub a few weeks ago. The cameras had caught him slipping bags of powder and pills to many of the clubbers. As unlikely as it was, he had slipped their net, escaping before Francesco's men could apprehend him, disappearing into the night.

He rubbed his eyes.

No matter how hard he tried to remove the dealers, there was always some other cocky upstart there to fill the breach. It was like trying to stop the tide.

The one good thing he could say about it was that at least he was making the effort to clean the place up, to counter some of the damage his father had done.

Salvatore had been responsible for channelling millions of euros' worth of drugs into Sicily and mainland Europe. How he had kept it secret from his son, Francesco would never understand; he could only guess Salvatore had known it was the one thing his son would never stand idly by and allow to happen. If Francesco *had* known, he would have ripped his father apart, but by the time he'd learned of his involvement, it had been too late to confront him. Salvatore had already been buried when he found out the truth.

It occurred to him, not for the first time, that his father had been afraid of him.

Slowly but surely, he was dismantling everything Salvatore Calvetti had built, closing it down brick by brick, taking care in his selection of which to dismantle first so as not to disturb the foundation and have it all crumble on top of him. Only a few days ago he had taken great delight in shutting down a restaurant that had been a hub for the distribution of arms, one of many in his father's great network.

While he'd been paying off Paolo di Luca, the man who'd run the restaurant on his father's behalf for thirty years, he had seen for the first time the old man Paolo had become. A man with liver spots and a rheumy wheeze. The more he thought about it, the more he realised all the old associates were exactly that—old.

When had they got so ancient?

These weren't the terrifying men of his childhood memories. Apart from a handful who hadn't taken kindly to being put out to pasture, most of them had been happy to be paid off, glad to spend their remaining years with their wives—or mistresses in many cases—and playing with their grandchildren and great-grandchildren.

There was a knock on the door, and the handle turned.

Mario and two of his other guards walked in, holding the young drug dealer up by the scruff of his neck.

With them came a burst of music from the club, a dreadful tune that hit him straight in his gut.

It was the same tune Hannah had been dancing to so badly in his London club, when he'd threatened the fool manhandling her.

The same Hannah who'd ignored her phone when he'd called and, in response to a message he'd sent saying he would be in London at the weekend, had sent him a simple message back saying she was busy. Since then…nothing. Not a peep from her.

It wasn't as if she never used her blasted phone. It was attached to her like an appendage.

There was no getting around it. She was avoiding him.

He looked at the belligerent drug dealer, but all he could see was the look of serenity on Hannah's face when he'd told her of calling the police on the casino cheat.

Hannah saved lives. She'd sworn an oath to never do harm.

What was it she'd said? *Who makes the rules?*

'Empty your pockets,' he ordered, not moving from his seat.

He could see how badly the drug dealer wanted to disobey him, but sanity prevailed and he emptied his pockets. He had two bags of what Francesco recognised as ecstasy tablets and a bag full of tiny cellophane wraps of white powder. Cocaine.

A cross between a smirk and a snarl played on the drug dealer's lips.

Francesco's hands clenched into fists. He rose.

The drug dealer turned puce, his belligerence dropping a touch when confronted by Francesco's sheer physical power.

Who makes the rules?

'You are throwing your life away,' he said harshly before turning to Mario. 'Call the police.'

'The police?' squeaked the dealer.

It was obvious that the same question echoed in Mario and his fellow guards' heads.

First the stealing, cheating gambler and now a drug dealer? He could see the consternation on all their faces, could feel them silently wondering if he was going soft.

Naturally, none of his men dared question him verbally, their faces expressionless.

'Yes. The police.' As he walked past the dealer, Francesco added, 'But know that when you're released from your long prison sentence, if I ever find you dealing in drugs again, I will personally break your legs. Take my advice—get yourself an education and go straight.'

With that, he strode out of his office, out of his nightclub, and into the dark Palermo night, oblivious to the cadre of bodyguards who'd snapped into action to keep up with him.

CHAPTER TEN

HANNAH BROUGHT HER bike to a stop outside her small front gate and smothered a yawn. She felt dead on her feet. The Friday-evening traffic had only compounded what had been a *very* long week.

She dismounted and wheeled her bike up the narrow path to her front door. Just as she placed her key in the lock, a loud beep made her turn.

A huge, gleaming black motorbike with an equally huge rider came to a stop right by her front gate.

No way...

Stunned, she watched as Francesco strode towards her, magnificent in his black leathers, removing his helmet, a thunderous look on his face.

'What are you doing here?' Her heart had flown into her mouth and it took all she had not to stand there gaping like a goldfish.

'Never mind that, what the hell are you doing back on that deathtrap?'

He loomed before her, blocking the late sun, his eyes blazing with fury.

Hannah blinked, totally nonplussed at seeing him again. Only years of practice at remaining calm while under fire from distressed patients and their next of kin alike allowed her to retain any composure. 'I don't drive.'

Breathing heavily through his nose, he snapped, 'There are other ways of getting around. I can't believe you're still using this…thing.'

'I'm not. It's a new one.'

'I gathered that, seeing as your old one crumpled like a biscuit tin,' he said, speaking through gritted teeth. 'I'm just struggling to understand why you would still cycle when you nearly died on a bicycle mere weeks ago.'

'I don't like using public transport. Plus, cycling helps shift some of the weight from my bottom,' she added, trying to inject some humour into her tone, hoping to defuse some of the anger still etched on his face. Her attempt failed miserably.

'There is nothing wrong with your bottom,' he said coldly. 'And even if there were—which there isn't—it's hardly worth risking your life for.'

The situation was so surreal Hannah was tempted to pinch herself.

Was she dreaming? She'd had so little sleep since returning from Sicily five days ago that it was quite possible.

'Like every other human on this planet, I could die at any time by any number of accidents. I'm not going to stay off my bike because of one idiot.' She kept her tone firm, making it clear the situation was no longer open for discussion. She was a grown woman. If she wanted to cycle, then that was her business. 'Anyway, you're hardly in a position to judge—do you have any idea the number of mangled motorcyclists I had to patch back together when I was doing my placement in Accident and Emergency?'

A cold snake crawled up her spine at the thought of Francesco being brought in on a trolley….

She blinked the thought away.

'My riding skills are second to none, as you know perfectly well,' he said with all the confidence of a man who knew he was the best at what he did. 'In any case, I do not ride around on a piece of cheap tin.'

'You can be incredibly arrogant, did you know that?'

'I've been called much worse, and if being arrogant is what it takes to keep you safe then I can live with that.'

His chocolate eyes held hers with an intensity so deep it almost burned. Her fingers itched to touch him, to rub her thumb over the angry set of his lips.

No matter how…shocked she felt at his sudden appearance, there was something incredibly touching about his anger, knowing it was concern for her safety propelling it.

She looked away, scared to look at him any longer. 'I appreciate your concern, but my safety is not your responsibility.'

Suddenly aware her helmet was still attached to her head, she unclipped it and whipped it off, smoothing her hair down as best she could.

God, since when had she suffered from vanity? Last weekend notwithstanding, not in fifteen years.

And why did she feel an incomprehensible urge to burst into tears?

It was a feeling she'd been stifling since she'd walked back into her home on Sunday night.

'What are you doing here?' she asked again, her cheeks burning as she recalled the two phone calls she'd ignored from him.

'That's not a conversation I wish to have on your doorstep.'

When she made no response, he inclined his head at her door. 'This is the point where you invite me into your home.'

Less than a week ago she'd invited him into her house, only to have him rudely decline.

Then, her heart had hammered with excitement for what

the weekend would bring. Now her heart thrummed just to see *him*…

'Look, you can come in for a little while, but I've had a long, difficult week and a *very* long, *very difficult* day, and I want to get to bed early.' Abruptly, she turned away and opened the door, terrified he would read something of her feelings on her face.

The last word she should be mentioning in front of Francesco was *bed*.

She could hardly credit how naive she'd been in sleeping with him. Had she seriously thought she could share a bed with the sexiest man on the planet and walk away feeling nothing more than a little mild contentment that she'd ticked something off her to-do list?

What a silly, naive fool she'd been.

Francesco thought he'd never been in a more depressing house than the place Hannah called home. It wasn't that there was anything intrinsically wrong with it—on the contrary, it was a pretty two-bedroom house with high ceilings and spacious rooms, but…

There was no feeling to it. Her furniture was minimal and bought for function. The walls were bare of any art or anything that would show the owner's tastes. It was a shell.

Hannah shoved her foldaway bike in a virtually empty cupboard under the stairs and faced him, a look of defiance—and was that fear?—on her face. Her hair had reverted back to its usual unkempt state, a sight that pleased him immeasurably.

'I need a shower,' she said.

'Is that an invitation?' he asked, saying it more as a challenge than from any expectation.

She ignored his innuendo. 'I've been puked on twice today.'

He grimaced. 'So not an invitation.'

'Give me five minutes, then you can tell me whatever it is you came all this way to discuss. While I'm gone, you can make yourself useful by making the coffee.' Thus saying, she headed up the wooden stairs without a backward glance, her peachy bottom showing beautifully in the functional black trousers she wore....

Quickly he averted his eyes. Too much looking at those gorgeous buttocks might just make him climb into that shower with her after all.

Besides, a few minutes to sort their respective heads out would probably be a good idea.

Hannah's reception had not been the most welcoming, but what had he expected? That she would take one look at him and throw herself into his arms?

No, he hadn't expected that. Her silence and polite rebuff by text message had made her feelings clear. Well, tough on her. He was here and they would talk whether she wanted to or not.

Yet there had been no faking the light that had shone briefly in her eyes when she'd first spotted him. It had been mingled with shock, but it had been there, that same light that had beamed straight into his heart the first time she'd opened her eyes to him.

Then he'd ruined it by biting her head off over her bike.

He cursed under his breath. If it took the rest of his life, he'd get her off that deathtrap.

He heard a door close and the sound of running water. Was she naked…?

He inhaled deeply, slung his leather jacket over the post of the stairs, and walked into the small square kitchen. He spotted the kettle easily enough and filled it, then set about finding mugs and coffee.

As he rootled through Hannah's cupboards, his chest slowly constricted.

He had never seen such bare cupboards. The only actual food he found was half a loaf of bread, a box of cereal, a large slice of chocolate cake, and some tomato sauce. And that was it. Nothing else, not even a box of eggs. The fridge wasn't much better, containing some margarine, a pint of milk, and an avocado.

What did she eat?

That question was answered when he opened her freezer.

It wasn't just his chest that felt constricted. His heart felt as if it had been placed in a vice.

The freezer was full. Three trays crammed with ready meals for one.

The ceiling above him creaked, jolting him out of the trance he hadn't realised he'd fallen into.

Experiencing a pang of guilt at rifling through her stuff, he shut the freezer door and went back to the jar of instant coffee he'd found and the small bag of sugar.

No wonder she had wanted to experience a little bit of life.

He'd never met anyone who lived such a solitary existence. Not that anyone would guess. Hannah wasn't antisocial. On the contrary, she was good company. Better than good. Warm, witty… Beautiful. Sexy.

Before too long she emerged to join him in the sparse living room, having changed into a pair of faded jeans and a black T-shirt.

'Your coffee's on the table,' he said, rising from the sofa he'd sat on. He would bet the small dining table in the corner was rarely used for eating on, loaded as it was with medical journals and heaps of paper neatly laid in piles.

'Thank you.' She picked it up and walked past him to

the single seat, leaving a waft of light, fruity fragrance in her wake. She curled up on it, cradling her mug.

Now her eyes met his properly, a brightness glistening from them. 'Francesco, what are you doing here?'

'I want to know why you're avoiding me.'

'I'm not.'

'Don't tell me lies.'

'I haven't seen you to avoid you.'

'You said you were busy this weekend, yet here you are, at home.'

Her head rolled back, her chest rising and falling even more sharply. 'I've only just got back from work, as you well know, and I'm on the rota for tomorrow's night shift. So yes, I am busy.'

'Look at me,' he commanded. He would keep control of his temper if it killed him.

With obvious reluctance, she met his gaze.

'Last weekend… You do realise what we shared was out of this world?'

Her cheeks pinked. 'It was very nice.'

'There are many words to describe it, but *nice* isn't one of them. You and me…'

'There is no you and me,' she blurted, interrupting him. 'I'm sorry to have to put it so crassly, but I don't want to see you again. Last weekend *was* very nice but there will be no repeat performance.'

'You think not?' he said, trying his hardest to keep his tone soft, but when she dug her hand into her pocket and pulled out her phone, the red mist seemed to descend as if from nowhere. 'Do *not* turn that thing on.'

Her eyes widened as if startled before narrowing. 'Don't tell me what I can and can't do. You're not my father.'

'I'm not trying…'

'You certainly are.'

'Will you stop interrupting me?' He raised his voice for the first time.

Her mouth dropped open.

'It's a bit much feeling as if I'm in competition with a phone,' he carried on, uncaring that she had turned a whiter shade of white. He knew without having to be told that there was no competition, because the phone had won without even trying. Because as far as Dr Hannah Chapman was concerned, her phone was all she needed.

He rose to his feet, his anger swelling like an awoken cobra, his venom primed. 'You hide behind it. I bet you sleep with it on your pillow.'

His comment was so close to the mark that Hannah cringed inwardly *and* outwardly. Dear God, why had he come here? Why hadn't he just taken the hint and kept away?

She hadn't asked for any of this. All she'd wanted was to experience one night as a real woman.

She'd ended up with so much more than she'd bargained for.

'Do you really want to spend the rest of your life with nothing but a phone to keep you warm at night?'

'What I want is none of your business,' she said, her tongue running away as she added, 'but just to clarify what I told you in your nightclub, I do *not* want a relationship—not with you, not with anyone.'

He threw his arms out, a sneer on his face. 'Of course you don't want a relationship. Your life is so fulfilling as it is.'

'It is to me.' How she stopped herself screaming that in his face she would never know.

'Look at you. Look at this place. You're hiding away from life. You're like one of those mussels we ate in the casino—you threw yourself at me to experience some of what you'd been missing out on, got what you wanted, then retreated right back into your shell without any thought to the consequences.'

She didn't have a clue what he was talking about. 'What consequences? We used protection.'

'I'm not talking about babies—I'm talking about what you've done to me!' If he'd been a lion he would have roared those last few words, of that she had no doubt. Francesco's fury was a sight to behold, making him appear taller and broader than ever, filling the living room.

She should be terrified. And there was no denying the panic gnawing furiously at the lining of her stomach, but it wasn't fear of him...

No, it was the fear of something far worse.

And this fear put her even further on the defensive.

Shoving her mug on the floor, she jumped to her feet. The calmness she had been wearing as a facade evaporated, leaving her jumbled, terrified emotions raw and exposed. 'I haven't done *anything* to you!'

'You've changed me. I don't know how the hell you did it—maybe you're some kind of witch—but whatever you did, it's real. I let a drug dealer escape without a beating last night, had my men turn him over to the police.'

'And that's a bad thing?'

'It's not how I work. That's never been how I work. Drugs killed my mother. Drug dealers are the scum of the earth and deserve everything they get.' Abruptly he stopped talking and took a long breath in. 'You gave me the best night of my life and I know as well as you do that you enjoyed every minute of it, too. You can deny it until you're blue in the face but we both know what we shared was special. *You* forced that night on *me*. It was what *you* wanted, and it's me that's paying the price for it.'

'You knew it was only for one night.'

'A one-night stand is never that good. Never. Not even close. But now you're treating me as if I'm a plague carrier, and I want to know why.'

'There's nothing to tell. I just don't want to see you again.'

'Will you stop lying?'

'I can't have sex with you again. I just can't. You've screwed with my brain enough as it is.'

'*I've* screwed with *your* brain?' His tone was incredulous. 'Do you have any idea what you've done to *me*?'

'Oh, yes, let's bring it all back to you,' she spat. 'The poor little gangster struggling to deal with his newly found conscience while I...'

Hannah took a deep breath, trying desperately to rein all her emotions back in and under her control. 'After my accident, you filled my mind. You were all I could think about. When I met you it only got worse. I came to you partly because I thought doing something about it would fix it. I thought we would have sex and that would be it— my life would return to normal, I'd be able to go back to concentrating on my job without any outside influences...'

'Didn't it work out exactly as you envisaged?' he asked, his tone mocking.

'No, it did not! I thought it would. But you're still there, filling my head, and I want you gone. My patients deserve all my focus. Every scrap of it. I want to experience more of life, but not to their detriment. This is all *too much* and I can't handle it.'

'I warned you of the consequences,' he said roughly. 'I told you a one-night stand wasn't for a woman like you.'

Something inside Hannah pinged. Taking three paces towards him, she pushed at his chest. 'You are a hypocrite,' she shouted. 'How many women have you used for sex? Double figures? Treble? How many lives have *you* ruined?'

'None. All the women before you knew it would only ever be sex. It meant nothing.'

'Ha! Exactly.' She shoved him again, hard enough to knock him off balance and onto the sofa. 'The minute the tables are turned, your fragile ego can't deal with it...'

She never got to finish her sentence for Francesco grabbed hold of her waist and yanked her onto the sofa with him, pinning her down before she could get a coherent thought in her head.

'You know as well as I do that what we shared meant something,' he said harshly, his hot breath tickling her skin. 'And contrary to your low opinion of my sex life, I am not some kind of male tart. Until last weekend I'd been celibate for ten months.'

She wanted to kick out, scream at him to get off her, but all the words died on her tongue when his mouth came crashing down on hers, a hard, furious kiss that her aching heart and body responded to like a moth to a flame.

That deep masculine taste and scent filled her senses, blocking out all her fears, blocking out everything but him. Francesco.

Just five days away from him, and she had pined. Pined for him. Pined for this.

She practically melted into him, winding her arms around his hard body, clinging to him, pressing every part of her into him.

And he clung to her, too, his hands roaming over her body, bunching her hair, his hot lips grazing her face, her neck, every available bit of flesh.

Being in his arms felt so *right*. Francesco made the coldness that had settled in her bones since she'd returned from Sicily disappear, replacing it with a warmth that seeped through to every part of her.

In a melee of limbs her T-shirt was pulled over her head

and thrown to the floor, quickly followed by Francesco's. Braless, her naked breasts crushed against his chest, the last remaining alarms ringing in her brain vanished and all she could do was savour the feel of his hard strength flush against her.

His strong capable hands playing with the buttons on her jeans, her smaller hands working on the zip of his leathers, somehow they managed to tug both down, using their feet to work them off to join the rest of their strewn clothing, in the process tumbling off the sofa and onto the soft carpet.

Only when they were both naked did Francesco reach for his leathers, pull out his wallet and produce a now familiar square foil.

In a matter of seconds he'd rolled it on and plunged inside her.

This time her body knew exactly what to do. *She* knew exactly what to do. No fears, no insecurities, just pure unadulterated pleasure.

The feel of him, huge inside her, his strength on the verge of crushing her, Hannah let all thoughts fly out of the window, giving in to this most wonderful of all sensations.

Later, lying in the puddle of their clothes on the floor, Francesco's face buried in her neck, his breaths hot against her skin, she opened her eyes and gazed at the ceiling. Hot tears burned the back of her retinas.

'Am I squashing you?' he asked, his breathing still ragged.

'No,' she lied, wrapping her arms even tighter around him.

Francesco lifted his head to look at her. There had been a definite hitch in her voice. 'What's the matter?'

'Nothing.'

'Stop lying to me.'

To his distress, two fat tears rolled down her cheeks.

'I'm so confused. *You* confuse me. I'd told myself I would never sleep with you again and look what's happened. You turn up and I might as well have succumbed to you the moment I let you in the door.'

Rolling onto his back, taking her with him so she rested on his chest, he held her tightly to him. 'All it proves is that we're not over. Not yet. Neither of us wants anything heavy,' he continued. 'For a start, neither of us has the *time* for anything heavy. But we enjoy each other's company, so where's the harm in seeing each other? I promise you, your patients will not suffer for you having a life.'

There was no room for Hannah in his life. Not in any meaningful way. The more he got to know her, the more he knew that what they shared could never be anything more than a fling.

Ever since he'd reached adulthood he'd assumed he would never meet a woman to settle down with. Even before he'd discovered his mother's diaries and learned of his father's despicable behaviour towards her, he'd known how badly she struggled to cope with his father's way of life.

His mother had been a good woman. Kind and loving, even when she was doped to her eyeballs on the drugs his father fed her by the trough. Not that he'd known his father fed them to her—back then he'd believed his father to be as despairing and worried about her habit as he was.

Elisabetta Calvetti had no more fitted into his father's world than Hannah fitted in his.

The women who did fit into Francesco's world and thrived were like poison. The rarer women—women like Hannah who did not fit in—he'd always known should never marry into such a dangerous life. To marry into it would destroy them, just as it had destroyed his mother.

Deep down, he knew he should have accepted her rebuffs and left her alone, but the past few days...

How could he concentrate on anything when his mind was full of Hannah?

The wolves, in the form of Luca Mastrangelo, were circling the Mayfair casino and Francesco needed to be on the ball. Otherwise the deal that would symbolise above all others that Salvatore Calvetti's empire was over, his legacy shrivelled to dust, would be lost.

He wasn't ready to let her go. Not yet. Knowing Hannah was in his life meant he could focus his attention entirely on the purchase of the casino and not have his mind filled with her.

'Okay,' she said slowly, pressing a kiss to his chest. 'As long as you promise not to make any demands on my time when I'm working, we can see each other.'

His arms tightened while the constriction in his chest loosened. He ignored the fact that her condition for seeing him—a condition he was used to dictating to his lovers and not the other way round—made his throat fill with bile.

CHAPTER ELEVEN

THE MAYFAIR CASINO was a lot shabbier than the ones Francesco owned, but the decoration was not something that concerned him. That was cosmetic and easily fixed. Even the accounts, usually his first consideration when buying a new business, mattered not at all. All he craved was what the business symbolised.

Tonight, though, symbolism and everything else could take a hike. He'd finally managed to drag Hannah out for the night.

Naturally, she'd been too busy to buy a new dress and had changed into the same dress she'd worn three weeks before in Sicily, confessing with an embarrassed smile that it was the only suitable item in her wardrobe.

He'd bitten back the offer of buying her a whole new wardrobe. He knew without having to ask that she would refuse. He was man enough to admit that it had been a blow to his pride when he'd learned she'd paid for the dress herself in Palermo. And her haircut. It surprised him, though, how much he respected her for it. She'd had free rein in that boutique. She could have easily racked up a bill for tens of thousands of euros, all in his name.

Tonight she looked beautiful. In the ten minutes she'd taken to get changed, she'd brushed her hair, but all this had done was bush it out even more. She'd applied only a little make-up. All she wore on her feet were her black ballet slippers.

In Francesco's eyes she looked far more ravishing than she had three weeks ago when she'd gone the whole nine yards with her appearance. Now she looked real. She looked like Hannah.

An elderly man with salt-and-pepper hair ambled towards them, his hand outstretched. 'Francesco, I didn't know you would be joining us this evening.' There was a definite tremor in both his hand and voice.

'I wanted to show my guest around the place,' he replied, shaking the wizened hand before introducing him to Hannah. 'This is Dr Hannah Chapman. Hannah, this is Sir Godfrey Renfrew, the current owner of this establishment.'

'Doctor?' Godfrey's eyes swept her up and down, a hint of confusion in them.

'Lovely to meet you,' Hannah said, smiling. Did Francesco *have* to keep referring to her by her title?

'The pleasure is mine,' he said quickly, before fixing his attention back on Francesco. 'I have some of your compatriots visiting me this evening.'

So that was the reason for Godfrey's discomfort.

Francesco glanced around the room, homing in on two tall men leaning against a far wall drinking beer.

So his spies had been onto something when they'd reported that Luca Mastrangelo was trying to usurp the deal. And it seemed as if Pepe was in on it, too.

If Francesco was in Sicily, all he would have to do was whisper a few well-chosen words into Godfrey's ear and the casino would be his.

But he wasn't in Sicily. And Godfrey had already proved himself immune to Sicilian threats, and much worse.

'I see them,' Francesco confirmed, keeping his tone steady, bored, even. 'They're old acquaintances of mine.'

'Yes…they said you had…history.'

That was one way of describing it. Smiling tightly, he bowed his head. 'I should go and say hello.'

Now wishing he hadn't brought Hannah out with him, Francesco bore her off towards the Mastrangelo brothers.

'Who are we going to say hello to?' she asked, surprising him by slipping her fingers through his.

Apart from when they were lying in bed together, she never held his hand. Not that they'd ever actually been out anywhere to hold hands, all their time together over the past fortnight having been spent eating takeaway food and making love.

'Old acquaintances of mine,' he said tightly, although the feel of her gentle fingers laced through his had a strangely calming reaction.

By the time they stood before the Mastrangelo brothers, his stomach felt a fraction more settled.

'Luca. Pepe.' He extended his hand. 'So the rumours are true,' he said, switching to Sicilian.

'What rumours would they be?' asked Luca, shaking his hand with a too-firm grip. Francesco squeezed a little tighter in turn before dropping the hold.

'I'd heard you were interested in this place.'

Luca shrugged.

'I thought you'd got out of the casino game.'

'Times change.'

'Clearly.' Francesco forced a smile. 'Does your little wife know you're going back into forbidden territory?'

Luca bared his teeth. 'You leave Grace out of this.'

'I wouldn't dream of bringing her into it, knowing how much she hates me.' Here, he looked at Pepe. 'I do believe your sister-in-law hates me more than you do.' Not giving either of them the chance to respond, he flashed his own teeth. 'I suggest the pair of you rethink your decision to try to buy this place. The documents for my ownership are on the verge of completion.'

Pepe finally spoke. 'But they're not completed yet, are they?'

'They will be soon. And if either of you try anything to stop the sale going through, you will live to regret it.'

'Are you threatening us?'

'You sound surprised, Luca,' he said, deliberately keeping his tone amicable. 'You should know I am not a man to deal with threats. Only promises.'

Luca pulled himself to his full height. 'I will not be threatened, Calvetti. Remember that.'

Only the gentle squeeze of Hannah's fingers lacing back through his stopped Francesco squaring up to his old friend.

He shook himself. He didn't want to be having this conversation in front of her, regardless of the fact that they were speaking in their native tongue and not in English.

'Don't start a war you'll never win, Mastrangelo.'

'I remember your father saying exactly the same thing to me when my father died. Your father thought he could take control of the Mastrangelo estate.' Luca smiled. 'He didn't succeed in getting his way. And nor will you.'

Baring his teeth one last time, Francesco said, 'But I am not my father. I have infinitely more patience.'

'Are you okay?' Hannah asked as soon as they were out of earshot.

'I'm fine. Let's get out of here.'

'But we've only just arrived.'

Expelling air slowly through his nose, he stopped himself from insisting they leave right now. He could insist and she would have no choice but to follow, but to do so would upset her, and that was the last thing he wanted to do.

Strangely enough, Hannah's presence tempered the

angry adrenaline flowing through him—not by much, but enough to take the edge off it.

Having promised to teach her how to play Blackjack, he found seats at a table for them to join in. Unlike at the tournament in Sicily, where her remarkable poker face was her biggest asset, there was no bluffing needed when playing against the dealer. She still picked it up like a pro. At one point he thought she would finish with more chips than him.

Watching her have fun eased a little more of his rage, enough so that there were moments he forgot the Mastrangelos were there, trying to muscle in on his territory. It pleased him enormously to watch her drink a full glass of champagne. She really was learning to switch off.

His driver was ready for them when they left. As soon as they were seated in the back, the partition separating them from the driver, Hannah squished right next to him and reached for his hand. Pulling it onto her lap, she rubbed her thumb in light circular motions over his inner wrist.

The breath of air he inhaled went into his lungs that bit easier.

'How do you know those two men?' she asked after a few moments of silence.

He could only respect her reticence in waiting until they were alone before starting her cross-examination. 'Luca and Pepe?'

'Is that their names?' she said drily. 'You forgot to introduce us.'

He sighed. 'I apologise. They're old friends. Were old friends. At least, Luca was.'

'Was?'

'Their father used to work for my father. And then he quit.'

He felt her blanch.

'Don't worry. My father didn't touch him—they'd been

childhood friends themselves, which saved Pietro from my father's vengeance. But the fact my father didn't put a bullet through him didn't mean the perceived slur could be forgotten. Once their professional relationship finished, family loyalty meant any friendship between Luca and I was finished, too. It's all about respect.' In his father's eyes, everything had been about respect. Everything.

How he'd envied the easy affection the two Mastrangelo boys shared with their father. It was the kind of relationship he'd longed for, but for Salvatore Calvetti a sign of affection for his only child consisted of a slap on the back if he pleased him.

'Have you not seen Luca since then?'

'He came to my father's funeral.' He looked away, not wanting her to see the expression on his face reflecting what he felt beneath his skin whenever he thought of his father's funeral. While a tiny part of him had felt relief that he could break free from Salvatore's shadow, he'd mourned the man. Truly mourned him.

If he'd known then what he knew now, he would have lit fireworks by his open graveside in celebration.

'My father's death freed me. It freed Luca and me to resume our old friendship. When we were kids we often used to play cards together, and always said that when we grew up we would open a casino together. We opened our first one three years ago, but then last year he decided he wanted out.'

'Why was that?'

He met her eyes. 'His wife thought I was bad for him.'

Her forehead furrowed. 'He said that?'

'Not in so many words. But it was obvious. She hates my guts.'

Still her forehead furrowed. 'But why?'

'Because I'm a big bad gangster.'

'No, your father was a big bad gangster,' she corrected.

'Even after everything you've witnessed, you still refuse to see it.' He planted a kiss on the end of her nose.

'No, I *do* see it. You are who you are, but you're nowhere near as bad as you like people to think.'

She wouldn't say that if she could read the thoughts going through his mind. Thoughts of revenge, not just against his father but against Luca Mastrangelo. And Pepe.

He would not allow the Mayfair casino to fall into Mastrangelo hands. It was *his* and he would do whatever was needed to ensure it.

'Do I take it that those men are also interested in buying the casino?' Hannah asked, swinging her legs onto his lap.

'I'd heard rumours they were after it. Being there tonight confirmed it.'

'And do I take it you threatened them?' At his surprised glance, she grinned ruefully. 'I might not speak Sicilian, but I can read body language.'

'And you think I have *good* in me?' Rubbing his hand absently over her calf, he couldn't help but notice the little bags that had formed under her eyes. Those little bags made his heart constrict.

This was a woman who worked so hard for such a good purpose she hardly slept. And *she* saw good in *him*?

'You won't hurt them,' she said with simple confidence.

He didn't answer. The one thing he would never do was lie to her. He'd lived a lifetime of lies.

Before she could question his silence, her phone vibrated. Dropping his hand, she reached into her bag.

'Is it work?' he asked, trying hard to keep the edge from his voice. The only time Hannah lost her sweet humour was when he mentioned her excessive use of her phone. On those occasions her claws came out.

She shook her head absently. 'Melanie.'

'She's back from her work trip?'

'Yep. She wants to know if I'm free tomorrow for the last fitting. For my bridesmaid dress,' she added heavily.

'Are you not going to answer?' When it came to work she would fire off a reply the second she read them.

'I suppose I should.'

Before he could question her reluctance, they pulled up outside his hotel.

'Shall we have a bath together?' he asked once they were safely ensconced in his suite.

Hannah's nose wrinkled. She felt all...out of sorts. Right then she needed something sweet to counteract the acidity that had formed in her throat. 'Can we have chocolate-fudge cake first?'

'Hot?'

She smiled. Already he knew her so well. Especially with regard to her hot chocolate-fudge cake addiction, which was fast becoming usurped by her Francesco addiction.

Was this how drug addicts started out? she wondered. A little fix here, a little fix there, then swearing never to do it again? But then temptation was placed right under their nose and they were too weak to resist? Because that was how she felt with him. Unable to resist.

Why did she even need to keep resisting? Addictions were bad things. How could Francesco possibly be classed as bad for her? Her work hadn't suffered for being with him.

The only reason to resist now was for the sake of her heart, and she'd already lost that battle. In reality, she hadn't stood a chance.

She looked at him, her big bear of a man.

What would he say if he knew that, despite all her protestations over not wanting a relationship, she'd fallen for him?

She'd watched him square up to those two men in the

casino and she'd wanted to dive between them and kung fu them into keeping away from him.

The strength of her protectiveness towards him had shocked her.

It was how she used to be with Beth. If you messed with one twin you messed with the other.

And like it had been with Beth, when she was with Francesco she felt safe. She felt complete. It was a different completeness but every bit as powerful.

'Will you come to Melanie's wedding with me?' She blurted out the words before she'd even properly thought of them.

Her heart lurched to see the palpable shock on his face.

'Sorry. Forget I said anything,' she said quickly. 'It's a silly…'

'You took me by surprise, that's all,' he cut in with a shake of his head. 'You want me to come to your sister's wedding?'

'Only if you're not too busy. I just…' She bit her lip. 'I just could do with…'

Francesco didn't know what she was trying to tell him, but the darting of her eyes and the way she wrung her hands together pierced something in him.

'Will there be room for me?' he asked, stalling for time while he tried to think.

A sound like a laugh spluttered from her lips. 'If I tell them I'm bringing a date they'll make room, even if it means sitting one of the grandparents on someone else's lap.'

'Okay,' he agreed, injecting more positivity than he felt inside. 'I'll come with you.'

The gratitude in her eyes pierced him even deeper.

It wasn't until midmorning they got into the enormous bath together. After a night of making love and snatches of tortured sleep, Hannah was happy to simply lie between Francesco's legs, her head resting against his chest, and enjoy the bubbly water.

Her phone, which she'd placed on the shelf above the sink, vibrated.

'Leave it,' he commanded, tightening his hold around her waist.

'It might be important.'

'It will still be there in ten minutes.'

'But…'

'Hannah, this can't continue. You're using your phone as an emotional crutch and it's not good for you.' There was a definite sharpness to his tone.

Since they'd started seeing each other properly, she'd been acutely aware of his loathing for her phone. Not her work, or the research papers or her studying; just her phone.

'I think it's a bit much you calling it an emotional crutch,' she said tightly. 'If one of my patients dies when I'm not on shift, then I want to know—I don't want to get to work and come face-to-face with bereaved parents in the car park or atrium or café or wherever and not know that they've just lost the most precious thing in their lives.'

The edge to his voice vanished. 'Is that what happened to you when Beth died?'

She jerked a nod. 'When Beth was first admitted, the doctor was very clinical in his approach, almost cold.' She fixed her gaze on Francesco's beautiful arms, adoring the way the water darkened the hair and flattened it over the olive skin. 'Beth died in the early hours of the morning, long after that first doctor had finished his shift. Luckily, she was in the care of some of the loveliest, most compassionate doctors and nurses you could wish for. They let us stay with her body for hours, right until the sun came up. I remember we had to go back to the children's ward as we'd left Beth's possessions there when she'd been taken off to Intensive Care. We got into the lift and that first doctor got in with us.'

She paused, swallowing away the acrid bile that formed in her throat.

'He looked right through us. Either he didn't recognise us as the family of the young girl he'd been treating twenty-four hours before, or he did recognise us and just didn't want to acknowledge us. Either way, I hated him for it. My sister was dead and that man didn't even care enough to remember our faces.'

'Do you still hate him?'

She shook her head. 'I understand it now. There are only so many times you can watch a child die before you grow a hard shell. We all do it. The difference is, he let his shell consume him at the expense of the patient. I will *never* allow myself to become like that. I never want any of my patients or their loved ones to think I don't care.'

'That must take its toll on you, though,' he observed. Francesco had only watched one person die: his mother. He'd made it to the hospital in time to say goodbye, but by that point the essence of *her* had already gone, her body kept alive by machines.

It had been the single most distressing event of his life.

To choose a profession where you were surrounded by illness and death... He could hardly begin to comprehend the dedication and selflessness needed to do such a job.

She shrugged, but her grip on his arms tightened. 'We send hundreds more children home healed than we lose. That more than makes up for it.'

He found himself at a loss for what to say.

Hannah had suffered the loss of the most precious person in her life—her twin—and she'd turned her grief into a force for good.

Hadn't he known from the start that she was too good for him? He still knew it, more than ever.

'Beth's death broke something inside me,' she said quietly. 'My parents tried very hard to comfort me, but they were grieving, too, and in any case I pushed them away. Melanie was desperate to comfort me, but I pushed her away, too. Since my accident I can see how badly I've treated my family. I've kept myself apart from them. I've kept myself apart from everyone...until you.'

His chest tightened. 'Your family was happy for you to isolate yourself?'

'No.' Her damp hair tickled his nose. 'They weren't happy. But what could they do about it? They couldn't *make* me.' Her voice became wistful. 'I think I wanted them to force the issue. I was so lost but I couldn't find the way out....'

There was so much Francesco wanted to say as her words trailed away. None of it would help.

'You're probably right about my phone,' she muttered. 'I guess I have been using it as a crutch. It's easier for me to interact with an object than a human. At least that was the case until I met you.'

She turned her head, resting her cheek on his shoulder as she stared at him. 'I'm so glad you're coming to the wedding with me.'

The very mention of the *W* word was enough to make his stomach roil.

'I've been dreading it for so long now,' she confessed.

'Is Beth the reason you're so anxious about it?' He dragged his question out. 'Because she can't be there?'

Her nails dug into his arms. 'This is the first real family event we've had since she died.' She placed a kiss to his neck and inhaled. 'With you by my side, I think I can endure it without ruining Melanie's day. The last thing I want is to spoil things for her, but I don't think even my poker face will be able to hide my feelings.' She swallowed. 'It's all feeling so raw again.'

Francesco cleared the sourness forming in his throat.

He hadn't bargained on this. None of it was part of his plan, whereby he would see her whilst spending lots of time in London finalising the Mayfair deal, after which they would head their separate ways.

None of this was in the script.

He hadn't for a minute imagined she would start needing him, not his self-sufficient doctor who didn't rely on anyone but herself.

Something gripped at his chest, a kind of panic.

If it wasn't for the tears spilling down her cheeks and the confidences she'd just entrusted him with, he would have dreamed up a good excuse not to go there and then.

But Hannah crying? In his mind there was no worse sight or sound. He would promise her anything to stop it.

Francesco slammed his phone down in fury.

The purchase agreement he'd spent months working on had been blown out of the water, with Godfrey Renfrew admitting he wanted time to 'consider an alternative offer'.

The Mastrangelos were standing in his way.

He picked the receiver up and dialled his lawyer's number. 'I want you to arrange a meeting between me and Luca Mastrangelo,' he said, his words delivered like ice picks. 'Tell him that unless he agrees to meet tomorrow, he will only have himself to blame for the consequences.'

The second he put the phone down, his mobile rang. It was Hannah. *'Ciao,'* he said, breathing heavily through his teeth.

'What's the matter?' she asked, picking up on his tone even though she was in London and he in Palermo.

'Nothing. I'm just busy. What can I do for you?' Looking at the clock on his wall, he could see it was lunchtime. She must be calling him on her break.

'I haven't heard from you in a couple of days. I just wanted to make sure you're okay.' There wasn't any accusation in her voice. All he heard was concern.

'I'm busy, that's all.'

Silence, then, 'Any idea what time you'll be over tomorrow?'

He rubbed his eyes. He'd promised he'd be back in London early Friday evening so they could head straight down to Devon. She'd even booked him a hotel room.

'I'll confirm tomorrow morning,' he said, wishing he could relieve the sharp pain digging in the back of his eyes. He would ensure his meeting with Luca and Pepe took place in the morning. That would give him plenty of time to get to her.

More silence. 'Are you sure you're okay?'

'Go back to your patients, Dr Chapman. I'll see you tomorrow.'

Hannah checked her watch for the umpteenth time. Her bags were all packed, butterflies playing merry havoc in her belly.

She felt sick with nerves and dread. Knowing Francesco would be by her side throughout it all dulled it a little but not as much as it should.

He'd sounded so distant on the phone. The plentiful text messages from him had whittled away to nothing.

Something niggled in her stomach, a foreboding she was too scared to analyse.

Twitching her curtain, relief poured through her to see the large black car pull up outside.

Her relief was short-lived when she opened the door

and saw the serious look on his face. 'You're not coming with me, are you?'

He stepped over the threshold and pushed the door shut behind him. 'I apologise for the short notice, but I have to meet with Luca and Pepe Mastrangelo tomorrow lunchtime. The sale of the Mayfair casino is under threat.'

For long moments she did nothing but stare at him. 'You bastard.'

He flinched, but a cold hostility set over his features. 'I do not have the power to be in two places at once. If I could then I would.'

'Liar,' she stated flatly, although her chest had tightened so much she struggled to find breath.

This could not be happening.

'You could have arranged the meeting for any time you like. Your life doesn't revolve around a set schedule.' Francesco's time was his to do as he pleased. One of the very things she'd been so attracted to had turned around and bitten her hard.

Francesco could do as he liked, and what he liked was to avoid her sister's wedding.

He was asking her to face it alone.

After everything she had confided and all the trust she'd placed in him, he was leaving her to face the wedding on her own.

'It has to be tomorrow.' He raked his hands through his hair. 'I wanted to organise it for today but tomorrow is the only day the three of us can be in the same country at the same time. Time is of the essence. I won't allow the Mastrangelos to steal the casino away from me. I've worked too long on the deal to let it slip through my fingers—it's far too important for me to lose. I've arranged for Mario to drive you to Devon.'

'Don't bother. I'll make my own way there.' She'd

rather cycle on her pushbike. She'd rather walk. 'You can leave now.'

'Hannah, I know you're disappointed. I've gone out of my way to tell you personally—'

'Well, that makes everything all right, then,' she snapped. 'You're blowing me out of the water so you can kneecap some old friends but, hey, no worries, *you told me to my face.*'

'I have spent the best part of a year demolishing my father's empire, eradicating the streets from the evils he peddled,' Francesco said, his voice rising, his cool facade disappearing before her eyes. 'The only business he wanted that he couldn't have was this casino. He did everything in his power to get it, including abducting Godfrey's son, and still he didn't win. But *I will.* It's taken me *months* to gain Godfrey's trust and I will not allow the Mastrangelos to snatch it away from me.'

His father? Hannah had known his relationship with his dead father had been difficult, had seen the way he tensed whenever Salvatore was mentioned, but she'd never suspected the depths of Francesco's animosity towards him.

He paused, his eyes a dark pit of loathing, his malevolence a living, breathing thing. 'You live your life imagining Beth watching over you. Well, I imagine mine with my father watching over me. I like the thought of him staring down watching me destroy everything he built, but more than anything I want him to see me succeed where he failed. I want him turning in his hellish coffin.'

Hannah didn't think she had ever witnessed such hatred before, a loathing that crawled under her skin and settled in the nauseous pit of her belly.

This was the Francesco he had warned her about right at the start. The Francesco she had refused to see.

And now she did see, all she felt was a burning anger that made her want to throw up.

'Go and take your vengeance. Go ruin your old friends. Go and show your dead father how much *better* you are than him by purchasing the very casino he could never have. Let it symbolise how *different* you are to him.'

Shoving him out of the way, she opened the front door. 'Now leave, and don't you *ever* contact me again.'

His chest heaving, he stared at her before his nostrils flared and he strode past her.

'Enjoy your vengeance, Francesco,' she spat. 'Try not to let it choke you.'

He didn't look back.

CHAPTER TWELVE

HANNAH FIXED THE back of her pearl earrings into place, trying desperately hard to contain her shaking hands. Since that awful confrontation with Francesco the night before, it had been a constant battle to stop the tremors racking through her. The long last-minute train journey to Devon had been a constant battle, too—a battle to stop any tears forming for the bastard who'd abandoned her when she needed him most.

She didn't want to think about him. Not now. Not when she was minutes away from leaving for the church to watch her little sister get married.

There was a tap on the door, and Melanie walked into the room carrying a small box.

'How do I look?' she asked, putting the box on the floor, extending her arms and giving a slow twirl.

'Oh, Mel, you look beautiful.' And she did, an angel in white.

'You look beautiful, too.' Careful not to crease each other's dresses—Hannah wore a baby-pink bridesmaid dress—they embraced, then stepped back from each other.

'The cars are here and our bouquets are ready,' Melanie said. Her eyes fixed on Hannah's bedside table, on which rested a photo of Hannah and Beth, aged eight. 'I've got a bouquet for her, too.'

'What do you mean?'

'Beth. I've got her a bouquet, too.'

Hannah had to strain to hear her sister's voice.

'If she was still here she'd be a bridesmaid with you.' A look of mischief suddenly crossed Melanie's face. 'The pair of you would probably follow me down the aisle trying to trip me up.'

A burst of mirth spluttered from Hannah's mouth. She and Beth together had been irrepressible. 'We were really mean to you.'

'No, you weren't.'

'Yes, we were. We hardly ever let you play with us and when we did it was to torment you. I remember we convinced you to let us make you into a princess.'

'Oh, yes! You coloured my hair pink with your felt tip pens and used red crayon as blusher. You treated me like a doll.'

'I'm sorry.'

'Don't be. I was just happy you wanted to play with me.'

'It must have been hard for you, though,' Hannah said, thinking of all the times Melanie had been desperate to join in with their games, how their mum would force them to let her tag along and they would spend the whole time ignoring her. Unless they found a good use for her.

Melanie didn't even pretend not to understand. 'It was hard. I was very jealous. You had each other. You didn't need me.'

Silence rent the room as they both stared at the photo. Despite all her vows, hot tears stung the back of Hannah's eyes. How desperately she wished Beth was there. And how desperately the pathetic side of her wished Francesco was there, too....

Thank God Melanie hadn't grilled her about the latest sudden change to the seating plan, simply giving her a quick hug and a 'No problem.'

Melanie cleared her throat. 'We should get going before we ruin our make-up.'

Looking at her, Hannah could see Melanie's eyes had filled, too, a solitary tear trickling down her cheek.

She reached over to wipe it away with her thumb, then pressed a kiss to her sister's cheek. 'You do look beautiful, Mel. Beth would be insanely jealous.'

Melanie laughed and snatched a tissue from the box on Hannah's bedside table. She blew her nose noisily, then crouched down to the box she'd brought in and removed the lid. 'Here's your bouquet, and here's the one for Beth. I thought you might like to give it to her.'

Hannah sniffed the delicate fragrance.

She looked at her sister. Melanie had been nine when Beth died. A little girl. Now she was a woman less than an hour away from marriage.

How had she missed her own sister growing up? It had happened right before her eyes and she'd been oblivious to it. Melanie had followed Hannah to London. She had been the one to keep the sisterly relationship going—she'd been the one who'd kept the whole family going. Unlike their parents, who still took Hannah's reclusiveness at face value, Melanie at least tried. It was always at her suggestion that they would go out for lunch. It was always Melanie who organised their monthly visits back to Devon, carefully selecting the weekends Hannah wasn't on shift. Melanie, who had never wanted anything more than the company of her big sister.

Her sister. The same flesh and blood as herself and Beth.

Hannah took another sniff of the flowers. 'Do you want to come with me and give them to her?'

'Really?' Melanie was too sweet to even pretend to fake nonchalance.

When it came to visiting Beth, Hannah preferred solitude. Alone, she could chat to her and fill her in on all the family and work gossip.

Since the funeral she had never visited with anyone else.

She had done far too many things alone.

All those wasted years hiding herself away, too numb from the pain of her broken heart to even consider letting anyone in—not her parents, not her sister. No one. And she hadn't even realised she was doing it, pretending to be content in her little cocoon.

She hadn't meant to let Francesco in. If she'd known the risk to her heart, she would have taken his advice at the first turn and found a safer method to start living her life.

But she had let him in. In return he'd dumped her in the cruellest of fashions.

She didn't care about his reasons. He'd left her to face this day alone and she would never forgive him.

Except she wasn't alone....

Her heart had opened for him, but it had also opened for her poor neglected family, who wanted nothing more than to love her. All those years spent hiding her heart from them had been wasted years, she could see that now.

She didn't want to hide any more. She couldn't. She needed them. She *loved* them.

Ironically, Francesco's rejection had helped in an unexpected fashion. She would *not* allow Melanie's big day to be ruined by *him*.

Fixing her old practised smile to her face, she took Melanie's hand in her own and gave it a squeeze. 'Why don't we leave now? We can do it before the ceremony starts.'

Melanie's eyes shone. 'I would really like that.'

'Beth would, too. And so would I.'

* * *

Francesco checked his watch. It was bang on half past one.

In thirty minutes Melanie Chapman would walk down the aisle, followed by her doctor sister.

He swatted the thought away.

Now was not the time to be wondering how Hannah was holding up.

Now was the time for action.

With Mario and Roberto by his side, he strolled through the lobby of the neutral hotel both parties had agreed upon and headed up in the lift to the private suite hired for the occasion.

Two men, equally as large as his own minders, guarded the door.

'Wait here,' he said to his men.

This conversation was private.

Sweeping past them, he stepped into the room and shut the door.

He could taste the malice in the air in his first inhalation.

Luca sat at the long dining table, his black eyes fixing on him.

Pepe leant against a wall, his arms folded.

Hannah would be on her way to the church...

Where had that thought come from?

He'd successfully pushed Hannah out of his mind since he'd left her home. He'd cut her out. He would *not* allow himself to think of her. Or the pain on her face. Or the words she'd said, her implication that he was exactly like his father.

He was not like his father.

If he was anything like his father, Luca and Pepe would both be long dead by now—Pepe when he'd tried to fight him all those years ago, Luca when he'd broken their partnership. He hadn't just broken their partnership, he'd severed their friendship, too.

'Well?' said Luca, breaking the silence. 'You're the one who wanted this meeting. What do you want, Calvetti?'

He'd thought he'd known. The casino. The final piece in the obliteration of Salvatore Calvetti's legacy.

His revenge against the man Francesco had learned too late had used his mother as a punchbag.

As hard as he tried to push her out, the only image in his head was Hannah, lying on the cold concrete and opening her eyes, that serene smile that had stolen his breath.

Stolen his heart.

'Well?' Luca's voice rose. 'What do you want?'

Francesco looked at the two brothers. His old friends. He looked at Pepe, the man whose girlfriend he'd stolen all those years ago. He hadn't known she was still seeing him, but he'd known damn well Pepe had been serious about her.

No wonder Pepe hated him.

He looked back at Luca. His oldest friend. A man who'd found that rare kind of love he would do anything to keep.

The rare kind of love he could have with Hannah.

Could have had if he hadn't abandoned her on the one day she needed him.

He'd known the second she'd asked him to go to the wedding with her that she'd fallen for him.

And he, stupid fool that he was, had thrown it back in her face so cruelly, and for what?

Vengeance against a man who was already rotting in hell.

His heart beat so loudly a drum could have been in his ear.

Hannah wasn't his mother. She wasn't a young, suggestible girl. She was a professional woman with more backbone than anyone he knew.

More important, he wasn't his father, something she'd known from the off.

Only two people in his entire life had looked at him and seen *him*, Francesco, and not just Salvatore's son. One of those had given birth to him. The other was at that very moment bleeding with pain for her dead twin who couldn't be there to celebrate their sister's marriage.

What had he done?

He took a step back and raised his hands. 'It's yours.' At their identical furrowed brows, he allowed the tiniest of smiles to form on his lips. 'The casino. If you want it so badly, you can have it.'

They exchanged glances, their bodies straightening.

'I'm serious. It's all yours. I'll call Godfrey and withdraw my offer.' When he reached the door he looked straight at Pepe. 'I was very sorry to hear about the loss of your baby.'

Pepe's eyes flickered.

Turning back to Luca, Francesco continued, 'Send my regards to Grace. She's far too good for you, but I think you already know that.'

He turned the handle of the door.

'Calvetti.' It was Luca's voice.

Francesco turned one last time.

'The casino's yours. Not ours.'

'Sorry?'

A rueful grin spread over Luca's face. 'Grace and Cara were already furious at us for looking at buying a casino, and they're just about ready to kill us for instigating a war with you. We've already told Godfrey to accept your offer.'

In spite of the agonies going on within him, Francesco managed a grin. 'See? I said Grace was too good for you.'

Just as Hannah was too good for him.

He looked at his watch again. At any moment the bridal party would start their slow walk down the aisle.

'I need to be somewhere.'

Hannah followed Melanie up the aisle, trying very hard to keep a straight face, a hard job considering the train of Melanie's dress was streaked with grass and mud.

Beth was buried in the cemetery attached to this very church, and the pair had left the rest of the bridal party to say a few words to her and leave the bouquet by her headstone.

All those years when she'd refused to visit Beth's grave with anyone... How selfish she'd been.

How glad she was that Melanie had found a man who put her first, who loved her enough to compensate for all the neglect she had suffered at the hands of her big sister. Not that Melanie saw it as neglect. Bless her heart, Melanie understood. It hadn't been said, not in so many words, but it didn't need to be.

In all the years Hannah had been grieving the loss of her twin, she had neglected to recognise there was another person in her life grieving, too—a young woman who was a part of her, just as Beth was. Sure, it wasn't exactly the same—how could it be? But then, what two relationships were ever the same? Their parents loved them equally but the relationships between them all were different. Hannah's relationship with them couldn't be any more different.

She looked at her father, walking with Melanie's arm tucked inside his. She might not be able to see his face but she could perfectly imagine the radiant smile on his face. And there was her mother, on her feet in a front pew, still a beautiful woman, looking from her beloved husband to her two surviving daughters, tears already leaking down her cheeks.

And there was the groom, his legs bouncing, his nerves

and excitement palpable. When he knelt before the priest by the side of his fiancée, titters echoed throughout the church at the *HE* written in white on the sole of his left shoe, and the *LP* on the right.

So much love. So much excitement for a new life being forged together.

As they exchanged their vows, the tears she'd successfully kept at bay since that terrible argument with Francesco broke free.

According to Francesco's satnav, the route from London to Devon should take three hours and forty-five minutes by car. By motorbike, he estimated he could make it in two hours.

What he hadn't accounted for was stationary traffic as hordes of holidaymakers took advantage of the late English summer to head to the coast.

This was a country of imbeciles, he thought scathingly as he snaked his way around motionless cars. Why couldn't they all be sensible like Hannah and travel down on the Friday night when the roads were empty?

The ceremony would be over by now, the wedding breakfast in full swing.

Hannah needed air. Her lungs felt too tight.

She'd tried. She really had. She'd smiled throughout the ceremony and wedding breakfast, held pleasant conversations with countless family members and old friends she hadn't seen in years. The number-one question she'd received was a variant of 'Have you met a nice man yet?' While she'd answered gracefully, 'Not yet, but I'm sure I will one day,' each time she was asked it felt as if a thorn were being pressed deep into her heart.

Now all the guests had congregated at the bar while the

function room was transformed for the evening bash, she saw her opportunity for escape.

She stepped out into the early-evening dusk and sat on a bench in the hotel garden. She closed her eyes, welcoming the slight breeze on her face.

Five minutes. That was all she needed. Five minutes of solitude to clamp back down on her emotions.

'Can I join you?'

Opening her eyes, she found her mother standing before her.

Unable to speak, she nodded.

'It's been a beautiful day,' her mum commented.

Hannah nodded again, scared to open her mouth lest she would no longer be able to hold on.

How could Francesco have left her alone like this?

How could she have got him so wrong?

She'd been so convinced he would never hurt her.

She'd been right about the physical aspect. In that respect he'd given her nothing but pleasure. Emotionally, though… he'd ripped her apart.

For the first time in fifteen years she'd reached out to someone for help. He'd known what a massive thing that was for her and still he'd abandoned her, and for what? For revenge on someone who wasn't even alive to see it.

Had she been too needy? Was that it? How could she know? She had nothing to compare it to. Until she'd barged her way into his life, she'd had no form of a relationship with anyone. Not even her family. Not since Beth…

'Why did you let me hide away after Beth died?' she asked suddenly. Francesco's probing questions about her relationship with her parents had been playing on her mind, making her question so many things she'd never considered before.

She felt her mother start beside her.

A long silence formed until her mum took Hannah's hand into her own tentatively, as if waiting for Hannah to snatch it away. 'That's a question your father and I often ask. When Beth died, we knew, no matter the pain we were going through and Mel was going through, that it was nothing compared to what you were living with. You and Beth… you were two peas in a pod. She was you and you were her.'

Hannah's chin wobbled.

'When you said you wanted to be a doctor, we were happy you had something to focus on. When you first hid yourself away, saying you were studying, we thought it was a good thing.' She rummaged in her handbag for a tissue and dabbed her eyes. 'We should have handled it better. We were all grieving, but we should never have allowed you to cut yourself off. At the time, though, we couldn't see it. It was so gradual that by the time we realised how isolated you'd become, we didn't know how to reach out to you anymore. To be honest, I still don't. I wish I could turn the clock back to your teenage years and insist you be a part of the family and not some lodger who shared the occasional meal with us.'

'I wish I could, too,' Hannah whispered. She gazed up at the emerging stars, then turned to look at her mother. 'Mum, can I have a hug?'

Her mum closed her eyes as if in prayer before pulling Hannah into her embrace, enveloping her tightly in that remembered mummy smell that comforted her more than any word could.

Hannah swallowed the last of her champagne. The bubbles playing on her tongue reminded her of Francesco. The optics behind the bar reminded her of Francesco. The man who'd just stepped into the function room, where the dancing was now in full swing, also reminded her of Francesco.

Unable to bear the reminder, she turned her attention back to the party surrounding her. The women from Melanie's hen party had hit the dance floor, dragging her dad up there with them. She couldn't stop the grin forming on her face as she watched his special brand of dad dancing. At least she knew where she got her rhythm from.

Why wasn't she up there with them?

Why was she hiding by the bar, observing rather than joining in?

She'd made it through the day with what was left of her shattered heart aching, but she'd *made* it. She'd come through the other side and she was still standing. She hadn't fallen apart at the seams.

A record that had been hugely popular when she was a kid came on. Her grin widening, Hannah weaved through the tables to the dance floor and grabbed her father's hands. His answering smile was puzzled, shocked, even, but delighted all the same.

Their special brand of nonrhythmic dancing took off, a crowd quickly forming around them, the bride and groom hitting the floor, too.

She could do this. She could be a part of life. She didn't have to sit alone on the sidelines.

One of her sister's hen party tapped Hannah on the shoulder. 'Isn't that the man from Calvetti's?' she yelled above the music, pointing across the room.

Following the pointing finger, Hannah's heart jolted to see the tall figure she'd spotted leaning against the wall watching the dancing. Watching *her*.

She gave an absent nod in response, tuning out everything around her—everything except him.

Francesco.

Her stomach lurched heavily, feeling as if it had become detached from the rest of her.

He began to move, snaking his way round the packed tables, revellers parting on his approach in a manner that evoked the strongest sense of déjà vu.

Her heart flipped over to see him so groomed and utterly gorgeous in a snazzy pinstriped suit, the top buttons of his crisp blue shirt undone, exposing the top of his broad chest and the cross he wore around his neck....

Up close he looked in control and terrifying, the intent in his eyes showing he could eat her alive if she refused him anything.

Francesco crossed the dividing line onto the dance floor.

After the road trip from hell, he'd finally made it to her.

Nothing had come easy that day, the puncture on his tyre the last straw. By the time the helicopter had illegally landed to collect him, he'd been ready to rip someone's head off.

At last he stood before her. She'd frozen on the spot, her eyes big hazel pools of pain and bewilderment.

What had he done to her?

He had no idea what was being played by the DJ and nor did he care. When he placed his hands on Hannah's hips and pulled her to him, the sound tuned out and he moved her in a rhythm all their own.

She looked so vulnerable in her traditional bridesmaid dress. She trembled in it, rigid in his arms yet quivering.

He could feel eyes from all directions fixed on them.

'What are you doing here?' she asked, not looking at him.

'I want us to talk.'

'I don't want to be anywhere near you.'

'I know.' He breathed her scent in. 'But *I* need to be near *you*.'

She moved to escape his arms but he tightened his hold, continuing to move her around the floor. 'I'm not letting you go anywhere, not until you've given me the chance to speak.'

'I'm not speaking to you here,' she hissed into his ear, her warm breath sending completely inappropriate tingles racing over his skin. 'This is my sister's wedding. These guests here are my family and my sister's friends.'

'And I should have been with you today, getting to know them, instead of leaving you to face it on your own, but I'm the bastard who let his thirst for revenge cause pain to the one person in the world he loves.'

He stopped dancing and looked at her. The pain in her eyes had gone, only stark bewilderment remaining.

'*You,*' he emphasised. 'I love *you.* I should have trusted fate when it brought you to me.'

'I don't want to hear it.' Her voice was hoarse, her cheeks flushed.

Her resistance was nothing less than he deserved. He released his tight hold and stepped back, keeping his hands on her arms so she couldn't run.

'Remember when I gave you five minutes of *my* time?' he said, reminding her of that time a month ago when she'd first begged for five minutes. If he'd known then what those five minutes would lead to, he would have locked himself away in his office without a second thought. What an arrogant fool he had been. 'Now I am asking for five minutes of *your* time.'

Had it really only been a month ago that she'd propositioned him?

How could his entire world transform in such a small timeframe?

'Believe me, if I could have that time again I would do everything differently,' she said, wriggling out of his hold. 'Let's go sit in the garden. But only because I don't want to have a scene in front of my family.'

* * *

The breeze had picked up since Hannah had sat in the garden with her mother. Now the evening party was in full swing, the peace she'd found then had gone, music and laughter echoing through the windows.

She sat on the same bench. A bunch of kids had escaped the party and were having a game of football with an empty can.

Francesco sat next to her, keeping a respectable distance. All the same, she could feel his heat. How she wished she didn't respond to him so physically. Her emotional reactions to him were bad enough without her treacherous body getting in on the act, too.

'Go on, then, what did you want to talk about?' she said, making a silent vow to not say another word for the duration of the next five minutes. If he started spouting any more nonsense about loving her she would walk away.

If he loved her he would never have let her face this day on her own.

'I want to tell you about my father,' Francesco said, surprising her with his opening thread.

Despite her vow to remain mute, she whispered, 'Your father?'

He breathed heavily. 'I always knew what a bastard he was, but he was my father and I respected him. God help me but I loved him. All I ever wanted was his respect. I turned a blind eye to so many of his activities but turned the blindest eye to what was happening right under my own roof.'

His eyes held hers, the chocolate fudge hard, almost black.

'I always knew my father was a violent man. To me that was normal. It was our way of life. I knew he craved respect. Again, that was normal. What I did not know until after his death four years ago was that he was one of mainland Europe's biggest suppliers of drugs. That was a blow, enough to make me despise him, but not enough to destroy all my memories of the man. But what I learned just a year ago when I discovered my mother's diaries was that he beat her throughout their marriage, cheated on her, and fed her the drugs that eventually killed her.'

When he reached for her hand she didn't pull away, not even when he clasped it so tightly she feared for her blood supply.

'She was seventeen when they married, an innocent. He was twenty-three years older and a brute from the start.' He practically spat the words out. 'He forced himself on her on their wedding night. He beat her for the first time on their honeymoon. I wish I'd known, but my mother did everything in her power to protect me from seeing too much. As a child it was normal for my mother to be bruised. We would laugh at how clumsy she was, but it was all a lie.'

He shook his head and dragged his fingers through his hair. 'I spent three days reading her diaries. When I finished I was filled with so much hate for the man. And *guilt*—how could I have been so blind? The man I hero-worshipped was nothing but a drug-peddling wife beater. He *wanted* her hooked—it was a means to control her. I swear if he hadn't been dead I would have killed him myself using my bare hands.'

Hannah shivered. Oh, poor, poor Francesco. She'd known he hated his father, but this? This was worse than she could ever have imagined.

Suddenly he let go of her hand and palmed her cheeks. 'I have spent the past eleven months eradicating everything that man built. Everything. The parties stopped, the womanising stopped. All I wanted was vengeance for my mother and, even though my father was rotting in hell, I was determined to destroy what was his. I'd already closed his drug dens, but I resolved to annihilate everything else—the armouries, the so-called legitimate businesses that were in fact a front for money laundering—every last brick of property. The one thing I wanted above all else, though, was the Mayfair casino.'

Here, his eyes seemed to drill into hers. 'Years ago, my father tried to get that casino. It was the only failure of his life. He tried everything to get his hands on that place, but Godfrey Renfrew refused to sell it to such a notorious gangster. That failure was a large thorn in my father's side. For me to purchase that same property would mean I had succeeded where he had failed, proof that I was a better man than him.'

'So you've won,' she said softly. 'You've got your vengeance.'

'No.' He shook his head for emphasis. 'I walked into that room with the Mastrangelos today and knew I had lost. I had lost because I had lost *you*. How could I be a better man than him when I had let the most important person in my world down for the sake of vengeance?'

He brushed his lips against hers, the heat of his breath filling her senses, expanding her shrivelled heart.

'After speaking with the Mastrangelos, I called Godfrey earlier and withdrew my offer for the casino,' he whispered. 'I don't want it anymore. It's tainted. All I want is you. That's if you'll have me. I wouldn't blame you if you didn't.' He sighed and nuzzled into her cheek. 'You asked me once if you scared me. The truth is you did—you scared me because you made me feel, and because I knew I wasn't worthy of you. The only real relationship I have as a reference is my parents', and witnessing that was like living in one of Dante's circles of hell. You deserve so much better.'

'Not all marriages and relationships are like that.'

'Intellectually, I know that. Emotionally, though, it's

taken me a lot longer to accept it. I wanted to protect you from me. I looked at you and saw the innocence my mother had before she married my father. I didn't want to taint you.'

'How could you do that? You are not your father, Francesco. You're a mixture of both your parents and the uniqueness that is *you*. You're just you. No one else.'

He almost crushed her in his embrace. 'I swear I'll never hurt you again. Never. *You* make me a better man. Even if we leave here and head our separate ways, I will still be a better man for having known you.'

Tears pricked her eyes. Her heart felt so full she now feared it could burst.

Head their separate ways? Was that really what she wanted?

'I know how important your work is to you and I would never want to get in the way of that. Medicine is your life, but what I want to know—*need* to know—is if you can fit me into your life, too. Forget what I said about you not fitting into my world—it's *your* world *I* need to fit into. Let me in, I beg of you. I'm not perfect, not by any stretch of the imagination, but I swear on my mother's memory that I will love and respect you for the rest of my life.'

Hannah's chin wobbled. But she kept it together, refusing to let the tears fall. All the same, her voice sounded broken to her own ears. 'I love that you're not perfect.'

He stilled and pulled away to look at her. His eyes glittered with questions.

'Neither of us is perfect but…' She took a deep breath, trying to keep a hold of her racing heart. If Francesco, her big, arrogant bear of a man, could put his heart and pride on the line… She cupped his warm cheek. 'I think you're perfect for me.'

She'd barely got the words out before his mouth came

crashing down on hers, a kiss of such passion and longing that this time the tears really did fall.

'Don't cry, *amore*. Don't cry.' Francesco wiped her tears away and pressed his lips to her forehead. He wrapped his arms around her and she nestled her cheek against his chest.

He gave a rueful chuckle. 'I can't believe I worried about *you* getting burned. I should have known from the start— deep down I think I did—that, of the two of us, I was the more likely to be.'

'Oh, no, but you were right,' she confessed. 'And I'm glad I was so blasé about your concerns because if I'd known how badly you *would* burn me I would have run a mile.'

She tilted her chin back up to look at him. She felt light, as if the weight that had been compressing her insides for what felt like for ever had been lifted. 'You've brought me back to life and let colour back into my world. You make me whole and I want to be in your life, too. Your past, everything you've been through has shaped you into the man you are today and that's the man I've fallen in love with.'

'You really love me?'

For the first time Hannah saw a hint of vulnerability in Francesco's cool, confident exterior.

'More than anything. I didn't think I needed anyone. You've shown me that I do. Not just you, but my family, too.' She kissed his neck then whispered into his ear, 'You've also weaned me off my addiction to my phone. I've only checked it three times today.'

He threaded his long fingers through her hair, a deep laugh escaping his throat that deepened when he snagged a couple of knots. 'If I could trust myself not to break every bone in his body, I would pay another visit to that bastard who knocked you off your bike and thank him.'

'For bringing us together?'

'The stars aligned for us that morning.'

'Shame about my broken collarbone and concussion.'

'Not forgetting your poor finger.'

She giggled. She hadn't thought of her finger in weeks. 'I'm surprised you let him walk away without any injury.'

'He took one look at me in his doorway and virtually wet himself. I didn't need to touch him. If the same thing were to happen to you now, I doubt I would be so restrained.'

'Yes, you would,' she chided, rubbing her nose into his linen shirt.

'And you know that how?'

'Because you would never hurt me, and to cause physical injury to another human, especially in my name, would be to hurt me.'

'You still believe that? After what I did to you last night, you still believe in me?'

'I believe it more than ever.' And she did. She, more than anyone, knew the hold the past had on the present. All that mattered was that they didn't allow the past to shape their futures. 'In any case, I bet he'll spend the rest of his life having nightmares that you'll turn up on his doorstep again.'

'Good. He deserves it.' He gave a humourless chuckle. 'We should invite him to our wedding.'

'Why, are we getting married?'

'Too right we are. I love you, Dr Chapman, and I will love you for the rest of my life.'

'I love you, too, Signor Calvetti.'

He kissed her again. 'Dottore Hannah Calvetti. It has a nice ring to it.'

'Hmm…' Her lips curved into a contented smile. Francesco was right. It had a wonderful ring to it.

EPILOGUE

HANNAH WALKED CAREFULLY up the steep steps to the front door of the villa, happily inhaling the scent emitted by the overabundance of ripe lemon trees.

Francesco opened the door before she got to the top.

'Buonasera, Dottore Calvetti,' he said.

'Good evening, Signor Calvetti,' she replied, before slipping into fluent Sicilian-Italian. 'How has Luciano been today?'

'An angel. Well, he's been an angel since I relieved the nanny. I think he might have given her an extra grey hair or two today. He's definitely worn himself out—he fell asleep fifteen minutes ago. But enough of the small talk— how did you do?'

She couldn't hide the beam that spread across her face. 'I got the job!'

Francesco's face spread into an identical grin. He drew her to him and kissed her, then rubbed his nose to hers. 'I knew you could do it, you clever lady. In fact, Tino is at this moment preparing your favourite meal to celebrate.'

'Mussels in white wine?'

He nodded with a definite hint of smugness. 'Followed by hot chocolate-fudge cake.'

'I love you!' Tino, their chef, made the best chocolate-fudge cake in the world.

He laughed and tapped her bottom. 'Go shower and get changed. I'll open a bottle of wine.'

This time it was she who kissed him, hard.

'Before I forget, Melanie messaged me earlier,' she said. 'They can definitely come for the weekend.'

'Great. Let me know the times and I'll get the jet over to England for them.'

With a spring in her step, Hannah climbed the stone staircase and headed down the uneven corridor to their bedroom. As she passed their eighteen-month-old son's nursery, she poked her head through the door to find him in deep sleep. He didn't stir when she lowered the side of the cot to press a gentle kiss to his cheek. 'Night, night, sleep tight,' she whispered before slipping back out.

She opened her bedroom door and there, on her dressing table, was the most enormous bunch of roses she had ever seen, huge even by Francesco's standards.

His faith in her never ceased to amaze her.

Luciano had come into their lives more quickly than either had anticipated. Within two months of their marriage she'd fallen pregnant, which hadn't been all that surprising considering the laissez-faire approach to contraception they'd adopted.

When it came time for Hannah to take maternity leave, they'd uprooted to Sicily. It had been agreed that when her maternity was up they would move back to London. Except…she'd fallen in love with Sicily, with the people and the language. Besides, it was easier for Francesco to run his empire from there, so she saw more of him during the week than she had in London, and they hated having to spend nights away from each other.

Full of determination, she'd set about learning the language. She'd employed a tutor and within weeks had refused to answer Francesco or any of his staff unless they spoke in their native tongue. She had been determined to master it. And they had all been determined to help her.

'I got the job, Beth,' she said, speaking aloud in English, just in case Beth hadn't bothered to learn Italian with her. Now that she couldn't visit her grave so regularly, she had taken to simply talking to her whenever the mood struck. Sometimes, in her dreams, her twin spoke back. 'I'm going to work at the hospital on the children's ward here in Palermo and train for my consultancy here, too.'

All the pieces had come together.

She could not be happier.

* * * * *

MILLS & BOON®

Why shop at millsandboon.co.uk?

Each year, thousands of romance readers find their perfect read at millsandboon.co.uk. That's because we're passionate about bringing you the very best romantic fiction. Here are some of the advantages of shopping at www.millsandboon.co.uk:

* **Get new books first**—you'll be able to buy your favourite books one month before they hit the shops

* **Get exclusive discounts**—you'll also be able to buy our specially created monthly collections, with up to 50% off the RRP

* **Find your favourite authors**—latest news, interviews and new releases for all your favourite authors and series on our website, plus ideas for what to try next

* **Join in**—once you've bought your favourite books, don't forget to register with us to rate, review and join in the discussions

Visit **www.millsandboon.co.uk** for all this and more today!